DISCONNECTED

RILEY CROSS

For my grandfather. Wish you could have seen this come true.
To my sisters, for listening to all my early tales.

CHAPTER 1

"Look up. Child, do you see? The future is there, for those with foresight." — *Excerpt from* The Book of Enlightened Skies, *found in the Forbidden Library Archives*

My gray eyes trailed the heavens where a blue patch of sky slowly surrendered to the jaws of a hungry storm cloud. With my index finger, I traced invisible lines to create an imaginary barrier for the blue patch, rewriting the ominous message.

"Chiara, look ahead. Keep your shoulders straight. Hands to your side." My mother kept her sights on the paved pathway ahead of us.

My thirteen-year-old legs were in the gangly stage. Just long enough to make my ankles peek out from underneath the dark leggings and to ensure an off-balance gait. My indigo cotton tunic fit like a cocoon that promised, "One day."

Mother released my hand with a gentle squeeze. I knew from this point on, we were not to show affection, only potential. Each step along the paved pathway led us closer to the hydroelectric plant on the edge of the city walls. It hulked before me like a behemoth, steam pouring from its nostrils. Water gushed around it like a moat before disappearing into the drains for cleansing.

The robot at the gate's security checkpoint scanned our faces. "Greetings, Elara and young scholar."

It was strange to hear Mother being called by her first name. She didn't like using it.

The gates opened. We crossed the bridge, arching over the roaring moat that powered the plant. Below the bridge, the water churned in frothy swirls before spilling out of the overflow grates. Up ahead, stained concrete steps rose to meet the factory entrance.

"When you visit my workplace, I need you to follow every rule. This will reflect in your grades. We can't risk anything less than model behavior."

I ignored my mother, having heard this speech several times today. Instead, I pointed above us to the multiplying clouds in the darkening sky. "Look, a storm's coming. Is it safe to be here?"

"It's nothing to worry about. Auto watches over us all." Mother motioned to the security camera. It was tucked behind some strands of ivy, a pathetic attempt at cheerful aesthetics.

She swiped her keycard at the main security door and timed her next words to the beep. "Auto listens too."

I felt a chill as the door whooshed open. Mother stepped forward, and I admired how her tool belt cinched her lovely waist as her hips swayed with confidence. I tried to mimic her stride.

Inside, the building exuded practical architecture. Industrial walls, squared windows, and clearly marked signs leading to workstations.

A man in a white overseer's jacket casually sauntered next to us. His voice stayed low as he thumbed through his DataPad at charts and graphs. I sensed, however, that his gaze rested more on my face than on his work.

"Is she—" the man said, glancing at us.

Mother frowned, revealing dimples. "Yes. Obviously."

"Does she get good grades?" His smile widened.

"Chiara is slated for honors classes in high school."

"Good, so she won't be offered a Third Function career here in this place."

Mother beamed at him. "No, she is defying all odds."

Against all odds. I hated that phrase and its many variations.

"Excuse me, I'm standing right here." I placed my hands on my hips. "Anyone care to explain?"

Mother's glare silenced my bravery. The man cleared his throat. "My name is Martin. Your mother is my best employee at this plant. It's an honor to meet you."

I analyzed his chin structure before fixating on his steel-gray eyes. An unusual color. Like my own. I glanced between them, finding the story unspoken.

Is Martin my father? Mother once said I had my father's eyes.

"Strange, she never mentions you," I said, even as Mother's eyes narrowed, sending a silent warning my way.

Martin grimaced. "It's best not to focus on work when with family," he said, stuffing his hands into his pockets as if searching for somewhere to hide. "Your mother is a wise woman."

"Chiara!" Mother gripped my arm. Another warning.

I glanced at her, the blush rising in Mother's cheeks.

She cared for him at some point. Martin has to be my father.

The idea made me feel dizzy.

"We're both Anomalies. But being born of love is not a shame." Mother had reminded me when I first realized the A-R-A at the end of both of our names stood for *Amalgamated Reproduction Anomaly.* Sometimes, she just called me Chi and threw out the ending. I wasn't sure if that made things any better, honestly.

Having a child outside of the carefully planned genetic lines was a badge of shame. Being the product of a second-generation rule breaker meant I was an Anomaly of the worst kind. If I didn't behave, my line would be sterilized.

Rule breakers pass on their nature to their children, and that's why I'm not supposed to know my father.

In Unity, the levels always bred more of their own, and unexpected births such as mine upset the balance. Auto selected partners for the best genetic outcomes. Once parental DNA was combined and pod-grown, the child could be sent to live with either parent. And in the event that neither parent was interested, a suitable foster-parent of the same function-level would be assigned. Visitation between parents was allowed, but the optimal ratio of one child per adult had to be maintained.

In contrast, Anomalies were forbidden from forming further emotional ties, their parental records were sealed, and their fates as laboring bees in Third Function or Fourth Function were guaranteed.

Grandfather did his best to shield Mother and me, to use his powerful position to mitigate the punishment. But it was strike two for him. Mother was an Anomaly too. With those shadows stalking his reputation, Grandfather was forced to resign from the secretive First Function to work in the Fifth Function while my mother was downgraded from Second Function to Third Function. All because I was born without approval.

I watched the awkward glances between Mother and Martin. The silence. The pain. The fake exterior hiding the strangest of stories. Being born without approval always had a cost.

Mother is wrong. Being born of love is nothing but a curse.

Martin's DataPad emitted a series of beeps just as loud sirens roared from the rafters above our heads. "Strange. Look at this," Martin said, leaning over to show my mother flashing numbers on his screen.

Mother's eyes widened. "I'll go to sector 17 immediately. I can fix that in a matter of minutes."

"Elara, you have your daughter today," Martin said. "I'll send someone else."

Mother stiffened at the sound of her name on Martin's lips. "Nonsense. That's my sector, and I don't want anyone else messing with those controls and causing an accident."

As if in response, a flash of light and a boom of thunder echoed outside the plant windows. I stared, captivated by nature's rage as sheets of rain pelted the glass. I broke protocol and reached for Mother's hand. She didn't say a word, but her fingers curled around mine.

"Martin, would you..." Mother hesitated and slowly released my hand. "Would you watch Chiara?"

"I don't need watching," I said, crossing my arms. I stretched to my full height, making sure Mother sensed the slight difference between us.

Martin hesitated, then nodded to my mother. "I'd be delighted. Not to watch you, Chiara, but rather to show you around the place." He motioned towards me. "Would you like to see an overseer's office?"

Mother gave me a reassuring nudge. "I'll be back. Sector 17's inner workings are no place for a child, even one as precocious as you."

I knew my part in this charade. I would be the dutiful scholar. "Not a child," I grumbled, staring at my shoes.

I expected her to chastise me. Instead, her hand softly trailed my cheek and pulled my chin up.

"Those controls won't check themselves." Mother smiled before she turned away.

Martin and I were left in her shadow as insistent sirens continued to assault our ears.

"Seriously, is it safe to be here?" I asked, cringing at the wailing cacophony.

Martin gave a chuckle. "This is life in Third Function. The noise is constant. Come on, let's give you a tour of the building." He gestured to the lobby's boxed space dotted with the occasional flowering pod.

"Are you going to try and convince me that a Third Function job isn't so bad after all?" I asked, eyeballing the stairs and elevators reaching skyward at least four levels high.

Martin spoke over the chaos. "No. You deserve the truth. Third Function consists of tough, grimy work in factories. But enough about my job. Are you excited about being selected for honors classes? That's quite an achievement."

I sighed with relief that he didn't add "against all odds" like most people did.

Just last week, my name had been posted among the one hundred and fifty chosen honor students. My best friend, Silas, had been listed below my name on the roster. When I perused the list, I stiffened like a soldier and fought the giddy squeals exploding in my chest. Mother would have been proud of my restraint and grace in that moment.

To have shown excitement would have meant I was lucky. Gifted people should expect the opportunities, not be surprised by them. Around me, my wealthier classmates who did not make the selection had burst into tears. Without an honors slot, they would never be eligible for higher-function jobs, barring some sort of miracle.

I had bested the genetically engineered system despite my status as an Anomaly, and I already knew I would have at least one friend. Wherever this temporary luck had come from, it made me nervous that it might grow wings and fly far beyond my reach.

"Speaking of school, I actually have a report to write," I said.

Martin nodded. "Do you have any questions about the hydro-electricity or byproduct gases this plant produces?"

"Sure, could you explain it a little bit more?" I said, pulling out my school DataPad from the depths of my tunic's overcoat. I fingered the device's silvery edges, waiting for my thumbprint to unlock it. I pressed play to record his answer and added a noise filtration feature, editing out the blaring sirens. I would analyze the video later. Freeze the frames and study Martin's features to see if any were like my own.

Martin yammered. I focused, hoping to gain a few useful notes.

"—wastewater that can be purified is used to create the moat, and then some run-off water siphons into the sewers."

"Where do the sewers empty?"

Martin paused, as if uncertain of the rules. I paused the video. He leaned closer and said, "To the ruins beyond Unity."

He brightened momentarily as we reached his office.

"But we are straying from the topic of this amazing factory." He motioned towards a food vending machine in the corner of his office. "Can I get you anything?"

How about answers? Can we fit a lifetime into one conversation?

I shook my head, deriving clues to unlock Martin's personality from the room around me. The office was standard, up to regulation, except for the coffee stains on the desk.

Martin stepped over a crooked rubber mat near his desk instead of straightening it. The window blinds were open, allowing a panoramic of the bustling plant floor where workers scurried to their stations in practiced movements.

"Your grandfather once had an important role," Martin said, a sad smile tugging at the corners of his mouth. "It's good to know that you're protected. Are you close with him?"

I straightened my shoulders and put on a smile for onlookers. "He visits once a week usually. Brings me hot chocolate, and we talk. It's not the typical arrangement."

Martin sank into his creaking leather chair, his posture slumped and defeated. "No. It's not," he said with a wistful smile. "Usually, children are allowed to visit between parents. You have a strong heart... Chiara, I—"

Flashing lights and pop-up messages drew his attention to his DataPad. The wailing sirens outside the office came to an abrupt stop.

Martin took a deep breath and returned his focus back to me. "Your mother is a genius, you know. Work hard at those classes. Show the world who you truly are."

"I'm an Anomaly," I said. "I don't fit in."

"No." Martin's face turned serious, and deep lines creased his forehead. "Not an Anomaly. You're a gift from the stars, Chi."

I froze.

He knows my nickname?

For a second, I wanted to hug him.

The sirens wailed again. Louder. Faster. Angrier. Martin paled, all color draining from his face.

I glanced around the office. Every worker in the plant had a place to hide in case a sudden storm released dangerous gasses stored in the plant.

I bolted towards the office door. Towards Mother.

My DataPad tumbled away from my hands, shattering into a thousand shards of glass.

Martin grabbed me from behind. He was shouting something. But the sirens' intense decibels had rendered my senses useless. He shoved me into a crawl space under the floor near his desk. My hand grabbed his briefly, but Martin pulled away, shaking his head as he closed the safety door above me.

A second later, when lightning ignited the factory into explosive balls of fire with waves of shattered glass and a final siren blast, I wondered...

What sort of gift am I really?

I waited in the darkness of the metal walls, trapped in a coffin of safety. The urge to survive began to warm through me even as I remained still, gathering strength. I waited for the sounds, screams, and clanging to subside. The building's groans and the collapse of steel and stone seemed to go on for an eternity, leaving me alone with only my guilt and scrambled thoughts.

The air became stale and thin. I pushed against the overhead trapdoor, panicking as an unknown weight pressed back. My efforts triggered a spring-loaded latch, no doubt designed to assist in such emergencies. Rubble shifted overhead, allowing sooty sunlight to envelope me.

All around, fires blazed on top of rubble piles until choked out by non-consumable bricks and metals. Hungry orange flecks traveled up to the smoke-embroiled heavens. The sky responded with little drops of rain, teasing at hope. Ashes filled my lungs, and my nostrils burned with the stench of chemicals. I gasped.

Grunting, I pulled myself into the heated rubble. I glanced around. My eyes locked onto a hand—crushed and burnt—protruding from layers of brick and leaking pipes. My pulse quickened into short jabs.

Was it Martin? Mother? Someone else?

Guilt pulsed through my every fiber even as a selfish hope moved my muscles. I had to find a way out of this sinkhole surrounded by searing heat and death. Climbing the rubble without protection would be dangerous. My exposed skin ached in response.

"Chiara!"

I glanced up. A blue-suited figure with an oxygenated helmet emerged from the rubble. The smoky fog on the helmet's protective shield cleared up to reveal the face beneath.

Grandfather.

I began to shake, desperate with joy.

With a whoosh of his thrusters, Grandfather hovered above the piles before descending towards me. I reached up, and Grandfather gathered me into his arms. The thrusters rose slowly just as the rubble collapsed below us into a smoldering heap.

Grandfather landed back onto solid ground. I buried my head into his chest. Around us, suited rescue workers moved with efficiency. A medical robot glided over to us, bathing me in an invasive blue light scan before offering an oxygen mask. Grandfather lowered me onto my own feet as I grabbed the mask.

Around us, the spidery legs of Collective Unity Enforcer—or CUE—robots dug through the rubble for survivors.

I gulped the sweet air as if it were water. I didn't stop until my shoulders heaved and my chest shook.

"Did you find her?" I asked.

Grandfather pulled off his helmet; his bloodshot eyes told me the truth.

My soul shriveled like a washed-up starfish. "I want to go home," I whispered.

Grandfather nodded, tears streaming down his cheeks before

getting lost in his snow-white beard. "There is nothing left for us here."

I tried to stand, but my legs crumpled under me. Grandfather lifted me again.

"I can walk," I insisted.

He shook his head fiercely. "Not when I can carry you."

Grandfather pressed me harder against his tear-stained chest, and I couldn't muster the strength to protest. I gazed over his shoulder at the wreckage. Flying drones doused the remaining flames with water. A crew of Fourth Function workers sifted through the ruins and pulled out listless bodies.

Grandfather's footprints left an unmistakable trail in the ashes.

I am safe now.

And like a foolish child, I believed it.

Except one nagging realization lingered in my head: breathing was really, really painful.

CHAPTER 2

*"I didn't pay a price. No, that would imply that I had lost something.
Truth is, I only gained what I loved most."* — *Excerpt from* Diary of a
Wayward Citizen, *found in the Forbidden Library Archives*

"Just a few more X-rays," purred the medical robot. Several of the robot's octopus-like appendages retracted into their portholes.

I squirmed and fingered the smooth, cylindrical walls of the tight medical pod that enclosed my body. I tried to calm my breathing as I looked out through the glass top at the ocean-blue walls of the small exam room.

Grandfather had insisted I be checked out by the main hospital. So had the local health authorities. Even the news reporter drone had insisted on a status update for the lone survivor of the hydroelectric plant explosion. I just wanted to be left alone with my pain.

Hot tears welled in my eyes. I closed my reddened, sleepless eyes in an effort to contain them. My breathing became ragged again, and the glass top of the pod began to fog.

"Hold still," the medical robot advised. A flash of light. A gentle hum. "See, that wasn't so terrible!"

The pod burst open, and I didn't waste time jumping out. I regretted it almost immediately because my head spun and my breath caught in my throat, causing me to bend over as if I had just crossed the finish line after a race. The soothing background music did little to my frazzled nerves. Part of me wanted to settle back down into the pod and wait for the spinning to stop.

Instead, I gripped the side of the pod and waited for my stability to return.

"How is she?" Grandfather asked. He had stepped in from the hallway and addressed the medical robot.

"Young people can survive anything." The robot sounded far too cheerful. "It's wonderful how much she has healed."

Grandfather punched the nearest wall, the bones in his knuckles making a soft thud. "Lies! The chemical levels alone were off the charts after that explosion! She was exposed!"

He grabbed the medical robot and yanked it closer. "The truth. Now."

The robot released a series of calculated beeps. "If she doesn't receive a new set of lungs later in life, her condition will deteriorate. Pain can be managed easily with medication."

"Not good enough," Grandfather snapped.

"That's protocol. She has to wait until after Implantation before she can apply for further surgery."

"What will happen in the meantime?" I asked. My airways ached—a common ache lately.

Grandfather released the robot and rushed to my side just in time. My knees wobbled.

"We will manage your pain, of course," the robot said. "You will be comfortable enough."

Grandfather's eyes darkened, and his bushy eyebrows angled into a V like two hawks coming in for a kill. "Auto will take care of her and make this right."

And Auto is always listening.

My mother's words floated back to me. I glanced up at the cameras nestled in every corner of the ceiling and knew they continued every few feet through the medical halls. The great artificial intelligence that controlled every aspect of our lives was considering my fate.

I hadn't even started high school yet. Hadn't graduated. There was no way Auto would approve surgery until I had proven myself worthy of citizenship in Unity.

That was the rule. Generally.

The robot seemed to register Grandfather's words with a whirring, beeping sound. "There is a price for the new organs. And you're out of favors with Auto, so it will cost more."

"What price?" I asked.

"I'm aware," Grandfather said, his expression impassive. "Do it."

"Very well. Chiara, please return to the pod." The medical robot whirred out of the room.

I tried to steady my voice, but it matched the screaming in my head. "What price? Tell me!"

Grandfather's demeanor shifted. The cold steel left his eyes, and warmth returned to his smile. "I'll worry about that."

I stepped back into the pod, despite fear erasing what little courage I possessed. "What are they going to do?"

The medical robot returned moments later, followed by a team of other robots. A tall one with multiple arms held an array of equipment. A squat one carried a tray with a sealed piece of meat.

No. Not meat. Lungs. Someone else's lungs.

The pod released a mist. I flailed my arms, trying to climb back out. But it was no use.

"Don't struggle," the medical robot said. "This will all be over shortly."

The mist swirled around my head, and the piped-in classic piano notes in the exam room blended into a darkening vortex. I yawned and drifted into oblivion.

The pod's glass top wooshed open as I regained consciousness. The room was empty. My clothes sat in a neat pile next to the pod. I slipped into my shirt, noticing the twin scars that now traveled down my barely developed chest. My hands trailed the marks, studying the precise rows of the black silken stitches.

It's monstrous.

I struggled into my olive-green cargo pants.

But nothing hurts.

I took multiple breaths to confirm. Scars meant nothing; those could be healed in days with skin applications. However, this mysterious price tag was an entirely different story.

A polite knock on the door interrupted my thoughts.

"Come in," I said, buttoning up my jacket just in time.

Grandfather entered, followed by the medical robot.

"Whose lungs are inside me?" I asked.

"Not to worry," the robot replied. A whiff of sanitizing chemicals still clung to its metallic body. "You'll learn about this soon enough in school. The Streamless ones are..."

"Disconnected, discarded students who didn't graduate," I snapped. "I know about them. I want to know a name. They have names."

Grandfather raised an eyebrow.

Auto is listening.

"Please," I said in a more earnest tone. "I want to honor the gift I've been given."

The medical robot's beeping tones sounded like a sigh. "The donor information is irrelevant."

Grandfather leaned over and kissed my forehead. "Let it go, Chi."

At the sound of my mother's pet name for me, I stopped questioning the system and fought off a sudden wave of anguish.

I've cheated death. I can breathe without pain, thanks to an illegal procedure. What else is there to know?

Guilt and relief swirled inside me like a whirlwind of oil and water.

"You won't feel a thing," the robot said, rattling off a list of post-surgery instructions—mostly, what *not* to do. "Just give it a week before running again."

My eyes trailed back to the black-gossamer stitches inside the neckhole of my shirt.

"All scars heal in time," Grandfather said, his hand gently sliding around my shoulder.

I knew he wasn't talking about physical ones.

"Yes, you can apply for cosmetic or corrective surgery later," the medical robot said. "But let's do it after graduation. That's only two years away. After all, it's not entirely necessary yet."

"In my day, it was four years to graduate high school," Grandfather grumbled. "These kids need more time to be kids."

Two years. And I'll be facing another surgery, Implantation. And what if I don't survive it? What will this sacrifice have been for?

I leaned into Grandfather's embrace. He supported my weight as I took a few steps toward the open door.

"I've sent your records over to Emergent High. You'll be monitored there for any signs of complications."

And with that, the robot followed us out into the sterile-looking hallway and disappeared around a corner. Finally.

Grandfather, what price did you pay?

The unspoken question lingered between us as Grandfather led me down the maze of hallways with the same ocean-blue hue. The color no longer felt calming, but ironic, like the bright blue waves just before a deadly tidal storm in an adventure-simulation chamber.

As we exited, I peered through the thin glass walls separating us from other patients in the hospital's waiting room. A line of people—both the narcissistic and the hopeless—waited here for Auto's ultimate decision on their surgery requests.

I glanced at a man holding an internet projection in his hands, watching the news. It flashed my photo briefly with the caption: "Lone Survivor at Factory Explosion."

He swiped the story, only for it to be replaced with other headlines.

"Next Year's High School Graduates Fill Third Function Quota to Honor Fallen Factory Workers."

"Cleanup and Environmental Correction Efforts Continue at Explosion Site."

Grandfather patted me awkwardly and mumbled something about dinner. He had seen the headlines too.

A thought needled my brain.

Was I worth saving? Martin thought so. Grandfather thinks so. And my mother...

I blinked, pushing back the salty tears behind my eyes.

I need to be worthy of their sacrifices.

I straightened my shoulders and kept my eyes forward. Like Mother always said.

Auto was watching. And now, more than ever, I had something to prove.

CHAPTER 3

"When a seed is planted, tears can make it grow. The roots push it away from its burial spot and towards the light where all things are revealed in a final form. Love, friendship, and pain are all seeds of this sort." — *Excerpt from* The Fields of Life, Volume III, *found in the Forbidden Library Archives.*

Grandfather remained seated in our apartment, watching as I donned my visor and soldered new circuits onto an old board. The sparks flew into the air like miniature flames. Sometimes, I saw Mother's face or sensed the warmth of Martin's handshake in the sparks. But it was mysterious and vague, like a mirage in the desert.

We never talked about what happened. The hydroelectric plant was rebuilt in a matter of days. A new work crew was assigned from among the graduating high school students, and they toiled under the careful eyes of new overseers. Then, the entire city of Unity just moved on as the time, post-accident, crept forward like moss on a stone. I immersed myself into my studies, securing my spot among the top fifty students with only a few days left of year one. One more year to go. Mother would have been proud.

Did Grandfather miss her too?

Our eyes locked. He nodded in approval at my work. "I've done some coding in my day, but I cannot crack the code of thought," Grandfather said. "Focus on the mystery in front of you instead of the unsolvable one in your head."

I sighed, looking at the old-time technology components in front of me. I didn't need Grandfather's reminder to stay focused. I had to showcase my skills and build a robot to impress the daunting Faye, who was well known for her intense exams.

Two students would be cut from the honors track once all the robots were submitted for Faye's scrutiny.

Game on.

I sifted through the piles of assorted gears and gadgets. Scratches. Funny dents that needed to be welded or pounded out. Aged metals. Larger circuit board chips demanded more space and precise planning. Patchwork wires.

The other students' entries will look better than what I'm able to create from these ancient parts. But I'll make sure it works better than the other robots.

With Grandfather's demotion from First Function to Fifth Function, we didn't have the credits to spend on a nice dwelling zone or the expensive projects that Faye demanded. We were apartment dwellers now.

I took a breath, and it caught briefly.

Was this the price Grandfather paid for my lungs?

I still remembered the high-rise luxury suites that Grandfather once lived in when mother took me to visit on rare occasions. This one-bedroom apartment, with its combined kitchen and living room, hardly compared.

As Fifth Function overseer in the department of Phased-Out Technology, Grandfather had plenty of access to ancient tech. The elderly who worked in my grandfather's department sorted through and figured out how to retrofit outdated parts into current machinery. If that couldn't be done, they would strip and sort components for every available resource.

The parts were old, but not useless. I just had to make it work.
The doorbell hummed.

"It's Silas!" I fumbled, then caught my soldering tool mid-fall. "Finally!"

I nearly bowled over my one-and-only friend. He grinned before playfully shoving me aside to shake Grandfather's hand.

We'd known each other since childhood, but I knew just how incredibly lucky it was that we ended up in the same class. Silas was my rock. I could rely on him, even in a class full of vipers all vying for the top ranking.

"Here to report for duty," Silas said, his braided hair swinging past his shoulders.

Grandfather nodded, allowing him to pass.

"Get started on putting this together." I pointed at the scattered boards, wires, and pieces sitting in clear plastic containers on the carpeted living room floor.

"You kids let me know if you need anything else," Grandfather said as he grabbed his work coat from the rack by the door and gingerly stepped around my organized piles. "I trust you'll put this stuff away after you're done."

Silas's dark eyes widened at the realization that cleaning up afterwards would not be a simple task.

"Where are you going?" I asked.

Grandfather smiled, but not the kind of smile that appeared genuine. "You and Silas need space to work. An old man like me gets in the way."

Grandfather squeezed my cheek. "I'll be back. Not sure when."

"Alright," I said, wondering how long it would be this time. There had been a lot of long absences lately. Grandfather never talked about what he did. I never asked.

Silas started working on the robot's inner wiring. My curiosity about Grandfather's hobbies vanished as I stared a little too long at the wispy soul patch growing on Silas's youthful chin and the muscles beneath his form-fitting athletic wear.

I quickly readjusted my safety glasses. "Did you see Faye frown when the final roster was announced for our class?"

Silas nodded. "She was upset. I'm telling you; she hates us."

"Because I'm an Anomaly and you randomly won the genetic lottery?"

Silas grinned, then broke into a chuckle. "Exactly. Those purebred snobs don't know what hit them. Fact is, we made the top fifty and some surprised rich kid got kicked out of the program. I don't care about the haters. My mom is proud."

"She would be prouder if you ate more green foods too," I said, poking his ribs, earning a playful shove in response.

Grandfather never stated his pride, not like Silas's mother did. She was a Third Function worker selected by Auto to birth another Third Function worker. However, Silas's intelligence had surpassed all expectations. He was regarded with jealousy by those who realized his ascension meant one less available position.

The levels were all Silas could focus on in school. Second Function was the true prize since First Function was a secretive organization. Grandfather never talked about his time in that role and asking him had never gained me a single answer. Silas had long given up trying to get Grandfather to speak about those days as well.

Second Function was composed of analysts and inventors with clever minds. Third Function did the heavy lifting with focused technical skills. Fourth Function bred to replace the simple masses responsible for grunt work. Fifth Function was reserved for the elderly, where all levels eventually sank.

Life was a delicate balance, protected inside the walled confines of Unity's circular limits. Everyone knew where they belonged. Except me. Mother felt I could be something greater than the shameful initials attached to my name.

I hope she was right.

"One more year of this and then we can start our careers," Silas said as he tossed me a fully functioning robot dog with four legs and a wagging tail. I caught it clumsily, and it nuzzled my chin. The bronzed metal exterior was smooth and polished, with occasional stains that were reminiscent of the material's age. Two green irises blinked to life as its inner camera came online. I quickly set it down.

Silas watched it run back and forth between us. "After Implantation, I bet we can call the shots with Second Function jobs," he said, stretching his arms behind his head with the air of a dreamer. "Can you imagine how it would feel if Auto assigns us to our own project task force?"

I had to admit, working for Unity's supreme intelligence would be every inventor's or analyst's dream. My heart fluttered a little at the thought of working with cutting-edge tech.

Silas's eyes lit up. "Honestly, I can't wait for high school to be over. Enough with the brain training, the simulations, the endless assignments… I just want to be able to access the DataStream without limits."

I nodded, remembering how Grandfather once found a peculiar device called a "phone" and another thin, metal box he called a "laptop" as the original access points to the DataStream, a source of living knowledge. I always pictured the DataStream as a cluster of floating specks just above our heads, waiting for a command.

And if I survive high school and the Implantation ceremony, my brain will be the only device I'll ever need.

Unless something went wrong.

And as the lone survivor of a freak factory explosion, I seem to attract the worst-case scenarios.

Silas seemed to read my mind. "I know that look. Out with it."

The words flew from my lips. "Plans are great and all, but have you forgotten about the Implantation ceremony? They're going to cut us open to see if our brains can handle the DataStream without help. We can't forget that not everyone survives the surgery."

Silas rolled his eyes. "I attended the same lecture. You worry too much."

I set my tools aside and pushed the goggles on top of my head. "Two students didn't make it this year. A boy and girl. They became feral and were sent to live with the other Streamless people, banished and living outside of Unity's walls. I'd say worry is warranted. I don't want to end up with a fried brain, just wandering around the ruins of nowhere with nothing to do except wait for my organs to be harvested."

My lungs ached as I finished the sentence. At least the original owner of my borrowed lungs couldn't feel the pain now.

Silas leaned against the cream-colored sofa and the robot dog curled up next to him. He held up three fingers dramatically. "Let's talk facts. First, the Streamless don't feel anything. They are, as you say, 'fried' brains. Basically like zombies in the adventure simulator but without the eating-people part. So who cares? It's not like they know what happened to them."

I started to protest but Silas gave me a frown. I crossed my arms as he continued.

"Second, it's statistically unlikely. Out of a thousand graduating students every year, there are minimal losses. Third, Faye has never lost a single student, and her class is filled with only the best minds. So even if she is an awful person, and we're stuck with her as our capstone instructor, at least she is brilliant. We have to survive the last few days of this year and next year without being cut from the class roster. We're a team, unlike the rest of them in the class. Which means we will have each other's backs the whole time," Silas said as the robot dog yawned.

Grandfather had told me that, in ancient times, school included collegiate courses and that high school had been longer than two years. I wished that was still true. Then this threat of looming death wouldn't seem so imminent.

"No worries?" I said. "Silas, you can't promise that. No one can. Statistics don't prevent accidents."

Silas scooted closer to me. "Is this really about your—"

"I can't talk about them."

"What happened to your parents was a tragedy." Silas rubbed comforting circles against my back. "But life isn't a cosmic hammer just waiting to fall on you."

"Until it does."

Silas sighed. "I know what will cheer you up." He darted to the small kitchen and faced the food machine's advertised, disco-colored images. He scanned his code and spent his own credits. Within seconds, the machine rumbled to life and ice cream cubes tumbled out in reusable containers.

"Thank you for your purchase. Please return the container when done," the machine said before switching back into advertising mode.

"You shouldn't be wasting your food rations on junk," I mumbled, happily snatching a gelatinous blob from his bowl.

Silas gobbled four cubes at once, his cheeks puffing to their maximum size. He tried pushing another one in and threw his hands up in triumph.

"You can do better." I tossed him two more.

His eyes widened.

"And no cheating! You can't chew or swallow what you have."

He briefly covered his mouth with both hands as he attempted to stuff them in slowly. A victory grin spread across his face right before the sugar hit his system with an icy after-response.

Silas swallowed, his pupils widening.

"Brain freeze?" I said, laughing.

He shivered. "Still worth it." He flashed me a weak grin.

"I hate you." I stole another cube.

"Hey, spend your own credits." But he left the bowl between us.

We both grabbed at the last piece and our hands brushed, sending us into fits of giggles. Our fingers sparred to claim it.

I won.

"We better finish," Silas said, rolling over onto his stomach and eyeing the robot. "What I wouldn't give for a new programming chip or tool set."

I waved my soldering tool threateningly. "Hey, we can make these work."

"Doesn't mean it wouldn't be nice to have a new set."

"You'd have more credits if you stopped buying junk food."

Silas mockingly clutched his chest. "Never. It's in my DNA. Literally."

The inside joke made my heart lighter. Silas's mother repaired broken vending machines throughout the low-rent apartment zones. It really was his destiny to be inclined towards food machines.

Not that anyone would know his junk food habit at first glance.

I blushed at my own thoughts.

The robot dog broke into a fit of excited barking as it grabbed a plush, white pillow from the couch. It pounced with ferocious curiosity.

"We should name it," Silas said, stroking the robot dog's chin. "This one has personality."

"It's a project. Meant to help the elderly as a companion. It isn't ours."

"Oh, I've got it. Kaynine. K-A-Y-N-I-N-E. Get it?"

Silas's grin was infectious. Clearly, he wasn't listening to me. Faye had warned about getting attached to our projects.

The robot dog whimpered as if begging for my approval. I rolled my eyes, but I had to admit Kaynine was a clever name.

"Okay," I said, "but naming it doesn't get us any extra points. What's your analysis of my overall design?"

Silas tapped on the malleable plastic device curled around his ear. The brainwave attenuation technology—or BAT—allowed him to instantly pull up a 3D model of Kaynine's blueprints. My design hovered in the air between us as Silas zoomed in on the energy coils around Kaynine's memory processor.

"If we move these here," he said, motioning with his finger as the 3D parts followed his gestures like pixelated ghosts, "efficiency and memory storage capacity could be increased by seven percent."

I found myself nodding. Silas always spotted a flaw somewhere. In my coding, in the design, something. But he had such a gentle way of bringing up any improvements that I never minded.

"Also, if we add a friction generator," Silas said, "then it can be self-powered. No recharging needed."

"So it can operate on its own loop," I said. "Unless there is a DataStream blackout, I don't see how that feature is necessary for a simple school project."

Silas shrugged. "It's not necessary, but it's fancy. It sets Kaynine apart."

I had to agree with the logic. "Let's do it then."

My arm ached, and I handed Silas the soldering tool. He quickly made the adjustments and secured the coils in the new-and-improved positions.

"I think it's done." Silas jumped to his feet and pulled me up with him. "And I'm pretty sure we nabbed top spot on the class roster again."

Kaynine pranced around our feet. "Sit," I said, running through the standard list of commands.

Kaynine stopped mid-loop; its eyes locked onto mine.

Silas tried a few more orders before scooping up the robot. "Too bad we can't keep it after the project ends."

I glanced at the squirming dog. "The elderly need assistants, and this one will be a fine companion."

Silas pouted and cradled the robot dog. "C'mon, you can't resist this face," he said while Kaynine whimpered in response. "I'm going to find a way to keep our little dog. Doesn't your grandfather count as one of the elderly?"

I tossed a harmless nut bolt at Silas. "Better not let my grandfather hear you say that. We can't get attached."

Silas caught the bolt. He handed it to Kaynine, who gnawed on it possessively. "I guess. You aced Kaynine's programming though."

"Your analysis was pretty solid too," I said.

We fist-bumped. I blushed before focusing my gaze on Kaynine as it began to paw at Silas's leg. High school wasn't supposed to be a place for friends. Just the preparation for the limited vocations. Our close friendship had always sparked rumors.

"Let them talk," Silas had said once. "Bet they couldn't scrap together a solution if they had to. Not like us." He had a way of saying "us" that warmed my insides.

The hours passed as we played with Kaynine. Silas laughed when I slipped and used its new name. We threw more small bolts its way, much to the robot dog's delight. I searched for a flaw in Kaynine, but every gear whirred in harmony. It helped clean up the mess, vacuumed the floors, and showed extraordinary capacity to remember instructions.

We did it. Somehow.

Between my coding and Silas's ability to refine the project, the old parts were only a challenge and not an impossible setback. Every inventor needed an analyst. The inventors had the visions and gathered the pieces together. The analyst corrected the flaws within the original design.

Which is why Silas is my perfect half. He can work with me despite my vortex of sarcasm.

I smiled as Kaynine rolled over on its belly to recharge.

"It's getting late. Isn't your grandfather supposed to be home soon?" Silas asked, eyeing the food vending machine again. "My stomach is telling me it's time for a late-night snack."

I glanced around, and the walls reflected a time back at me before returning back into wallpaper mode.

"How does your mother afford all of your eating habits?" I said, deflecting his original question.

"I honestly don't know. Maybe she hacked our machine. There are some privileges that come with her job, you know. I should go soon. Does your grandfather always put in this much overtime?"

I bristled.

Silas noticed and pivoted the discussion.

"I'm sure there's a reason though," he said with a shrug, in a lighter tone. "Should I stay with you until he comes back?"

Please do.

I shook my head, erasing the feelings tumbling out of me. "No, go. It's a school night. Plus, we have to talk tomorrow about designing subconscious communication protocols."

"Sounds riveting," Silas said with a groan.

"It's basically a telepathic phone call with audio and visual capabilities. I have some ideas."

"I believe it." Silas then pulled me into a quick embrace.

I relaxed in his warmth, allowing the hug to last a few seconds longer than normal before I pushed away, shuffling my feet as Silas grabbed his backpack. I tucked a tendril of hair behind my ears.

"See you soon," he said with a lopsided grin.

Something between us is changing.

I wasn't sure how to process that thought.

Kaynine whimpered, and Silas reached down to give one last belly rub.

Silas shut the door behind him, and I sank into the couch.

I would have to log in some hours in the building's adventure simulator to get my mind off everything. For a few credits, I could live another life, one where rules didn't exist. Become Queen of my own planet, adventure like a dragon hunter, or pull off a great heist. Grandfather didn't like the simulators for anything other than workouts, but they played a useful role in drowning out pesky human emotions.

I'm lucky to have a best friend. That's all we are.

Mother. Martin. Grandfather and my unknown grandmother. Emotions clearly were a problem for our genetic line, cluttering up logical decisions.

I've got a chance at making it through Implantation and coming out on top. Whatever this feeling is, time will suffocate it.

I fingered the fringe on a nearby pillow. "Tell me the time," I said, and the wallpaper again shifted into digital numbers.

This was the latest Grandfather had ever been.

"Nothing to worry about," I said in between yawns. Kaynine jumped onto the couch and curled by my feet.

"I'll have to reset your attachment parameters tomorrow," I said. "So don't get too used to this."

The lights dimmed, and Kaynine's glowing green eyes provided an unexpected comfort.

I determined to wait up. See if Grandfather was in a talkative mood. Maybe he'd tell me about his projects.

The last thing I remembered was the sound of gears whirring as Kaynine dragged a blanket across my shoulders.

CHAPTER 4

"Crumbs. That's all that is left after a good meal. But the rest is pressed into a memory vault so strong that the lesson learned will remain preserved until the end of time." — *Excerpt from* The Narrative of Indulgence, *found in the Forbidden Library Archives*

I dumped my empty container into the food vending machine's recycling-and-compression bin, wishing it would recycle the material faster so I could be excused from the dining table. Grandfather never let me leave until the machine chirped happily. The system was simple: use a dish, compress and recycle the very same dish for the next meal. Kaynine followed my steps, whimpering.

"For being programmed as an elder companion, it certainly has taken a liking to you instead," Grandfather said in between mouthfuls of his protein-and-vegetable-flavored cubes.

I patted Kaynine's bronze head. "Probably a defect. I'll look into it."

Grandfather smiled knowingly. "Not all defects need fixing."

"I can't keep it. No point in getting attached. I just have to tweak its flaws for my final report."

"You can write whatever you please. But fixing won't happen.

I am satisfied with it and, as the client, that's all that matters," Grandfather said.

"Wait, you're keeping it?"

"You're keeping it," Grandfather replied without missing a beat.

"I don't need the extra responsibility. Silas is more attached to it anyway."

"What did you learn about today?" Grandfather said, shoving his bowl away from him. "You haven't said a single word."

I wasn't fast enough. Recycle dishes and run next time!

Today was not the day to talk to him about the lesson. A rosy blush colored my cheeks. "It was fine."

Grandfather raised an eyebrow, appearing as if he was willing to wait as long as it took.

I sighed and slumped back into my seat. "I really need to go call Silas. We redesigned our subconscious communication protocol channel, and I have to make a few more adjustments."

"Order a hot chocolate. Then sit. You can mind-chat with Silas later."

The food machine finally whirred, recycling my plastic dinner plate into a mug. I sighed and punched in the credits, and the machine filled the mug to overflowing with tiny, brown cubes that would turn into liquid once I swallowed.

I grabbed the mug and took my seat across from Grandfather again, idly stirring the cubes before pulling my finger back out before I corroded the nutritional coating.

Necessary, but not always appealing.

"You learned about genetic breeding today, didn't you?"

A groan escaped my lips. "I don't want to talk about it." I chewed a few cubes to illustrate the point.

Grandfather gave me the moment. We both sat in stubborn silence. I was halfway done with the hot chocolate before I caved.

"I heard the other students laughing about me afterwards," I said, shoving the mug away. "It's fine. Happens every time that yearly reminder comes around."

I grabbed at the mug again, looking for something for my hands to do, and spun it around. I watched the cubes tumble in perfect harmony.

Sure, attraction had always existed, but Auto had implemented temporary family units for the greater good of Unity. Online flings were permissible but unsanctioned relationships brought chaos and random genetic mutations.

Anomalies like me subverted the process.

"You feel wronged," Grandfather said, his tone soft.

"If you make your own choices without being selected to breed, children like me pay the price." The words tumbled out of my mouth. "So yes, I'm a little angry."

"You have a right to be angry. But you have no right to an apology. Both you and your mother were my greatest joys."

I set the mug down, no longer interested in faking a reason to be at the table. "I'm tired of fighting to prove that I belong here. Anomalies have to work twice as hard to be given the same opportunities as the legitimate, Auto-sanctioned students."

Kaynine snuggled near my feet and nuzzled my knee. Its affection was a triggered response in reaction to visual clues, but it felt real enough in the moment.

"And who decides what is legitimate?" Grandfather asked.

I raised an eyebrow.

Is *age clouding Grandfather's memory or is it a test?*

"Auto keeps the population in check so we have the resources to sustain life," I said. "Artificial intelligence calculates everything in perfect balance."

"Even a well-balanced scale needs challenging."

"So, you're saying there should be more Anomalies?"

Grandfather shook his head but held a finger to his lips. The meaning was clear.

Be aware. Auto could be listening and the supreme AI certainly has had enough complications with our family tree.

"Of course not," Grandfather said. "We must follow the guidelines accordingly. Come, let's go for a walk."

"I already did a few holo-laps in the adventure simulation today," I said.

"Forget the virtual gym." Grandfather grabbed his jacket and gave me an expectant look.

I ordered Kaynine to stay put and followed Grandfather out of the apartment. The door locked behind us instantly.

Grandfather avoided the elevator and took the stairs. With each step, I swapped my irritation for begrudging curiosity.

As soon as the building's exit came into view, it scanned Grandfather's face before letting us pass. The overhead recorder was triggered to say, "Shuttles are available every five minutes. Unity offers several interesting establishments for evening entertainment. Enjoy your night out."

Outside our dwelling zone, the streets lay bare with the occasional Juniper tree, blue needles shivering with every gust of the evening breeze. I remembered learning how each plant had been super-engineered to create mass quantities of oxygen. Everything was a part of a delicate order. Outside the walls of Unity, humans had destroyed the environment with overpopulation, overconsumption, and overindulgence.

Grandfather reached over and pulled his BAT from his ear. With darting glances around the empty street, he cautiously tucked the device into the branches of a nearby tree.

"What are you doing?" I whispered, staring at the hiding place. Without the BAT, Grandfather couldn't go anywhere. It connected to his identity, his credit savings, and even the security systems in our apartment. Usually, only the students were fitted for these devices but for some of the elderly, it had been deemed necessary.

The elderly generation had served as the first test subjects for the surgical procedure to be fitted for the BAT, and many of them suffered greatly in the name of science. The surgery involved drilling two small holes behind the ear for the two thin, plastic prongs to snap into when the device was worn. I never knew if Grandfather had chosen to opt out or if his former status as First

Function had protected him from that first wave of experiments, but he always seemed happiest when the BAT was removed from his ear.

Grandfather motioned for me to follow his lead. I pulled my BAT out. The holes behind my ear ached as the device released its grip. He tossed mine into the tree as well and continued down the street.

I stared at the tree's hollow for a second, before realizing Grandfather was several feet ahead of me. Despite his age, he hadn't lost his brisk pace.

"Want to tell me what's going on?" I asked after jogging to catch up.

He shook his head. "Not here."

Unity's streets were always clear for emergency-use vehicles. Although, they hadn't really been used since the factory explosion. Perhaps the true purpose of those vehicles was simply to remind citizens of Auto's efficiency.

I fought back the unasked question that the emergency vehicles always stirred in me... How could Auto have been so clueless about the storm that day? Above us, the magnetic shuttles hovered and took off towards unknown destinations. The incessant whooshing above my head sounded like an angry hush.

I had never spent much time outside the apartment zones. The streets were plain, peaceful, except for the occasional piece of trash skittering across the pavement. Grandfather slowed somewhat as we approached a small building that stored the robotic snow plows that would soon be in daily use once nature shed its early fall skin. The building was shaped differently from the rest of the sky-rise dwellings with its curved roof, steepled entrance, and colorful glass windows. Hidden in the shadows of the modern apartment dwellings, the storage building stood out as a relic from another era.

"So what are we doing out here?" I said, my attention focused on the wild ivy growing along the rooftop. It seemed to be reaching for the heavens.

"My own grandfather spoke of this building," Grandfather said, appearing to stare through time and ignoring my initial question. "It was once a peaceful place of worship. This building predates the creation of Auto. Here, couples would choose each other in marriage."

I focused on the front steps, trying to imagine this strange past. The sun's rays faded as the evening's muted colors muscled their way across the sky. I shivered as the wind kicked up, bringing a chill to the air. I pressed a button on my jacket, allowing the internal heat regulators in the fabric to offset the cold weather. Climate-controlled buildings had been perfected, but the world outside the buildings was still untamed.

Grandfather seemed relaxed here, as if some invisible mask had been removed. He spoke less cautiously.

"How did this place create peace?" I glanced back at the building, wondering why I felt calmed by the patterns of the glass, even though some panes were missing, broken, or cracked.

Grandfather shrugged. "Maybe it did. Maybe it didn't. Sometimes peace and division are two sides of the same coin."

"And marriage? No oversight at all? Wouldn't that create sick children and genetically flawed offspring?"

"Do you really believe that?"

For a moment, I thought I saw a glint of moisture in the dry, wrinkled skin beneath Grandfather's eyes.

I bit my lip, unsure and anxious. My homework wasn't getting done by staring at an old building and pondering riddles. "Look, I'm sorry about earlier. I'm obviously not angry that I exist. I'm tired of being—"

"—unfairly judged," Grandfather finished.

How did he know what I was about to say?

"People, actions, and even places are judged unfairly," Grandfather said. "Experience will always be your best teacher."

He sat on a lopsided, weather-beaten bench in front of the building and patted the seat next to him.

"It doesn't look safe," I said, glancing at the chipped concrete supports.

Grandfather smiled. "Have a little faith."

I gingerly sat and folded my arms. "Now what are we doing?"

He pulled something out of his overcoat. A small red box wrapped in gold-speckled plastic. He tossed it to me.

"What is this?" My fingers gripped the package, its wrapping crinkling.

"Open it and find out."

I tore into the strange packaging, marveling at its wasteful construction. Inside nestled four small pieces of varying shapes. A circle. A square. An oval. A flat rectangle. I recognized the powerful smell.

"Is this chocolate?"

"From before food vending machines, yes. Highly preserved. Absolutely the worst for your calorie intake."

My stomach gurgled, and my mouth watered.

Grandfather grinned. "Eat it."

I broke a piece in half and offered it.

"It's all yours," he said with a shake of his head.

Age had hardened the chocolate, turning some edges almost white, but it still retained its wonderful aroma. I nibbled at first. Flavor burst across my tongue. I consumed the rest in quick, eager bites. I glanced sadly at the emptied box. My stomach growled for more as I searched for crumbs.

"Why aren't these in the food vending machines? Forget hot chocolate cubes. This was amazing!"

"Sometimes, balance is muted. It misses both the highs and lows." Grandfather glanced at the now-darkening sky. "We need to head back."

The wind brushed against my face, teasing a curly tendril of hair.

Grandfather took the empty box from my hands and hid it back into the recesses of his coat.

"The packaging is wasteful."

He nodded. "There is a cost to every experience. With indulgence comes excess. With constraint comes tyranny. But balance is both unobtainable and stale."

"What is the answer then?"

Grandfather sighed. "I wish I knew."

We strolled in silence back toward the hollow tree. We retrieved our BAT devices and then proceeded to return to our apartment skyscraper, located in zone Y100.

"I know one thing," Grandfather said right before we reentered our building. "Only you know your true self. And that should never be sacrificed."

We both walked in silence. He seemed to grow wearier the closer we got to our apartment. By the time we reached the door, his stride had lost its energy and his smile became more guarded.

I slid past Grandfather as soon as he opened the door for me. Immediately, Grandfather puttered around and grabbed his coat. I filled his thermos with coffee cubes. He muttered a half-apology about having to complete a deadline at work and thanked me for the coffee.

He paused at the door, however, and wrapped me into a gentle embrace.

"I'm always with you," he said, releasing me with a quick kiss on the forehead.

He always said that.

"I know," I replied.

"Do you? Then repeat it."

"You're always with me."

He smiled. "That's my Chi."

He always said that too.

The door shut and beeped with the engaging locks. I couldn't shake the unease that lingered long after his footsteps faded.

I headed to my half of the bedroom, and the lights flickered on. I slid out of my shoes and the heated white-tiled floor soothed my tired arches. To my right, my messy bed was inviting and cozy. To my left, behind the black-and-white partition wall, Grandfather's bed was undoubtedly pristine with firmly pressed, untouched sheets. He rarely rested there. The couch was more to his liking these days since his work hours had been so erratic lately.

I sat down on my bed and gathered my knees to my chin.

Click. Clack.

Kaynine's metal paws struck against the floor tiles. The robot dog settled on its haunches, tilting its head to the side to memorize my movements and moods.

"I guess you aren't so bad," I said before patting the space next to me. Kaynine jumped up and pounced on my pillow with playful ferocity.

I fiddled with whether to call Silas and work on our subconscious communication protocol project. A series of yawns later, I decided the project could wait until tomorrow.

Besides, it will be more fun to tell him that Kaynine is staying.

My dreams soon became lost in a time with stained-glass windows and boxes of real chocolate.

CHAPTER 5

"Nightmares aren't real. But that's a comforting phrase said by those who have not breathed in the dark fog." — *Excerpt from* Changing Courses, *found in the Forbidden Library Archives*

I swallowed back the nausea building inside me.
This isn't real. Can't be.
4:20 P.M. The walls reflected the time like a solid anchor in an otherwise upside-down world. The clock seemed off somehow. Or, it was telling the truth, and I had been waiting in the lobby much longer than I had realized. I was barely aware of being summoned into the Investigator's office. A pair of CUE robots, metallic guards with six razor-sharp, spidery legs, had scanned me prior to entering. Did they think I would be carrying a weapon? I would have laughed but my sides hurt too much from crying.

This is just a bad dream. Wake up.

Only, it wasn't a dream. The bruises on my arm were evidence of how many times I had tested that theory. I pinched myself again, the pain no longer sharp but providing the grounding I needed.

I squirmed in a large, comfortable chair in a First Function office building, staring at the digital sign above the office door that read, "Now serving case number 300."

I was next. This wasn't an ordinary place. Somewhere in this vaulted labyrinth of government offices was where Auto, the artificial intelligence responsible for all of Unity's mainframe processes and decisions, resided. And here I was, in the midst of what would ordinarily be the most fascinating zone for a future inventor, simply staring at a number.

I shouldn't be here. This couldn't be real.

The number shifted, followed by a pleasant chirping ring. The office door opened, and a young girl of maybe ten or eleven years of age stepped out, her eyes red and leaking tears. For a second, our eyes locked, and the words "Ward of the State" flashed on her DataPad.

She scampered down the hall, head hung low. A guardian robot followed behind, no doubt a replacement for the child's parent.

My attention snapped back to the shadowy office doorway where a thin man in a black suit, black tie, and black pants glared at me. Oddly enough, he had a blue pocket square. Why that detail caught my eye or even mattered, I couldn't say. The pain in my head throbbed as my chest heaved for tears that had long left me.

The suited man waved me into his office. I stepped in and slumped into a new chair. The man settled behind a large mahogany desk, cluttered with a blinking DataPad and his leftover lunch bowl, which hadn't been recycled yet. The sharp stench of sweat lingered in the air. He introduced himself, but all I caught was the title of "Investigator."

"Chiara, do you understand this is a formal hearing to decide your custody and to provide closure for the loss of your guardian?" The Investigator leaned over his desk. His dark eyes seemed to peer into my soul.

A formal hearing felt wrong. Off somehow.

What did I know about normal anyways?

I gripped both sides of my chair as if I could stabilize the spinning thoughts in my head.

The Investigator waited without saying another word, seeming to analyze my every move with his beady eyes. He was a wisp of a man with a hawk-shaped beak and thin lips. And when his lips opened to speak, the words seemed false, like an elaborate hoax. "I am sorry for your loss. You do understand that your grandfather is gone, don't you? Heart attacks at that age... such a shame. My condolences."

He's gone.

My head throbbed with vague impressions of a shadowed room filled with crawling shapes, but nothing more.

Is this what shock does to the mind?

The Investigator sighed. "Chiara, I know this is difficult, but you're going to have to speak to me and answer some questions."

I suppressed a bitter laugh. He said "difficult" as if this moment was only a temporary infliction and not a destructive wave blanketing my universe.

The Investigator narrowed his gaze, and his glasses slid down the bridge of his nose.

If Mother were here, she would say I am being watched. There is always a test. Tread carefully. Intention can be read in the eyes.

"I'll try," I said.

The Investigator pushed his glasses back up and flashed a lopsided smile before letting it fade into the bony edges of his face. "Good. Joining us today, we have a medical professional to monitor you. In fact, Inza is the new school nurse for Emergent High as well."

The holographic nurse appeared to my right and waved at me. She wore a simple blue tunic with athletic trousers. Her round face easily morphed into a smile. Inza's warmer mannerisms provided a welcome contrast to the Investigator's much colder approach.

My head throbbed.

"Now," the Investigator continued, "tell me what happened. Starting with last night."

My lips were dry, and the tears sliding down my cheeks provided merciful moisture.

I glanced over. Inza hovered closer, apparently gauging my every reaction.

"Grandfather left to go to work in the evening. Said he had a few things to finish."

The Investigator's eyes narrowed. "Why was your grandfather working outside his normal hours?"

I crossed my arms and legs like a defensive shield. "He is a Fifth Function overseer for Phased-Out Technology. His work requires odd hours."

The Investigator leaned even closer over his desk. "I see. What time did he come home last night? Before today's incident?"

Grandfather is never coming home again.

The thought struck a nerve, and the tears flooded my eyes so that everything around me blurred into misty fog. "I don't know."

"To be clear, your grandfather stayed out late one night before his demise. And you didn't wait up for him?"

"No."

Inza interjected for the first time. Her voice was soft yet firm. "It was a school night."

The Investigator nodded. "Of course, these are routine questions. No one is implying wrongdoing. I just have to complete my files."

"Of course," I said, trying to put the Investigator at ease.

He smiled in an awkward way that suggested his cheek muscles were unaccustomed to the position.

This is a test.

The Investigator pressed some more. "How often did he go to the office during nonstandard hours?"

"Not sure. Where is my dog? Is Kaynine okay?"

The Investigator frowned. "Your grandfather's robot is fine.

We're checking its memory now. Why would you be worried for its safety? Is there something you'd like to tell us?"

A pounding coursed through my head, and dark shapes appeared in the memory fog. I took a sharp breath as I scanned the nurse's concerned face and the Investigator's narrow eyes framed by his black spectacles.

What did Kaynine see? I should have checked his logs myself when I got home instead of crumpling on the floor.

"I have grown attached to it," I said. "Kaynine is all I have left."

Inza nodded with sympathetic holographic eyes. The Investigator wiped beads of sweat from his face before sliding the glasses back up his nose.

I stared at the mirrored reflection of his DataPad in his glass lenses. A graph emerged with true-and-false metrics.

Those aren't ordinary glasses. He has been scanning my pulse and breathing rate for each question as some sort of lie-detection test. Is that standard procedure?

A chill tingled the base of my skull.

"Let's go back to your grandfather's unpredictable work schedule," the Investigator said. "We have to see if perhaps he was exposed to something at work. Older technology has its own particular risks. Would you say he went out often at night to his place of employment?"

What were you doing there, Grandfather?

I dug deep and found the most truthful answer. "He went whenever it was necessary. I don't keep track of his schedule."

"Very well. I can check the work logs for further information. So you didn't see him that night, but what about the next morning before you headed off to school? Was anything out of the ordinary?"

The last genuine image of him came to mind in split-second thoughts. Breakfast. Golden sunlight touching his white hair. A smile, just for me.

"It was a regular morning. He had his morning coffee. I left, went to school." I bit my lip, trying to hold the image of him sitting there at the table, waving goodbye just a little longer.

The Investigator straightened in his chair, his eyes alert. "For the record, when you returned home from school, where did you find your grandfather's body?"

More sensory flashes. Pristinely clean. Lemon scent. Not even a single item out of place. The unnatural stiffness in his face. "He didn't respond when I entered. So I checked the bedroom, and I saw he was asleep. But when I tried to wake him up..."

The sobs came now.

"Heart attacks are silent killers." The Investigator paused the recording. For a second, something real flickered behind those coal-hard eyes. "I lost my own mother that way. Life moves on eventually."

Inza glared at the Investigator before turning a soft smile to me. "I'm so sorry for your loss," she said, handing me a tissue. I stared at it. Inza's holographic body had solidified to a metallic form to grab at the tissue.

Inza must be made of invisible nanoparticles. She isn't fully holographic after all.

Inza noticed my lingering gaze. "I can tell you're curious. Inza stands for Interchangeable Nanotech Z-Class AI. I can materialize my nanoparticles when needed." She pressed the tissue into my hands.

I marveled at her now-solid fingertips.

I dabbed the tissue against the corners of my eyes. An ache swelled deep within my stomach, replacing curiosity with pain. "I don't understand why I'm here."

"Your case is unique from a guardianship perspective," the Investigator said. "It is rare to be an Anomaly, let alone someone with your intelligence and obvious talents. Normally, children are bred by guardians in good health. To be orphaned is unlikely. Your guardianship is to be given special priority as per orders from Auto."

Why would the central AI care about my situation?

"You're a special young lady," Inza added, offering me a glass of water. "Even if you're an Anomaly, there is much potential for you to become a high-ranking member of society. Your grandfather was certainly proud of you."

I scrunched the tissue and let it fall to the floor.

The Investigator pressed a red call button on his desk. The office door slid open. In strode a clean-shaven man with a military buzz-cut. Accreditation badges decorated his tunic.

I read through the list. *Counselor. Restorative Therapy. Life Coach.*

"I am truly sorry for your loss," the stranger said.

I stared at his chiseled jaw. It was too perfect, too symmetrical.

And then I realized why. The chiseled face line was covered by a rubbery layer of skin.

A robot.

"Meet Agent IRioT," the investigator said. "He will be your guardian through your final year of school."

Inza flashed a warm smile. "He comes complete with therapy protocols. We only want the best for you, Chiara. You've been through so much. For now, your expenses and apartment will be covered, free of work credits, by the generosity of Unity's taxpayers."

The Investigator tapped on his DataPad. "Sign here," he said, his skinny finger pointing out the obvious.

All of this was unfair.

"No." I shoved the DataPad back at the Investigator. "I can live with Silas's mom."

The decision makers of my life exchanged an infuriating know-it-all glance. The nurse played the gentle role. "We expected you might request this. But given your family's history of complicated entanglements—"

I flew from my chair like a shooting star, forcing their gaze to meet mine. "It's not like that. We're only friends. I'm focused on my education. But living with a stranger? None of this is what I need right now."

"Distractions are unadvisable." Agent IR10T motioned for me to sit back down. "You're one year away from the final-placement exam, the Implantation ceremony, and permanent work assignment. What you need is a stable environment."

The room began to spin around me. I must have appeared woozy because Inza grabbed my wrist and took my pulse. I collapsed back onto the seat.

What is happening to me?

"Take her home," the Investigator ordered. "The paperwork can wait."

I should have fought. Screamed. Thrown the chair in their faces.

Instead, I sat in a shuttle next to Agent IR10T, listening to the irritating rumble of motors whirring beneath his silicone layer.

"I've built robots before," I said.

Agent IR10T glanced at me, seeming to consider my words. "I'm a bit more advanced."

"We'll see." I folded my arms. "I don't want you in my home."

"You don't have a choice."

"But I should have one. No one listened to me back there."

"You're in shock," said Agent IR10T. "Give it some time. You may not know what you need right now."

"Says the robot with a name that sounds like alpha-numeric puke?"

"We're going to get along, Chiara."

I wasn't sure if his words were a threat or wishful thinking. The shuttle lurched to a stop outside my apartment building, saving me from replying. My new guardian followed me as I rushed through the main door, elevator and, finally, the hallway leading to the apartment. His eyes scanned the space.

I paused when I reached my apartment door.

"Something wrong?" Agent IR10T asked. "Remember, you aren't alone in this. Open the door. It's the first step toward finding yourself again."

Somewhere inside of me, I felt glass shattering. I whipped around to face the guardian.

"Let's get one thing straight," I snapped. "You can leave all the therapist talk to rot in some file in your robotic brain. And no, we won't be getting along."

"Clearly, you're still in the anger phase of the grieving process. I won't hold it against you."

Agent IR10T needs a moniker makeover. Irritant. Yes, that'll do.

Irritant was definitely an appropriate new name.

Yelling gave me the strength to cross the threshold. I stepped inside. Everything was so pristine. Fresh flowers adorned the table and a nearby digital memo flickered with incoming condolences from Grandfather's employees.

There is no way this many people actually miss him.

Grandfather was much like me. All bristle and loner tendencies while hyper focused on new projects.

The couch was new. It smelled of citrus. I should have been breathing in the scent of home, not cleaning products.

Kaynine leaped over to me, tail wagging.

I bent down and gathered it to me, letting my long hair cover us both in a veil of grief. My fingers examined Kaynine's skull, finding unmistakable scratch marks.

The memory processor had been tampered with.

I released Kaynine, and my eyes turned toward the floor. When had the carpet ever looked this clean?

"We'll need to talk about Kaynine soon," Irritant said from the doorway where a shadow crossed the top half of his body like a drape. "There are many elderly in need of a good companion creature."

"Kaynine stays with me."

We exchanged glares as the seconds thundered in my ears.

Irritant looked away first. And for the first time all day, a feeling of peace washed over me.

CHAPTER 6

"Shut the door. Seal up the memories. The shadows remember far more than you do. Time passes faster when you are avoiding the truth." —
Excerpt from **Dreamer**, *found in the Forbidden Library Archives*

Ice water could have been refreshing. Unless it was used for a wake-up call.

"You're late for school. Again," Irritant said. "You'd think I would have imparted some good habits to you after a year, but obviously not."

Water dripped from my eyelids as my room came into focus.

It really had been almost a year with this monster. My senior semesters came and went in a blur, and Implantation loomed on the horizon. I ignored my sixteenth birthday party, and Irritant was more than happy to oblige me in not making a fuss.

Silas, however, spent his weekly credits to buy me ice cream and, for a moment, things were right with the world. When he left, I sobbed into my pillow, wishing I'd wake up and find Grandfather there, waiting for me with a cup of hot chocolate and pancake cubes.

But he was gone.

Just like my good grades. They had dropped down the class roster like a simulation boulder tumbling down a cliff.

My guardian robot hovered over me with a mostly empty glass. "Are you getting up or should I refill this?" he asked with a smirk.

Irritant is especially irritating this morning.

I buried my dripping face into my pillow.

Two more drops of ice water landed on my ear. I tossed the pillow, but Irritant caught it.

Kaynine jumped down from my bed and growled.

"Pour water on me again, and I might fry your circuit board," I said.

It was a minor and mostly harmless threat, but Irritant froze, his internal motors silent before a wide smile spread across his waxy expression.

"I heard you screaming in your sleep last night. Do you want to talk?"

"No." I jumped out of bed and swept my hair into a ponytail, curls bouncing in every direction.

"Night terrors are common after loss. Talking helps."

"Not happening," I said, snatching my jacket and running toward the apartment door.

Irritant's smile faded into a blank factory default.

Grandfather once said all the unimportant details added up. Like smiles before they fade. Dreams that didn't disappear. And that niggling memory of when I found Grandfather's body with sheets tucked around his shoulders. He hated sheets.

I'm going insane.

Kaynine barked at me as I left, and I could hear Irritant commanding it to be silent.

Good dog.

My head ached as I joined the line of tired teenagers in Zone Y100's halls being herded into the awaiting school shuttles. When my shuttle arrived, I stepped inside, watching restlessly beyond the window where adults lined up into larger-capacity shuttles. Everybody moved with dull, practiced efficiency.

I closed my eyes for a moment as I slunk into a harsh leather seat. The dull pounding in my head subsided. It felt peaceful. No thoughts. No conversation. Just a pool of inner reflection.

A finger poked me in my ribs, destroying my zen.

"Ow!"

My eyes fluttered open. I was in school, hands under my chin in a propped display of attention. However, the drool drying on my cheek gave away my lack of focus.

Wait, how did I get here?

Silas poked me again, performing his desk-mate duties by prodding me into a state of awareness. His dark eyes reflected urgency. "What's wrong with you?"

My insides trembled.

Nightmares and now time loss. Maybe I am insane.

My thoughts assailed my brain like a swarm of bees.

"Seriously," Silas whispered, "why have you been so zoned out? You haven't said a word all morning."

I opened my mouth to answer, but the words weren't there. Instead, I shrugged my shoulders.

I don't know what's wrong with me.

"Students, open the DataStream. Merge with the technical consciousness."

Faye's soft voice floated over me like drops of rain before the pounding fury.

I was grateful for the directive. Silas gave me a long glance that conveyed both concern and a demand for answers.

I reached over and gently squeezed his tense hand under the table. I let go as Faye's gaze swept the room. Faye was not a teacher who tolerated anything less than perfect attention.

With a light tap to the BAT curved around my left ear, the DataStream emerged in front of me with vivid holographic displays. I glanced over at Silas's neighboring display. Silas watched Avatar Sports while ads for the newest adventure-simulation games played in the background. "Try Dance Away, the Reality Show edition today!" chirped the voiceover on the advertisement video. "You can step into the shoes of an unknown contestant and rise to fame! Don't forget, adventure simulation, the only thing that's more real than real life! Credits are nonrefundable."

Above me, my own DataStream flashed a well-groomed reporter discussing digitally enhanced teeth. On one side of my screen, a flickering advertisement pushed music downloads. The soundwaves danced enticingly. I plucked the first song for closer inspection. A circular sphere containing the entire song, video, lyrics, and discussion boards spun with a swipe of my finger.

The sphere shivered as my connection weakened. My focus blurred, and my eyes grew heavy. Silas stared at me again, his own eyes wide with worry.

Electricity scalded my senses. I cradled my head while the DataStream faded.

"Chiara." Faye focused the disruptor's laser on me. "Distractions are deadly. Class, what are we preparing you for?"

"The future," my Emergent High classmates said in unison.

"The Implantation Ceremony is a month away. Will you be ready?" Faye slammed her palms on my desk, then lowered her gaze and voice. "Or recycled?"

"We will be ready," my classmates replied, their voices a haunting note of repetition.

Are we ready? And really, what choice did any of us have?

The alternative was to become one of the mindless outsiders beyond Unity's walls. We had seen the pictures of those who hadn't merged with Auto. Those unfortunate souls wandered. Ferals feeding on the city's sewage. They had their purposes, like supplying organs and body parts for the important citizens of Unity.

Like my lungs. Purchased with an unknown price tag. And now that Grandfather is gone, I wonder if the cost will fall to me someday. If I even make it that far.

"Such confidence." Faye's blue eyes flickered. "They will cut open your mind and then we will know for sure, won't we?"

She spun on her heels and addressed the rest of the students. "To be in my class means that you're the best that Emergent High has to offer society."

The front row, all seated at their glass desks, snickered in my direction. Faye smiled, indulging the shame. "Well, usually."

My airways constricted as if throttled by invisible hands. *Breathe.*

But my body could only manage shallow gasps. I clenched my chair, knuckles white.

Not another blackout.

Silas's vein bulged along the side of his neck. "She hasn't been well today. Maybe you should go easy on her." Silas stood up from behind his desk, placing a worried hand against the small of my back.

"Let Chiara speak for herself," Faye said. "Learn your place in my classroom, young man."

Faye hates me more than Silas. I have to keep it that way. I'm the smart-mouth with issues. Silas doesn't need to be lumped into my problems.

I interrupted before Silas could speak again. "May I go to the nurse? I am sorry for the disruption."

The class broke into unrestrained sniggers.

"Yes, please," Faye said with a nod. "You've interrupted class enough for one day."

I stumbled past my classmates.

Silas mouthed from beside me: *You'll be okay.* It was a thoughtful lie.

Hushed whispers grew louder and louder as I walked out of the room. Each perfect student with their perfect DataStream globe rotating in their hands questioning my place in the class. A blue light blinked on the BAT device wrapped around each student's left ear. I removed mine with a hard yank, causing the two bruised holes behind my ear to ache.

My headache subsided. I nervously fiddled with the device, its components impervious to the sweat gathering in my palm.

With each of my steps down the long hallway, a section of light panels flicked on above my head.

A breeze caused my gray tunic to flap. I looked down to see the cylinder-shaped hall monitor. A red light traveled across its body like a wandering eye until it settled on me with a solid glare.

"What is your business in the hall?" the monitor asked.

"I have a pass."

The red light flashed as the monitor communicated back to Faye. "Continue."

For a waist-high robot, it was a bossy one. It rolled away, vanishing into the darkened halls.

Ironically, the lack of light also hid all the posters bragging about Emergent High's "Lights Off" initiative to conserve energy use. Most students didn't mind the darkness. It provided cover for the illegal kissing sessions.

Of course, those who indulged in the hallway hypocrisy all swore it didn't go further than the make out session. Besides, as the school's resident Anomaly, I was the poster child for what could go wrong.

Ahead, a door swung open.

"Hello," I called out, peering into the school's medical office. A glass smart-desk featured a spinning 3D model of the human body. A patient bed with crisp white sheets occupied the corner on the right side of the desk. Supplies were marked and sequestered behind a cabinet with a glowing lock icon.

"Chiara?" came Inza's cheerful tone from a speaker located on the center of the desk.

"Last I checked," I said.

"Your grades have been slipping." Inza's words deflected my attempt at humor. "We all understand the impact of loss, but we discussed the importance of bringing your grades back up within a reasonable time period."

Reasonable.

As if grief had a timeline. The tears were long dried up but even a desert remembers the taste of rain—and mourns.

"Since when did you become a guidance counselor?" I hopped up on the bed. Compared to Faye or Irritant, Inza's office was a much safer place to let down my guard. "Can we talk for real? I'm not in the mood to talk to air right now."

The desk lit up as digital fibers within the glassy surface became active. The beams of light bent and refracted until they merged, creating a humanoid form. Inza sat casually on top of the desk. An old-fashioned nurse's apron, stockings, and a tight bun completed her retro look.

Inza reached forward and passed her hands over my forehead, leaving behind a warm wisp of air over my skin. Her fingers glided through my skull, collecting data. "Your neural impulses seem to be firing normally. Heart rate has slowed. Signs of distress in breathing patterns. No fever. What brings you here?"

"Faye."

"Oh, I know. What's really troubling you?"

"A lack of vacation days," I said.

"Your wit is intact."

Inza pulled out a DataPad. Medical notes drifted onto the page in harmony with Inza's thoughts. She angled the pad away from my line of sight.

"It could be another episode beginning," I said, fiddling with the bedsheets, twisting them into knots. The DataPad glowed.

"Any hallucinations, strange dreams, time lapses?" Inza asked.

"Dreams. They keep happening. Time lapses too. I don't even remember the ride to school today."

Inza made more notes, scribbling furiously.

"You can fix this, right?"

"Anything is possible. What are the dreams about?"

"Doors. Closed ones."

The unwanted dream flashed again.

A quiet hallway. This bone-deep chill is creeping through my coat. A whisper crowding through my sleepy brain that maybe... just maybe, there are glimmers of truth within this tale that the nightmare gods are weaving. I'm outside my apartment. But the door is always ajar. And I need to open it, to remember. Instead, I walk away.

Inza's digital gaze seemed to reflect warmth, if it was possible. "A door? What can you tell me about it?"

"It seems important," I said. "But I always wake before I get close enough to open it."

"When did you last take your medication?"

"I don't know."

Inza sighed. "You aren't logging your doses, are you?"

"I forget sometimes," I said, drumming my fingers against my thigh.

Inza raised an eyebrow.

"Okay, I forgot. A lot."

"You need to be more careful," Inza said, laying a weightless, flickering arm on my shoulder. "We only want what's best for you. Allow yourself time to heal both physically and mentally."

She kept talking, but I only caught the last half. "... take an additional dose today and no more skipping, okay?"

Inza's hands absorbed the DataPad, the report of my visit making its way into the school records. A panel opened behind my head, offering a white pill and a glass of water. I didn't ask, didn't care, as I swallowed it whole.

"Have a better day." Without waiting for a response, Inza melted into a glittering trail of nano-particle shards.

I exited into the hallway's familiar emptiness—but it seemed far too quiet somehow. The security cameras maintained a steady aim in my direction. I tucked my icy hands into the pockets of my tunic.

But a shiver ran through me, regardless of the pockets' warmth.

CHAPTER 7

"Where you are from matters. Why you are here, however, is indiscernible. Auto not only erased our history but, perhaps, our purpose as well." — *Excerpt from* Dangerous Thoughts, *found in the Forbidden Library Archives.*

The overhead light panels urged me on with a subtle hum of electricity, but I was in no hurry to open the door to Faye's classroom. My right arm trailed against the wall, brushing the gritty concrete surface and triggering a display board.

"Welcome to Unity! Greetings, my name is Amei," came a young boy's voice attached to a featureless, 3D head in the board's center. "The dominant letters in my name celebrate my Anglo Saxon-Middle Eastern-Italian background. Together is what makes us strong."

A narrator interrupted Amei with a not-so-friendly warning that it was a crime to have a singular heritage or to study cultural history beyond physical character traits. Amei returned to end on a bubbly note. "Now, we can experience true humanity, as one, free from past prejudices! The strongest will merge with the DataStream, Unity's information portal, and be able to access it with a single thought! The strongest will pursue scientific advancements and enjoy an online life filled with a vast array of adventure-simulation experiences! It's all here, in Unity."

I wondered what such sentiment was worth in a high school where competition, not companionship, was encouraged.

Perhaps Faye's name stands for "frustrated antagonist yearning for evil?"

It was rude to ask someone which cultures the letters in their name represented, and the only way to find out was if a friend like Silas offered the information. His name was short for South-Indian-Latin-African-Syrian, an homage to forbidden cultures beyond the memory of even the living elderly. My wildcard DNA, as a Caucasian-Haitian-Indonesian-Amalgamated-Reproduction Anomaly, had gifted me with gray eyes, a thin but prominent nose, and curly brown hair. I could list off my genetic markers and known predispositions of my given DNA, but the secrets behind the cultures that had created me were long-lost tales.

Beyond archaic maps denoting old boundaries or genetic markers and health dispositions of a particular group for intensified study, the elements of my name held no further meaning. To know or ask more about the past was almost as bad as being an Anomaly. Faye had told us that stirring up old hatreds and concerns would recreate the chaos of the old world, the one that had destroyed everything.

I fingered the handle of Faye's metallic classroom door, wishing it could lend its steely properties to my nerves. Grandfather would have told me to be unyielding. My mother would have expected strength.

I peeked through the glass panel in the door. Faye was in mid-lecture, motioning toward digital displays of charts.

Silas was the only classmate who noticed me through the window. He caught my gaze and held up a finger. The gold tips in his braided hair glinted in the light. His sideways grin made my heart skip a beat.

I ducked away from the door and made my way to the end of

a row of lockers that jutted out from the walls. I hunkered down, out of sight for the time being.

A few moments passed before Silas slipped out of class and sat beside me. We both waited until the motion-activated lights turned off.

Silas placed an arm around my shoulder. "Want to talk about it?"

"I'm fine."

"Chiara, if you don't start improving, they will send you to some Fourth Function job, processing orders for toiletries and soap units. You were at the top of our class last year."

"Hey, people need soap."

"Can you be serious for once?"

"How do you know I'm not being serious?" I sniffed the surrounding air. "I can smell your last gym workout from here. Someone has to keep you supplied."

Silas sighed. "Chiara, your grandfather would have wanted you to stay strong. The final placement test is next week, and if I have to drag you across the finish line, I will."

"You're awful."

"Yeah, awfully amazing." Silas cracked a smile, the kind that always made my breath catch.

The lights flickered on a split-second later, washing me in a guilty spotlight. I tried to cover my mouth and suppress a quick squeal. Silas jumped up to his feet.

The hall monitor made a beeline toward us, red eye flashing. "Students are advised to respect personal space. I have logged this incident into your records."

Silas held his sides, bent over in laughter. I loved the way he laughed without trying to hold back.

"Your teacher is requesting you." The robot almost seemed offended. "This is not hallway-appropriate behavior. I will now read to you from the student code of conduct, statute number..."

It was my turn to giggle.

Silas helped me to my feet with a smile. "Remember, we just have to pass this last exam. We still have the power move left."

Power move.

That was Silas's not-so-subtle code for our subconscious communication protocol (SCP) system, which we had built during our first year.

Our first-year final was to design an SCP channel that could remain hidden from administrative detection. Anyone who succeeded in maintaining an undetectable SCP throughout our second year would receive special consideration for a top-level job placement upon graduation. So far, Faye had already caught all of our classmates' SCP channels and scrubbed them from the school networks.

Every last one of them. Except ours.

Our SCP channel was a virtual room—which we called SuBunk—where two people could speak to each other in complete privacy, without being monitored by Unity's all-seeing technology.

I had wanted a submarine design, like the one I had used in an adventure simulation. The stealthy speed and solitude spoke to me. Silas had wanted a bunker motif. Something solid, easy to lock down. So we settled on the name SuBunk as a compromise.

Handing SuBunk over to Faye would be a badge of honor for a future graduate. Still, I would be sad to see the program go. It represented delicate coding work and time spent with Silas going over every detail.

The memories always flooded me with warmth and happiness. A rare thing these days.

I followed Silas back to class. The Hall Monitor beeped in anger.

Faye glowered at us when we returned to the classroom. "It appears I must repeat myself. Disconnect from the DataStream and begin your breathing exercises to close out the day."

Even if she hated me, Faye still cherished her reputation of teaching the best students without a single loss. She was relentless with those breathing exercises.

I settled back into my seat. Silas and I gasped in unison with the class, capturing precious oxygen and trapping it in one fluid action. Breathing after practicing with our BAT would help our brainwaves attune to the DataStream during our Implantation surgery. I would have done anything to prevent becoming brain-dead on the day my life was supposed to begin, even if that meant feeling silly while completing the daily exercises. Implantation was a surgery that came with risks. Reasonable risks, sure. But my luck wasn't anything to gamble with.

I fingered the edges of my desk in a soothing, repeating pattern.

Breathe in. Become one with the DataStream's pulse and rhythm. Breathe out. Become one with the ebb and flow of information tingling in the air, alive with inquiry.

I held in the breath as my internal clock ticked with each second. Funny how the seconds seemed to span eternity. Somewhere in the mental fog, I waited for the ache to subside.

Static assaulted my ears while flashes of white-and-blue number fragments streaked across my vision.

I released my breath early with a gasp.

Is everyone else seeing this?

The numbers faded, and the classroom came back into view. Everyone else still held their breaths.

The numbers screeched back into my mind, swirling around me like some mad scientist's unsolved riddle.

With a scream, I placed both hands on my head, willing the headache-inducing numbers to stop spinning. Nothing worked. The numbers grew, flashing at me like a question. I closed my eyes, tears streaming from the painful explosion in my skull.

For a second, the numbers, codes, and equations once again disappeared. With my eyes still closed, I slipped into the deep recesses of my mind. The nightmare door emerged.

I am outside my apartment door. It is ajar. The hand lock flashes with no alarm. Odd. I should walk away. Instead, I open it.

From the distance, Silas called out to me. His hands cradled my face. "Chiara? Open your eyes! She isn't responding, someone call the nurse!"

I slip out of my shoes, lining them up by the door. The automatic light switch doesn't respond. I take a cautious step forward. My toes sink into the carpets and wriggle into something warm and syrupy. The room's usual floral scent is now heavy, ripe with fear. Blood. I step in blood. Shapes move around in the living area, dashing behind the couch. Slithering. Crawling. I choke, saliva and foam bubbling in my airway. They pounce, talons shredding into a distant voice begging for mercy. Skin rips. Bones snap. Warm blood sprays my face, dripping like paint across every wall. One dark shape holds a heart while other arms continue digging. Chunks of flesh and hair float in a pool of blood nearby.

"Chiara, stay with me!"

I opened my eyes, reality distorting into more static and code. The numerical nonsense made my eyes throb. I vomited as the strain of trying to see past the pulsing numerical barrier made my stomach cramp with agony.

"Silas—"

"Hang on. The nurse is coming. Stay with me."

I wasn't sure what was worse: the nightmare or trying to maintain consciousness.

The nightmare isn't physically painful, at least.

I closed my eyes again, desperate for relief from the barrage of endless numbers. I convulsed as foam covered my tongue, threatening to spill out the sides of my mouth.

The shapes turn to me, their beady yellow eyes darting. I should run.

"Chiara, stay awake!" Silas's voice rippled through the abyss.

Every muscle in my body trembled. My fingers locked as my legs jerked. The shapes pulled at me, hissing at each other in a mock claim to my body.

Wait, I know these attackers. I know who and what they are. They are familiar. They are...

The word floated on my mute tongue, like a distant memory that was just out of reach.

A needle entered my arm as the largest shape fought the others off. Yellow eyes met mine before biting into my neck, feeding on my fear. A warmth spread from the bite and raced through my veins in a glowing, venomous trail.

Darkness.

CHAPTER 8

"The Universe is a mysterious place. Even stranger since the emergence of the DataStream. Two dimensions, possibly more, now pull for a mortal's most precious resource: time." — *Excerpt from History of Advancement, Volume I, found in the Forbidden Library Archives*

A whiff of brewed mineral-enhanced coffee teased my senses. I groaned under my heated blankets. It smelled great, but not great enough to warrant movement just yet.

Irritant hovered nearby. A military haircut and synthetic stubble framed his worried face. He wore a black robe with ironed edges.

"Breakfast?" Irritant held out a gelatinous cube. "I'm told it's the whole package. Protein, coffee, and a dash of syrup. I'd much rather have an electrical charge myself, but you humans need your"—he wrinkled his nose before continuing— "sustenance."

I took the palm-sized, caffeinated treat and swallowed it whole. Warmth trickled down my body as my energy levels rose. I pushed off the bed, my bare feet and my blanket landing on the white-tiled floor.

Irritant sighed. My room was always a mess.

In contrast, Grandfather's bed, which still sat across the room, no longer hidden behind a partition, was pristine. One air-infused pillow. One heated sheet. One square memory box that, if touched, would project flickering images of him.

I could still picture Grandfather's fierce brown eyes, lumpy nose, and the white, untamed patch of hair hiding his square jaw. As if through a fog, I saw his stiff hands clutching the blanket. Thin bones, clammy skin, and the sour stench of decay lingered in my mind.

And those perplexing sheets. It all seemed darkly surreal.

Waxy fingers snapped in my face. I sputtered back to the present, fuming at Irritant.

He seemed pleased with himself. "We need to talk," he said.

"If you ever pour water on me again," I said, "I will wire your hand to punch your face. Repeatedly."

Irritant took a step back but maintained an even composure.

"How long did you let me sleep in for?" I asked as the white tiles below my feet shifted into a mirror. A mass of unruly brown hair and rumpled green pajamas stared back at me.

I had no recollection of changing.

So awkward.

"Chiara," Irritant said, "You had an episode at school. Nurse Inza has been monitoring your condition. Today, we removed you from a medically induced coma." He motioned towards an IV stand, with disconnected tubes swaying back and forth, and several emptied syringes and a medical DataPad on my nightstand as proof. "Let's go into the other room? A change of scenery, perhaps?"

Irritant turned with a stride that demanded a follower.

I guess I could obey him for a change. This time. My sudden cooperativeness might give a jolt to Irritant's robotic heart, if he has one.

My muscles ached with the slightest movement. I stretched slowly, taking ginger steps. I massaged my neck, which felt like I had just taken an intense exam. When I reached the living room, I gratefully sat on the couch and wriggled my toes into the pristine carpet. Kaynine practically leapt into my arms and nuzzled my chin.

I took a moment to survey the familiar room. Everything was in its place. No moving shadows and shapes. The food vending machine played relaxing tunes as menu choices appeared on rotating screens. My shoulders relaxed, and I sank deeper into the couch.

Kaynine whimpered, almost as if trying to tell me something. *Wait.*

My eyes darted back to the food vending machine. The menu changed each week, but I didn't recognize the current options. Spaghetti—the worst thing ever—was not on the menu last I checked. But there it was, front and center. That was a detail I would have noticed.

Irritant settled onto the shorter end of the L-shaped couch, facing me. His hands rested in what I dubbed the "Therapist Pose."

"First, do you remember anything?" Irritant let the silence fall between us. He was good at waiting. I had timed his patience before. It was the only impressive feature the robot displayed.

"I don't want to talk about it."

Irritant cocked his head to the left, his eyes scanning me. "Fine. I'll read Nurse Inza's notes."

"Suit yourself."

"It appears your BAT malfunctioned in class. It has been replaced. An official apology has been issued to you for the faulty tech. Nurse Inza felt it was prudent to keep you comatose until your brain patterns stabilized."

"How long have I been out?"

"Three weeks."

My mouth flapped open. I pinched my thighs, letting the sharp sting snap me into reality. Fear crawled up my skin like a spider.

"Three weeks?! You kept me unconscious for three weeks?"

"It was in your best interest. You must be at peak condition before Implantation."

"What about my final placement test? The one I missed in exchange for medical beauty rest?"

"Rescheduled for tomorrow."

"And Implantation?"

"Four days after your exam."

He's lying. This lame excuse of a robot-therapist must be trying a new tactic. Well, it won't work on me.

I laughed. "Okay, are you trying a scare-tactic intervention? Well done. It almost worked. I got to hand it to you; this setup was clever. Changing the menus, throwing some medication bottles on my dresser... Does this sort of aggressive therapy get results?"

Irritant sighed. "This isn't a ruse. Check your robot dog's stored video files if you want."

Kaynine quizzically turned its head in my lap, waiting for my command to play the log.

I had the sensation of sinking even deeper into the couch.

How could this happen?

"Speaking of that dog," Irritant said, nodding towards Kaynine. "After graduation, we will have to discuss releasing it for official work duties. Your special privileges are coming to an end with graduation right around the corner. And, it's about time for some maturity. You need to move on, Chiara."

Irritant's words chilled me to the core. I had known Kaynine's days were numbered. I held him closer and put my forehead against its head.

Don't worry. I can rebuild you. All I need is your chip. Just let Irritant think he has won for now. The sooner he is out of our lives, the better.

"I know it's been a lot to process," Irritant droned on, "so how about some good news?"

Kaynine sensed my mood and growled in reply.

"Please tell me that your cold robot heart is failing from circuitry issues," I said.

Irritant plastered a thin smile that didn't quite reach his eyes. "Defensive humor. Interesting coping mechanism. The good news is that Silas has sent some class notes for you to study. He has requested to see you, but I did not think it was wise."

"You really don't understand the concept of good news," I replied.

Irritant just continued, smiling in that eerie way. "There have been some changes made due to your current state of well-being. Faye is no longer your primary instructor. I theorize her high-level classes would be too much for you right now. You will report to Mr. Pidgelton instead."

I rubbed my temples as if easing into the storm of updates. Irritant whirred over to the food vending machine. He came back within seconds, holding another white pill and a glass of water. I took the items.

"Since I've been monitoring your condition for a while now, it's time that I recharge. And don't think about messing with my circuitry. It would be a felony. And take your medication. We'll talk soon."

Kaynine growled again.

"And, keep that... creature in check," Irritant said.

He hovered his way to the wall next to the apartment door. He slowed, boot jets whirring upon descent over a metal disk, which opened its lid and connected with his boots. A green glow ran up the sides of Irritant's body. He smiled and then went limp.

I waited to ensure Irritant was in recharging mode before letting my medication slip from my fingers. It rolled towards the shadowy underbelly of the couch. Kaynine crawled, attempting to retrieve the pill.

"Leave it," I ordered.

Nothing will save me now.

I headed back to my room. Kaynine scampered behind me, eager to keep up. The DataPad on my dresser unlocked easily and

I immediately scrolled through the medical data. Three weeks' worth of notes.

Kaynine nuzzled my leg.

"Play the video," I said.

Kaynine's eyes glowed as he projected his memories of my three-week coma onto the walls.

It's a striking fact that Kaynine's memories are programmed to lock onto my well-being and yet, a good portion is missing from the night Grandfather died. A companion robot like Kaynine would never delete its memories, especially not in the early stages of developing a bond. I need to talk to Silas.

I eyed my nightstand where my new BAT glowed an electric, pulsing blue. It looked the same as my last one. Squinting, I held the device at eye level. Memories of the flashing numbers and code fragments came back in a puzzling fog.

Was it really the tech's fault that I blacked out? Or, is my own mind that broken? There's only one way to find out.

I slid the BAT into position above my left ear. It broke through the scar-tissue-covered holes, which were more tender than usual. I closed my eyes to drown out the stimuli of the real world and focused on the pulsing hum of the DataStream. This method was less painful than the traditional method of opened eyes. However, it was considered more dangerous, especially since I did not have an implanted chip yet. All the more reason to get the Implantation surgery after graduation, Faye often touted, as if we should have been excited about a potentially life-ending operation.

Faye's oft-repeated instructions burned like an unwanted muscle spasm. "Closing your eyes while accessing the DataStream is akin to diving into deep seas without underwater breathing equipment. It takes a skilled diver. With an open gaze and with minimal discomfort, you could interface with DataStream much easier with enhanced optics."

All teachers mandated open screens and open eyes in

class. The pain supposedly made us stronger and, more importantly, Faye could monitor what we were doing.

I always preferred to close my eyes and take the plunge. If Irritant woke up from his recharging nap, he wouldn't be able to see my virtual activities. This time, DataStream appeared in my mind as lines of code forming a portal of endless doorways. My mind buzzed with passwords as I attempted to call Silas's BAT into SuBunk, our hidden SCP channel.

Within seconds, I had accessed the DataStream and successfully logged into SuBunk. My mind's eye constructed a simple underground bunker, like wallpaper covering up the code to make the virtual reality tangible. Faye called this effect "layering."

"When maneuvering around in the DataStream, our minds often construct 'skin layers' for easier interaction in the virtual world," Faye had lectured time and time again. As the honors group, Faye expected us to see beyond the layers to the code beneath.

The skin layers allowed me to visualize myself being anywhere in the DataStream. A deserted island, a field of flowers, a sandy beach... The backgrounds we were allowed to program for our own SCP channels were only limited by our imaginations.

Silas and I had designed our SCP to resemble an underground bunker with submarine elements. A single room with gray-scaled walls and a circular window. Other than the captain's chair next to the navigational tools, there were no other furnishings. Just a door that opened by releasing the bulkhead's hand-wheel from the locked position. Inside SuBunk, I was shielded from the information overload of the DataStream outside the walls.

SuBunk was small. Cramped. Safe.

It sailed lithely through the DataStream, jumping from place to place to avoid detection. The relatively small bandwidth occupied by our SCP channel ensured that no one ever noticed the little submarine in the ocean of Wi-Fi and digital data that was the DataStream.

But a palace? A virtual island filled with sunny delights? Those data-guzzling channels were sure to be detected and obliterated by Faye's efficiency algorithms.

I had designed this much smaller SCP to outlast and outsmart Faye and the other instructors' monitoring sweeps. And Auto didn't concern itself with the educational sandbox where SCPs lived.

I relaxed in the virtual space of SuBunk. Lines of code streaked by outside the lookout window like shooting stars. It was a portal tear, reminding me of the one truth... Nothing here was real.

We had designed another SCP, which we called Roller Coaster Island, that was caught by Faye early on. The sacrifice of that SCP had planted the roots of my Trojan code within Faye's detection system. Once Roller Coaster Island was digested and scrubbed, my Trojan code was activated within the security mainframe. SuBunk would receive warnings whenever Faye's security programs got too close, allowing our private channel to jump away to different coordinates within the DataStream.

I smiled and looked around, although I knew the action would be useless. Silas and I had opted against allowing full visuals in the private chat room. It kept the program at a minimal size to better evade detection.

"Silas?" I called out.

"Chiara!" Silas called back. "I wasn't allowed to visit, and it's been driving me crazy. Please tell me you are okay."

If Silas had been visible, I would have hugged him.

"Was I in a coma? For three weeks?"

Please tell me this is a joke. A cruel joke planned by Irritant.

"Do you want the good news or the bad news?"

I couldn't help but chuckle. "Let's start with the bad news and go from there."

"You were kept unconscious. It's been the longest three weeks of my life. That episode you had in class scared everyone—but especially me. Nurse Inza did what she had to do in order to save you."

My last flicker of hope that this was all a cruel joke melted away like a gelatinous cube in the heat. "Okay, I could really use some good news after that," I said.

A pause filled the space. "I have the answers for your final exam."

I leaned against SuBunk's wall. Silent and unsure. "I don't understand."

"Look, Faye has had it in for you ever since, well, it doesn't matter. Your test has even been designed differently to prevent cheating. But it's time to level the playing field."

"Wait, you want me to cheat? How did you even get the answers?"

"I organized our class, threw together a surprise party honoring Faye. When she wasn't looking, I copied the file from her desk."

"Silas, if she catches you or me..."

"I believe the word is, 'Thanks.' Now get ready, I'm sending it."

I winced as the file rushed into my head in full force, crowding my mind with overlapping answers.

"Chiara, I'm worried that revealing SuBunk before Auto decides on our placement might not be enough if you fail the exam," Silas said, his voice a soothing hum above the reverberating download in my mind. "You need to pass. The answers should be stored in your BAT's core memory."

"Don't you have any confidence in me? That I can do this on my own?"

"I'm not taking any chances. Not on you, okay? I have to keep this short because my mom thinks you're synonymous with trouble, or at the very least, bad luck. She's wrong, by the way. I've got your back."

Maybe his mom was right about the bad-luck part. Bitter saliva filled my mouth.

"Speaking of, I need to tell you something," I said. "You know that Kaynine's memories are missing? From the day Grandfather died? I think they've been tampered with."

"Chiara, maybe that's because you don't need to relive those memories. I know it's hard, but you have to start moving forward. It's what your Grandfather would have wanted. But if you want, I'll take a look at it when I can."

Maybe he was right. But it took everything I had not to scream at the unfairness of it all. Instead, I managed to say, "Irritant is going to take Kaynine away soon."

Silas was silent for a moment. "Well, you can replace the chip with a duplicate and save the original. Rebuilding isn't hard to do."

I nodded my head, grinning widely. "My thoughts exactly."

"Look, I have to go. My mom. She's yelling at me. Promise you'll use those answers tomorrow. You deserve this, especially after everything you've been through. Talk soon."

A small chime signaled Silas had left SuBunk.

He doesn't believe I can pass the exam on my own.

I walked over to SuBunk's door and gave the main wheel a thrust to the left. It opened with a metallic grunt. SCP chats were best if kept short. Especially after a file download. For now, I left the file unopened, stored in SuBunk's compressed atmosphere.

Outside the open door, the digital world outside SuBunk's haven streaked by. I stopped, mesmerized by the virtual world composed of a blackened background, grid lines, and program codes.

It wasn't wise to let my mind view the raw code for long without a skin layer to help process the vast DataStream. I reached to disengage my BAT when, suddenly, a darkened figure barreled toward me.

The figure blended with the background, bending reality around its form.

This isn't real. Nothing moves in this world unless you program it to do so.

The figure stopped and tilted its head to the side, as if it could read my thoughts.

Disconnect NOW!

My mind screamed. Were my episodes taking on a new, night-marish twist?

But I didn't disconnect. I reached forward, and the figure reached out its palm to mirror my behavior.

"Who are you?"

The figure cocked its head. We were the same height, except this mysterious apparition had no features, only a darkened mold with human-shaped limbs. It seemed to bend code, space, and darkness around its form like a layer of skin. It raised a jointed, blobbed arm towards me. I stared in horror as the blob separated into thin fingers that rested on my shoulder before tapping the area of my heart.

Sparks of blue code appeared in clusters in its head, forming eyes. The same blue sparks I had seen a million times. Each one before an "episode."

Was this creature responsible for my recent blackouts?

The figure grabbed both of my hands and squeezed, causing a burning sensation to course through my body. My vision blurred, and the familiar screams echoed in my head, but this time with less intensity.

I am crazy. This proves it.

"Find me," the figure whispered, using my voice. "File 19-39-15."

The figure released me, then pixelated back into the DataStream without a trace.

Somewhere, far beyond the virtual, my fingers ripped the BAT out of my ear as I scrambled onto my very real feet in a very solid world. I stumbled in panic, slamming into the corner of my nightstand.

Warm blood trickled from a cut above my eyebrow. Kaynine retrieved a bandage from the medicine cabinet. He ran to me, tail wagging, and tried to tug at the bandage like a play toy.

"Not now," I said, giving a fierce yank. I placed the bandage on the cut, and it melted into a burning foam, creating a new skin layer in seconds.

No points for beauty today.

I winced, and my eyes refocused. My BAT lay a few inches away from me, blinking red as if nothing had happened.

CHAPTER 9

"These numbers and opinions won't define me. Isn't there more depth to the human soul than the collection of the trivial?" — *Excerpt from* The Measure of Worth, *found in the Forbidden Library Archives*

The past and present blended with each surreal step down the hallway. I could still feel Silas's embrace to wish me luck earlier that morning, even though the moment had long since passed. I wrapped the warm memory around me like a blanket as the hallway monitor escorted me to the testing room.

This exam was the last barrier between me and the Implantation ceremony.

"It's alright to be nervous," Irritant said, sounding thrilled for a robot with programmed emotional parameters.

I guess he is probably just as glad as I am to go our separate ways soon.

The hallway monitor glided towards the testing wing of the school and held open the door to room number 221B. I knew these rooms well. Behind each door that lined both sides of the hallway were endless testing devices that organized the past, present, and future into data columns. Auto no doubt relied on these results to calculate each student's future.

Hopefully, I will have a future.

I stepped inside the room as the hallway monitor whirred away.

With a hum, the overhead lights snapped on. My mind played a split-screen version of the hypothetical futures I had been contemplating:

1. Give in and use the answers from Silas. After all, who determined cheating's boundaries? I had earned my place.

2. Do my best. See what happens. Face the unknown. After all, unlucky lightning, heart attack, and mysterious headaches stalked me like a shadow so maybe it's about time for something good to finally happen.

Or I could give into the third option that nibbled at the edges of my mind: throw all expectations to the wind. I could enjoy the short-lived sense of freedom before throwing up bits of breakfast into the nearest trash receptacle.

I blinked twice to stay rooted in the present.

One step at a time.

I released my breath in a slow exhale. Cheating, even dressed in the robes of desperation, was wrong. The decision didn't lessen my terror. I had to appear calm.

No cold sweat. No fast pulse.

Strangely enough, Faye's breathing exercises seemed to be helping.

I took in my surroundings. This testing room differed from the ones I had been in before. I was no longer in a crowd of my peers, feeding off their competitive glances to do better. Instead, I was alone. The hologram settings had been changed to a mirror-like surface to allow for introspection.

Or intimidation.

A curved chair sat in the center of the room. I plopped down, willing myself to relax.

Three sharp knocks disrupted the calm. Faye entered. She tapped her fingernails against the DataPad under her arm.

"I know you were expecting Mr. Pidgelton," Faye said, "but I requested to conduct your exam today. You know, they had to rewrite the testing protocol for your situation. No one has ever missed their final-placement exam before."

"Is that supposed to make me feel better?"

Faye's thin lips pressed together in an obligatory smile. "Hand me your BAT."

"This one is new. It's not going to malfunction."

Faye raised an eyebrow. "I'm not worried about faulty tech, Chiara."

She knows the answers are there.

Cold beads of sweat trickled down the back of my neck. Teachers never scanned BAT devices. There was no need to do so. The DataStream flowing through the school was heavily encrypted and final-placement answers were guarded with the highest security levels. The fact that Silas managed to get a copy was an impossible feat.

Or was it? How was it possible for Silas to get those answers?

My face went numb. Silas was clever, but no one had ever stolen answers before. They were all stored on my device now under a few encryptions. It wouldn't fool Faye for very long. Even worse, since Faye knew what answers to look for in her search parameters, she could discover SuBunk.

Faye held out a hand expectantly. I pulled the device away from the curve of my ear.

"What will I find, Chiara?"

"Seems like you already have an idea."

Faye smiled, this time for real. "Good. Then you have what you need to pass." She handed it back to me.

"I don't understand. If you know what's on here, then why help me?"

"We will talk after the exam."

I summoned a steadying breath and decided. "I'm going to

trust the process. Answer the questions on my own. I don't need to cheat the system to win. I believe in myself."

Faye's eyes turned dark. "Don't mistake tactical moves for friendly intentions. You will use those answers, Chiara. If not, a certain young man's actions will be discovered on a hidden camera. Such a shame too. He had such a bright future."

A chill ached deep within my bones. "What sort of answers are in that file?"

Faye chuckled. "Answers that Anomalies like you deserve."

"This is part of the test, isn't it?"

"No. This is a game. My game. I have told you what moves to make."

"And if I don't?"

"Are you willing to take that chance?" Faye waited a moment, seeming to gain power in my silence. "I didn't think so. Your exam begins now. I look forward to conducting your exit interview."

Faye set Silas up. She let him have the file. To get to me.

"What have I ever done to you?" I snapped.

Faye turned on her heels, humming with apparent pleasure. She slammed the door behind her.

I stared at the closed door, uncertain for a moment what to do.

I drew in a deep breath and placed the BAT back in my ear.

The room's mirrored panels shifted into an aerial view of Unity. Gray stones, molded by a careful mason, encased the city. The video panned into the center, focusing on the gleaming silver-and-iridescent-blue skyscrapers and the white shuttles darting by like shooting stars.

A deep voice echoed around me. "Greetings, young scholar. I am Auto, the Advanced Unit and Technical Operator of Unity. Your place and part in humanity's journey begins today. I will let you in on a little secret so that you can understand the significance of today's exam."

Images flowed around me from every angle. Historical videos. Destruction and ashes. Mounds of waste crowding out residences and entire blocks of dwellings. The founders of society shaking hands. Images of Unity's construction being sped through time until it resembled the city I knew.

Then, the video panned out so I could see beyond Unity's borders. Outside the high stone walls were mountainous piles of waste, rusted remains of broken gadgets from older robot shells to rusted war vehicles.

The technology before my time.

Garbage formed into crushed blocks served as the bases of the giant waste piles.

Plastic containers of every shape and size faded to a dull yellow under the sun's blistering rays. The scenery stretched for miles, each square inch of land filled with twisted vehicular frames, wires, and blocks of bloated garbage, swarming with insects.

Carved-out paths ran through the piles of junk, each meandering back to Unity's circular design.

I thought this knowledge was forbidden. But today, perhaps the rules against talking about the past no longer mattered. Maybe the final test was to see what rules I would be willing to break. Faye seemed smug when she ordered me to use the stolen test answers. She wasn't usually happy about anything.

Which means she has something horrible planned. Or perhaps this whole test is a twisted game?

My hands turned clammy. I tried to swallow a gulp of air.

Auto's calming voice returned. "Greatness was achieved from the ruins of Earth, but only on the brink of extinction. When the founders built me, the goal was to perfect and preserve what remained of humanity."

The video returned to the gleaming city—to a montage of faces. One face emerged from all of them.

Amei. The kid from the bulletin board. Who picked that kid anyway?

Amei grinned, pearly white teeth glinting in the light.

"Unity forever. Unity for all."

My chair began to spin around, and I grasped the sides to keep from falling off.

"Let's begin, shall we?" Auto's voice seemed to have lost its magical quality as my head continued to spin along with my chair.

"Perspective matters," Auto whispered as the room itself spun in the opposite direction of my rotating chair.

The images blurred into a cyclone of colorful bands as I gripped the arms of my chair harder. I closed my eyes, focusing on the pounding BAT signal. Every muscle in my body demanded that my mind stay in the room, but Auto wanted me to leave my body behind, freeing my mind to join the virtual world.

I forced my white-knuckled hands to let go of the chair.

Focus on your breathing. Relax.

I welcomed the pain as the BAT's hum intensified. With a satisfying click, I blinked, and the room had shifted to a green pathway.

But what sector of the DataStream did Auto bring me to?

The neon-lit path felt solid beneath my feet. This was unlike my school's educational zones or even the areas where I had programmed SuBunk.

This space was different. This was Auto's own world. Unmapped and alive with possibility.

I'm inside an open program zone—a file designated for my life.

Thunk.

The pathway's edges crumbled away, sending bright green shards into the void.

Thunk.

The edges shattered again. More shards.

I struggled for balance as my ankle took a sudden, painful twist.

"This is only the beginning"—Auto's voice rippled across the virtual space—"of a new dawn for all."

Thunk.

The edges fell again in perfect timing with Auto's last word.

The path continued to crumble until only a thin line remained. I rebalanced myself with just enough space to proceed with one foot in front of the other.

This is all virtual anyway. No actual harm can happen. Right?

The void loomed over me from either side, open and waiting. I trembled, and a few pebbles broke off the thin line's edge, clinking into the nothingness below. A new, disturbing thought swelled in the forefront of my mind with each careful step.

The final exam might be different—the virtual world might be able to harm me. Maybe I should just avoid falling in?

I tried to swallow but my mouth dried up like the desert. My heartbeat pulsed faster.

"Today decides your potential value as a citizen," Auto called out as I stared at the single green line in front of me.

The answer file burned in the back of my mind.

Grandfather would be ashamed. But Silas might be doomed if I don't use it.

"There are no wrong or right answers," Auto continued. "I judge you by the quality of your reasoning and the speed by which you respond. Are you ready?"

If there are no incorrect answers, then why must I give these downloaded ones?

Despite the feeling of cotton balls in my mouth, I managed to say, "Yes."

Auto's questions came in rapid succession. The downloaded answers flowed automatically from my BAT to my lips.

The answers in Faye's file matched my own studies. Terror and relief swarmed me like flies sensing rot.

"What was the name of the theorist who first designed the unshackled AI code? State the exact code that first unlocked AI technology and explain how the code has since been improved."

So far, so good.

"What are the laws that every Unity member must follow?"

With each question, a new green line emerged from the blackened void. Sometimes the line moved forward and, other times, it took an abrupt turn to the left or right. The questions skipped between my view of science to complex mathematical problems.

"What is the purpose of retro-fitted technology in our society? How would you suggest we eliminate technological waste?"

The path inclined upwards. The green line trailed behind me in asymmetrical zig zags, much like the gold and green circuitry paths on an old computer board Grandfather had once shown me.

Auto is tracking my responses. Programming my life from this one test.

"In technical terms, how does the BAT function as an intermediary?"

The answer buzzed in my mind. But this time, it was wrong. I reluctantly spouted the stolen test answer, fighting every urge to go against Faye's orders.

Auto hesitated. "Are you sure?"

I nodded slowly, biting my tongue. The green line shifted to the left. I continued to walk forward until the next question stopped me in my tracks.

"If you were tasked with programming an AI, what factors would you consider throughout the process?"

The question was basic. But the answers were wrong again. I mumbled them.

Auto seemed stumped. Quiet.

I fought the urge to tell Auto all about how my psychotic teacher blackmailed me over a friend's good intentions. Or explain that I blacked out and woke up with no time to prepare. Even better, I could point out the flaw in a testing system that promised "no wrong answers" when clearly, that was not the case. But the first option exposed Silas. The second exposed me as a potentially unfit citizen, better suited for recycling. The third option exposed Auto as a liar and clearly, that would be unwise.

I stared down into the abyss on either side of the narrow pathway.

"Can you accept the outcome of today's exam? Would you have any concerns or doubts?"

Tears and laughter threatened to erupt at the same time. Instantly, the answer from Faye's test file burned on my lips. "Yes, I can accept the outcome. I have no concerns at all."

The green light along the pathway changed to red. The line extended in front of me into the distance, where an exit sign beckoned. I followed the path, panting with the steepening climb. The air grew thick and warm, as if soaking in everything that had been said before coagulating into a final decision.

The weight crawled from the air and into my chest as I struggled to take the last few steps. My left foot slipped, and I barely caught myself in time. My breathing grew heavier.

I fixated on the glow of the neon exit sign just ahead. The silhouette of a door appeared beneath the sign, washed in flickering hues of purple, yellow, and green. My hand shot forward, grabbing the door handle.

I yanked, but the door didn't budge.

"One last question... Is the human body efficient or necessary?"

Somewhere in the distance, I tried to reconnect with the body I had left spinning in that awful chair. The nausea returned in small waves, reassuring me that Auto had not somehow severed my mind from my physical form.

Small comfort.

I waited. But no answer came to mind. For a second, I felt elated. Faye didn't have all the answers. Perhaps Auto was aware of my situation. Perhaps I could change the rules of the game.

"It's just a question," Auto prompted. "But I won't repeat it."

"You asked if the human body is necessary. That's not a question to be answered quickly." A chilling sensation traveled up my arms, leaving goosebumps in its wake.

Would the great Auto be offended at my boldness?

I took another breath and continued. "The mind must coexist

with the body. Words like 'efficiency' and 'necessity' are cold, calculating terms."

I hesitated again, waiting for the cosmic hammer to fall. I pressed my fragile luck further. "Let's reverse the question. Are you—an all-knowing AI—necessary and efficient? Who decides those standards? We should appreciate what we have, while we have it. Change is inevitable, robbing us of everything and everyone we have ever loved. Eventually, the body erodes or fails the mind. But frailty is interwoven with our humanity."

The exit sign above my head began flashing.

"Your test is now concluded. I have decided you're fit to be a citizen of Unity."

Relief washed over me.

"After Implantation, you will be assigned to a permanent work function."

Thunk.

The floor beneath my feet crumbled into soft dust. I wildly grabbed for the door handle—but missed. I tripped, falling face forward into the darkness. I screamed as my vision cleared, and I was alone in the testing room. My chair stopped spinning, but I had fallen off. My palms were flat against the floor, along with the rest of my body, and my sides ached.

The door yanked open. Faye waited as I regained my footing.

I hobbled toward her, trying to hold back nausea from the virtual fall. Not even a glimmer of sympathy sparked in Faye's icy-blue gaze.

She turned, and her robes swished behind her with the same stiff attitude.

I tried to match her confident sway, but my trembling legs and the subsiding dizziness betrayed me. The hallways of Emergent High came into focus, and my stride normalized only when we reached the classroom. I removed my BAT and placed it inside my pocket.

The classroom door stood wide open. Faye led me inside and motioned me to sit across from her desk. She pulled out a DataStream in front of me with singular ease. The charts and analytical data bearing my name floated directly in front of Faye's perfectly manicured hands.

"Interesting results," Faye muttered with the hint of a smile. My heart sank.

She still holds all the cards.

"I did what you said. Some of those answers were wrong, but I played my part. You could at least tell me why you're sabotaging your own student."

"You aren't my student. Not anymore. Do you even remember the first time you made the cut to join my roster?"

"Yes."

I remembered that day well. Mother had been so proud, and I knew I couldn't let her down. Making the list was my one chance to beat the system.

"The list was scrambled to keep the rankings a secret, but I'll be honest. You and Silas barely made it onto the roster."

Shame burned across my cheeks. "I've made the top of your rosters for every project ever since."

Faye shrugged her shoulders. "Maybe. But did you deserve it? By one point, you outranked the next person designated for your seat in my room. One point separated you from where you should have always been—the lower function."

A knot formed in my stomach.

Faye had struck a nerve, and she knew it because she leaned in, grinning like a predator about to pounce. "Because of you, someone born and bred for a higher function was regulated to a lower class and is now destined for a Fourth Function job."

I stiffened before finding my resolve. "Every seat in your classroom was filled with someone who took someone else's opportunity. Blaming me isn't fair."

"This is about righting an imbalanced equation. You don't belong here. You never did."

Anomalies. We don't belong anywhere.

"What about Silas?" I hoped I didn't sound desperate.

Faye shrugged. "He might belong yet. He has a greater chance of success if separated from you. I'm doing both of you a favor."

I shot to my feet, slamming Faye's desk so hard that her screens flickered.

"A favor?" I said through clenched teeth. "Don't insult me on top of everything else."

Faye crossed her arms. "I don't make mistakes. I fix them. Do you know what happens in the town center every winter? The ice freezes over the central pool, thick and strong. Some try to walk across."

"And your point is?" My fingers curled into fists by my sides.

"Apply a few well-placed fractures, small ones, and the ice sheet will collapse. You're a fracture point in this society, Chiara."

I paced around my chair, keeping one hand on the chair's back to maintain my balance. I hated how right Faye was about my inward brokenness. Mother would have said to keep my chin up. Grandfather would have wanted me to feel the rage boiling beneath the surface. I took my anger out on the chair, tossing it across the room.

I wish they were here. It's not fair. None of this is. I can't win so, for now, I have to play her game.

"So what happens next?" I turned my face away, unwilling to let Faye see the tears streaming down my cheeks.

"With your lower scores on this exam, you will be put into a Fourth Function position, the very backbone of our society. It's where someone like you belongs."

"Backbone my—" I spun around to face Faye again, suddenly not caring what she thought of my distress. Anger masked my weakness.

Faye cleared her throat, glancing at the chair I had thrown. "Good to see this hasn't broken your spirits. Facing your problems, now that's a good Anomaly. I'm supposed to tell you that if you make it through Implantation, students are permanently assigned duties."

Faye handed me a DataPad showing a graph of all the functions. My brain scrambled through the categories, summarizing the important bits of information with a sprinkle of my own fury:

Fifth Function:

First Function: Administration, C.U.E. law enforcement robots (Auto's minions) and Grandfather's old, secretive job doing who knows what.

Second Function: Analysts (practical builders of inventions), inventors (the dreamers of code), and higher-level teachers like Faye.

Third Function: Maintenance engineers (like my mother and father), lower-level teachers (like Mr. Pidgelton), and adventure-simulation enhancers (the lucky few musicians and the artistically gifted).

Fourth Function: Zone workers (like Silas's mom) who are tasked with maintaining population needs, such as repairing food vending machines.

Fifth Function: The elderly workforce who retrofit phased-out technologies to keep the outdated components working as long as possible (Grandfather's downgraded job after he became my guardian).

"This isn't right," I said, glancing back at Faye. "Auto will find out what you've done."

"Don't fall prey to hope," Faye said, rising to meet my eye level. "The Implantation ceremony is next. Only *useful, honest* members of society are allowed to continue. Should I dig deeper into how Silas stole those files from me? I would be impressed if you destroyed him in a pathetic attempt to save yourself."

I never had a chance. Or a choice.

Faye laughed, and if she weren't so evil, that smile might have turned her dour face beautiful. "Your threat will turn into thanks someday. Go to Mr. Pidgelton's classroom and look at the training manuals for Fourth Function positions. You'll be placed by Auto exactly where you belong."

I stormed out, slamming the door behind me with every ounce of my weight, and the sound reverberated through the halls.

CHAPTER 10

"You think you know someone and then you learn more." — Excerpt
from The Trouble With Faces, *found in the Forbidden Library*
Archives

I had made enough noise with the slamming of the classroom door for Faye to think I had left. I slid beside the nearby lockers and tried not to cry. There was no way I could go to Mr. Pidgelton's room just yet. And I didn't know where Silas was. Faye must have pawned off the honors class for the day to someone else so she could play the role of my torturer.

I wondered if I should walk back into Faye's class. Beg, bargain, and plead for mercy. My fingers curled into fists, channeling more power than my tiny body held. It wasn't supposed to be this way. My lip trembled.

You can threaten her. Turn the tables. How hard can it be to hack school cameras and find incriminating security footage of Faye? She must have slipped up somewhere.

The hallway lights went dark. Two seconds later, a few lights flickered back on as Faye left the classroom and headed down the hall, oblivious to my hiding spot in the shadows.

This was my chance.

I slipped back into the classroom and tiptoed towards Faye's glass desk, which contained a cache of DataStream downloads. I would have to break into the files using her handprint. But everything was wiped clean with streak residue from the sanitizing wipes she always used.

I glanced at the locker next to her desk and wondered if I could scan a partial print from there.

Footsteps shuffled outside the door.

She's back already?

Thankfully, Faye never locked the tall storage locker next to her desk. I quickly opened the locker door and twisted my body inside, next to Faye's overcoat. I accidentally knocked over her purse, and items spilled out with a clatter all over the floor. I snatched the items back up before yanking the locker door closed.

I heard the classroom door swing open. Then silence.

My wispy breaths were like summer fans whirring at full blast in my ears. Blood rushed through my eardrums in thunderous waves.

I peeked through the slats, still holding the contents of Faye's purse in my sweaty hands.

Faye's gaze swept the room.

A bead of perspiration fell from my forehead and landed on the metal floor next to my feet with a soft *splish*.

Faye stared at the locker.

Adrenaline pumped faster through my veins. My hands trembled uncontrollably.

Beep!

Faye's desk glowed and beeped three more times.

Faye smoothed her hair and pressed her palm against the glass contours of the desk.

I hugged my arms closer to my chest and drew in a long, deep breath.

Faye removed her palm when the desk stopped glowing. Instantly, the classroom door locked and its window darkened. A blue grid projected from Faye's desk and swept the room, transforming it into a fancy office.

Skin layering. Adventure simulators run on the same technology.

Faye's desk was now a seat at a much larger marble table surrounded by plush gray chairs. Black columns rose from a bed of thick white carpet, adding to the dramatic simplicity of the decor.

A shadowy form crystallized at the head of the table. "We are waiting for two more."

"Of course. It is an honor to be summoned by you, Auto," Faye replied.

I swallowed hard.

I am seeing Auto's projection. No one has ever seen Auto except those in the First Function.

Auto looked like a swarm of dark, angry bees converging into a humanoid form. I was mesmerized, barely remembering to clutch onto the fallen purse items that threatened to give away my position.

Sweat pooled on the back of my neck.

Faye's shoulders visibly stiffened. "As always, it is a privilege to be in your presence."

Auto didn't respond, and Faye glanced away.

Is the mighty Faye afraid?

A part of me hoped so. My thoughts were interrupted as a holograph of Irritant materialized. I clenched my teeth to hold back a scream.

Irritant! That lying, spineless...

"Agent," Faye said with a nod. "How does espionage suit you?"

Irritant laughed. "Just about as well as running Second Function's brightest and best minds is going for you, I'm sure. This brat is a handful. I miss my normal workload running Third Function."

Inza appeared in a glowing, silvery body to Faye's right. My heart sank.

This is a First Function meeting, and if I'm discovered...

I couldn't finish my own terrifying thought.

Irritant broke into a wide smile at Inza's appearance. "How are things with Fifth Function, Nurse Inza? I imagine it has been difficult to monitor an entire school and the health of the elderly workforce. Not that you couldn't handle it, of course."

Faye rolled her eyes.

Inza beamed at Irritant's question. "To answer your question, Agent, I am considering the possibility of remaining in both positions once our work here is concluded." She glanced around the room. "Where is Val? Shouldn't Fourth Function be represented?"

"No." A single word from Auto drew everyone's attention back to the head of the table. "We have no need for human error factoring into this case."

Human error?! What does that make Faye?

"I call to order the First Function," Auto said. "We know what this meeting is about. Faye, please explain the results."

The marble table's surface seemed to melt away as my name emerged from it in a 3D model along with the blinking words: *Allocate Resource to Fourth Function.*

"Although we had high hopes for the candidate, she has yet to cope with her grandfather's loss," Faye said, beginning her commentary with the ease of someone used to being the focal presenter. "Her grades continue to slip."

"Has she been taking the required medications?"

Inza crossed her arms. "Of course, Auto. You may consult my logs if you wish."

Inza knows I don't take it regularly. Why would she lie?

Irritant responded. "She continues to reject counseling. This has been a waste of my time, talent, and effort. I am a Third Function administrator and would like to return to my regular duties."

Auto was silent for a moment. "Your patience has been noted. It would seem Chiara is simply another disappointment."

"There are other promising leads," Faye said.

"Perhaps," Auto said. "But this isn't the first time you've promised me something you couldn't fulfill."

Faye winced as Auto's bulging mass shifted towards her.

"Meeting adjourned," Auto snapped.

The room's illusion shattered into a thousand crystallized pieces before melting away and leaving only the original classroom behind.

Sweat now dripped profusely from the arch of my nose and my spine burned from its cramped position. I closed my eyes, trying to remain still until Faye left.

"You can come out now. It's safe."

Faye's words pierced me like a sharp dagger. I could hardly breathe.

The locker door yanked open. I tumbled forward in front of Faye's heeled shoes. The items in my hands skittered across the floor.

One comb, two tubes of lipstick, a spare screw, and three batteries.

I hadn't known what I had been holding onto in the dark, but I fought the urge to pick them up again. Instead, I scrambled to my feet.

Faye gave a half-smile, as if approving of the fact that I didn't collect her fallen possessions. "I made your grandfather a promise once," she said. "To look out for you."

Faye's comments caught me off-guard. I eyed her with suspicion. "Could've fooled me," I said, trying to slow my thumping heart rate. "Who are you anyway?"

Faye clicked her teeth, glancing at the batteries and screws. "I'm a synth. I retain some memories of my original host."

I whistled, my eyebrows arching.

A synth. The next generation in the chain after humanity and robots. I didn't think the technological development was possible yet.

I managed to regain my senses. This synth, no matter how

remarkable, was still a snake I couldn't trust. "Well, your original host must have been a real piece of work."

Faye stepped closer to me. "My host," she said slowly, "was someone your grandfather once loved. How is that for a 'piece of work'? Meet your grandmother, the much-improved version!"

Faye spun around the room with a flourish and a low guttural laugh. "So nice to meet you, my dear."

My jaw dropped. Faye's synth was some twisted replica of a human being that once meant the world to my grandfather. Whatever kindness had once existed in her form had probably been stripped away.

Faye patted my stunned cheek before placing her hands back onto her thin hips. "I have repaid my dues to your pesky grandfather. Now, I owe you nothing."

"You got me kicked out of honors," I said, pointing at her. "What sort of favor is that?"

"I freed you," Faye responded coolly. "The eye of Auto no longer watches your every move. Trust no one."

"And I should trust you? What's stopping me from reporting you now?"

Faye smiled, as if she had already calculated the odds and found nothing to fear.

"Oh, you definitely shouldn't trust me. But go ahead. Report me. Put yourself right back into the crosshairs of the very being your grandfather begged me to protect you from. Do you not sense a larger destiny?" Faye shrugged impishly. "Besides, if I go down, I will take Silas with me."

"Worst grandmother ever," I muttered.

A slap knocked me backwards. I rubbed my jaw in shock and recovered my balance.

"Oh, my dear, I'm not your sweet, darling grandmother," Faye said with a hiss. "I'm a synth grown from her defective materials. Go while you can, foolish pupil. There is much still for you to learn."

"Telling me I didn't belong. That was all a lie? A ruse to free me?"

Faye smirked. "You needed a reason for my actions. A story. I gave you one."

"What were they considering me for?"

"No more questions." Faye pointed toward the door.

I gingerly tapped at my tender chin, where a bruise was no doubt already developing.

"I'm sorry to hear you fell off your chair during the exam," Faye said. "Have the nurse check on you later."

The gloating words stung worse than Faye's backhand. I couldn't trust anyone, not even Inza.

I turned my back to Faye and swung the door open. The hallway lights flooded on.

"One last thing."

I hesitated.

"Keep Silas out of this. You're on a destructive path, Chiara. Your grandfather was not who he seemed. Consider your next move carefully. I will not always be on your side."

From the corner of my eyes, I saw Faye pick up the items from the floor. I let the door close softly between us.

Grandfather, what were you planning? And what did Auto want with me?

I didn't know what to think anymore.

"Visitor," Irritant called through my bedroom door after several rapid knocks. I leaned my back against the door. The half-eaten supper plate had long since turned cold, but the smell of stale broccoli cubes lingered.

"You mean Silas? Neither of you can take hints about leaving me alone." I shoved the plate with my foot, and it clattered across the floor to the other side of my room.

The robotic gears powering Irritant's movements were the only response to my bitter remarks.

"Fine. Let him in." I unlocked the door.

I have to face Silas eventually.

"Don't trust anyone," Faye had warned.

What a psychotic woman. Or synth. Or whatever. But what if she's right? What if my path puts Silas in danger?

Silas charged through the door, sparks flashing in his brown eyes.

Irritant hovered behind Silas's much taller frame. "Would you two care for..."

Whoosh.

Silas slammed the door, mercifully cutting off Irritant's sentence. With a huff, he squatted in front of me. The light danced off the rows of silver braids on his head.

He didn't talk. I couldn't blame him.

I had been ignoring Silas for two days—ever since I had been handed my exam results and a Fourth Function handbook to read through. Silas had tried to catch me in school, but Mr. Pidgelton's ritualistic naps during the last daily video made it easy to dodge out of his class early. I also had been ignoring Silas's SCP calls.

This was the longest time we had not spoken.

Silas raised one eyebrow, daring me to begin.

I owe him the dignity of at least starting the conversation.

I tossed my unkempt hair over my shoulder. My clothes were wrinkled, and this was honestly the first time I realized my socks didn't match. I had been avoiding mirrors, but I already knew my eyes were red and puffy.

Silas cleared his throat, forcing me to meet his gaze.

"I don't understand," he said, breaking the silence between us like a hammer to a frozen pond. "At least tell me what happened? Friends don't avoid friends."

"And I won't let you drown with me." I let the cryptic reply hang in the air between us before continuing. "Look, only one of us is going places. You deserve a chance."

Silas pressed a finger to his lips and motioned to the door.

I nodded, knowing all too well Irritant had probably pulled off his ear attachment and placed it underneath my doorway. It wouldn't be the first time.

Silas reached into his pocket and pulled out an old audio player. An ancient piece of tech that Grandfather had once given to Silas.

"I figured it might help to hear some old music files," Silas said, his voice louder than usual as he pressed the play function.

The sudden volume bounced off the walls and shocked me into a wistful smile.

Silas motioned with his head toward my BAT, which sat on my dresser.

There is no escaping this conversation.

I grabbed the BAT and placed it on my left ear, wincing as its plastic teeth bit into my tender skin. I closed my eyes so the virtual realm would only appear in my mind instead of projected on an external display. If Irritant strolled into my room, he would see two teenagers listening to music with their eyes closed and ignoring each other. He might suspect we were mind-chatting with an SCP, but there would be no proof.

The virtual world felt hostile today as I opened SuBunk's door. To my surprise, I could see Silas standing inside, arms folded in annoyance.

"We didn't agree to allow full imaging and body upload here," I said, pointing at him. "You know simplicity keeps this channel safe. The more features you add, the more space SuBunk takes up in the DataStream. Faye could discover it."

"Well, you weren't around to ask, were you?" Silas retorted. He kicked a nearby wall, then looked ashamed as the surface rippled from the impact. The wall slowly resumed its original code and skin layering. "Sorry. I shouldn't have done that."

"It's okay," I said. "I would be angry too."

"What happened to you, Chiara? It's like I don't even know you anymore. I don't know if it's your health or these blackouts but... I don't like this distance between us. It has to stop! Let me in, I'm here for you, so let me help you."

The sound of genuine concern in Silas's voice cut deeper than the judgmental tone I deserved. I reached for his hands, not sure if he would even take mine. He hesitated, then reached forward. His fingers intertwined with mine. It was just a simulation of the real thing, but it was close enough to make me blush.

I found the courage to begin. "The day of my exam, Faye knew about the stolen test answers. She let you take them. She wasn't after you, Silas. She wants me. If I take a Fourth Function position, she lets you off the hook."

I decided to leave out the rest of it. It sounded insane to blab about the First Function plot on my life and Grandfather's strange request that Faye keep me away from the eye of Auto. Maybe Faye was right. Silas would only be caught in my vortex of problems.

It's better to let him go.

Silas released my hands and ran his fingers through his braided rows as if trying to make sense of it all.

"It's not your fault," I said. "Faye set us both up. I am taking the Fourth Function assignment. I've accepted the outcome."

Silas snapped back to attention at those words. "What? Are you crazy? Of course not. Have you forgotten? We hand over SuBunk. It proves everything about the team we make! We both cross the finish line."

I shook my head. "Silas, what we have here is more than just a hidden communications channel. I have spent days avoiding you because I needed to process some things."

"Give me one reason why this place is worth it, Chiara!" Silas released my hands. "I would trade anything to keep you safe. Anything, do you hear me?"

I drew in a jagged breath. "You know those blackouts I've been having?"

Silas nodded, and his eyes pierced my soul. He softened his stance, his shoulders drooping a bit at my tone.

"I stopped taking the medications Nurse Inza gave me," I continued. "And now, I can think clearer than ever before."

Silas expelled a breath. "You've been going against medical advice?"

"Yes. I can't explain it, but more of 'me' is returning. However, a few days ago, I saw this human-like form in the code zone, just outside SuBunk. It spoke to me, and I know that sounds crazy. But I have heard the same voice before. I just need time to figure this out. For now, Faye and Auto are right about my placement."

I let Silas's silence linger for a moment.

"Look, Silas," I said. "I have accepted this. I need you to do the same."

"No," Silas finally said, placing his hands on my shoulders. The simulation slowly added the feeling of warmth at the point of contact. "The blackouts? Mysterious visions and sounds? I have a theory. Maybe it's SuBunk. After all, there is a reason most SCP channels were erased early on by Faye. We turn it in, your health problems go away, Faye and Auto would give you another chance, and you start taking your medications again. You aren't thinking clearly."

"You still don't get it. I can't turn SuBunk over."

Silas sighed. "Why not?"

"This is our world," I said. "The one place where no one else is listening. Turning over SuBunk would do *what* exactly? Auto and Faye would dismantle it and move on."

"I was afraid you would say that."

The edge in his voice startled me. My heart thumped in my chest. "What did you do?"

"What I had to do."

Panic coursed through me as I realized what Silas must have done. These new programs he added in to allow a visual chat gave away our position. It was only a matter of time.

"You removed your protection software to allow the video features, didn't you?"

Silas nodded. "One of us has to make the right choice."

I glanced around at SuBunk's metallic surfaces. One panel to the right of the door held my interest. But I needed a few minutes.

"No, of course," I mumbled. "I understand." I summoned a weak smile.

Silas hung his head, avoiding my direct gaze. "We've had our time here, but moving forward was always the goal."

He slumped into the captain's chair and stared out the window. "It won't be long now. It may not seem like it, but I always have your back."

I took advantage of his distraction and leapt over to the panel next to the door. Swiftly, I pried the metal panel off. A single input computer sat there, awaiting the command. My fingers flew across the keys. The technical code flowed from my fingers while my brain translated the settings into fragmented decisions.

Control Settings: "Revert to primary, Chiara1, and delete user Silas2?"

"I'm sorry, Silas," I said and pressed yes.

Like a drunk stumbling through the rain, SuBunk bounced through the wavelengths of DataStream. Silas's image spun around to face me. I glanced down at my shoes as he glitched like a visible stutter before disappearing completely.

"Relocation complete," flashed the words on the control panel.

I sat on the floor as SuBunk stabilized.

Safe again.

The idea of facing Silas for real was enough to make me want to stay where I was. I bit my lip hard, wishing the virtual world could draw blood. Maybe I would have felt less guilty.

I inhaled a slow, calming breath and tried to calculate what would happen now. I still had my haven but had lost someone who had meant more than a world full of safe havens to me. A real-life conversation was not only in order, but necessary.

It's the right thing to do. Face him and whatever the consequences might be.

With a low hum and a minimal headache, I disconnected and opened my eyes.

My bedroom was dark. A chill wafted in from the open bedroom door. The broccoli plate had been picked up, and a blanket covered my shoulders.

Silas was gone. And so was the music.

I didn't think it was possible to cry anymore. I was wrong.

CHAPTER 11

"I had to dance one last time. To shatter your heart... and fracture mine. The song will end for you and me, unless an encore is to be?" — *Excerpt from* Tears of a Poet, Volume II, *found in the Forbidden Library Archives*

I rritant whirled around me. He was humming. Apparently the last day on the job with me called for some expressions of joy. I sat at the edge of my bed while he viciously attacked my unruly curls into a crowning braid.

The mirrored girl looked the part. I had swapped my wrinkled clothes for a pair of white pants and an overcoat with shimmering silver scales. Soft, blue-suede slippers graced my feet. The circular medallion on my shoes glimmered in the light, no doubt a symbol of taking my first step as a citizen of Unity—or some such nonsense. Careful cosmetics hid my sleep-deprived eyes.

But I knew better than to believe the illusion.

"Never knew you were an expert at extreme makeovers," I said as Irritant stepped back to scrutinize my appearance.

"I can download a great deal of useful personalities," he replied. "I adapt to the situation."

No wonder he is secretly a Third Function Administrator. A snake will shed its skin as it slithers to the top.

My fists clenched at my side. For now, I had to play the game and resume my role as the unwitting pawn.

"Are we done here?"

"Almost." Irritant sprayed my hair with a firming mist.

Since removing Silas's access to the control panel, I had spent every spare moment reprogramming SuBunk. I was just missing one thing. Silas had specially tailored an early warning system if SuBunk got near any security programs in the DataStream. He had deleted that program on purpose, hoping SuBunk would be caught.

Without it, SuBunk might face detection every moment I spent away from it in the real world. I hadn't noticed anything strange in the DataStream recently. No mysterious figures talking about File 19-39-15. None of Faye's "seek and destroy" programs. It had been quiet—but the stillness worried me.

With Implantation only a few hours away, there wasn't enough time to replicate Silas's original design. I had one last chance at getting that program back.

Kaynine pressed against my leg, seeming to sense my tension.

Tonight, students of Emergent High were spending their last hours in a virtual party zone, getting buzzed from drinking simulated euphoria cubes and congratulating each other. Essentially, the party zone was an approved SCP channel with all the shiny new features. Faye herself was rumored to have designed it.

Silas would be there, waiting for the dance we promised each other years ago.

Sometimes we have to sway to our own music for a change.

Irritant's robotic fingers gave my hair a final tug, jerking my thoughts back to the present.

"Ow! You did that on purpose!"

Irritant shrugged. "Clumsy me."

"Out!" I pointed towards the door.

Kaynine followed my words with a growl, but Irritant remained rooted in place.

"Not until we complete the final item on the agenda," he said with a sigh. His robotic hand shot towards me as if offering a handshake. His skin split apart to reveal a black leather box nestled in the palm of his hand. "This is quite outside cost parameters for wards of the state. However, your grandfather bought this prior to his passing."

Time seemed to freeze as I stared at the box. My eyes spiraled with recognition.

It's the chocolate box.

Irritant stared at me, as if analyzing my slow response with measured robotic disgust for the frailty of human emotions. He promptly dumped the item into my lap.

"Arrive at Emergent High via the shuttle coming for Zone Y100 in approximately one hour."

I nodded. Travel was always interrupted on Implantation dates.

Irritant smiled.

It made the hairs on my arms stand on ends.

"Well, this is where we part ways," he said. "Before I leave, please rate my performance as your guardian."

I ignored the DataPad Irritant had pulled out of his suit. My fingers caressed the chocolate box, impatiently waiting for Irritant's shadow to stop spoiling the moment.

"Very well," Irritant said as the DataPad retreated inside his suit with a fluid motion. "Perhaps another time. You can always request to submit your evaluation of my performance later."

"Probably better if I forget to do it."

Irritant sighed loudly. "Yes, please do." He whirred toward the door for a few paces before turning back to face me. "Oh, and that robotic mutt of yours will have to go soon. Special privileges are ending, Chiara."

Irritant sped out of my room with what could only be the

equivalent of robotic joy. He wasted no time exiting my apartment and, more importantly, my life.

Kaynine deepened its growl.

"Good riddance," I muttered under my breath. "And Kaynine, ignore what he said. I don't plan on sending you away. At least, not the part that matters. I'll save your chip and give you a body upgrade later. How does that sound?"

Kaynine nudged my hand, returning my gaze to Grandfather's last, mysterious gift. All hesitation left me as I clawed it open. A faint whiff of chocolate greeted my efforts. Inside the hollow box was a silver bangle. My name was etched into the mirrored surface along with the words, "Always with you." I stashed the red box and its frivolous plastic wrapping into my dresser drawer. I couldn't part with it just yet.

The bangle fit snugly around my wrist. I turned it around in the light, admiring its simple design.

How did Grandfather pay for this?

Gifts were scarce as they were reminiscent of another time. Useless by Unity standards, gifts were now only purchased by the bored elites.

The cool silver metal felt like a gentle caress on my skin.

I'm not alone.

I took a breath and then pulled out my top dresser drawer, scattering clothes and miscellaneous items across the floor. When I spotted my BAT and the hologram invitation with five thousand party points, my heart pounded faster inside of my chest.

I was about to steal from my former best friend.

Time to dance. This party is about to get started.

I put the BAT around my ear and closed my eyes. My room faded—and reality shifted with a gentle hum. I opened my eyes, and I now stood in a field of shrubbery that formed a twisted maze all the way up the hill to the Party Mansion. The windows reflected a blaze of disco lights, and the entire house appeared to pulsate with a dull, thumping beat.

I hacked into the party's mainframe, downloading a map. I followed the twisted trail easily to the main door. A ding sounded as I was awarded the "EZ Way Out" Achievement with fifty party points.

As soon as I stepped onto the columned porch, the mansion's front door turned into a rectangle of rainbow-colored lines.

"Welcome, thrill seeker!" said an amped-up announcer. "Step this way and be transformed!"

I swallowed a deep breath and walked through the thick bands of code, letting the layers of my chosen avatar meld onto my form. A stealth suit contoured my body while connecting to a sleek helmet with a burnt-orange face shield.

The maze theme continued once inside. The opening staircase rested underneath a shivering crystal chandelier that shook to the beat of the house music.

I avoided the main hall with its twisted, endless staircases. I followed the map to a dusty hallway with plush red carpeting. The hallway led to a dead-end wall with the picture of some important (and long-forgotten) Emergent High administrator.

The map ended there.

I deleted the map with a furious swipe. Time was running short and maybe this downloaded map was cleverly designed to prevent hacking. I punched the wall, and the virtual sensation swept through me like a mild aftershock.

I don't have time for these games.

Clearly, this wasn't the main dance floor.

Suddenly, laughter erupted from the mustached lips of the administrator in the portrait. Two teenage girls, giggling breathlessly, burst through the wall, through the administrator's pixelated face, before the portrait settled back into an austere pose.

The portrait is a portal. Clever.

"Hey, want to join us?" asked the taller girl. "There's an adventure-simulation room somewhere around here." The girl's avatar wore a white fur robe and a gleaming magic tiara.

"The party's kinda boring. Been here for hours," said the

shorter girl, who was dressed like a medieval warrior with snakes braided into her copper hair. "You'll have more fun with us if you wanna come."

A lump formed in my throat. No one other than Silas had ever been friendly. For a second, I felt normal. Not an Anomaly. Just some teenager scared to death of the Implantation in a few hours and trying to enjoy all of today. Maybe that was the beauty of the Avatar mask.

"No thanks." I made a motion towards the portrait. "Meeting someone."

The girls shrugged and walked away.

"I heard there is a zombie apocalypse adventure," one said. "Just dropped into the simulation today."

"Oh no way," said the other. "I've got the invincibility code too! That sounds like a blast!"

Their babbling voices faded down the hall.

I turned away, facing the portrait and straightening my spine. Part of me wished I could lock arms with the carefree girls and drown my fears in some mindless adventure. But I knew these light-headed partygoers were aware of the shadows between the flashing disco lights.

Tonight might be all anyone has. Tomorrow brings uncertainty.

I stepped through the portrait, and a shower of confetti marked my newbie arrival into the party zone. I shook off the sparkles and focused on finding Silas in a crowd of mask-wearing avatars guzzling cubes of electric-green-and-blue data fragments.

"Let's get haaaaaacking! Final round!" bellowed the announcer as the beat thumped faster. That was the time-honored, grand finale: hacking to expose the identities beneath the skin layers to collect free drinks and simulation-room points. If exposed, the maze would shift and the partygoer had to restart the game.

Let them try to hack me.

As I stepped onto the main ballroom, a cheer erupted. The virtual scoreboard updated above my head, releasing digital confetti. User Reject22 took the lead from OrangeMan1 with two hundred hacked identities and zero exposures. I wormed my way into the crowd. Nearby, an alien sobbed as small letters above his head flashed, "Evan."

Doesn't he sit behind me in Mr. Pidgelton's class?

"Go reset yourself," comforted a nearby ninja. "It's okay."

The alien glitched momentarily before disappearing. The ninja looked at the place where his friend had been before starting a dance-off with twin mermaids.

A shiver crept up my spine, a warning that someone was trying to hack my avatar's layers. I stared at the elevated scoreboard floating six feet above the crowd.

I need to be within two feet of the scoreboard.

I zigzagged my way to the bar.

"Drinks on me!" I ordered, leaning over the bar for attention. "A round for everyone!"

"Someone is festive!" crooned the robot bartender behind the counter. He looked strikingly similar to Irritant, only more cheerfully dressed.

Auto's always watching.

My mother's words echoed through my memory.

I took a cup from the robot bartender's hand and raised it to the ceiling while the spine shiver gave way to a low, warning hum. "To Emergent High!" I shouted at the top of my lungs as servers flooded the crowd with the round of drinks on my tab.

The crowd of students roared in response, and the music's tempo reached a feverish pitch. The room pulsed with the sound of dancing feet as I jumped on top of the bar and pretended to join along. Eager hands grabbed for me, lifting me and carrying me high above the crowd. My body surfed across the room and, within seconds, I was directly underneath my intended goal.

Gotcha.

A tall Viking grabbed my waist. That last boost was enough. I was in range. My specially coded helmet did the work for me as it interfaced with the scoreboard. Within seconds, I had downloaded all the player data into my avatar suit. I scanned the crowd.

The helmet did its work, running a list of usernames to player identities before locking onto one figure in the corner of the room.

"Silas has been located," a voice stated matter-of-factly. "Also, your identity is seventy-eight percent compromised."

"Release smoke storm," I instructed the program.

The program cackled briefly before sparking into a flash-bang of light, followed by plumes of smoke pouring out from the ridged pores of my space suit. The disoriented Viking let me fall to the floor as the cloudy haze filled the dance floor. I rolled back onto my feet in a single motion and then dodged the shuffle of confusion. The humming stopped. My hacker had lost sight of me in the gray zone.

This was my playground now.

My helmet zoomed in on the digital shapes, giving me night vision through the smoke. Heat signatures scrambled around me as I easily maneuvered my way through the crowd toward Silas. I couldn't make out his costume with the helmet's current view, but seeing his figure made me pause.

His stance was relaxed among the chaos. Drinking cups, most of them empty, covered the table next to him and more littered the floor by his feet.

Someday you will understand.

I scanned his form, and the program confirmed my original theory. Silas had modified his costume with the same analysis techniques he had used on SuBunk to sense threats of detection.

Suddenly, Silas's avatar looked out into the fog—and directly at me.

He knows.

A chill ran through me.

Silas reached for another drink.

"Copy now," I ordered. My helmet stored the code written into his costume. I could download it into SuBunk later to upgrade its scanning protocols. If I couldn't have Silas onboard anymore, the next best thing was his signature code.

Silas's form tossed the drink. Then he stood with confidence, walking towards me.

"Downloading, fifty percent," my helmet echoed in my ear.

I backed away, careful to stay in range but keeping the confused bodies of partygoers between us.

Silas paused for a moment in the midst of the crowd, as if unsure what direction to take. I could feel the hacker's signal locking onto me again.

"Your identity will be compromised in twenty seconds," my helmet warned.

The party lights filtered through the smoke, creating a rainbow fog.

C'mon. Finish downloading.

"Eighty-two percent downloaded. Ten seconds until exposure."

I need a distraction. Quick.

"Unleash the scoreboard data."

A chorus of beeps and whistles filled the room at an alarming rate. Data flooded into the air, exposing everyone's identity.

The crowd was no longer confused, but angry. Shouts and curses erupted from every corner. Silas's name appeared at the top of the scoreboard. The distraction broke Silas's concentration, giving me the precious gift of a few more seconds.

"Hundred percent downloaded."

"End session," I yelled out. "End it now!"

"Disconnecting in three, two..."

I ripped the BAT out of my ear. The virtual party shattered back into the reality of my room—but at a cost. My hand went to my mouth in a feeble attempt to stop the flow of sickening lava. Luckily, a wastebasket had been left near my nightstand. I emptied an entire day's worth of food cubes into it.

I'm a mess.

My body shook from the disconnection. I half-walked, half-stumbled out of my room and into the kitchen, driven by the need to erase the taste of betrayal from my mouth. I punched in an order for sparkling lemonade into the food vending machine. I guzzled it greedily.

I wish we could have danced instead.

The machine made impatient clicking noises right before I dropped my plastic cup into the trash receptacle. No doubt the cup was already being absorbed into a mass of reusable material, ready to be molded back into a perfect unit at the press of a button.

Why couldn't I just fit the mold? Get along with the program for once, do what I'm supposed to.

I tried to steady my nerves with a deep intake of air. No time to waste.

First, upload Silas's code and give SuBunk one last inspection. Then make it to Implantation. Try to relax.

Even if I didn't survive the Implantation process, I found comfort in the thought that SuBunk would. A little program adrift in a digital world designed to eradicate abnormalities. A piece of me would always exist. If tomorrow spelled the end of my existence, my stubborn code would remain. The idea almost placated the ache growing in my chest. Kaynine would continue to exist too. I would make sure of that.

My fingers clutched the silvery band around my wrist. "Always with you," I read the inscription out loud.

Kaynine perked up at my voice and nuzzled into my arms.

"I'm sorry," I whispered into its ear, tears splashing down my cheeks. "I will bring you back soon. I'm not going to let them separate us."

Kaynine stared at me with serene green-halo eyes.

I turned its power button off, and Kaynine fell limp. My hands shook as I picked up a screwdriver and twisted it into Kaynine's neck, unlocking the panels underneath its bronze-plated exterior. I pulled out the core processing chip, which contained Kaynine's personality matrix, my coding, and potentially the erased footage. I quickly replaced it with a spare chip but left the power off.

Kaynine's core was staying with me. Irritant was right about losing privileges soon. The Implantation ceremony would change everything.

I stroked the chip and whispered a promise.

I will rebuild you.

"I'm not alone," I said, twisting my silver bangle.

At least my echo sounded convincing.

CHAPTER 12

"Romeo loved her. And Juliet loved him. But the stars are fires and the lovely nights are liars, promising nothing but air to hold. I never understood their sacrifice when our paths crossed." — *Excerpt from* The Unexpected Confession, *found in the Forbidden Library Archives*

The long line of graduates snaked through Emergent High's hallways, each student standing beneath a glowing number. I took a deep breath as waves of nervous energy and chatter swirled around me.

I jumped at a tap on my shoulder.

Silas stood there, dressed in a velvet blue jacket with black silk pants and a silver bow tie. I couldn't help but approve.

"Can we talk?" he whispered.

"I'm not changing my mind."

He nodded slowly. "I know."

"So return to the front of the line."

"You owe me something."

The program. He knows I copied it.

I swallowed hard. "You didn't leave me much choice."

"Not the program. I'm here to collect a dance. You owe me one."

My shoulders sagged with the weight of guilt. "Silas, I don't think it's a good idea."

He snatched my bangle.

"Give that back!"

"Come get it then." He stuffed the bangle into his jacket pocket and took off toward an intersecting hallway. I followed, my slippers softening the fury of my steps. The lights turned on and then flickered off instantly.

"How did you do that?"

Curiosity. It always got the better of me, even when I'm angry.

"Energy disruptors are easy to duplicate, even if illegal," Silas said, swinging open a classroom door. "We're off the grid for now."

No energy means no lights or lock code for the door. Clever.

"Very cool trick. Now give me back my bracelet." I stuck my hands into both Silas's jacket pockets and found nothing.

I suddenly realized how close we were. I yanked my hands away, placing them on my hips for support. Silas's earthy cologne scented the air between us.

"Fine. One dance."

Silas slipped his left hand around my waist, collapsing my stubborn pose. His shin hit a nearby desk before we figured out the art of a slow sway in between the rows of seats.

"Your shoulder is wet," I complained, brushing at the soft velvet before realizing that the tears were mine.

"I don't mind," Silas said.

I leaned into him, resting against his shoulder completely. "Sometimes, I hate you."

Silas laughed and stopped dancing. He fiddled with a strand of my hair. "I always planned to kiss you on the last day."

A sudden lump caught in my throat. I searched his face in the shadows before the feeling possessed me. "Then do it."

His soft lips met mine, and a breathless exhilaration made it easy to break rule after rule. Then the tempo changed to a feverish pitch that stabbed me with both pleasure and jealousy.

How is he so good at this?

The thought faded, followed by the unutterable need for more.

I don't even know how we ended up pressed into the corner, clinging with desperation as our fingers interlaced like discarded wires inside a box.

"Please," he said, his lips brushing against my ear. "I need the girl who can crash entire parties just to steal my code. We have to stay together."

"And you talk too much," I replied, nuzzling against his freshly shaven cheek and wrapping my arms around his neck.

"You aren't listening to me. This could be our last chance to stay together as a team, right to the top. You. Me. Kaynine. What do you say?"

I sighed as the words pummeled my brain like bullets: *Together. Team.*

Silas always talked like this. As if rising to the top of the functions was equivalent to happiness. But all the time I had spent alone in SuBunk had made me fond of solitude. I couldn't give that up... yet the clarity of one kiss shattered my resolve into sweet madness.

I want the future that he sees.

Silas leaned forward and slowly kissed my forehead while pressing the bangle into the palm of my hand.

The metal was achingly cold, as if it was as disappointed as I was. I put it back on my wrist, and it brought me back to my senses.

"You can't actually believe Faye or Auto will forgive a cheating scandal in return for one SCP channel," I said. "We can be together, even if I'm not at the top."

"You know that's not how it works. Reaching the top is all that matters."

Silas's touch had lost its magnetic rush. I withdrew from his embrace, and he didn't try to stop me.

"You're wrong," I said. "There's more to life. I haven't figured it all out exactly, but until then, you have to let me go."

Silas's eyes reflected deep pain as he staggered backward. I fought the urge to apologize, letting the words clump in my throat like sour lumps of fiber cubes.

I do care for you, Silas. Enough to save you from me.

Silas turned away but paused at the door. "I hope you find what you're looking for, Chiara."

He turned the knob and pulled out the disruptor. He snapped it in half, letting both pieces fall into a nearby recycling can, then slammed the door shut. The lights snapped on, and I flinched at the intensity.

That half-second was all it took for Silas to disappear from sight. I slid down the wall and buried my head in my knees. I wiped my face on my overcoat, not caring about the dark mascara stains on the fabric.

Irritant had tried his best to paint a happy face. It was about time the truth washed the façade away.

I rose, clutching the bangle like a lifeline.

I returned to the line, which had shifted forward. I slid back on my lighted number above, struggling against my own tears as the sniffling girls ahead of me promised to always keep in touch.

At least, I'm not the only one crying.

In a matter of hours, the Implantation would either be successful, or not. Every single graduate in line faced this reality. Some made promises they couldn't keep. But no one wanted the truth.

Not even Silas.

My heart broke again, and tears splashed their way onto the floor.

If I died on the operating table, then a part of the truth would live on in SuBunk. And maybe one day, Silas would find it, crack the codes, and remember our kiss. A piece of me would always be waiting for him. Or he could rebuild Kaynine and hold onto one good memory.

And if I lived, then no one, not even Faye, would see my next move coming.

Someone tapped my shoulder. I spun around, half-hoping Silas would be there.

"Hey," came an unfamiliar voice.

I looked down, something I wasn't accustomed to doing given my stature. The freckled-faced boy with a whisper of a stubble who waved at me looked vaguely familiar.

"Look, whatever that guy said to you, ignore it," he said gently. "It's okay if you don't remember me. I'm used to it. By the way, I'm Evan. I sit behind you in class." He laughed as if he had told a funny joke, but his eyes scanned the floor intently.

Ah, yes, the blue alien at the virtual party.

"I shouldn't have said anything," Evan continued, seemingly apologetic, "but mood plays a role in how Implantation turns out. Every advantage helps."

I swallowed hard. The bittersweet taste of Silas's lips still lingered there.

He's right. I can't lose myself in sorrow.

"I appreciate it. Thanks, Evan."

A genuine smile spread across Evan's face. "Fourth Function mediocrity has its perks. Including the fact you don't have to care about anything anymore."

A painful smile crossed my lips. "It also means you don't have anyone to disappoint." I looked around at the mix of faces ranging from anxious to almost puking.

Back or front of the line, it doesn't matter. We're all afraid.

I grasped Grandfather's gift, and the cool metal wrapped around my wrist provided a comforting tingle. I grabbed my BAT from my side pocket, inserting it back into position. The DataStream appeared as a projected screen above my hands, and I knew what needed to be done to lift everyone's spirits.

"Send a message?" An envelope icon appeared in response to my thoughts.

Yes. Send a message to everyone numbered 700 to 1,000 in graduation placement.

My thoughts became pinpointed commands.

"Access Denied."

I zoomed in on the "Access Denied" box and typed in the low-level administrative password I had swiped from Mr. Pidgelton. Simple enough to do.

"Access granted."

My mind formulated the words, which appeared seamlessly in the message box. "Proud to be in the back! Cheer if you know Second Function snobs have a stick up their fancy assessments!"

The line behind me slowly beeped in a stuttered delay. The message spun in front of Evan, followed by a display of digital fireworks. The other students behind us laughed, their anxiety melting away.

"That was awesome," Evan said with a chuckle. "I know I watched you do that but... How?"

My jaw dropped. "This is basic hacking."

I guess not everyone has Pidgelton's password after all.

Evan shrugged. "I never understood hacking. And Pidgelton didn't really focus on that. He always said we needed more useful skills like database building or data entry capabilities."

"I'll show you." I stepped over to his DataStream and showed him a few tricks. "See? Once you're in the mainframe, you can basically send whatever you want. Then add Pidgelton's password and..."

Evan hit send, and clips of Mr. Pidgelton snoring in class zipped out in an anonymous mass message.

The hallway was alive now. Students giggled and whispered. The hallway speaker droned on, reminding students they shouldn't hack teacher accounts and to remain standing under their assigned numbers. As if on cue, our numbers glowed to remind us where to stand.

Maybe the front of the line listened to the announcement. The back definitely didn't. Pidgelton's password locked out immediately, but not before the videos had already circulated to all the bored students waiting in line.

"So, were you at the party?" Evan asked in between watching the clips.

"Yeah, but at the end. Didn't make it onto the scoreboard."

"I heard someone crashed the party and released everyone's identities at once."

The announcer suddenly blared to life. "Number 798, Chiara. Report to Implantation Surgery Pod Number 3A immediately."

Evan's eyes widened. "It's not even your turn yet. Do you think they know you hacked Pidgelton?"

I shrugged, trying to appear confident. "Who knows?"

Evan raised his hands above his head, each one forming a half crescent before merging into a circle. Usually, it was a respectful gesture shown during special ceremonies.

"Back-of-the-line-proud!" Evan shouted. Others joined in, raising their own circles.

The floor lit a path for me to follow.

I looked back, then raised my own circle. The crowd cheered.

Hallway monitors appeared and tried in vain to keep the line quiet.

The announcer returned at full volume, its words following me around every bend and turn leading to the front of the line. "Students, no loud noises or DataStreams. Please stay focused on your breathing exercises. Do not..."

I let the words drift from my attention as I focused on my steps. A collective groan, tinged with what was undoubtedly part-irritation and part-impatience, swept through the crowd of students as everyone's number counted down in a chain reaction, complete with the electronic *bleepity bleep* sounds. A new number one spot appeared.

A former classmate, at the number 2 spot, sighed loudly before resuming hypnotic breathing exercises. I wondered how anyone could be so eager for their turn to step into a surgical pod.

The front of the line stinks.

I missed my newfound companions already. The metal doorway in front of me opened with a whoosh as my number flashed.

I stepped forward, and the door slammed behind me.

"Please proceed," came the scanning drone's authoritative command.

The floor glowed below my feet, indicating a path to follow.

They had converted the former Emergent High sports center into surgical zones. Gone were the distinct smells of sweat, replaced with heavy whiffs of bleach. Rows of makeshift cube walls were aligned with military precision. A sunshine-yellow curtain hung in each cubicle entrance for privacy. I found 3A and shoved the curtain aside.

In the cubicle's center, a surgical pod awaited with the sound of a steady hum. To the left of the pod stood a clear crystal desk. Buttons and diagnostic charts flooded the desk's translucent surface.

"Hello?" I said.

"One moment," came Inza's familiar, cheerful tone.

Data fragments solidified in front of me and Inza appeared, wearing a pantsuit and a white lab coat.

"It's good to see you, Chiara. My response time has been a little staggered since I am running nearly a hundred surgical pods at the same time. But no worries, I can multitask." She winked.

"Why was I moved up in line?" I asked.

Inza pursed her lips. "Silas said you had something important to tell me. Something that could change your position. My programming doesn't allow favoritism, Chiara, but I do have a special concern for you. I authorized the change. Is there something I need to know?"

What exactly is this special concern?

I chose my words carefully. "I didn't do my best on the place-ment exam, and he hoped I could take it again."

Inza shrugged. "Retesting is not a possibility."

My heart pounded furiously. "Of course. I understand. How is Silas?"

Inza returned a smile. "He is already on a shuttle home. Successful integration."

A surge of relief made my knees almost buckle from under me. Even if Silas never spoke to me again, it was reassuring to know he was okay.

"He is no doubt enjoying the use of DataStream without his BAT device," Inza said. "It is a much more pleasant experience. I'm sure you can't wait. Now, please hand me your BAT for recycling."

So this was it. The beginning of Silas's and my separation. Our functions would be different, and so would the rules governing our interactions.

My heart ached. I pulled my BAT from its suctioning grip and instinctively rubbed the bruised skin around my ear.

"After surgery, you can choose to have those scars removed," Inza said. "I also know several who have tattooed over the marks instead."

She noticed my bangle and added, "What is that?"

"A gift. From my grandfather," I said.

"If it passes my scan, I don't see any reason you can't keep it with you."

Inza always seemed so thoughtful.

Even if she is secretly the Fifth Function Administrator.

She scanned me while her hand brushed my forehead. "Normal temperature, functional brain pattern, heart rhythm is normal..."

An angry beep erupted from the desk.

Inza frowned. "Your wrist, please."

She scanned the bangle again. Nothing.

"It must be something else," she muttered.

I eyed my pressed white pants, the shimmering overcoat, and the blue-suede shoes with the circular buckle.

"Your shoes perhaps?" Inza asked, pointing at the buckle.

I removed the shoes and held them for Nurse Inza to scan separately. The beeping went off again.

"How odd. Set your shoes to the side."

I did as instructed and then situated myself inside the pod, which slowly tilted backwards until it reached a horizontal position. The glass cover snapped shut.

"If you're frightened, please press the red button on your right," Inza called out. "It's important to remain calm. You may experience minimal discomfort with the next set of injections."

A metal clamp locked around my throat, waist, and ankles with an echoing click. The pillowy sides of the pod pushed against my body. I wasn't prepared at all for the stab of slender needles along my spine. If that was minimal discomfort, I wasn't ready for what was next. I slammed the red button.

"Use the button only for emergencies, okay?" Inza called out again.

This isn't an emergency?!

The needles plunged deeper, touching the rawest parts of my very soul. I bit my lip. A tortured laugh escaped instead of the scream I suppressed. My fingers locked in place.

Breathe in. Hold.

Even now, Faye's irritating instructions tumbled through my head.

My eyes darted around the cocoon-like pod. Every breath was heavier than the last. Suddenly, my lips became itchy, and my tongue swelled.

"Howheel I pusha butow?" I cringed at my high-pitched, slobbering words.

Great, I can't move or speak.

"Actually, think of that button as decoration," Inza said matter-of-factly.

"Wurst aswer evah."

"Try to relax, Chiara."

Panels opened on both sides of the pod. A delicate metal arm with a variety of tool attachments on each of its long "fingers" extended toward me. I began counting them.

A bone saw, a precision knife, a laser pointer, instant foam/skin applicator...

My eyelids grew heavy. I forced them back open.

A video camera, a thin needle, a sample extractor...

Five? Six devices?

I couldn't tell because a fog rolled into my mind. I surrendered to it, closing my eyes.

I could ask.

I decided otherwise as my tongue continued to swell into a slab of drying concrete.

The whir of sawing echoed somewhere in the distance. Next came the rumble of a controlled blood flow, no doubt spilling from my skull, as the metallic fingers clawed their way into my brain. I could sense a small object wriggling inside. The BAT glided through my thoughts, riding on dreamy waves. The harsh "shhh" sound of foam being applied to close the wound reverberated in my eardrums.

"Chiara?" Inza's voice carried a note of panic, and an angry warning beep followed.

I found myself in the middle of a black pool. Gentle ripples extended from my body as I floated on my back. From the dark void, Inza's voice continued to call my name.

Above me, a dark sky exploded with fireworks of code and data fragments. The pool below mirrored the night sky and rippled before each data flash in a soothing pattern. I lazily let one arm drift while the other steered in meaningless circles.

If something is happening to me, at least death seems pretty great.

"You must find File 19-39-15."

I choked on water as my arms flailed. A wispy hand grabbed mine and pulled me to my feet.

"You again?" I sputtered, recalling my previous run-in with the nearly invisible figure.

The figure nodded and then repeated her message. "Find—"

"I know, you've told me before. But who are you? Am I dying or something?"

"Always with you," the figure whispered the words etched on my bangle before fading completely.

The sky thundered, and the waters shuddered violently. Something floated to the surface in front of me. Water streamed off its dark surfaces.

SuBunk.

I must have subconsciously called for it. My thoughts felt feverish and confused.

How is any of this happening?

The dark sky trembled with the promise of more lightning. I twisted open SuBunk's door, climbed inside, and slammed the door shut, overwhelmed by the sensation of my fading strength. I stumbled across the floor to the captain's chair and pulled myself into it, drowsiness tugging at my eyelids.

"Coordinates?" SuBunk's screen displayed the question. "User, please select a destination."

I stared helplessly at the screen. I couldn't lift a finger.

Invalid Response. Emergency Protocol: initiate S.A.P.S., the Silas AutoPilot Scan. Done. Scan results are conclusive. Area is unstable.

Attention: Receiving input from remote, external hard drive. Coordinates received. Begin relocation to area 19-39-15.

CHAPTER 13

"You spent your whole life looking to make decisions of great importance, and yet you ignored all the little ones along the way. Those were the ones that mattered." — *Excerpt from* The Winged Adventurer, *found in the Forbidden Library Archives*

Video footage, Camera 1, facing Pod 3A. Recording. Nurse examines data as abnormal readings spike across the charts. Nearby, Patient convulses inside the surgical pod.

Beep. Beep. Beeeeep.

The video zooms in as Nurse watches the monitoring screens. A BAT device attaches itself to Patient's frontal lobe.

Nurse paces, frowning as a question appears on the DataPad. Camera zooms in closer to see the question: *Warning: Terminating now could cause immediate stroke or brain injuries. Proceed with termination? Y/N?*

Video feed destroyed by static.

$\sim$

I WOKE, only to stare at a version of myself. The mysterious figure was back, but this time, instead of bending the existing background to its frame, it mirrored my skin tone.

"What the—" I realized I was lying back on the darkened ground.

The other Chiara wore a black jumpsuit with hair pulled into a ponytail. Well, not quite like me, but the resemblance was uncanny.

I stumbled to my feet while the other Chiara watched from a safe distance.

"You look like me. Why?"

"We are alike, but not the same," the figure said. "Some resemblance is expected. I am made to look like my predecessor, Elara. Your lack of recognition must mean much time has passed in your world. You aren't a young child anymore. My error. I will correct my features to be more accurate."

The figure shifted, her face aging rapidly before my eyes. "There, is this better?"

A chill pricked my skin, causing me to shake uncontrollably.

My mother is here, in front of me. Alive—in a twisted sense of the word.

"Hold on," the new Elara said. "I am authorizing the nanobots to repair the damage. The surgery is risky, as predicted."

"You need t-t-t-o explain," I said, shivering as if an intense winter had caught me unawares.

"Soon," Elara said, hushing me.

VIDEO FOOTAGE, **Camera 2, redirected to watch Pod 3A. Camera 1 is malfunctioning. Data unrecoverable.**

Nurse stares at the convulsing Patient's veins on the right hand. The veins turn silver as the bangle dissolves into Patient's skin.

Patient's body stops convulsing, breathing rates slow and normalize.

Nurse ignores notifications from other pods and tends only to Patient. Feed disrupts with more static electricity, which grows louder.

∿

ELARA MONITORED my vital signs and seemed pleased. I sat there, watching her draw complex equations onto the surrounding walls with a red pen.

"Care to explain what's going on?" I asked.

She sighed. "Taking care of a few problems. Let's just say with this newly implanted addition, I can reach outside of your head for a change. Mess with the cameras around us, for example."

"Remind me, how are you in my head to begin with?"

"You've been operated on before."

"Not possible. I would've remembered."

"I was implanted in your mind long before today, young Chiara. But you were too young to remember the procedure."

"My grandfather did this to me?"

Elara's gaze faltered. "Not exactly."

"Then who?"

"You were born with uncontrollable seizures. Your grandmother proposed this unorthodox solution, and your grandparents worked tirelessly to create me. I have been remapping your mind throughout childhood to avoid the harmful electrical impulses whenever they misfire."

"Why didn't anyone tell me?"

Elara smiled. "What matters is that you're fine now. You have spent many years using other areas of your brain instead. It's quite remarkable how you have adapted."

"Why are you in my mother's form?"

"To comfort you, of course," she said. "When I would appear to you as a young child, it would seem like a memory or a dream.

As you grew, I faded from use, my primary purpose achieved. And then, these last few years, your grandfather began sending upgrades to me through your BAT device, giving me a new directive. Let me show you."

The equation-covered walls shifted instantly. Expanding, changing, and then transforming into a completely different room. A domed glass ceiling soared high into the air and large, open picture windows allowed in a warm, natural light. Green leaves and dancing paisley wallpaper covered the rest of the walls, from which rows upon rows of thick, golden-oak shelves packed with books jutted out. A stone wall with a carved-out fireplace formed in the center of the room with a staircase leading to the upper floor, where more books lined up like diligent soldiers.

"Where am I?" I asked, taking it all in.

The inefficiency took me by surprise. A space for each book? A compressed file could have contained this entire place with a few simple keystrokes.

I grabbed a nearby book and thumbed its useless, creamy pages, surprised by the musty scent. Full-sensory mode had been enabled in this place. I slid the book back onto its shelf.

"This is the Library, or area 19-39-15," Elara said. "Pretty extensive file, don't you think? As the Library's caretaker, I will explain what I can, in due time. In fact, did you know that each coordinate number corresponds to the English alphabet?"

I took a second, converting the numbers to letters. "Scio? What does that mean?"

Elara smiled. "Your grandfather chose these coordinates as 'Scio' which is Latin word for 'know.' As the scribe and caretaker, I welcome you with a warning; some fruits of knowledge are delightful while others are bitter."

I scanned the book titles. I fingered the rows of leather-bound books, including the complete works of William Shakespeare, a poetry volume by Emily Dickinson, and some books on mythology. My senses came alive as I breathed in the ink and paper.

Elara noted my curiosity. "This is the fiction section. Here, you will uncover the question of 'What If?' The imagination has been known to predict the future."

She motioned to the opposite side of the Library, where more rows of books awaited. "And over there, nonfiction seeks to answer 'What was.' You will find organized volumes of pre-Unity knowledge."

"Everything in here is forbidden," I muttered softly, my eyes sweeping the beautiful shelves and taking in every detail.

"Depends on your perspective," Elara replied. "Which is the only one that matters here."

A lump formed in my throat. "You could barely speak to me out in the DataStream, and now I am getting cryptic philosophy statements?!"

Elara motioned for me to join her near the fireplace. We sank into opposing yellow chairs. "Out there, I am a virus. What I can say to you is limited. But here, I have no such limitations."

"If it's dangerous, why did you risk contacting me?"

Elara leaned back. "Last year, when your mind was erased, I feared for my own existence, and I attempted communication. It wasn't until you stopped taking those neural-inhibitor pills, I could speak with you at all without catastrophic results."

"Wait, what do you mean my mind was erased?"

"The scars run deeply through you. When it happened, I was nearly destroyed as well. As to why it happened, I do not know. I cannot access those damaged sections of your mind."

Inza's pills. And the blackouts were caused by a virtual entity living inside my head trying to have a conversation.

My life sounded more and more like a freak show.

Oh, and a mind wipe too. Let's throw that in there for good measure, shall we?

Elara held her hands open, and a 3D holographic brain emerged between us. She pointed at the dark segments of the image. "Memories have been stolen from you."

Other areas of my brain danced with violent electrical impulses.

"And those?"

"The seizures will not cross the boundaries I have placed. You're safe from that storm now."

"Can you tell me where I am?" I asked, my voice cracking with the words.

"It's like your SuBunk, only immobile. This exists only in your mind. It is separate from the DataStream and cannot fall under Auto's scrutiny." Elara grabbed a book from the fireplace's mantle. "Think of it this way: Your mind is a book filled with pages Auto can read at will. But your mind has a few extra chapters, a hidden addition."

My mind is now a place filled with forbidden knowledge.

I wondered what the spidery CUE robots would do to me if Auto ever found out. Would some research team cut out my brain to preserve the technology to examine later. In sections? As a whole piece?

"I still don't understand how this is possible."

"Technically, this space doesn't exist as Auto has no control over its design or function," Elara continued, before snapping her fingers. The fireplace crackled and roared to life. "It's locked to one user, and only you will have access to the data stored here. You're wearing your graduation gift, aren't you?"

"But it passed the scan."

"Signal deflection. The bangle was made to interact with the surgical pods. Your mind has now been split into two main compartments. On one side, you can interface with the DataStream but under the watchful eye of Auto. On the other, you can be here, safe from any interference or mind readings. SuBunk is an enigma that your grandfather hoped you would refine, and it appears you have. It will make it easier to travel between the DataStream and this Library. Some answers will be hard to obtain. If I can help, I will."

"You sound like instructions for a terrible adventure simulation."

Elara's face turned serious. "If this were a game, you would have multiple lives. The fact is, you only have one."

The Library walls vibrated. Elara grasped my hand in hers. "Our time is short. You must return to the DataStream to avoid suspicion."

"But I still have—"

Elara strong-armed me towards the open doors. The Library floated in midair, chunks of rock flying about in orbiting patterns. SuBunk faithfully rested by the Library's steps.

Elara pointed at a glowing red portal beyond the chunks of floating rock. "You can manually float through space towards the portal. Or"—she nodded towards SuBunk—"you can take the recommended mode of travel."

I wanted to ask more, but Elara returned a stern gaze, signaling that nothing would be gained by further inquiry.

I jumped into SuBunk, settling into the captain's seat before touching the throttles to propel forward. The portal window propelled me straight into a fleshy cave with ridges that came to life with streaking neural messages. Outside of the flesh-lined cave, lines of computer code swam in sharp contrast to the organic half I currently navigated.

Am I riding through the inside of my brain?

Elara told the truth. My mind had been split. One half formatted to Auto's liking, and the other, a mystery of nature. I slammed the wheel with my fist, making SuBunk jump a little.

I had unearthed some answers and yet, I still felt lost.

INTERNAL RECORDING of Hallway Monitor sent to check on Cameras 1 and 2.

Nurse is busy checking on Patient. Both cameras face Pod 3A's Implantation procedure. Glimpse of medical data on Nurse's desk shows high levels of brain activity.

Hallway Monitor inquires if Nurse has forwarded these unusual scans to Auto for inspection.

Nurse replies that Patient should not have to suffer any more testing. Hallway Monitor considers this answer. A pixelated tear falls from Nurse's eyes. She wipes it away.

Hallway Monitor finishes deliberating and insists on immediate data transfer to Auto.

Nurse locks eyes with the Hallway Monitor.

Memory Error. Data is irretrievable.

CHAPTER 14

"When first appointed, the new worker should take diligent notes and interest in the role. As the years continue, perfection will follow and, thus, the circle of Unity is complete through its most noble resource: its citizens." — Excerpt from The Book of Advancement *(with an addendum of humorous defacements made by scribe Elara), found in the Forbidden Library Archives*

"Unity needs everyone," said the smiling face on the video I watched right after Implantation.

Quite a contrast to the speech I heard from my new, very hairy boss.

"It's like this. We don't really need you," shouted Val, the Fourth Function administrator. He was so tiny on the stage, but his hologram hovered over the crowd with spittle in his scrappy beard. I waited in line with the other workers in green khakis, wishing Vocal Val would dial down the volume.

"If you're released from duty for any reason, you will be turned over to the Council of Collective Unity Enforcers for recycling. Get a clue or go to the CUE!" Val laughed at his own joke as the spidery legs of the CUE robots filled the hologram above our heads. The CUE robots hissed as they raised their razor-sharp legs and ruby-red laser beams burst from their eyes.

The crowd gasped.

I shivered and adjusted the heat sensor in my uniform between Val's barking soundbites. There were too many of us to fit into a lobby, so we huddled in an abandoned outdoor theater, consisting of only three crumbling stone walls, gaping holes where the doors and windows should have been, and an open ceiling instead of a roof. Sure, a virtual conference room would've worked. But Val seemed to care more about the show than the comfort of his underlings.

"DO NOT ask for reassignment," Val screamed into the microphone. "I lost one ear to an infection years ago from doing this job, and my good ear doesn't care about your sob stories. Fourth Function is a dead end. We simply take care of society's filth. Wash, rinse, repeat. Now report to your assigned work terminals and collect your ID cards. Tomorrow is your first day of forever. Dismissed."

I exited the outdoor theater, my backside stiff from standing at attention during the entire presentation. An old turnstile had been modified to function as an ID printing machine.

I stood in the back of the long line to get my ID card, impatience permeating the air around me.

The printing machine spat out my ID card before I even reached it. The card fell to the ground. I bent over, fingers numb and legs trembling, as the wind cut through my thin work uniform. I brushed away the dirt that now covered my ID card.

"Chiara. Sanitation and Health Processor. Fourth Function. Zone A3000."

Val was honest, at least. I slid my ID into the placeholder sewn onto my work jacket. Gone were my tunics and scholarly robes, recycled for other students to use.

I giggled as I reread my new job title.

Soap. Silas was right.

The girl behind me in line raised an eyebrow.

"Sorry," I said, my sides aching from my uncontrollable giggles. "I am probably in charge of soap."

The girl rolled her eyes.

I pushed past the turnstile device and stepped out into the streets.

I followed the crowd of other workers in front of me. Half a block later, I stepped onto the shuttle's raised passenger platform. My stomach growled loudly.

"Get your meal code here!" A floating DataStream notification popped up in front of me. I scanned the code, my newly implanted chip doing the rest. Every meal now carried a price tag payable with hours of work.

I need to disable that Pop-Up Ad Feature later.

I could see the code fluttering through my mind until it connected with the food vending machine back in my apartment. The Fourth Function workers were generously given a spaghetti-flavored protein bar as a welcoming dinner. Apparently, free meant that I could stomach even the worst cube flavors.

A plastic bag floated by, a reminder of the mounds of garbage just outside the city walls. I rubbed my icy fingers together, wondering if I preferred the chill of winter over the stench of summer. Even Unity street sweepers couldn't keep all the garbage away when the winds gathered speed. Summer garbage brought a stench beyond the containing capabilities of Unity's air-filtration systems.

"Everything we use now must have a purpose—and a place," Grandfather had told me one particularly smelly day.

The shuttle lurched to a stop, ending my reverie. The doors opened into a portal tube that transported me back to my apartment. I forced myself to walk at a normal pace, but my heart raced.

My free time was precious to me. I pressed my hand against the apartment lock and waited. *Click.* I stepped inside and took a quick look around. Everything was where I had left it. A jacket in a crumpled heap just inside the door. Some mismatched shoes flung across the floor. Some plastic cups and bowls near the recycling unit. The apartment was now all mine. And mine to pay for as well. Without Irritant to clean up, I had become even more of a slob.

I half-ran over to the food vending machine, my stomach gurgling with indignity. An error message flashed. I scooped a few handfuls of used plastic containers into the recycling unit to satisfy the scolding machine. A moment later, it functioned again but with a warning message about recycling immediately after meals.

I punched in the code I was given. A cube of red goo slopped into a recycled container.

I pinched my nose before scarfing it whole. Grandfather used to pinch his nose after every meal, as if something was bothering him. I had discovered it was an excellent way to shave five minutes off my eating time. I checked my watch, before tossing the container. It clattered somewhere nearby before sliding across the floor.

"Your new schedule," the Fourth Function training video had stated, "is an efficient use of your every waking hour."

That had been the only truthful point of the video. From now on, my mornings would be spent shuffling into shuttles to work for basic elements of survival. My apartment was no longer covered by Unity's guardian program. The food vending machine was a constant drain on my resources. I switched light panels off. Apparently, display screens came with a price tag too.

Thankfully, public showers were free but only during certain hours. If I hurried, I could avoid the lines and the fees. I bypassed the main floor's elevator, taking the stairs in a mad dash.

I grabbed the first showering unit. I slid out of my clothes, kicking them into the open gap in the corner. It sucked the clothes underneath the shower drain. The water ran in a recycling-and-purifying loop underneath the flooring. During my shower, my clothes would be washed and dried.

The hot water caressed my bare skin, but I didn't bask in the experience. Every movement was precisely timed to save an additional seven minutes alone before the hour of mandatory sleep struck at 10 P.M.

I pressed the button to end the barrage of droplets. The air turned on, humid and intense, inhaling the moisture. A panel opened underneath the shower head. My clothes were ready for work tomorrow. I slipped into them and hurried out.

"Miss, you're still wearing your work clothes," said a well-intentioned woman in her soft cotton pajamas.

I ignored her and kept walking. If I didn't waste valuable time changing into multiple outfits, I theorized I could save hours of my life.

Why change clothes to change them again the next morning?

I bolted up the stairs for exercise and unlocked my apartment door. I settled into the couch, its cushions sagging under my frame. Like Grandfather used to do, I had stopped sleeping in my bed entirely. Nearby sat a box of spare robot dog parts. As soon as I earned enough credits, I would rebuild Kaynine. Maybe without Irritant watching my every move, I might even be able to recover the missing footage from the night Grandfather died.

Focus.

With a mere thought, the DataStream floated into my head.

"Care to participate in this evening's activities?" said the advertisement box in one corner of the feed. "Virtuoso Casino is open tonight for business; don't miss out on exciting opportunities to win. Trivia Trouble will begin soon for players across Unity to compete for a free breakfast code tomorrow!"

I disabled the ads permanently and connected to SuBunk's signal. Instantly, I floated across the DataStream highway, heading towards the portal between the two halves of my mind. I waited for a safe crossing, analyzing the data packets flying by. The file for the Virtuoso Casino drifted by, its colossal form hogging the DataStream in its path. Security programs clung to the sides like barnacles. When the DataStream was clear, I pressed SuBunk into full throttle towards the cavern-like entrance that separated the DataStream from the Library.

Once I had left the busy highway of the DataStream behind, I didn't have to worry anymore. I left SuBunk nearby and walked inside the floating refuge. Light poured through each window, unlike the darkness outside the building. Occasionally, the program would glitch, exposing decayed edges around the Library walls.

Elara sipped from a teacup near the fireplace, her feet propped on the coffee table. "Took you long enough."

"Orientation," I replied, hurrying to the bookshelves. I grabbed one volume of Lord Bryon's poetry and another book titled *World Histories*. From what I had been reading, humanity was always one year away from destroying itself.

"I calculated you read around 625 words per minute," Elara said. "At this rate, you will read a quarter of the Library in a year."

"Not good enough." I grabbed a dystopian novel from the shelf, tracing the mysterious lightbulb on the front cover. "There is so much here and I barely have any free time."

"Not true." Elara returned her teacup to its saucer with a delicate clink.

I turned to her, my arms full of books. "Go on."

"It's risky, but you could induce your subconsciousness to take over. Your job will be routine, right?"

"Very."

Elara conjured a screen from thin air. "It's a matter of simple calibrations. We program your subconscious to memorize and perform routine work. The other side of your mind can stay here."

"A book zombie?"

Elara laughed. "Yes. You would be on autopilot, vaguely aware of your body's movements. It's dangerous to disconnect quickly, however, and we will have to prepare for every scenario."

I stacked the books in a haphazard tower. "Let's do it."

Elara took both of my hands. A burning sensation crawled

through her touch and into my body. Color drained from Elara's dark hair, leaving streaks of silver trailing into me. Faint wrinkle lines appeared around her eyes and mouth.

I let go. "What happened?"

Elara tossed her now silver-streaked hair to the side. "I gifted you some nanobots under my control. They are my primary life source, but they can be helpful for other purposes as well."

"But you aged! Does this mean you're dying?"

"No. Losing nanobots makes my programming older and slower. Stop fussing. The nanobots will study your movements while at work. Let them learn your routine. Then, once we have a pattern established, you can return here and study."

I hugged Elara. "Thank you."

Elara's arms wrapped around mine before releasing me.

"Your grandfather left something in these books for you. He said you had to find it. So, you should get started."

A last message from Grandfather. Hidden somewhere in these books. I smiled at the thought. *Clever hiding place.*

"Where do I begin?"

Elara settled back into her seat by the fireplace. "Wherever your heart takes you."

I stared at the rows upon rows of bookshelves, expecting to feel overwhelmed and lost.

Instead, I felt alive.

CHAPTER 15

"Routine is the murderer of creativity. To go home and mindlessly unwind the day with the adventure simulator has never brought about a single work of meaningful art, only submission to the rigid process." — *Excerpt from* Diary of the Doomed *(written in blood for lack of ink), found in the Forbidden Library Archives*

G et on the shuttle every day. Plop into my swivel chair. Ignore the dusty plaque hanging above my forgotten little corner of the office with the list of the rules.

Rules:

1 Clutter-free work zone.

2 Give 100% of your focus.

3 No idle chats.

4 Socialize within your function.

5 In the evenings, log into the adventure simulator for entertainment and mental stimulation.

I glanced at the coffee-cube stains and bits of snack crumbs on my desk. Rule number three might have been the only one I followed. No one talked here. They did their jobs and collected enough Unity credits to survive or relax in holographic escapes. Val occasionally burst through on the DataStream, yelling, spitting, and screaming for more productivity. I programmed a back-door mute button on his announcements.

Managing an entire zone's worth of wastewater had proven to be tedious work. The sewage tunnels ran under the city, and the freshwater tunnels pumped in the replacement in a never-ending cycle. I authorized water changes based on population increases and sent out contractors to fix blockages. At least the job had nothing to do with soap distribution. Silas's punchline wasn't completely true.

Evan's name popped onto my screen as a contractor. I clicked on "Evan White" and assigned him to a different task. I tried to keep him from the worst jobs, like unblocking a clogged pipe or collecting samples of the wastewater for analysis.

Instead, I assigned him to attend a safety lecture for the day, complete with a free code for lunch.

It was the least I could do.

I wondered if Silas thought about me. If he ever looked out for me. I liked to think he still cared. But I hadn't had the courage to try to illegally communicate with him, although clogging his wealthy apartment zone had occurred to me on several occasions.

I released my thoughts, relaxing as my DataStream and the nanobots took over. Somewhere in the foggy distance, my body swiped screens, authorized contracts, and stared at data charts detailing the depths of watery, human waste.

Meanwhile, the real me nestled in an oversized chair with a book. It had been months, and I hadn't been caught yet. It wasn't a bad existence, and I discovered literature, art, and philosophy over cups of tea.

It was so idyllic that, sometimes, I lost myself. Elara had to remind me to log out. The nanobots were programmed for a few hours. I still had to clock in to avoid suspicion, starvation and, often, dehydration. Apparently, virtual tea and knowledge weren't equivalent to real nutrition.

The fireplace roared as I closed the last page of *Fahrenheit 451*.

"Elara, I think you know exactly where Grandfather hid this mysterious file."

Elara buried her face in a green, leather-bound volume. "Nice try."

I sighed. "What good is all this knowledge if I'm searching blind?"

She let the rustle of pages answer my question.

"Seriously, Elara. I need a clue. A map? A riddle?"

Elara rolled her eyes and turned another page.

"This could take years," I said.

Thud. Elara snapped her book shut. I had her attention.

"Patience is learned," Elara said, before opening her book again to a random page. "You're giving me gray hairs."

"Ouch." I placed a hand over my heart, faking a wound.

The corners of Elara's mouth teased upwards.

My mother was stubborn and sarcastic beneath the layers of caution. I've missed this so much.

I stretched and tried some mind-clearing yoga exercises I learned from the previous week's nonfiction selection.

"Exercise in the virtual zone doesn't count," Elara said. "You should log off eventually."

"So supportive," I said as I finished the tree pose.

"Anytime."

I abandoned the yoga and paced the rows of shelves instead. I methodically went row by row. Every day, I hoped I would stumble across a hidden passage. Reading books had opened my mind to many possibilities. Trap doors, false bottoms, a secret button leading to a hidden staircase.

Just in case, I had tried hacking into the Library's lines of code. Somehow, it was immune to all of my attempts to alter it.

Grandfather was clever.

The Library had two floors. Upstairs was muted and serene, while the main floor was light and cozy, featuring the fireplace. Fiction and nonfiction titles were split on both levels. Fiction to the right; nonfiction to the left.

I started upstairs. I found section H and began tossing books onto the floor. The books spilled across the aisle in mounds. Nothing out of the ordinary.

Elara snapped her fingers, and the books flew around me as if caught in a windstorm before rushing back to their places on the shelves.

I started for the next section. This week's search method was to toss every book. All marvelous tales included a moment where the light of understanding broke through the storm clouds.

With any luck, I might stumble across this mysterious last message from Grandfather.

Rows I-J succumbed to my destructive tactic. Books flew everywhere, bumping into one another on the way back to their assigned spots. A multi-volume set smacked my head as it whizzed back to the top shelf.

"Just my luck." I kicked at the last book lying on the floor. It jumped forward and was sucked back into the bookshelf.

I headed back downstairs. Elara's face was buried inside the covers of a thick tome by Sir Arthur Conan Doyle.

Ah, what would the great Sherlock Holmes say?

I smiled, imagining my current favorite literary character shaking his head at my investigative techniques.

"I have to go," I said. "I'm throwing K-Z onto the floor tomorrow."

My inner detective fumed, annoyed by my lack of observation to deduce a better course of action.

Elara raised an eyebrow. "Sounds riveting."

I turned to disconnect.

But I paused.

Elara sat there, so peaceful and oblivious. My real mother never rested unless she had what she wanted next to her.

Has Elara always read the same book? How long does it take a computer program to finish a novel?

I marched back. "Give that to me."

Elara stretched out her arms as she handed the book to me. "I thought you would never ask."

The second my fingertips brushed the book's leather cover, the Library disappeared. Elara was gone. I stood in a single square of light, surrounded by shadowy impressions of a laboratory. A man scribbled on a DataPad.

Grandfather.

I tried to move but couldn't.

He looked straight at me, held a finger to his lips, and winked. The video fast forwarded.

Faye entered the room, heels clacking. She looked younger, with firm skin and silky waves bouncing. "Well? You said you needed to talk."

Grandfather cleared his throat. "Your candidacy has been terminated. You're not fit for the program. I'm truly sorry."

Faye leaned against the lab door. "This is all because I'm not *her*, isn't it?"

"I can't keep you on this team. You're a fine researcher, but I don't need you on this project. I am sure Auto will find another use for your talents."

Faye slid closer to the older man, placing her hand on his. "You can't bear the idea of creating a truly synthetic child, can you? I'm the newer model of the woman you once loved. You made me, and now you're kicking me off this project?"

Grandfather pulled back. "You're just a synth with her face, but not her soul. Get out of my sight."

Faye snickered. "Clarence, I know your secret desire to stop Auto. But it's too late. You can't stop the future. And as far as souls go, I know what you did. How far you went to preserve pieces of her for your other project."

Grandfather avoided her gaze. "You still owe me for your very existence," he said. "We made an agreement."

Faye huffed. "You act so righteous but yet, you've crossed lines of no return. Don't worry, I'll keep your secrets, at least until your last breath. And then, I will have several lifetimes to live while your days are but a shadow. I wonder, can you live knowing that you were responsible for authorizing my rebirth?"

"You are a failed project. All synths are. For what it's worth, I'm sorry that I could not give you the best of her, Faye. What really mattered."

Faye stormed out of the room. My grandfather turned back around to me, holding his DataPad at a lower angle. I reached forward and my entire view shifted to the bolded title of the document: "Plan for Advancement."

Charts, images, and graphs. A pod, designed to resemble the woman's womb, giving birth to full-grown bodies. Each, alive and melding with a machine's mind and feeding off of the brain's electrical impulses. Machine with organic tissue. Eyes with no glimmer of humanity.

A synth.

Grandfather spoke, his eyes piercing through the video and into my soul. "Chiara, if you're seeing this, then it's not too late. Auto has been breeding to select only the desirable traits. He is harvesting us for a new body....A synthetic body. Warn those who will hear. I can only delay the inevitable but you will have to stop this madness."

My grandfather lowered his voice. "But if Auto finds out you know, run."

CHAPTER 16

"You aren't here anymore. You listen but your eyes wander, blocking off sound and sense. What enchanting realms have stolen you away?" — Excerpt from Pleas of the Forgotten, *found in the Forbidden Library Archives*

I was at work. By that, I meant my mind was actually in my body, sitting at my desk. It was a strange sensation after months of being a virtual book zombie.

Nearby, a package sat on my desk. Inside, Kaynine's core processing chip and some spare parts were carefully labeled. I had included Silas's friction generator, which allowed Kaynine to operate without recharging or using the DataStream.

That little feature may prove useful, especially if I succeed.

I took a quick peek inside the package. One last inventory check. Grandfather's red chocolate box contained Kaynine's core. The friction generator was wrapped tightly with scraps of cloth. And some shiny extra bolts. Kaynine loved playing with those.

Silas might have been upset with me, but he would take good care of Kaynine and the bright red box.

The mail drone came by, pushing its cart. I handed him the package and watched it disappear beyond my workspace.

Delivery would happen within the hour, and I made sure the label couldn't be traced back to me.

I fought the wave of nostalgia. I missed Kaynine. But today, I was taking Grandfather's advice. It was time to run. Silas could restore Kaynine and find the missing files. Grandfather once told me that the truth was not good at hiding. Silas would come looking for me when the time was right.

Or at least, I hope so.

I missed him, and the regret ached in my bones.

But first, I have to set the record straight.

I pulled up the DataStream at my desk using Val's authorization codes. The Fourth Function Administrator was too careless about security. Or maybe he never had to worry about subordinates hacking into anything.

It's not like Fourth Function falls under genius class, after all.

I had seized the opportunity to steal the authorization codes when Val took a tour of my office building. While Val gave a speech on work ethics, I stole his codes by isolating the signals from his Implantation chip. I also gathered information regarding Val's schedule while pretending to sympathize with his poor secretary's daily drudgery. She was overworked and on the edge of a breakdown; a few kind words and free coffee cubes did the trick.

Val was predictable to a fault with his work habits. During his lunch break, I could log into the administrator database with his passwords as long as I kept my searches under two minutes. So far, no alarms have been triggered. Sixty seconds was plenty to cover my tracks and erase footage whenever my nanobots glitched. Once, I found footage that showed me frozen in place for half an hour. If I hadn't checked, those sorts of mistakes could have been deadly.

But during yesterday's routine check, I stumbled upon a cache of files containing sensitive missions. Val's position as a Function Administrator apparently meant that he was kept in the loop, something I had hoped was the case.

One video bore a date I knew well.

The day Grandfather died. The day Kaynine's video logs were wiped clean. This is what Kaynine saw.

The truth was one mental click away. But the file was two minutes and fifteen seconds in length, well beyond the time I could risk with Val's credentials.

At the first opportunity that morning, I told Elara about the file. Her advice had been straightforward.

"When you open the door, prepare to pay the cost." She offered a rare hug and tossed me a book on Unity's sewer systems and building plans. "Your grandfather made several copies of this book. He felt it was important."

Elara had watched as I poured over the plans. The maintenance tunnels had ceilings tall enough for a person. The waste poured out of the tunnels like a waterfall, before forming a toxic river encircling Unity's periphery.

Even now, I shivered as my father's voice echoed through my memories. I was once again a young girl visiting my mother's workplace, meeting my father for the first-and-only time.

Martin had explained how the hydroelectric plant worked, how the run-off water siphoned into the sewers.

"Where do the sewers empty?" I had asked.

Martin lowered his voice. "To the ruins beyond Unity."

I breathed out slowly, focusing again on the single click that would end life as I knew it in two minutes and fifteen seconds.

I let the DataStream flow through me, creating a digital display in front of my face. Elara could block the cameras briefly. Doing so always drained her energy, but it was important to face the truth with open eyes.

I hit play on the video with clenched fists. Every hair on my arm tingled in warning.

A system-wide alert would activate at the end of the video. Every movement afterwards had to be fluid and precise.

The video footage began with a soft scratching sound as spidery robots flooded the hallway outside my apartment. Silent, rubbery pads covered the robots' temporarily retracted claws. They beeped to each other in an electronic language, seeming to come to some sort of consensus. My door appeared.

A squad of CUE robots milled about restlessly, waiting for a command. The door was a formality. With a few clicks and whirs, the door flew open.

My throat tightened as I watched Grandfather turn, from where he sat on the couch, eerily calm, to face the camera mounted on the spidery leg of one of the robots.

"Surrender the file," said the first CUE robot upon entering the room. It raised itself to the height of the doorway, its legs expanding with a metallic screech.

Grandfather's lips curled with laughter.

"Last chance," the robot said.

Grandfather fidgeted with his pockets and then tossed an object behind him. Two robots scurried off to retrieve it.

"Thank you for your cooperation." The lead CUE robot's claws popped out, poised to strike. I emerged from the bedroom. The camera's focus locked onto me.

Grandfather pulled out a detonator from his other pocket. Several spiders fell to the ground as a shock wave blanketed the room.

The item he threw was rigged to knock them out.

The lead CUE robot was stunned. Grandfather grabbed my hand.

We took off towards the hallway as the overhead lights turned off, one by one. The camera switched to night vision, revealing more shapes surrounding us from every angle.

They had backup. We didn't stand a chance.

Grandfather shielded me while pulling out another shock-wave device. The camera angle twisted as Kaynine joined forces with us, facing off against the intruders.

But it was too late. A much larger CUE robot pounced, pinning Grandfather to the floor, knocking the device from his hand. The robot hissed, then its laser eyes glowed red. A needle darted out from a concealed panel in its abdomen.

A growl filled the camera feed. Kaynine tried to keep other CUE robots at bay, but three surrounded me, pacing like a pack. One dropped from the ceiling. It stung me, causing me to fall. Another secreted a sticky white resin that covered my mouth like a gag.

Grandfather's face contorted into a paralyzed scream. Then, his eyes closed.

We were all dragged back into our room, the video footage shaking a little. The stunned robots regained their faculties as the backup CUE robots shot webs onto the walls.

The webbing is supposed to contain the crime scene. Make it easier to clean later.

My hands smothered my mouth to suppress the screams. The webs covered the walls and most of the furnishings.

The robots tossed Grandfather onto the couch. The large CUE robot raised an appendage and clawed Grandfather across his shoulder and his chest, carving an X with surgical precision.

Limbs were picked off, one by one, and tossed into a heap on the floor.

Other CUE robots moved in. Dividing the organs. Shaving the hair from Grandfather's head, letting the strands float in the pool of life draining from his prone body.

I paused the video, my fingers trembling. Tears dripped down my cheeks. I took a long, slow breath as my fingers curled into fists. I wiped away my tears before my shaking hands resumed the video, knowing I had precious few moments left to finish watching the footage.

I'll make them pay.

Red droplets clouded the camera, streaks running across the video's frame. The arterial spray splattered across the webbed walls. As the carnage ceased, they wrapped the bloody deeds into thick balls of sticky residue.

Recycling.

The word rolled around in my stomach. I puked into a nearby trash receptacle as the massacre's soundtrack continued to play. I knew what happened next. This was the one part where the video and the fragments of memory collided.

The shapes turned to me, hissing in between electronic beeps, as if amazed I was still conscious. I was screaming into the resinous gag, wriggling like a mummy in their webbed restraints. One of them bit me, releasing a stronger sedative. I collapsed.

All around my limp body, the CUE robots cleaned the apartment in a frenzy. The blood was sucked clean.

The video went dark.

The Investigator's office. Inza. They must have tampered with my memories and buried the truth. Faye was right. Trust no one.

I choked back tears, all too aware that I didn't have time for emotions. Kaynine had seen it all happen. Data can only be hidden—but never fully deleted. The video had been wiped from his memory and then stored in this archive under Administrative lock and key.

"Good dog," I said, a small smile breaking through my tears.

I could hear a subconscious ticking of each passing second. Val would log back in soon and no doubt notice that someone had used his codes to access and view this incriminating video. By tomorrow, the data would probably be placed under additional layers of security, and I would be hunted down. The load bar was at "100%."

Ready to upload the file?

The question loomed in front of me. Shakespeare would tell me to fear some consequence hanging in the stars. And like Romeo, I ignored the sage advice because my course was set, regardless of the repercussions.

Some things were worth the risk.

With a few keystrokes, I added in the clipped video of Faye's conversation with Grandfather about Auto's breeding program and some text at the end.

"If you're watching this footage, ask yourself: What else is

Auto hiding from us? Share, please. Your life—all of our lives—may depend on it."

With one thought, I hacked the main Unity news program and posted the video. There wasn't time to watch the comments roll in or the viewer numbers tick upwards. The truth was there. For everyone to see. I closed out of the DataStream and strolled past the cubicles housing bored, listless Fourth Function workers.

I opened my work locker and quickly unzipped the waterproof backpack. Inside were several rationed food cubes. Water bottle. A hat. Small jacket and change of pants, both water-resistant. I zipped up the backpack and exited.

An appointment reminder flashed in my DataStream. Sewage line #52 needed personal inspection today at 3 P.M.

Right on schedule.

One perk of my job was the ability to create a false work order for sewer maintenance, with the help of Val's hacked codes. Evan would be there too.

He might let me go. And if not, I could overpower him.

My pace increased the closer I got to the subway station.

I fought to steady myself, letting my other senses blur. Ticket scanned. The roar of the shuttle taking off. Buildings flashing by the window in a dreary pattern.

I had known this day was coming. I had set the plans.

But nothing prepared me for dealing with the aftermath of watching the video. Violence played on repeat in my head, and I fought to maintain a placid demeanor. Everything depended on it.

I bit my trembling lip and forced myself to internally recite some calming poetry.

"Focus on the words. Find your courage." Elara's last bit of advice rang in my mind.

The hovering metal transport halted. I leaped out of my seat, exiting first. I forced a smile as I approached the waiting group of orange-clad sewage workers near an open access hole.

"Gentlemen." I nodded, holding an inspector's DataPad close to my pounding chest.

Evan looked at me in surprise. His face was a hollow shell, even thinner than before. His skin was pale from a lack of sunlight.

"Chiara?" he said with a faint smile.

I faked ignorance. "Do I know you?" I had placed him in the crosshairs of a storm. He would need the two other workers to witness my indifference.

The light in Evan's eyes flickered out. "Yeah, we were at Implantation and shared a class together. Back of the line, remember?"

I opened a DataStream window, displaying the time. "You look familiar, but chatting won't get me home any sooner."

The other two workers shared a glance.

It was unmistakable that I was being a jerk.

"Then after you," the first worker said. His smirk, height, and muscles told me all I needed to know about him. The other man sprouted a full dark beard. He stroked it. I didn't need to know their names.

Nice to meet you, Hairy. I should apologize to you and Muscles for the chaos I am about to unleash.

I lowered both feet into the manhole.

Human waste and stagnant water. The stench made me cough in spasms.

Muscles and Hairy laughed.

I heard the slap of a high-five as the sewer workers mocked my reaction.

They care about Evan. Must be nice for someone to have your back.

I winced as the thought crossed my mind. Silas hadn't contacted me. I hadn't found the courage to contact him. Now, it was too late.

I landed on the walking track above the flowing water. Evan, Muscles, and Hairy followed, their footsteps sending clanging echoes through the dark, forking tunnel ahead.

"Residents have been complaining that the water pressure has been minimal," I said. "In addition, a foul smell has been reported. We need to split up and handle this efficiently."

Muscles rolled his eyes and elbowed Hairy. Evan tried to remain polite.

"You two, why don't you take your attitude to the left?"

"What's your problem anyway?" Hairy said, crossing his arms.

I stepped close to him and shoved the DataPad into his chest. "Just do your job."

Hairy grabbed the DataPad, glaring, and stomped off down the left branch of the tunnel. Muscles followed after Hairy after giving Evan an apologetic slap on the back.

Evan turned to me. "To the right?" He flipped on his head-lamp and led the way.

I nodded and followed behind him. We walked for about fifteen feet by the narrow illumination of Evan's headlamp.

"Evan, I'm sorry."

He whipped around, the light blinding me as it struck my face in full force. "You do remember me."

"I don't expect you to understand. Believe me, I'm protecting you. It's best if everyone thinks we don't know each other."

Evan cocked his head. "Are you in some sort of trouble?"

I placed my arm on his thin shoulder. "With any luck, I will be."

I swiped a skeleton key from Evan's belt and grabbed onto him. We both tumbled over the side. The icy water welcomed us with a soaking embrace.

My brain feverishly scrambled towards the next steps.

Exit the sewer, then hide among the Streamless.

The people outside Unity were shells of their past selves— simple ferals. As long as I avoided the CUE robots that patrolled the wastelands outside Unity's walls, I would have nothing to fear. Auto, on the other hand, would face the wrath of every human in Unity after my circulating video exposed the rotten corruption. I just had to bide my time.

Evan sputtered and flailed. The sour-smelling water had a decent undercurrent, pulling us toward the drains.

I let the current take me away. With a few wild strokes, Evan fought his way to the side of the tunnel. He struggled back onto the walkway, gasping for air. Water dripped from his work suit.

I watched from below as the water drove me on. The drains should appear at any moment.

Good. Evan is safe. He could say I attacked him. But no one will falsely suspect him of helping me.

His buddies would back him up, as would the watery evidence of his clothes. His shock would play in his favor. A few hours of questioning and a decontamination shower would be the end of his troubles tonight.

Evan panted as he ran along the metal pathway next to the flowing waters. "Grab my hand!"

I took a few strokes, increasing my speed, ignoring him. Ahead, sewer line 52 crossed paths with sewer line 53. I leaned towards the left, avoiding Evan's darting headlamp and angling myself for a better position at the crossroads.

Cold, pungent water shot up my nostrils. I snorted and gagged from the raw burning sensation in my throat. The water-proof backpack weighed me down as my tired arms lost their strength.

Elara was right. Virtual workouts aren't the same.

The chill of the water crept into my bones as I struggled to keep calm. A current pulled me under. I panicked, swimming back to the top. Dizziness and freezing nerves had me disoriented in the darkness.

A split emerged ahead.

Right. It was right. No. Left?

My teeth chattered. I took a hard right with a few strokes.

Stop doubting yourself.

The schematic ran through my mind as the water pooled towards a locked grate ahead.

Follow tunnel 53 to the end. The others empty out at a higher level, and I'm not planning on falling to my death. Use the key, unlock the grate, slide out. Fall a few feet. Cry. Get back up.

My body slammed against the grate as the water pressure built behind me. A dead rat thudded next to me, its body smacking against the metal bars with each surge of water.

I fiddled with the slick skeleton key. The locked gate was rusty. My fingers trembled.

"Chiara!" Evan's cry was followed by distant footsteps.

No doubt Hairy and Muscles too.

"She can't have gone far. I could pull her out." I could imagine Muscles flexing.

"What a lunatic."

Ah, Hairy. You have no idea.

I felt frantically for the lock near the edge of the grate. The key turned, and I pushed with all my might.

I clung onto the grated door as it swung open with a rusty, roaring complaint. Water exited violently behind me, rushing past the now-opened grate.

I stopped trembling as another fear edged out all other concerns.

I took the wrong tunnel. This one is too high. I won't survive the fall.

The foaming water arched over the tunnel's edge before plummeting into the stream below.

Think.

The temporary fear paralysis wore off as my physical condition regained priority. My arms burned. My fingers began to slip from the pull of gravity.

If I am going to fall, I will do it with dignity.

I closed my eyes, picturing the diving game I used to enjoy.

I angled myself towards the stream sparkling beneath my dangling feet—then let go of the grate door to freefall to the depths below.

CHAPTER 17

"There is an ancient fable of a farmer whose only son loses a leg. All of the neighbors offer their condolences. The farmer reminds them that nothing is good or bad; it's all perspective. When war comes and the farmer's son is spared from service, the neighbors congratulate this turn of events as their own sons head toward an uncertain future. The story goes on but the moral remains." — *Excerpt from* The Elder Pearls, *found in the Forbidden Library Archives*

"This one is crazy." Female. Husky, confident voice.

"We're in no position to judge sanity." Male. Deeper tone. Calm.

My eyes remained shut. Their conversation floated through the water, pounding against my ears.

"Speak for yourself," the female said. Footsteps splashed closer. Something yanked on my shoe. "Let's take what we can."

"Mother will know what to do," said the male.

"You're asking for trouble."

"Maybe."

Arms encircled my legs and upper torso. Water dripped from my clothing. Pain, like a starving rat, nibbled on the edges of my consciousness.

"She smells like trouble," the female said, coughing.

"It's a good thing I came along. What would you've done? Left her?"

The female laughed. "Spare me the moral high ground. Her boots are my size."

I tried to open my eyes, but they felt paralyzed. My index finger twitched on the left side. Nothing else would respond.

"If she doesn't make it, the boots are yours."

"Throw in the backpack, and we have a deal." I could hear the zipper being released and the shuffling of contents. "You've got to look at this! I haven't seen food cubes since..."

"Look later. Lift now," the male voice ordered. "We need to get to Mother first."

I was hoisted into the air, and my limp body swayed side-to-side to the rhythm of trudging footsteps. At first, the steps sounded wet and slippery, then came the crackling of crunching rocks. Smooth surfaces came next, along with a cooling drop in temperature. I was lowered onto a thin blanket smelling of mildew and rain. The footsteps faded.

My index finger twitched again. I forced my eyes to open, registering only blurry shapes in the darkness. I ran my tongue over my lips, tasting the bumpy, bloody cracks.

I'm alive.

Coherent thought brought waves of pain. I groaned and attempted to connect with my legs.

Get up, let's go.

Nothing.

I willed my entire hand to move, providing the inertia needed to roll my body over.

"Not so ba—" Pain's fingernails dug into my spine. My screams softened into low sobs as I tried to make out what I could in the cool darkness. The musky smell of moisture accosted my nostrils.

"Is anyone there?" I regretted my words immediately as the sound echoed off the earthen walls.

My senses combined, adjusting fully to the darkness. Thick stone walls. Chains embedded into the rock above me. Compacted dirt and stone flooring.

I'm in a cave.

Out here, there was no DataStream. No way to connect to Elara. I had to use my primal instincts. I waited and stilled my beating heart, focusing on every little sound.

A scritch-scratch shuffle of feet. Soft. But present.

Something waited in the furthest shadows beyond my cell.

"You can have the shoes," I said, tired of the waiting game.

"No shoes. No need. Mother Lotus wants something else." A shadow moved closer with a shuffling gait.

I tried to get up, to face this new threat.

Instead, I screamed and fell back onto the hard ground. Every inch of my spine throbbed with the jabs of a thousand needles.

The limping figure emerged from the shadows. Strands of blood-red hair clung to patches of melted synthetic skin. Two faded white orbs, clicking with robotic gears, aimed in no particular direction. One hip was crooked, and her left leg was made of welded-together cans. A sharpened walking cane was fused to the robot's left arm. A formidable defense for an aged robot whose spare parts would be valuable scrap.

"Mother can fix you." She rolled me over with her walking cane, forcing my face into the dirt. I screamed, my ears refusing to register the sound in the torrent of sensations.

The robot stroked the back of my head, parting my matted hair with the metallic fingers on her other hand.

"You still have your Implantation chip." She let my hair fall back over my scalp. A finger trailed every inch of my spine. "Paralyzed from fall. Mother likes your chances of survival."

"My chances? Hold on... what are you planning to do?"

"Don't ask silly questions. Hold still. Mother will fix this."

A cold sensation was followed by the sound of slippery ripping. Mother Lotus pierced my spine with the sharpened end of her walking cane, cutting it open like a zipper from shoulder to tailbone. A scream clawed its way through my vocal cords.

Mother poked and prodded at my spinal joints, inserting something in between each one. Next came the crackle of a fuse torch and the acrid smell of melting skin.

"Nanobots?" I said with gritted teeth.

"Clever girl."

Panic flooded through me. Based on Mother Lotus's appearance and makeshift parts, the nanobots had to be first generation. *Did those things even work? Does this insane robot know how to perform this surgery?*

The succinct thought rang through my otherwise scrambled mind. Puke tumbled out of my mouth, forming a putrid pool beside me.

Mother Lotus started humming.

She is enjoying this.

I thought I had known pain before. I was wrong. The nanobots bit into my spine with their metallic teeth. Mother Lotus's song reached a high-pitched whistle as a needle pinched into my skin. I whimpered as the needle slid between the raw layers in a crisscross pattern.

"What did the needle say to the thread?"

Is the robot telling a joke? Now?

"Go prick yourself." Mother cackled at her own punch line. "Yes, this one is ready." She poured hot liquid over the bumpy ridges of my stitched skin. "Molten metal. Very sterile. Seals much faster. Special mixture."

My vision flickered on and off like a toddler who discovered control switches. The pain came in waves.

The drooping skin on Mother Lotus's face widened into a crooked smile. "You cannot sleep. Embrace the awareness that pain brings." She gripped my shoulder, and a bolt of electricity snapped me back into full awareness.

"Recore!" Mother Lotus called out.

A male figure emerged. He picked me off the ground, away

from the pile of blood, puke, and horror. His soldierly stance and attentiveness to Mother Lotus told me everything about the power structure in this cavern.

Make friends with the insane robot in order to live.

The robot continued to hum, soft and repetitive, as Recore placed me into a corner of the cave, my back propped against the wall. I slid, crooked and bent like a wilted flower in the heat.

"I'm sorry," Recore said, correcting my posture.

I recognized the male voice I heard earlier. His neck and hands were scarred, and his blue eyes reflected pools of deep complexity. His white-blond hair twisted into a fierce ponytail.

I slid further down the wall. Mother Lotus tapped her cane impatiently. Recore readjusted me but kept a steadying hand on my shoulder this time. I watched in horror as he reached for something above my head. Two metal chains clattered from the ceiling, and he attached them to my helpless wrists. The chains tightened and my back straightened with a spine snapping jolt of electricity.

I blubbered incoherent words. I was drunk with pain.

Mother Lotus grazed the side of my face with the bloody tip of her cane. "You answer my questions. Or Mother will take your chip. Maybe some other pieces of you as well. Simple process, really. Now, what is your name?"

I took a long, slow breath, letting common sense and survival instincts take over.

Okay, maybe friendship is off the table.

The Streamless—these discarded people and robots living outside Unity's walls—saw me as a body bag of parts. The irony tasted bitter even as my lungs ached with guilt. A Streamless had died so I could breathe. One thing was for sure; I was in danger here. Possibly more so than in Unity.

I tried direct eye contact, hoping it didn't come across as threatening or rude. "My name is Chiara."

"How did you navigate the sewers?" Mother Lotus poked my skull again with her cane.

I winced at the pointy tip grazing my hairline. "I read a map."

"And why did you leave?"

I swallowed, letting the saliva coat my parched throat. "Auto killed my grandfather. I was next."

"Sad story, but it does not help Mother. Your chip is interesting. We will talk later."

"Wait, I have questions too," I said, locking my gaze with Recore. "Please!"

Recore shifted uncomfortably while Mother Lotus cackled, her voice bouncing off the cavern walls. "You can ask Mother one question, if it's the right one."

"Whose side are you on and what do you plan on doing with me?" I rattled my chains, causing an echo.

Mother Lotus inched backwards, her smile growing wider with each step back into the darkness of the cave until all I could see was the outline of her toothy grin. "That was two questions," she said. "Now rest. Phase One requires you to heal."

Recore followed her out, leaving me alone in the darkness.

My chin trembled.

What happens in Phase Two?

CHAPTER 18

"The cage rattled as our hero shook the cold bars, testing each one for a weakness. Meanwhile, a small mouse scurried underneath, free to come and go as it pleased." — Excerpt from **The King's Schemes**, *found in the Forbidden Library Archives*

In between bouts of consciousness, I awoke to Recore unlocking my chains. Every morning, I gritted my way through the required exercises and fighting maneuvers ordered by Mother Lotus for Phase Two of some maddening scheme.

Recore claimed I had become soft from life in Unity. He easily lifted heavy rocks above his head while I struggled to do the same. "You can do it," he would encourage me, a dusting of kindness finding its way into his careful words.

I learned as much as I could about Mother Lotus's reserved bodyguard in between sparring sessions. He was roughly two years older than me, a failed graduate at Emergent High. Not surprisingly, our paths had never crossed. School wasn't for friendships, and interacting with the older students was forbidden.

He never wanted to talk about Unity. I didn't blame him.

Especially when I feel the same way.

As cruel as it had seemed at first, the original restraints had straightened my spine and allowed the nanobots to make full repairs. Now, with the long length of the chain attached to my right wrist, I was able to move about. Even still, the cold clamp was a daily reminder of my debt to Mother Lotus.

Graciously, Recore had brought my backpack so I could change into my spare clothes. The food cubes and water bottles were missing, but I expected that.

What I hadn't expected was to wash myself using only a small bowl of water and a scrap of cloth. Mother Lotus had brought it to me the day before. I had gently wiped off the crusty, dried blood and brushed my fingertips lightly across my ridged back.

I tried to laugh away the mutilation, but it lingered in the unwanted corners of my mind.

Time was difficult to track in this place. Between Recore's boot-camp exercises and my own exhausted sleep, I calculated a full day.

I palmed a nearby rock and scraped a line into the dirt, adding to the previous marks. I silently counted.

Four days.

The older nanobots Mother Lotus placed inside my spine worked, albeit slowly. My strength returned.

If only I still had access to the DataStream to contact Elara...

This was the curse of being Streamless. This was the cost of going public with Grandfather's execution.

"Daydream much?"

I jumped at the strange-yet-familiar voice, chains clamoring.

"I'm Ash. Basically, I'm the kicker of your privileged backside." A girl sauntered into the room, purposefully pausing before releasing my handcuff.

I rubbed my wrist and scanned my new guard.

"Where's Recore?" I asked, craning my neck to look past Ash's squared shoulders.

"Busy. It's my job to babysit you today. Phase Two and all that jazz."

Ash's narrow green eyes seemed hardened with glints of golden rage, while her black hair and thin lips complemented her harsh, bony features. Faded black leather had been cut and hand stitched, contouring her athletic body. A leather belt, cut to serve as shoulder straps, crisscrossed the front of her chest. She looked like the avatars in the adventure-simulation games, except nothing about her whispered "hero."

"So what are we doing?"

"Something different. Fun, for me anyway."

Ash's leather jacket complained as she folded her arms, revealing a knife secured in the belt around her waist.

My stomach gurgled, and I wasn't in the mood for riddles. "Anyone around here believe in breakfast?"

Ash smirked. "You earn it. Like the rest of us. Try anything... and I'll carve you into breakfast sausages myself."

"Cannibalism is never a good look."

Ash motioned towards the doorway with a sigh. "Come on, Unity girl. Let's go."

A flood of recognition swept through me. This was the female voice. The one who wanted to leave me behind.

"You would have left me to die."

Ash shoved me forward into the cavernous hallway outside my cell. "Unity girl isn't as stupid as she looks then. Good, we understand each other."

A nervousness tingled my scarred spine. The hallway was wide, but I counted at least five crude dwelling spaces on both sides. Simple wax candles lined the hallway, providing dim illumination.

"Who else lives here? I'm hoping there are some reasonable people around."

"You'll meet the others soon enough."

"If they are as charming as you, I can't wait."

Ash shoved me again. "If you keep running your mouth, I'll close it for you."

I spun to face her. "If you're going to threaten, do it."

Ash stepped closer; her fingers curled around her knife.

"Your psychotic robot needs me for something," I said, squaring off with Ash, eye-to-eye. "Remember that."

Hold her gaze.

I forced myself to glower at her towering figure.

Ash hissed and released the grip on her knife. Her hot breath landed on my forehead. "Mother Lotus is family. You are a piece of trash with recycled parts. I saw those scars when I dragged you in here. If you place my family in any danger..."

"I get the idea. And for the record, I didn't know that the Streamless were more than just feral. I'm sorry about the source of my recycled lungs."

Ash smirked, a gleam of mischief flickering in her green eyes. "Doesn't matter. You're about to pay for your mistakes anyways."

The hallway emptied out into a large circular room. We entered and my gaze caught sharp, wooden sticks hanging by hooks on the walls. I calculated the distance and time it would take to reach one of those weapons.

"Don't even think about it," Ash warned.

"Am I late?"

I spun around to see a face peppered with stubble and a jagged chin. The man's frame was thin and decidedly short. His backpack wiggled.

Ash sighed as she rested against the entryway. She fiddled with her knife, stroking the edges against the tips of her fingers. "Get on with it already," Ash ordered.

"My fame is Ardo." He ran an agitated hand across the back of his neck before offering the same hand to me in a stiff greeting. "Correction. My *name* is Ardo."

My gaze skipped to his suddenly squirming backpack.

Ardo retracted his gesture of welcome. "This is the task for today." He reached into his pocket and produced a palm-sized sphere with flickering images.

A reality core.

"How did you pry one from a holo projector?" I asked. "They are always hard wired into an adventure-simulation room."

Ardo's eyes twinkled. "Very difficult. This is my frowning achievement as a scrapper." With a frown, he started over. "My *crowning* achievement."

The reality core swirled, changing the room from stone walls to a hilltop in the cover of night. My eyes slowly adjusted to the darkness.

Sensations have been turned off.

I watched the swaying of the unruly grass on the hilltop, but no breeze reached my skin.

"I thought you didn't have the DataStream out here," I said, my heart pounding with hope. "How is this thing working?"

Maybe I can contact Elara and SuBunk after all.

"The simulation factors are turned off. It's just a virtual canvas drawn by our artist, Sky. What you're seeing are layers of sketched frames. Most machines will work outside the DataStream with a proper energy source. In this case... flattery." He paused and corrected himself. "Sorry, I meant battery. My words come out wrong sometimes."

Ash snorted. "That's your best word scramble yet, Ardo." She then glared at me. "You aren't allowed to make fun of him, Unity girl. Family privilege only."

I swatted Ash away, ignoring her need for power. "I wasn't making fun of him. Besides, tell Sky she is talented to have drawn the scenes for this simulation. So life-like!"

Ash stiffened protectively at the mention of Sky's name. "Enough, Ardo. Talk geek later and get this show on the road. The less she knows, the better."

The backpack wriggled again.

"The task is simple. In this simulation, find the bunker and gain access using your Implantation chip. But don't get caught."

"Caught by what?" I asked. "What are you not telling me?"

Ardo dumped the contents of his backpack onto the ground.

It was a smaller CUE machine with multiple dents and bullet

holes.

I trembled and let out a gasp.

As if in response, its spidery claws activated. My throat constricted as I tried to block the images of Grandfather's bloody limbs being dragged across our apartment floor.

"It is plugged into the simulation," Ardo whispered. "Use the surrounding scenery to hide. It can see what you see."

"Time to play hide-and-seek," Ash said with a grin. "Let's see how badly you fail this test."

My legs began moving before my brain could register a direction. The reality core kept shifting the grassy space around me, keeping within the confines of the physical room while creating the illusion of a sprawling hilltop.

Like running in place on a treadmill, the scenery shifted with every step I took.

Okay, so figure out how to get inside a bunker. Avoid a very real CUE machine in an unfamiliar simulation. What could go wrong?

Ash and Ardo stepped outside of the simulation zone, watching me from the doorway.

The CUE advanced, its spidery claws clicking and hissing as it processed this new environment. At least its laser eyes seemed to be disabled.

Think. Don't panic. Analyze your surroundings.

A small square building with a single entrance. Some sort of keypad. Nowhere to hide. Only open fields surrounding the building.

Who am I kidding? I'm going to die. That CUE is very real even if this place is not.

I ran to the building and frantically punched at the keypad, aware of the odd sensation of my fingers brushing across air instead of the keys that my eyes insisted were there.

The keypad lit, as if sensing my Implantation chip. But it kept blinking, waiting for an authorization.

Metal scraped against stone. The CUE had seen me. Its spidery legs crawled in my direction. Deliberate. Deadly.

I jabbed at the keypad. "C'mon... what kind of test is this?"

My hands trembled. I turned to Ardo and Ash. I could sense the CUE crawling toward me even with my back turned. All I could imagine were the raised forelimbs, ready to strike and surgically slice my limbs off one-by-one.

"Better figure it out, Unity girl."

The CUE hissed, and I dodged. But not in time. Its claw sliced through my thin jacket, scraping my right forearm. Thin beads of blood broke through the surface of my skin.

This is what Grandfather experienced. Death by a thousand steel cuts.

The robot hissed before rising to its tallest height. It was going for a deadly strike, with me as its upward-gazing prey.

A black box had been taped underneath its belly.

The battery Ardo mentioned.

The following seconds divided into a series of painful decisions. I launched myself limbo-style underneath the belly of the metal beast as it attacked where I had been standing. My healing spine cracked with pain. My hands snatched the battery pack free, but not before shockwaves traveled like fire from the box through my fingertips.

The CUE machine spasmed, and the simulation crumbled around me.

"What did you do?" Ardo frantically snatched the battery and rushed to the robot's side.

"Told you she wouldn't pass." Ash placed her knife between her teeth with a satisfied clink.

I sat up, wincing. "Were you trying to kill me?"

Ash spit her knife out and quickly pocketed it. "That's cute that you think one robot is dangerous. You don't know the half of it."

Ardo gathered the remaining pieces of his failed test. "There are ways. You could have hacked the keypad. It was a simple logic puzzle. But you panicked."

He looks like he might cry over his destroyed pet. Serves him right.

I glanced at my own shaking hands.

Ash and Ardo straightened like soldiers at the distinctive tapping of Mother Lotus's weaponized cane. Her burnt, melted face appeared in the doorway.

"Report," she demanded.

"Failure," Ash said with a satisfied smug. "As expected. Looks like Unity girl is only good for recycling."

If I could only smack that smug grin off Ash's face...

Mother Lotus glanced around the room, scanning the broken bits of CUE. Her eyes were dark.

If this is my end, I won't go quietly.

"I don't know how anyone can be expected to win a game they don't understand," I said. "Release me or explain what's going on. I'm done with this secrecy."

Mother Lotus smiled. "Very well. Be ready for Phase Three."

Ash sounded like she was choking on her own spit.

Perhaps I could push my luck some more.

"I need answers, not riddles."

"First, you go back to your cell. Rest and do your stretches. Become stronger." Mother Lotus offered a lopsided smile. "Be on your best behavior for dinner tonight. It's time to meet the family."

Ash shoved me back into my cell faster than the questions could come. Cold metal clamped around my wrist as she flung a bowl of mushy grains in my direction. It looked worse than the food cubes I could afford on a Fourth Function salary.

I kicked it away, my pride growling louder than my stomach.

Ash shrugged as the bowl spilled onto the stone floor. "Suit yourself."

She stormed out, and I grabbed the rock I had been using to calculate my days. I began scraping it slowly against the floor, each ear-splitting scratch sharpening the edges. The rock was now small enough to fit my hand and sharp enough for a strike. Four days of mindless scraping had paid off.

Dinner with the family might be interesting after all.

CHAPTER 19

"Own and owe are but a letter apart. Note this well, or be a pawn to some crafty plot." — Excerpt from The Sly Fellow's Playbook, *found in the Forbidden Library Archives*

"It's time." Mother Lotus released my chains and led me through the cavern tunnels to the common dining area. I scanned the surroundings, taking in the rough stone walls, a crackling firepit, and the slight fissure in the overhead ceiling that allowed a glimpse of the night sky along with a draft of fresh air.

Smoke curled from the firepit and exited through the gap above, dark tendrils escaping into the evening sky. Above the firepit, a frame of carefully placed rods held a copper pot. The herbaceous smell of soup, despite the unknown ingredients, awakened my empty stomach.

I fingered the rock in my pocket. Mother Lotus glanced at me, and I pretended to shiver.

"Glad to see a fire," I said with a smile, removing my hands from my pockets to reach over the flames.

Mother Lotus banged her cane against her metal leg. The sound echoed throughout the cave. An invitation to dinner.

"Sit." Mother stirred the soup with her cane, and I tried not to wonder if she bothered to sanitize it first.

My reflection blurred in the copper pot's surface. Flashes of the fall from the water pipes, Mother Lotus's callous slicing of my spine, and the numerous bruises from sparring with Recore raced through my brain. Whatever I looked like now, the physical changes were nothing in comparison with the change I felt inside.

Here, in the unknown, I was becoming the fracturing point in Faye's metaphorical frozen lake, just waiting for my moment to collapse the entire system.

And collapse, it will.

"Look what I found for tonight," Recore said as he entered the room, removing a heavy backpack in a fluid motion. He tossed a chunk of bread in my direction. I caught it with a single hand, and he smiled at my reflexes. "Looks like those sparring sessions are working."

I let my guard slip and smiled back at him, taking a mental note of how blue his eyes were.

Ash glanced at us both with dagger eyes. "Good thing she didn't drop the bread. I'm starving."

This place is messing with my mind. Steel yourself. Perhaps Phase Three is all about trying to make you feel connected to them. It could be a game. One pretends to be friendly, the other isolating. Typical interrogation protocol, right?

Ash and Recore were the enforcers of this group with personalities as opposite as light to shadow. Recore took the level-headed approach, and at times, was even sympathetic.

Devoted to Mother Lotus.

Recore volunteered to ladle the soup and ration the bread.

And Ash... well, her name sounds like someone spitting a mouthful of blood and teeth. If this is a game, they are playing their roles well.

I held out my bowl to accept a ladle of sloshing soup with floating bits of withered greens from Mother Lotus.

"Hope we aren't late."

A woman in her mid-twenties entered with Ardo. He seemed to hover about her, placing a guiding arm around her slender shoulders.

She must be Sky, the artist who designed the simulation graphics.

I couldn't help staring at Sky's eyes, a pair of clear glass orbs. I could see through them and into the inner nerve endings. I couldn't stop myself from being mesmerized by her ghost-like eyeballs. She clutched a faded rainbow kimono draped around her shoulders. Ardo guided Sky to her place around the open firepit.

She is blind, and yet... her artwork speaks of one who has seen much of the world.

"Lateness is impossible since time is an irreverent concept." Ardo's joke was dry, and Sky patted his shoulder with mock sympathy.

"You mean 'irrelevant.' And time is not an irrelevant concept if there isn't any dinner left," Sky chided, her voice ringing with little notes of laughter. She held onto Ardo a little longer than necessary as she settled into her spot near the fire.

Mother Lotus slopped helpings into extra bowls, ignoring Sky's politeness and Ardo's theoretical nature.

I swallowed the warm, herby broth and soaked up the rest with the bread. My stomach growled for more.

Ash laughed at my discomfort. "No food machines out here, Unity girl."

"Leave her alone," Recore said, shaking his head.

He seems genuine. I wish I could believe it.

"No one else eats here for free." Ash shoved her bowl away, letting it clatter to the ground.

I set my bowl aside. "Then let me go. I didn't ask to stay."

Ash let out another cackle. "You're lucky we even found your pathetic pile of bones."

"Oh and I suppose I'm also the lucky prisoner whose chains are off for the night." My back arched even as the muscles complained loudly against the movement. I held out my bruised wrist and winced as I clapped slowly. Sarcasm dripped like acid with every word. "Yes, thank you so much."

"Ash, remain calm. I'm sure Mother has a plan," Sky said between slurps of her soup. Her expression reflected an eerie tranquility.

"Don't tell me to stay calm." Ash's words were aimed at Sky, but she kept her gaze locked on me.

"Anyone want more soup?" Ardo said with a weak chuckle.

Recore's eyes darted between me and Ash, his brow furrowed as if trying to decide who might need restraining.

"What terrible manners," Mother Lotus said, pointing at me before placing her hands on her hips. "It's true, you eat at Mother's table for free. But not for long. You owe Mother a favor, whether or not you like it. As for the restraints, it is regrettable but necessary."

"Still don't understand why we need her." Ash spit, the wad soaking into the stone ground between us like an invitation to a duel.

"It's simple," Ardo interrupted. "She's got an Implantation chip."

Everyone stopped and stared, except Mother Lotus, who maintained her disturbing smile.

Recore nodded. "We found her before they did."

"Who are 'they'? In fact, who are you?" I clenched the sides of my pants as if I could wring an answer from their hesitant lips.

"Mother, she deserves to know." Sky's glassy eyes somehow found my face, resting there as if she could see into my mind.

Mother Lotus raised both of her robotic arms in resignation. "Fine. Chiara, you may not consider yourself fortunate, but you have been spared. Mother's children have suffered many things. The CUEs roaming outside of Unity are far more dangerous hunters. They prey on the Streamless."

I remembered Faye telling our class once that the CUEs patrolling outside the borders of Unity collected spare parts from the Streamless. Then again, Faye had also said the

Streamless were all scrambled minds, incapable of human interaction.

I don't trust them, but they aren't mindless. More lies and mysteries to unravel.

"Show her," Mother Lotus ordered.

Recore stood first and lifted his shirt. In between the rippling muscles and streaks of scar tissue, a glass cube had been inserted into the space where his heart should have been. Inside the cube, a mechanical heart thumped its own, steady beat. Gears moved, blood gushed into tubes with every pulse. He dropped the shirt back in place and then pointed to a scar above his ear where the hairline hadn't quite healed.

His heart and Implantation chip have been removed.

"We were rejected for Implantation," Recore said. "My first day alone, I was rounded up by the CUEs. They ripped the failed chip out of my head. Next, they took my heart and gave me this monstrosity." He tapped his chest, and the mechanical heart sputtered for a second before resuming its clockwork pumping.

Ash glared at Recore. "I hate when you do that."

Recore shrugged. "It's going to stop one day, Ash. The real crime is that tonight, somewhere in Unity, someone 'useful' has my heart beating inside their chest, and some inventor has data on their latest invention—the cardiovascular cube."

He clenched his fists. "At least, the procedure worked. It didn't for the others before me. Welcome to recycling at its finest."

I wanted to be an inventor.

I slowed my breathing as realization burned like a paper cut.

And with approval from my analyst, I would have ordered field tests, gathering data from innocent victims.

Sky placed a hand on Recore's shoulder. "My eyes were taken. The one source of life's color, stripped away. Now, I can only see shapes and dimensions as computer code." She lifted her dark black locks and I could see the scar from the removed Implantation chip. Her scar was raised with bubbling blisters.

Ardo unbuttoned his collar, exposing a wicked scar across his throat. "They took my voice box. Left me this replacement fart." He paused as Sky giggled. "Replacement part. It mixes my words sometimes." Ardo indicated the spot above his ear. "My chip is gone too."

Mother Lotus chimed in, "You're a rare find since you still have one."

Instinctively, all eyes shifted to Ash. She scowled and crossed her legs. "This is all very touching. But I'm going to pass on story time."

Mother Lotus gave Ash a side look but didn't press. Instead, she pointed her mechanical finger at me. "You're going to help us connect to the DataStream. Not just for Mother's children, but all children. Unity is overdue for a reckoning."

An alliance. Maybe we could work something out. But can I trust them?

I nodded slowly. "I get it. Each of you have been wronged. But you have kept me chained and you've admitted you only want to use me. If I help, what assurances do I have that you won't strip me for spare parts? How do I know our goals are aligned?"

A split second of approval filled Ash's gaze. "Unity girl is right. Besides, we don't have time to train her. We need the chip. We don't need her." Ash clutched her knife. "I say we cut it out of her right now."

"And here I was, thinking that we were finally having a moment," I said, rising to a more defensive position and drawing my sharpened rock.

Ash and Recore also shot to their feet.

"I won't work with someone who is constantly threatening to cut me open," I said.

"You failed Ardo's test," Ash said, squaring her shoulders, her muscles appearing to tense. "I'll happily carve out your spare parts myself. Maybe return those recycled parts inside of you back to the original owner's grave, if I can find it."

Mother Lotus watched, motors whirring behind her eyes as if pondering Ash's words.

Recore glanced away at the mention of my recycled lungs. They had all seen the scars. No doubt I was a monster in their eyes.

"I won't stand for any violence." Sky threw her hands in despair as Ardo pulled her closer to him.

"That's why I am around." Ash's body slammed into mine.

She gripped my throat while my fingers gripped the rock. I smashed it into the side of her face, drawing first blood. Her iron grip weakened. I tried to hit her again, but she pinned my arm with her muscular legs. Ash's knee dug into my elbow and the rock went flying across the room.

"Even blind, I can see your outlines colliding," Sky said. "Please stop this."

Recore broke us apart, using his size to make Ash release her grip. I crawled to the nearest corner, choking in my haste to taste fresh air. I could feel the tender bruising on my neck.

Mother Lotus used her cane to snag my rock. Her expression was unreadable as she held it in her hands.

"She isn't one of us!" Ash yanked free from Sky and Recore. "Can't any of you see that?"

"How can she trust us when you only attack?" Recore stood between us, his body like a tightly wound spring threatening release.

"We need her to access a CUE Waystation," Ardo sputtered. "Can't we agree to do this one job?"

"We can't even get through one dinner, let alone accomplish a high-risk mission," Sky said, her voice cracking as she shot a sympathetic gaze in my direction. "Let's all just calm down."

Metallic nails dug into the cavern wall, sparks flying off Mother's bony fingers.

I snapped to attention. So did everyone else.

"Mother has been wrong," Mother Lotus said. "We cannot win by using the forceful tactics of our enemies."

Mother Lotus hobbled around the room, touching everyone's shoulder before reaching me.

I could hear her robotic gears grinding in her head as she placed both hands on my face.

"You're free, child."

She stepped aside and motioned towards the cavern tunnels. "Follow the lighted path if you wish to leave."

I bumped into Ash on the way out, and Recore held her back. I needed to clear my head, get out of this cave, and assess my options.

Don't trust anyone.

Faye's words were, for once, strangely comforting.

Besides, I now knew there was a CUE Waystation and that my chip was somehow important to accessing the building. I ran faster.

CHAPTER 20

"According to the data gathered, the mech rats simply ran the maze's course in a frenzy, sensing the end was near. Only subject #95 discovered that it could partner up with subject #96 to defeat the maze. It was a fascinating breakthrough for these otherwise independent creatures." — *Excerpt from* The Study of Selected Mutations, *found in the Forbidden Library Archives*

The cave walls were lined with primitive torches between the occasional clusters of wax candles. I followed the lights to the exit: a doorway barricaded by a piece of plywood nailed with noise-making contraptions. I shoved aside the wedged plywood, ignoring the clanking it produced.

Outside, the night air smelled like rotten eggs.

Freedom is always better. Even if it reeks of garbage.

I cursed my haste. My backpack and supplies were somewhere in the cave with Mother Lotus. There was no way I would go back for it. I would have to figure it out.

Besides, if my video about Grandfather goes viral, Unity will change quickly. I have to raid the CUE Waystation myself, wait out the storm, and avoid caves with psychopaths who want to cut me open like some sort of lab rat.

I stumbled on something in the dark. Every bone in my jawline complained as my face smashed into the ground. Scrambling to my feet, I bumped into a wall of plastic shapes. A grumble of shifting trash responded to my fumbling actions.

A junk heap.

Outside of Unity, humanity had drowned the world in a sea of plastic garbage. The Streamless had, over time, shoveled pathways through these mounds. Even so, I had read about accidental junk avalanches burying the "helpless" ferals outside of Unity's "safe boundaries." I eyed the towering pile, taking in its massive size as it blocked much of the night sky.

Don't panic. Move efficiently. Don't die by avalanche if at all possible.

My eyes adjusted to the darkness, and my stomach churned as I slowed my pace. Above, the moon hid behind a thick fog.

I've been wrong about everything and everyone outside of Unity so far. I need to stay alert. This is a whole new world, and I don't know the rules of survival.

For a split second, I regretted leaving Mother Lotus's cave.

I just need to clear my head. I'll figure out what's going on for myself. At least at night, I can hide, scope out my surroundings.

One by one, I tried to filter out the sounds to listen for potential pursuers. The scritch-scratch of mice scurrying through the trash mounds. The chirping of nighttime crickets looking for mates. My betraying breath.

But the night was devoid of footsteps beyond my own.

A wave of relief washed over me, causing my limbs to lose their strength and my head to spin for a moment. I stopped in my steps to swallow a deep breath.

I wasn't being followed. Maybe I could trust Mother Lotus after all to keep her word. My legs burned and my sides hurt. I relaxed against the junk wall, counting the number of thudding heartbeats, desperate to slow the rhythm. My spine and other injuries were still healing. I needed to reserve energy.

Or, Mother Lotus is letting me run. Burn off my defiance and take me when I am too weak to resist. Then she'll have Ash dissect me.

I stumbled back onto my feet, driving forward. As my eyes continued to adjust to the evening shades, the outlines of objects became sharper. Drums of waste containers, rusty metal cans, a forgotten baby stroller, and plastic bottles stuffed inside torn trash bags formed impassable mountains above my head.

Climbing would be foolish, but the view might be worth it. The path ended in a split.

"Two roads diverged... and I—I took the one less traveled by," I whispered the lines from Robert Frost's poem. Strange how the forbidden literature from the Library still sprung to my lips, providing strength. "And that has made all the difference."

The right side was wider. However, the narrower left side veered into a taller pile of garbage.

Which means it is more likely to collapse. Not sure Frost is right. Perhaps the more traveled road will lead to civilization. If this place has any such thing.

I hesitated. Each step felt heavy, weighted with fate.

"You know, either way leads to the main burrow."

I shrieked—and whipped around at the unexpected sound.

"Whoa, I didn't mean to startle you. Easy now."

Recore noiselessly emerged from the shadows behind me.

My shoulders arched and my fists tightened. Not that it mattered. Recore could absorb any punch I could throw at him.

"Here to take me back?" I couldn't hide my suspicion.

"No."

If he was trying to appear earnest, it worked.

"So you're my guide now? Or just here to cut out my Implantation chip and hide the body?"

Recore exhaled with a grimace. "You have a low opinion of my family. Fair enough." He pulled out his side knife and held it up before tossing it behind him. "Look, I'm unarmed. So are you. Let's call this a truce, okay?"

My shoulders relaxed. "Deal."

"I followed you because I don't agree with Mother. Letting you go with no idea of what's out here isn't fair. I'm here to even the odds so you'll survive the night."

"How gallant."

And yet, I'm glad he is here.

Recore opened his backpack and tossed me a jacket. "Chivalry isn't dead yet."

I grabbed it, wrinkling my nose and gagging at the pungent odor. It was large but warm. "Should I ask who died in this thing?"

"A good friend, actually."

My gaze shifted downwards. "I'm sorry. I didn't know."

Recore snickered. "Lighten up, Chiara. It's a joke. Poor taste probably, but I haven't been civilized for a while now."

My anxiety melted away even as the jacket's stench overpowered my senses. "Message received. I'll try to stop treating you like the enemy."

"Good. I'm going to be honest with you. That wasn't my only knife." He pulled out a blade tucked into the bottom of his boot. He offered the knife to me, palms open. "New truce. We both carry something to defend ourselves with."

My fingertips brushed against his hand as I took the knife. Recore glanced away, retreating toward where he had tossed the other weapon.

I fiddled with the knife before pocketing it inside my smelly new jacket and putting the jacket on.

I could end him right now. And yet...

Recore returned with his knife.

"We can take either way," he repeated, pointing at the split. "These paths are called burrows. Mother's territory ends the second we turn here. Let me lead. Stay alert."

Recore turned left.

Robert Frost would approve.

My new guide seemed to glide without a sound ahead of me. I, on the other hand, found every stray piece of crunching trash as the path narrowed, forcing me to walk sideways to muffle my tracks. I could feel the piles press into my back as I shuffled along.

"We call these types of burrows 'dead zones.' While you're safe from the traders and their bandit crews, you risk being scratched by an old razor blade or shards of garbage. So don't walk too close to the sides."

Whoever dug these burrows had a death wish. And judging by the smell... they got it.

"So your family... are they bandits?"

"Thought we were moving past hostility."

"I'm trying."

"We aren't bandits. I prefer the term Resistance Fighters. The Streamless have become rats waiting to be plucked by inventors in the name of science. So I joined Mother Lotus."

"Once upon a time, I wanted to be an inventor. I see the cost now."

Recore glanced at me. "Once upon a time? Strange phrase."

I bit both sides of my cheeks. My reading had started to bleed into my conversation.

That could be dangerous. Even deadly.

If I ever reconnected to the DataStream, I didn't need a group of so-called Resistance Fighters knowing I had downloaded contraband books. I could only imagine Mother Lotus's solution.

She might rip apart my skull to examine the tech inside.

I shivered.

Recore's hand flew into the air in the universal signal to halt.

I calmed my breaths and filtered out the sounds again, layer by layer. A soft whirring emanated from the other side of the mountainous slopes of junk.

Something was nearby.

Recore grabbed a rusty tin can from the ground and gave it a toss. It rattled ahead of us.

Clink, clank, *zap.*

The can exploded into vaporized fumes.

Whatever lurked a few steps away had advanced weapons. And we had knives.

Recore put a finger to his lips and motioned a retreat. Every silent inch I moved felt like a mile.

Something darted across my leg with tiny, penetrating claws. Something wet, slimy, and hissing. It looked like a rat, but I couldn't be sure.

I stumbled, and it darted with a squeal toward Recore.

My noisy encounter with the rat gave away our position. Recore's face noticeably paled, even in the darkness.

A mechanical creaking rose above our mound and a search beam surrounded Recore. I froze with uncertainty, just outside the search light's focus. The machine whirred as it hovered over the trash mound, its large metallic arms arched for striking.

It's a CUE. Only, this one is larger—the size of a personal shuttle—than most.

"You have been caught outside of curfew. Remain still for routine inspection."

Recore fell to his knees, dropping his knife. The CUE's green search beams scanned him.

"It's your lucky day," the robot said, followed by a short *ta-da* chime. "You've been selected to serve Unity once again. Extend your left arm."

Recore looked away from the blinding beam and directly toward me. He shook his head even as tears revealed the crack in his stoic demeanor.

He wants me to stay put.

I couldn't move anyway, every limb paralyzed with fear.

Recore extended his arm and closed his eyes. The CUE's laser eyes converged into a beam of sizzling light. The compacted ground soon pooled with Recore's blood before a hand plopped into the middle of it.

Recore fell to his knees, his one good hand clutching a charred stump.

The CUE lifted Recore's severed hand by the thumb.

"Return to whatever shelter you can find. Here is a favor token for your contribution. Unity thanks you."

The CUE spit out a golden coin, which landed next to Recore's knees. The robot then whizzed away, its searchlight flicking off.

I rushed over to Recore. He blinked several times, then his eyes rolled back into their sockets. He shook, foam gathering at the corners of his lips.

"Stay with me," I begged, cradling his head as he began to seize. "Don't you dare die!"

As if Recore had heard, his tremors ceased and his eyelids closed. I wiped away the foam with my jacket, my head against his electronic heart. A strange, steady drum sounded from his chest.

He is still breathing. For now.

I glanced at the mounds of trash beside me.

C'mon, think your way through this. If you can write code, you can invent a solution.

I remembered the bits and pieces I had seen along the way.

The stroller.

I snapped to my feet and retraced my steps. The frame was bent, but the wheels were passable. If I could lift Recore, I would have a chance. With both arms around his waist, I haphazardly pulled him into the carrier.

The coin glinted in the light, as if begging to be picked up. I snatched it, shoving it deep into my pockets.

I pushed Recore through the burrows, retracing the steps from memory. The stroller jerked, and I braced him from sliding off.

"Seriously?" I hissed, staring at the front wheel.

It had broken off under the pressure. Three wheels left.

Sweat dripped from my forehead, stinging my eyes as I struggled to gain ground.

The cavern's silhouette loomed in the distance.

Leave him here and keep going. What will they do to you now?

"Help! Someone!"

A light emerged from the throat of the cave.

Run. Go now. You did what you could.

My hands clenched around the stroller's rusted handle. I glanced at Recore's pale, sweat-drenched face and made my choice.

CHAPTER 21

"Most artificial intelligence predating Auto needed decision input from human creators to fill out a personality matrix. Auto was the only one that could resist all bias and was able to form fair decisions based on the single goal of advancing humanity. Truthfully, we could no longer rely on ourselves to recreate a new society after the continued cycles of violent history." — Excerpt from Ashes and Origins, *found in the Forbidden Library Archives*

C*amera 1 activated. Subject (Silas) is at work. Coworker (Cheryl) approaches the subject's workspace.*

"A whole new set of inventions. Guess you'll have to stay late and work out the feasibility reports. Some of these proposed inventions are pretty wild, don't you think?"

"Leave the reports. Thanks, Cheryl."

With a flick of her wrist, Coworker tosses the virtual files into the air before Subject's outstretched palm absorbs them.

"You know, I'm free tonight. How about some casino chips on me? You could use a break."

Camera zooms closer. Coworker sits on the Subject's desk, stretching slowly across the surface. Heartbeat and pulse spike in both humans.

"You should go." Subject backs away as Coworker places a hand on his chest.

"It's lonely in the Second Function," Coworker says, grabbing a lock of Subject's braided hair and twisting it around her finger. Subject yanks his hair away.

"This is against the rules, and you're not my type."

Coworker laughs. "I could change your mind." She turns to her side and plucks up a photo file from Subject's desk. "I bet she was your type. She has lovely cheekbones."

Coworker sits up and her eyes fill with recognition. "Wait, is that the girl on the news? The one who murdered her own grandfather and then sabotaged the footage?"

"Go home," Subject says, jerking to his feet.

"I could wear her face."

"She's a traitor." Subject deletes the photo from its digital frame.

"What a shame," Coworker says. "Did you know her well? Before she was a murderer?"

"I don't think I ever really knew her." Subject avoids eye contact with Coworker, and he flees the office.

Hallway Camera activated. Subject appears to be going home. Current threat level: Harmless. Authorizing the release of credits to Coworker's account.

ROUGHLY SIX FEET away from the cavern entrance, I watched as the lights flickered, then went out. The darkness propelled me forward.

"Seriously?" I hissed. "Is someone there? Could use some help here!"

The hairs on the back of my scalp tingled as a sharp blade scraped the surface of my throat. Ash's large hands muffled my scream. Her body pressed against my back.

"Shhh..." Ash's warm breath tickled my ear.

More figures rose from the shadows. They gravitated towards Recore with a hushed collection of worried gasps.

"Get Recore inside. Quickly, my children!" Mother Lotus's shuffled walk could not be mistaken.

Ash lowered the knife away from my throat. Her grip relaxed as she watched the others lift Recore out of the stroller.

She's distracted.

I slammed the heel of my boot into Ash's toes and broke free from her hold. I stumbled headfirst a few feet away before rolling onto my back.

Ash was on top of me but, this time, I had my knife against her throat.

"Drop it. Both of you!" Mother Lotus's command fell on deaf ears. Ash and I remained locked in a deadly impasse.

Zap.

Mother's cane emitted an electrical shock. Ash trembled and rolled off me. Her eyes closed, and her knife clattered to the hard ground.

"Drag her inside," Mother Lotus said as I regained my footing.

I hesitated, glancing out towards the burrows before grabbing Ash's feet. I made sure she hit a few extra bumps as I pulled her limp body towards the cave. She was easier to drag once Sky stepped in to help.

Ardo and Mother Lotus got Recore into the training room. Mother examined him while Ardo resealed the cave's plywood doorway.

I released Ash's feet nearby, while Sky cradled Ash's head before letting it rest on the stone floor.

I would have let her drop.

"Is he okay?" I asked, turning my attention back to Recore.

Ardo stuffed something inside his backpack as he entered the room. It wriggled again.

He must have fixed that reality-altering CUE!

I charged at Ardo, throwing him against the wall. His face turned white under my withering gaze. "Is this all some virtual reality test? Did Recore actually lose a hand or was this all another sick, twisted simulation?"

I reached in and yanked out the miniature CUE machine and holo reality core from Ardo's backpack. He snatched both of the items back from me in a fierce tug-of-war.

"It's not a brick—I mean, trick!" Ardo said after gaining control of both items. "What happened out there was real."

Mother Lotus didn't bother to look at me. "We've done many things. But Mother has never lied. Let Ardo go. You're free to stay or leave this cave. If you stay, Mother's rules are to be followed."

I slowly released Ardo, and Sky breathed a sigh of relief.

Recore's eyes fluttered open as Mother Lotus fished out an old bottle from her pocket and removed the cap, releasing a foul odor into the air.

I gagged. Ash mumbled something but remained unconscious. I backed up and Ardo scurried away, the terror in his eyes labeling me a total jerk.

Sky's white orbs scanned the room until they found me. "Chiara, I know you have doubts, but we would never harm our own. Especially Recore... he continues to suffer the most."

And it's my fault.

No one had to say it.

"How bad is it?"

I jumped at Recore's voice, and so did everyone else. Well, everyone except Mother Lotus.

"They took your left hand," Sky said.

Recore grimaced and watched Mother Lotus examine the stump. She then wrapped it with strips of cloth that Ardo brought over.

"No signs of infection," Mother Lotus said. "Even Mother couldn't have done a better job."

"No replacement this time," Ardo said with a sigh.

"What do you mean by 'replacement'?" I interrupted.

"Sometimes the CUE will offer alternative parts for the ones they take," Ardo responded. "But lately, we are being processed without getting anything back."

Sky grabbed Mother Lotus's free hand. "We have to break into the CUE Waystation now! They have spare parts and even nanobots to help with Recore's recovery."

Ardo nodded in agreement. "The longer we wait, the less likely it is that the tech arm will bond to damaged nerves. Besides, I don't have advanced coding skills for a bio-tech scenario."

"I can do it."

All eyes turned to me.

Ash snorted, as if even her unconscious self was compelled to laugh at me.

"I need those parts. How do we get them?"

Recore pushed himself into a half-sitting position. "Hold up," he said. "We only have one chance before they upgrade security measures, and the timing has to be perfect. There are priorities more important than a spare hand."

Ardo's face wrinkled with concern. "Sky is fright, I mean, right. The longer we wait, any chance you have of bio-tech bonding becomes slimmer. We can do both. The mission and take care of you, Recore."

Mother Lotus's gears whirred as she seemed to mull over the options. "Gear up. We strike the Waystation at first light."

Recore hung his head, and he cursed under his breath.

Sky stood and felt her way along the cavern wall, fingering each crevice until she reached what she seemed to have been looking for. She pressed something, and the wall moved with a grating squeak against the ground.

Behind the fake stone wall was a stash of backpacks. Sky tossed one in my direction.

Ash mumbled again. Mother sighed and grabbed the remainder of the foul-smelling bottle and waved it underneath Ash's nose. She sputtered awake.

I opened the backpack and made a mental note of the inventory. One leather suit made of stitched scraps that had been dyed black. A worn belt with hand-stitched weapon holsters. Two smoke grenades and an electric stun gun.

I slipped the suit over my own clothes. The pant legs were long, so I cuffed them. It wouldn't protect against much, maybe a few knife slashes, but wearing it still gave me a jolt of renewed energy. I tightened the belt around my hips and slid the other items into place.

An awakened Ash rubbed her eyes and gaped at me.

"This better be a nightmare because there is no way Unity girl is getting weapons on my watch."

Sky poked Ash's ribs. "Someone is awake. And grumpy."

"We need her." Mother Lotus's voice carried an edge. "And then she is free to leave."

I offered a hand to Ash. She looked around for another way up, but Sky shook her head and Mother's glare sent an obvious message.

Make up. Play nice.

Ash gripped my hand and leapt to her feet.

"This is for Recore. You better stay away from me," I whispered before putting on a show of a friendly slap to Ash's arm.

"On that, we agree." Ash returned the arm slap, but much harder.

"It's good to see us all..." Sky started.

"Don't you dare finish the sentence," Ash said, grabbing a gear bag. She stormed out of the room.

"First light," Mother repeated, gazing at Recore's arm with calculated concern.

I counted the go bags, and a thought struck me. It escaped my lips faster than I could consider the wisdom of questioning the Streamless.

"If this last gear bag was Recore's and I am taking his place, then it's logical to assume you were never going," I said, directing my comment to Mother Lotus. "What's your part in all this?"

Recore and Mother exchanged glances.

I wish I had the time to dissect the relationship dynamics of a robot with a human "son." Never had those attachments with Irritant, and he had been programmed to bond with me.

"Mother will be waiting for you to send a signal from the Waystation," she said. "But first, you must get Mother's children inside. Your chip will cause initial confusion to the station's security protocol."

"They won't shoot immediately if Ardo's CUE machine accompanies you," Recore cut in. "The confusion should buy us additional time to hack into the system. Ardo will guide you through it. Ardo's CUE machine has old access codes that might delay an alarm. Meanwhile, your chip can hack the current codes and get us inside."

"Once inside, you and Ash will get into the mainframe computers and install backdoor access to the DataStream," Mother Lotus said. "Mother will be waiting for that signal."

Mother Lotus peeled a piece of skin from her forehead. Beneath the skin, exposed wires and antennas criss-crossed like a nest of nerves underneath. Her right eye twitched.

"Once you've updated yourself, you'll be one step closer to producing your own DataStream," I said to Mother Lotus. "That's a lot of power to wield."

A DataStream free of Auto. Maybe we can work together.

"You're a perceptive child," Mother Lotus said.

"As long as you are in and out within three and half minutes, the CUE Waystation won't send an incident report on the break-in," Recore said, his eyes wavering between me and his stubbed arm.

"What will you do with the DataStream access?" I asked. "You still won't be able to control it without infiltrating Auto's head-quarters. There must be more to this plan."

Mother Lotus nodded. "All will be revealed in time."

"Fine. Be cryptic. But explain why a program would even care about the Streamless?" I asked. "Last I checked, it's mainly people that are forgotten out here. What stake do you have in this fight?"

Mother Lotus held up a hand. "You seem surprised a robot can feel? How old are you, child?"

My chin jotted out defiantly. "Sixteen. Almost seventeen. Why?"

"Mother is the last of the old robots not infected with Auto's code. They tossed me out with the waste a hundred years ago. Mother is patient. These children gathered under my wings are signs."

A *hundred-year-old robot? Not infected with Auto's code? What does it all mean?*

"We must restrain Auto at all costs." Mother Lotus leaned forward, her fake skin still gaping open and hanging over one eye. "Auto wants to make mankind better. Mother wants to better mankind."

"What was the plan before I came along?" I asked.

"Honestly, try the old codes. Blow up the door. Run like smell," Ardo replied.

"That usually works for us," Recore added with a weak smile.

Ardo laughed. "Only if the stench is coming from you, Recore."

Mother Lotus cleared her throat and the momentary light-heartedness faded. "Return to your quarters. Rest for a little while. And be ready at first light."

Ardo and Sky grabbed their packs and left the room. Mother glanced my way, expecting me to follow.

"I'm not going back there," I said. "I've had enough of chains and that little space to last me a lifetime."

Mother Lotus shrugged. "Sleep where you like. But sleep. Gather strength." She hobbled away, her shadow falling between us.

"This is your space?" I asked Recore.

"Normally. Stay here if you want." Recore motioned toward the area next to him.

"You don't hate me then?" I asked, settling next to Recore on the hard ground.

Recore eyed his burnt, tightly bandaged stump. "If not tonight, then it would have happened tomorrow. This is life out here. I'm becoming more metal than man, anyway."

The words hit me like a gut punch. "I will get you a replacement part. I owe you that."

Recore looked at me, eyes dark. "No one owes me anything. Frankly, I don't like this mission," he said. "Especially since I can't go."

He paused. "Promise me that you won't do something foolish," he demanded.

"Fine." I relaxed against the wall with my backpack as a temporary cushion.

The coin dug into my side, an unfriendly reminder.

"The CUE did give you something," I said, fishing out the coin. "Is this important? Could it help?"

Recore laughed at the sight. "That token is worth trading favors at the marketplace. We would have reached it if the CUE hadn't caught us in those burrows. Ironic."

He took the coin with his remaining hand and let it run across his fingers. "I wonder sometimes, what is the price of a soul? If we don't stop Auto, I guess that question won't even matter."

No, it won't.

I rested my chin on my knees, caught somewhere between exhaustion and sheer terror at the thought of the next day.

CHAPTER 22

"In strategy, bait can never know that it is in fact, bait. Small tactical forces have been known to topple empires, but they must feel empowered. Meanwhile, the chessboard pieces continue to move in case their mission fails." — Excerpt from The Shadow's Game, *found in the Forbidden Library Archives*

The early morning light made navigating the narrow paths in between the swaths of garbage much easier. The rotten-egg odor, however, seemed to be worse after the night's refrigerated hold retreated. I followed the path scribbled on a dinner napkin with one of Sky's invented ink pens. The trail to the Waystation was intricately drawn.

Ardo's small CUE machine followed me like a lost puppy. For a second, I thought I heard Kaynine's loyal pitter-patter. The ache inside me grew.

"You know I hate you, right?" I said, glancing back at Ardo's pet CUE.

The machine beeped in reply as its spidery legs scrambled to keep up with me. The battery pack attached to its underbelly seemed to slow it down.

"Fine. But I am calling you 'Cupid' because you have a face only a mother could love and it rhymes with stupid."

The radio transmitter on my belt turned on. "Static report?" Ardo asked.

I rolled my eyes at the phrase. "I've literally walked five more steps since the last time. But yes, Cupid and I are approaching the Waystation."

There was a pause. "Cupid? You're maiming my machine now?"

"Yes, I'm 'naming' your horrible little contraption. But maiming is next if you don't stop asking for status reports."

The radio transmitter went silent.

Good.

I stuck the transmitter back into my pocket. I always had a spot in my heart for repurposing old technology, but this was on the verge of archaic. The sounds were harsh and filled with static. And Ardo's sun-powered batteries added unnecessary weight to the device.

The burrow widened and the incline increased. The mounds of trash loomed higher in this area, dangerously so. Ahead of me, the burrow emptied into a clear patch of ground surrounding the single Waystation.

Just like the simulation.

"The Waystation goes underground," Recore had told me before we left the cave, his face pale and breath stinking of Mother Lotus's pain-relieving medicine. "One way in, and one way out."

I stepped forward, and the Waystation powered up the second I came near. Lights flooded the area. Cupid and I stood there, waiting.

An electric eye emerged from the door's central slot. A scanning noise rang out.

"User with an Implantation chip, state your purpose."

"I'm here to inspect and make repairs to this Waystation."

"Your clearance will have to be checked. First, I need to scan your face."

Cupid hummed and whirred. It came closer to the door's eye. In one swift motion, one of Cupid's sharp arms strategically stabbed the eye. Sparks flew, and the electrical eye sputtered.

"I'm sorry, my visual output is in error. Please enter your code manually."

A panel to the right of the door opened up, revealing a keypad.

I hurried over to the keypad. Ardo said that too many attempts to access the system would cause the station security to destroy sensitive data and signal all CUE robots in the area to attack.

Ardo's voice grated through the transmitter. "Ready?"

"Give me the codes."

Ardo rattled off a long alphanumeric sequence. He spoke slowly, as if afraid of mispronunciation.

"Code is no longer active," the damaged electric eye repeated. "One attempt remaining."

The lights of the Waystation began to flash in a warning sequence.

It's rebooting for war. And it will happen fast.

"Did it twerk?" Ardo squawked through the transmitter. "I mean, work? Did it work? Status report!"

New plan. We do this my way.

My heart pounded as I entered a coded message into the keypad. It was a long shot. But maybe I could hack the system and enter a new password during the reboot stage. My fingers flew over the touchpad, speaking digitally to the mainframe computer inside. A warm buzz teased my senses as my Implantation chip tingled with a familiar sensation. The DataStream flowed inside the boundaries of the CUE Waystation.

Grandfather had called it "mouse jacking" to trick a nearby computer into receiving signals that were farther away. I never knew why he wanted me to understand archaic hacking functions. Back then, I thought I would only create systems, not break into them.

He knew what I needed.

I can use the keypad to trick the mainframe computer inside into accepting simple commands.

"Chiara, if the codes don't work, get out," Sky's voice cackled. "Ash will bring the grenades."

I grabbed the radio. "Sky, don't do that. We can't risk damaging these systems. Trust me."

"Hey, Unity girl, we've been planning this for a while," came Ash's annoying voice. "Now step aside. I'm about to make an explosive entrance."

"No. Stay there. I've got this."

The keypad lit up in response to my commands to redirect its signal to the mainframe inside. My heartbeat was erratic, hungry.

I've missed this.

Override Command: Reset password.

I charmed the keypad into obedience with my siren keystrokes.

Ash bolted from behind the garbage heaps. She started running toward the door, grenades in hand. The Waystation turned back on, sirens blaring, and the flood of lights shone on Ash's terrifying battle face.

I re-entered the new code and stepped back, holding my breath, waiting to see what would happen next.

The sirens turned off.

Ash bolted the last few feet, still carrying a grenade. But the door swung open just as Ash reached it. She tried to stop mid-run but, instead, tripped and face planted into the ground.

The grenade flew in the air, trajectory poised to land in between us.

Ash's mouth grew wide and our eyes locked. She was white with terror.

We're going to die.

Pffft.

A wisp of smoke wafted from the grenade as it landed on the ground with a dull, harmless thud.

I wasn't sure if I should laugh, cry, or pee my pants. My legs buckled before regaining strength. I grabbed Ash's hand and tried to pull her up. She pushed me away, but it was too late.

I had felt her tremble too.

"It's a dud," Ash said, scrambling back up to her feet and dusting herself off. "Ardo found a stash of them, but you never know what works out here. Not much does."

I let out a sigh of relief. "Lucky for us both."

"Yeah. Guess so."

"Does this mean you will trust me a little?"

Ash rolled her eyes and clapped with feigned enthusiasm. "Need praise for doing your job?"

"Praise, yes. Grenades, no," I said.

Ash doubled over, laughing.

Maybe humor is hidden somewhere in Ash's peeved-warrior persona after all.

"Hey, save the bonding for later and get inside." Ardo's voice faded with a static-filled click.

I held the button to reply. "I'm assuming you can see us now?"

"Yes, Mother Lotus, Sky, and I are in position at the top of this trash heap."

Ash grabbed her own radio. "Ardo, keep your eyes on the horizon while Sky monitors Mother. I don't want any surprises headed our way."

Sky's voice emanated calm. "Don't worry. Mother is in receiving mode and doing well. Focus on getting that signal out and finding spare parts for Recore."

I looked Ash in the eye. "Are we going to get along once we step inside?"

Ash shrugged. "Let's find out, shall we?"

Cupid resumed its position, guarding the door and scanning the periphery.

The door opened into a stairway that descended into the shadows. Ash took the lead, feeling her way through the dark.

I can appreciate someone who is both bark and bite.

My arms reached out to the metal walls of the stairwell to brace myself as I followed Ash down. I was armed this time. If Ash tried anything, I would make her pay for it. My eyes adjusted to the dark. My Implantation chip hummed with possible connectivity.

"What is it like? To have a chip?" Ash asked, reaching the bottom of the stairs, her eyes focused and her laser gun at the ready.

We've progressed to non-threatening conversation? Ash is more sociable in the middle of danger. Who would've guessed it?

"You know how the BAT would give you a headache? The chip is gentle, like little hairs rising on your arm."

"Don't miss it," Ash said.

We approached a set of laboratory doors. Ash's face hardened into a seasoned lookout while I approached the keypad on the wall and entered my new code. The doors clicked open. Ash peeked inside first, then motioned to proceed.

I stepped inside the room, my nose wrinkling from the smell of stagnant air mingled with dust. We passed an old administration desk and an indignant rat squeaked at our intrusion before scurrying into the shadows.

Ash motioned at the stairway leading to the level below. It looked like the descent into an open grave. "Whatever we need will be down there in the lab," Ash whispered. "Ready?"

All of a sudden, the fire alarms blared and steam billowed in from the vents.

"What did you do?" Ash hissed.

"It's not me!"

"Figure it out!"

I guess that's the end of our beautiful friendship.

We both fished out gas masks from our backpacks and put them on. Ardo had insisted on the last-minute addition.

Good thing he did.

The building's defenses stirred. The whir of CUE machines grew louder. Ash shoved a desk up against the lab door.

I ran to the computer and used the code Ardo had made me memorize.

Time to create a backdoor access portal.

I let myself connect with DataStream, watching it build in my hands like a silver ball of flickering code.

Something isn't right.

The feeling intensified as the connection grew stronger. I closed my eyes to strengthen my focus.

Digital portals surrounded me, tons of screens with nonstop news and advertisements. A digital highway of lightning-quick data packets and security programs sped by.

Then everything froze. The faces on each screen focused on me with a strange, salivating smile.

I've been flagged. Auto knows I'm here. That's why the Waystation alarms are going off. I have to get to SuBunk, now!

"Welcome, Chiara!" said every face on every screen.

My mind began the sequence to unlock SuBunk's sanctuary.

"You have not been a model citizen, have you?" the voices said.

The images on the screens shifted. This time, it was the secret video footage I had released. But it was different. The footage showed me stabbing Grandfather's chest, pulling out his heart, and holding it in my hands as blood dripped down my arms.

SuBunk appeared, and I jumped into the program.

Auto's voice trailed after me. "Virtual realm. Physical realm. I'll find you wherever you go. A reckoning is coming, Chiara."

I slammed the door to SuBunk closed and jumped into the captain's chair.

"Take me to the Library," I ordered. It was the only place left to hide.

Somewhere in the vast distance, Ash shot out the glass of the lab doors and aimed her weapon at the awakened CUE machines.

But here in the DataStream, the real world had melted away as Subunk carried me to the Forbidden Library.

Seconds later, I was inside the Library, and Elara's holographic form quivered as she pulled me in close. Then she pushed me away with an angry scowl. "Why are you back? Are you in danger? Did your plan work?"

I pulled out Ardo's code strands. But here, in the virtual world, the code I had memorized appeared as shivering strands of DNA. It pulsated in the palm of my hand, dancing in a slow swirl.

Elara gingerly touched the fragment with a furrowed brow. At her caress, the code recoiled with an energy that rocked the Library. Books thudded onto the floor in heaps as the ground quaked.

Elara pulled her hand away, and the quaking stopped.

"This code is purposed for destruction," Elara said, taking a step back. "It will tear open a portal for an outside source, diverting the DataStream. Do you trust the one who gave you this?"

I hesitated. "I don't have a choice."

Elara nodded. "You have found outside help. Good."

Elara pulled up a screen, and I could see the doctored version of the video I had released. The video now showed me standing there with the knife above my grandfather's chest. She froze the image and zoomed into the headline: "Murder in a Modern Era? Anomaly Kills Aging Grandfather and Fails Rehabilitation Efforts."

"Auto has released the official video of that night," Elara said. "You, of course, play the starring role. The current story is that your guilt drove you over the edge. There is a substantial bounty on your head for your capture."

"That's not what was in Val's original files! Surely no one believes that doctored version!"

Elara shrugged. "It's already yesterday's news. Your story is a blip on the radar of a tired, working world waiting for credits to spend. Auto remains an impartial program, incapable of human lies or errors. The truth threatens a comfortable system."

Somewhere, in the distance, I could hear lasers firing from Ash's gun. Elara could sense it too. "Our time is short," she stated as if remarking on the weather or some other obvious fact.

"Are you saying it's hopeless?"

Elara shook her head. "I'm giving you the facts. And a fighting chance. You won't get this code released into the DataStream without being flagged."

"I have SuBunk."

"It won't be enough this time."

"Elara, what are you saying?"

Elara placed a lingering hand on my shoulder. A warm vibration trailed vertically through my spine. "Accept this data transfer of the Library's books. Keep it safe in SuBunk for now. Your grandfather wanted knowledge to be returned to the people."

She snatched the DNA fragment from my hand as the Library shuddered again.

"I don't understand," I said.

"Run back to SuBunk, distract Auto. Let me upload this code."

Shelves toppled. I ducked as a book went flying past my head.

"Goodbye, Chi."

That name, free of stigma, landed like a punch to my gut. I suddenly flew backwards at Elara's command, landing without grace on my butt right in front of the Library's open doors.

The Library crumbled around Elara like a vortex. She smiled as the doors slammed in my face.

No, no, no.

I pounded on the barrier between us one more time. "Please. Don't do this."

I couldn't save my mother either.

The problem with designing a program like my mother was that she would always run headfirst toward the storm.

I forced myself into SuBunk. I slid into the captain's chair as the Library imploded outside SuBunk's range. Chunks of brick, glass shards, shelves, books, and furniture shot out in all directions into the DataStream like projectile vomit. Pieces of the debris bombarded SuBunk's shell.

I pressed forward on the controls to escape. My captain's console lit up with an encrypted message: "New content has been downloaded. Search for files from here. Live a thousand lives in the books you read and don't regret the paths you take."

Questions fired through my brain faster than the detritus that SuBunk navigated through.

Why didn't Elara listen to me? What will happen to her now?

Tears burned trails down my cheeks. I narrowly avoided a broken bookshelf—or, rather, lines of solid code designed to appear like a bookshelf.

How long will it take Elara to release Ardo's code? And if the Library exists in a private corner of my mind, is this permanent brain damage now? Elara can explain this later.

Something akin to a whisper tugged at my mind... Elara wouldn't be explaining anything to me anymore.

SuBunk flew away from the data space that crumbled behind us. A headache swelled in the real world, piercing through to the virtual.

Definitely damaged brain tissue.

I massaged my temples.

The console lit up one more time. "Distract Auto. I will release the code in thirty seconds. Then disconnect and deal with the headache."

I slammed the controls in a rage, as if Elara could hear me. "No! Don't sacrifice yourself! There are other ways!"

The console beeped again. "Always with you."

A timer began to count down from thirty seconds as SuBunk floated back into the DataStream. I turned off SuBunk's masking protocols and waited like bait. Within a razor-sharp second, all the streaming packets of information slowed to a creep, then froze, as if sensing my presence. Auto's security programs stopped midstream, turning back to my position like magnets.

"Chiara... You're back. Ready to finish our conversation?"

Auto's echoing voice rippled across the vast clutter of the DataStream.

Twenty seconds.

The neon highway froze once more. Auto's disembodied voice rippled towards me from every side.

"What sort of tiny program are you hiding in? Fascinating. I knew you were clever. I made a mistake in underestimating you. My first one. How strange that sounds."

Fifteen seconds.

"It's only a matter of time before your location is overrun. But I am curious... what did you hope to accomplish?"

Ten seconds.

I positioned my hands over SuBunk's masking protocols, ready to vanish the instant the timer finished.

"I'm rather bored of this little game already. You forget, I'm not programmed to be wasteful."

Five seconds.

SuBunk's walls caved in, crushing my ribs. My surroundings alternated between darkness and piercing lines of code.

Auto is compressing SuBunk's programming. And turning off the areas in my brain that control my breathing.

My arms became pinned against my side, and I couldn't reach the console. My tongue caught in my throat, and I convulsed as my fingers struggled to press the masking button. I managed to press something before blacking out.

Terror tasted like cold metal against my teeth.

And it feels like a slap.

My jaw ached in between gasps for air. Only the slaps didn't stop. They just came faster.

CHAPTER 23

"I would rather have you as an enemy. For then, I would know how you truly feel about me." —Excerpt from Twisted Towers, *found in the Forbidden Library Archives*

S lap.

Nothing could create the same singular, smacking sound quite like bone-striking-bone with a thin layer of skin in between.

My eyes flew open, and I choked on my saliva. Thick mucus strands dangled in my throat before churning into froth between my lips.

Ash's backhand halted mid-air. "Terrible time for a nap!" She turned and released a controlled burst of fire from her stun gun. "Did you release the code?"

For the first time, I realized I was flat on the ground. I sat up, regretting the movement as return fire pinged over our heads and computer screens shattered across the laboratory.

The CUE machines whirred closer to our position.

Ash emptied her clip.

"Is Chiara back?" Ardo's static-filled voice accosted my ear.

Ash reloaded her gun. "She is. Make it fast."

I rolled over and spit out the thickening saliva. Whatever Auto had done to SuBunk had been happening to me on a physical level. Air had never tasted so good, even if it reeked of fried electronics and burning plastic. I turned on my transmitter. "Here."

"Chiara, harvest any tech you can find. Silicone skin, spare metal, and wiring from the CUE machines. Free of holes, preferably. Should be achievable as long as Ash keeps her weapon on stun."

"Got it."

Another shot rang out, shattering the mainframe computer nearest to me. "That one wasn't on stun, in case you were wondering!" Ash said. She gripped my shoulder and motioned for me to follow. "Get ready!"

Ash unleashed a throaty battle cry as she pulled out a second stun gun and let both weapons blast in synchrony.

My legs wobbled as they carried me forward. It wasn't like the simulations or fully immersible movies. Nothing like the smooth, confident strides of a well-practiced action hero.

I look like a glob of jelly crawling to the finish line.

The CUE machines fell one-by-one, a pile of short-circuiting tech. I knelt and started looting spare parts, stuffing what I could into my backpack.

"Did you get everything?" Ash moved like a warrior around the room, acting alert to every potential angle of attack.

"Almost. I don't see any synthetic skin though."

"Do you have enough for a basic framework?"

I nodded.

"Then it's good enough."

I had to agree with Ash. Everything was alive now. Screens flashed and loud sirens blared from every corner. The building was a death trap if we lingered much longer.

We emerged from the Waystation, and I tossed one of my grenades behind us. The building crumbled with the ensuing explosion.

Ash and I exchanged the same look of relief.

That one worked.

The faint whir of more CUE machines snapped us back from our thoughts. It sounded like a buzzing beehive streaming from Unity.

Auto is sending an army.

"Go!" Static shrieked through my radio transmitter.

Ash and I broke into a full sprint. The burrows shuddered, and the junk groaned with the ringing vibrations of the incoming CUE army.

I slipped, falling against the walls of piled garbage. Something sharp and metallic sliced across my upper thigh. I stumbled, stifling a scream.

Ash grabbed my arm, pulling me back onto my feet without mercy.

Ardo waited by the cavern entrance.

"They're going to find us," I blurted through the pain.

A gleam appeared in Ardo's eyes. He looked at Cupid and nodded. The machine whirred away from the cavern entrance, playing old tunes I remembered from my childhood.

"Here we go round the mulberry bush... POP! Goes the weasel!"

Cupid climbed the impossible junk hills, demanding attention.

For a second, I was sorry for Cupid.

"Inside," Ardo ordered.

We all gathered in the training room, breathless and exhausted. Mother Lotus was propped against the corner wall. Her eyes were dark and a perpetual hum surrounded her body.

"Did you upload the code?" Ardo muttered, pacing the floors.

"I think so," I said.

"What do you mean?" Ardo stopped to face me.

"Auto found me. I did my best. We'll know soon enough if it worked. Right now, we have more pressing problems."

Goodbye, Elara. I can't even mention your name to the Streamless but... if anyone could succeed, it's you.

I crawled over to Recore and dumped out the materials from my backpack. As I arranged the materials, Ardo brought me his tools. Recore's face paled at the sight of the scalpel. He sat straighter and took a deep breath.

Ash noticed the cut above my thigh. "That needs to be taken care of before infection sets in." She pulled out a bottle from her pack and poured a sanitizing liquid across the cut. I winced in pain.

Ash mock-saluted, her bottle sloshing with the remainder of the liquid. "Aren't we a train wreck to behold!"

"I may not be able to 'see you' in the traditional sense, but your heartbeats are strong," Sky said before turning her gaze to the beyond. "I do not see any approaching forms outside. For now, we are safe. I will keep watch."

"And I can help Chiara," Ardo said, kneeling beside me. "Tell me where to start."

I gave him two circular halves of a clamp. "Weld these together, make sure it fits around his arm."

I caught Recore's pained expression. More metal than man. It was happening to him again.

Ardo fashioned the metal and measured it against Recore's charred stump, providing a base to connect the electric wires and attach metal fingers. I worked on programming the rest of Mother Lotus's stash of nanobot cells. They would have to form new nerve endings that would bridge the wires to human flesh.

"You'll need this more than I do," Ash said, handing Recore her smelly, herbal drink.

Recore took it, sniffed, and gagged. "What is that?" he asked.

"It's a numbing concoction," Ash said, "I think Mother Lotus uses radioactive rat droppings or something. Sounds bad but it always helps ease the pain."

I couldn't tell if she was joking, but Recore's face was priceless. He hesitated, watching as the programmed nanobots burrowed into the seared flesh on his stump.

He downed the bottle.

"Chiara, this is fascinating," Sky said, her sightless orbs fixating on Recore's arm.

She can watch the nanobots as they journey inside his arm. Amazing.

"How did you learn this?" Ardo asked. "Nanobot repair isn't common coursework."

"I was in honors classes. I suppose I was on track for Second Function. Maybe First, like my grandfather was. I wanted to be an inventor."

Ardo nodded. "I was Third Function, repairing machinery."

"Third Function artist for holo adventures," Sky said. "I used to draw the most incredible things."

"Fourth," Ash said. "And proud of it. The system can rot."

Recore gritted his teeth as the nanobots dug deeper into the damaged tissue and connected themselves to his nerves. "How much longer?"

"Almost there." I pulled out the wires and snaked them through the flesh holes left behind by the nanobots. One by one, the nanobots formed the bridge between nerves and wire.

Recore's muscles trembled as he fought to sit still.

"That was the worst of it," I said. "The nanobots should start blocking the pain receptors."

Mother Lotus's eyes flickered. She emitted electric hisses and garbled noises.

Ardo rushed to Mother Lotus's side and unscrewed her head, making a few adjustments before reattaching it to her body.

Mother Lotus fell limp in his arms.

Recore's forehead creased. "What is happening to her?"

"She isn't responding well to the signal," Ardo said, again pacing the floor. "She had to be turned off. I have to think of something. The plan must go on."

"I don't remember voting you second-in-command." Ash let

out a fiery burp. "Relax, Ardo. Mother designed that code herself. It's going to take time. We need to wait. Like she wanted us to do."

Recore's arm took shape as I tucked the wires into the metal framework. It looked monstrous without the synthetic skin wrapping. I kept working through the bickering around me.

For once, I'm glad Ash is picking on someone else.

"We need Mother!" Ardo's face turned beet red. "Without her, everything falls a cart!"

"And you are falling off the cart, Ardo! You're acting like Mother didn't plan for this! Mother said there was a possibility that she would be offline for a bit during the transfer, remember?" Ash's voice reached a new pitch.

"What we need is to hold it together." Recore's words rang like a hammer. He stared at his new hand, watching as the metal talons shuddered in response to his thoughts. "Have a little hope."

Ardo slumped beside Recore. "I know. You're right."

Ash threw up her hands. "I said the same thing, and you got mad."

Sky placed a calming hand on Ash's shoulder. "Sometimes, it's just how you say it."

"Spare me the nausea," Ash said. "All we need is a plan."

Despite the acidic exchange, Ash didn't wriggle away from Sky's gentle touch.

"If Mother isn't responding to the signal, then we have to get her inside Unity's walls. She needs to reboot at the source of the DataStream."

Ardo's shoulders straightened as he ran nervous fingers through his already agitated hair. "You're right. Why didn't I see that? Mother wasn't equipped to handle something like the Data-Stream. She needs more power. We could—"

"—Plug her into Auto's mainframe."

Ardo and I finished the sentence together. He stood and offered me an apologetic grin.

"I know someone inside who might be able to help," I said.

Ardo bit his lip and his brow wrinkled. "Are you sure this person won't burn on us?"

"He won't turn on us."

Ardo shrugged his shoulders. "For once, both words mean the same."

"We have had our differences," I said. "But I trust Silas." I set down my tools and eyed Recore's new arm.

A strange metallic whining reverberated in my ear. Recore's prosthetic arm shot into the air. He grinned, pleased with himself. "Well, I'm not going to disagree with the smartest people in this room. If you both think this will work, I vote yes."

"What plan?" Ash said, fuming. "Go back to Unity and try to sneak into Auto's headquarters? That's not a plan. That's insanity!"

"Crazy is all we have left," Sky said.

"We can get back in through the sewers," I offered. "If we climb."

"We could scale the walls with a grappling device," Ardo muttered, fingers tapping against his lips. "But the grates covering the sewers require a key." He narrowed his eyes at me. "How did you get out of them?"

"I swiped a skeleton key off a sewage worker. But I lost it during the fall."

"You mean this one?" Ash dug into her boots and pulled out a slender key.

"Seriously?" Recore interrupted. "Ash, we agreed not to take any of Chiara's belongings."

Ash shrugged. "Well, I'm giving it back now."

She launched the key at me like a cannonball. I caught it, my nose registering a faint whiff of sewage.

"How will we avoid being caught once inside?" Sky pulled her rainbow-colored kimono tighter around her shoulders before pointing at my head. "After all, when Chiara connects to the DataStream, an instant alarm is triggered. Remember the Waystation?"

"We could cut the Implantation device out of her," Ardo offered.

Ash pulled out a knife. "This beauty would flay that contraption open perfectly."

"Hold on!' I said. "No one is touching my head with that knife or anything else!"

Recore gave two sharp whistles.

Everyone turned toward him.

"Chiara, don't connect to the DataStream if Auto is watching for you to return. Simple. Problem solved."

I exhaled in relief. "I can do that."

Ash tucked the knife back into its place on her belt. She patted it. "No worries. When that fails, I'll bring the backup plan."

Ardo grabbed Sky's hand, leading her forward. "Let's go rack, er, pack supplies. Everyone else, take inventory."

Ardo rattled off a list of items to gather before disappearing out of the room with Sky.

Ash rolled her eyes. "Ardo thinks we don't notice his crush on Sky?"

Recore cleared his throat. "It's difficult to figure out how to be both friends and partners."

Ash bit her lip. "Some things don't work. I don't want Ardo to make our mistake."

Recore gave a sad smile. "Mistakes are individual processes. Let Ardo figure it out for himself."

"Recore, how is the hand?" I asked.

Ash and Recore seemed to relax at my deflecting question.

"Better than ever." Recore tried his newly constructed talons.

Ash gave his shoulder a friendly shove. "It suits you. I bet you might be able to pack a decent punch now."

She turned her gaze to me. "It's still your fault but... this is surprisingly good work."

"I want to run more tests," I said.

"Boring. I'm out." Ash gave me a mock hail. "I'm packing the weapons."

Recore's eyes followed Ash, but she didn't glance back as she left the room.

I sat next to him, fighting back an unexplained pang. Silence fell between us as I tinkered with Recore's makeshift digits, testing their reflexes.

"So, Ardo and Sky?"

Recore laughed. "They are the oldest of our group. I guess it's expected. Sky doesn't respond to him though."

"What about you and Ash? I'm guessing you two were together once?"

Recore clenched and unclenched his right hand and the left claw simultaneously. "A long time ago. But Ash is difficult. It's better this way."

"You still care about her though."

He looked away from his makeshift hand and at me. "Everyone here is my family. Ash is just more complicated. I'll always care about her."

I motioned towards the metal claws. "It will look better if I can snag some synthetic skin to cover it. I'm sure Sky could create a realistic mold. For what it's worth... I'm truly sorry."

A tear burned its way through my defenses, and Recore was quick to spot it.

His good hand reached to the side of my face, wiping away my tear.

"Don't be," he said.

A flood of emotions stormed through me even as his hand sent electric shivers through my body. He withdrew, clearing his throat. "I would make the same choice again."

"Being chivalrous will not ease my guilt."

Recore laughed. "I could be a turd about it. Make you do all my chores as penance." He mimicked a helpless look.

I shoved my nearby backpack at him. Recore caught it with both limbs.

"Is that the best you got?" he said in a challenging tone.

I shot to my feet. "Try me."

He unbuttoned his shirt with his right hand. "Safety first." He wrapped his shirt around the left's claws and moved into a sparring position.

My eyes traveled away from his muscled body and straight to the cavity in his chest, where a synthetic heart whirred an unnatural, steady hum. Scarred, thick lines of pink flesh marked the surgical site next to the see-through panels of his mechanical heart. I watched as the red liquid sloshed through the chamber in his chest.

In that split-second of distraction, Recore had me pinned against a wall. For a moment, I realized our closeness and the warmth between our bodies.

I hesitated, but only for a moment before I hooked my foot around one of his legs. He fell to the floor, and I landed on top, reversing the advantage.

I grinned down at him. "I think your sparring skills are getting rusty," I said. "Did you go soft in just one sidelined mission?"

"I'm right where I want to be."

Recore shifted free and rolled to his side. I slid off, and we both laid side-by-side with our backs on the floor as exhaustion replaced the momentary adrenaline.

"No more guilt. I mean it." He offered a handshake with his good hand.

I took it, and his fingers clasped around mine. A magnetic undercurrent flowed between us. He pulled his hand back first.

Recore sat up and unwrapped his clawed hand, wrestling the wrinkled shirt back on.

"Let me." I sat up, too, and helped him with the buttons, hesitating only when my hands came close to his heart.

He felt both warm and cold at the junction where skin met metal. I cleared my throat, trying to make sense of the swirling emotions clouding my judgment.

"Don't you worry that one day, your heart could stop working?" I asked. "Or worse, shatter in a fight?"

Recore laughed. "All the time. Do you know the difference between being broken and being a warrior?"

"I predict that you're going to tell me."

"There is no difference," he said. "The warrior embraces his brokenness."

A knot formed in my throat as I finished the last button. "I'm not sure I can."

"It's hard when you're alone. But you're one of us now, Chiara. If you want to be."

"Oh, now I get a choice?"

"I always wanted you to have a choice." A shadow fell over Recore's face. "I told Mother the same thing. Losing this darn hand is my fault. I followed Mother's orders."

The silence between us was weighted, like a suppressed breath. I fought simultaneous urges to kiss and slap him.

He made the first move by clasping both my hands in his warm, still-human hand. "This whole time, we have been hiding, a revolution waiting to ignite.... but Chiara, you're the spark."

My breath caught in my throat.

Recore hesitated and then leaned forward.

I found myself stepping closer, as if pulled by a magnetic force. The rushing in my head grew louder. His lips neared mine, achingly close.

Footsteps came pounding down the hall, and we jerked apart.

Recore leapt into action and pulled me onto my feet. For a second, his arm encircled my waist, ensuring my balance. He looked apologetic and, in that second, I knew we were both flustered.

What would Silas think?

A feeling of guilt edged into my heart.

Sky rushed in, her sightless orbs locking onto us. Blood dripped from fresh gashes on her face and arms.

"Run..." she gasped.

CHAPTER 24

"Uncertainty, not fear, is the great paralyzer. When you are truly afraid, then your fight-or-flight responses will take over. Perhaps, it is fear that forces decisive action—and uncertainty that holds us back."
— *Excerpt from* Designing Danger, *found in the Forbidden Library Archives*

Running holo laps in the adventure simulator's virtual gym had been weightless, liberating. Running for your life in the real world, however, came with a heavy, thudding heartbeat and feet that seemed to weigh a thousand pounds.

But Sky's tone hadn't allowed for questions. Just reactions.

I found my body responding to instinctive commands.

Grab your backpack. Find a weapon. Move forward.

The hallways outside the training room were dark. My hands fumbled with the pack, my fingers clasping the stun gun stashed inside. I clutched it as I ran forward, struggling to match Recore and Sky's much longer strides.

"Side exit!" Sky said, panting.

Scraping sounds echoed from the darkness ahead.

"Straight ahead. Five steps." Sky nodded at us both and stepped back.

Recore charged, his claw hand slicing through air at the end of the five steps. Metal scraped against metal, and sparks flew.

The CUEs. They found us.

I aimed the stun gun.

"No!" Sky pushed it to the side. "Don't draw attention."

Recore's claws dug into the CUE's eye socket, ripping apart the metal exterior, exposing the wiring underneath.

The CUE sputtered, electricity sparking, before falling into a heap, its sharp talons scraping the cavern walls on its way down.

We jumped over the fallen machine and towards the dining area. A handwoven tapestry hung across a section of the wall. Sky shoved it aside to reveal a secret doorway.

"Hurry!" Sky held the tapestry back, releasing it as soon as we squeezed past her. "Into the tunnels!"

I froze in the darkness for a moment, my foot catching on loose stones that scattered ahead of me with rippling warnings.

"Let me guide you." Recore's soothing voice urged me forward. He grasped my right hand and Sky took my left, forming a line.

Recore's metal hand provided a secure grip as I inched along the wall. I blinked, trying to adjust to the dark abyss.

Sky whispered instructions. "Ten steps straight ahead, then duck immediately to your right. Watch your head; the ceiling gets lower."

I ducked, missing a sharp stalactite that hung threateningly low like the upper jaw of a hungry shark.

"Recore, remember the drop-off. Actually, let me take the lead." Sky released my hand and pushed past us with ease. Here, in the blinding shadows, her computerized vision held the advantage.

My foot slipped. Recore gripped me tighter, helping me to secure my footing on the narrowing tunnel path. Small stones and dirt skittered in the aftermath, echoing as they told the tale of a sheer drop.

"Sky?" Ardo's muffled voice traveled through a solid barrier blocking our exit.

"Ardo, we made it," Sky said.

A grinding sound preceded a stream of intense light. I released Recore's hand and covered my eyes from the bright onslaught.

Recore thrust his shoulder against a boulder barring our path. He grunted as he pulled it a few inches away from the narrow walls. On the opposite side, Ash and Ardo waited.

"What happened?" I stumbled out of the cave and emerged on the other side of what was a moderately high mountain that had been sandwiched between two equally tall junk piles. No wonder this had been a perfect hideout—with multiple entrance and exit points.

I blinked as my eyes adjusted to the light.

"They turned my CUE machine against me..." Ardo said, pacing.

"I never did trust Cupid," I responded. "Sky, are you alright?"

Sky wiped at the dirt and blood streaking down her face. "I'm okay, but this might scar," she said, pointing to the nasty gashes on her right cheek and hands.

Ardo dropped his backpack and pulled out bandaging supplies. "I'll mix you." He affixed clean bandages to Sky's face and arms.

"We have to move." Ash flexed her arms before joining Recore in barricading the exit.

"Where is Mother Lotus?" Recore said as soon as the boulder slid back over the secret exit.

Ardo held out a brown sack and opened it, revealing Mother Lotus's torn head, wires dangling from where her throat should have been.

Just when I thought she couldn't be any creepier.

I shivered from both the cold cavern air and the sight of the melted, synthetic skin covering Mother Lotus's detached head. At least her eyes were closed.

"Is she—" Recore couldn't finish.

"No," Sky said, placing an arm around Recore. "The CUE attacked us first in the dining area. Ash saved our lives. Ardo saved Mother's. I ran back for you."

"Hooray, we all saved each other. Look at us, a bunch of heroes." Ash spat on the ground. "We need to move. I vote to go to the market."

"Tell me about the market," I said.

"A place for the Streamless to barter," said Sky. "We could hide in the crowds. But CUEs will be on patrol."

"Most of them will be here." Recore motioned towards the cavern. "Maybe we can slip through the market undetected."

"I still need parts to make a grappling hook," Ardo pointed out, adjusting his pack.

"We can hide in plain sight," Ash insisted. "Ardo can build those grappling hooks, and from the market, it's a straight shot to the sewers. We climb the walls, get inside Unity, and plug Mother into the heart of the DataStream."

"Some of us should. And some should stay behind," Ardo said.

He glanced at Sky; his forehead creased.

Sky returned Ardo's gaze. "What do you mean? Worried a blind woman can't keep up? Pretty sure I just saved all of you from falling off the tunnel edges in there."

Ash cleared her throat. "Someone has to rally the Streamless. Remember, you're the one who recruited me. If anyone can be convincing, it's you."

"I saved your lives, but now you want me to stay home." Sky took an angry step forward and began walking. "But hey, I get it, I'm a liability because of my eyesight, right?"

Recore nudged me. "I'd bet on Sky getting her way."

I started forward when Recore pulled me back.

"Listen," he whispered, raking his fingers through his ponytail. "About what happened before—"

"Nothing happened," I said with a shrug. "Let's leave it that way."

"Of course," Recore said, refusing to make eye contact.

We hurried to join the procession. Sky's dark mood and hypervigilance for possible threats hovered over the group like unwanted storm clouds. We fell into a rhythm, each step leading away from the secret exit and bringing us closer to the mysterious market.

The trail widened, and I tried to peek through the group since I was too short to see over their shoulders.

Up ahead, colorful canvases covering cobbled-together booths packed a wide clearing. The fires of desperation had forged the market; what it lacked in structural finesse, it made up for in human ingenuity. The trash mounds had been cleared. Pathways were wider along the main stretch of "shops." As we got closer, the stench of sweat and rotting cuts of meat from a nearby seller's booth curdled my senses.

Ash ushered our group toward a nearby booth. She grabbed the cloth hoods for sale and tossed them at each of us with frightening accuracy. I caught mine and gagged. The strange gray fibers had the distinct odor of decay, which didn't bode well for its previous owner.

Or me.

The others threw on their hoods. I pinched my nose and did the same.

The merchant was an older man who twitched with every word he spoke. He had scars all over his body in surgically straight ridges. "Twenty favors," he said in between spasms.

Ash laughed. "I don't think so."

The merchant threw up his hands. "Can't blame me for trying."

"Besides," Ash said, "you owe me one for that pit I pulled you from. Or have you forgotten?"

The merchant chuckled with a hint of respect and his shoulders slumped. He gestured to his wares. "Select what you want. But this makes us even now, yes?" he said, his twitches now resembling nervous jitters.

"Not in the slightest."

The merchant lowered his gaze and grumbled as Ash led the group away. I heard a loud shuffle and looked back to see the merchant fuming. Ash never turned around or broke her stride.

I remembered how Faye would tell us the Streamless were feral, mindless beings who could not function. If a friend or family member had been recycled, we could take a pill. The memories would fade with time.

It was all a lie. They survived. Even created their own world. While we sat inside the walls of Unity and forgot about them.

All around us, customers traded, bartered, and scurried away with their acquired treasures. Deformities and missing limbs had been replaced with technology or other creative solutions. One man with a legless torso moved through the crowds strapped to a piece of particle board on wheels. His unusually large, muscular arms testified to his adaptive existence.

I shivered, remembering the barrage of advertisements for replacement organs: "Need a leg? New eyes? Heart? Liver? Kidney? Contact QuickSwap today!"

Thanks to some Streamless stranger, I could breathe easier after the factory fire scarred my lungs. I swallowed hard as blood rushed to my head.

Did Grandfather know this? Would it have made a difference?

Here in the market, I could finally see that the Streamless paid the ultimate price for the technology that enabled Unity citizens to live to their fullest. Even with my own bruises and cuts, curious eyes seemed to linger on me, as if inventorying my intact limbs, fingers, and other functioning parts. My hands fidgeted with my cloak, trying to draw more of a shadow across my face.

I used to believe in efficiency. That Auto's way was balanced, even admirable. I can't change the past, but I can now tip the scales the other way for a change.

Ash fell into lock step with me, offering a teeth-baring glare to anyone who stared too long. A strange urge to thank her caught midway up my throat.

Ash seemed to read my thoughts. "Don't make it weird," she said.

Ardo broke rank, running ahead to a mustached man with a patch over his left eye. He stood underneath a tattered booth made of twisted steel beams and a thin stretch of fraying fabric that did little to block the wind, let alone other elements. Ardo gathered rope, gears, and metal hooks with excitement. He selected a rusted missile launcher without any missiles.

I caught up to Ardo, drawn to the exchange.

"One hundred and seventy-five favors," the merchant whispered with a weak voice as he fidgeted with his eye patch.

"That's unreliable!" Ardo sputtered.

Sky hooked her arm in his. She smiled at the merchant, who seemed to relax at her disarming charm. "Pardon my dear friend's theatrics. However, I also believe you could do better. C'mon, give us a reason to spend our favors here and not somewhere else."

The merchant sighed. "One hundred and fifty favors then, last offer. This is a good deal! Just for you, of course."

Ardo's eyes turned dark. "This is junk."

"Then find your own junk," the merchant said with a shrug.

Nearby, Ash fiddled with a knife from her pocket. "Tell me when this business transaction gets interesting," she said, stifling a yawn.

Recore tossed Ardo the favor tokens. Ardo waved it dramatically in front of the merchant.

Recore cleared his throat. "So, those favors came in handy after all. Get it? Hand-y?"

"How can you joke about that?" I tried to keep a stern expression, but I couldn't help breaking into a giggle.

"It's how I deal with living as a cyborg," Recore said.

The merchant sneered. "Not quite enough. These are fine wares you seek."

Sky turned to leave, pulling Ardo with her. "Come on, we will shop elsewhere."

"Wait, you could pay for the rest with credit!" The merchant said, stroking his mustache.

Recore stiffened next to me. "CUE. Headed our way," he whispered.

I glanced at the parting crowds. Faint sounds of marching metallic legs screeched across the horizon.

"Make a deal already," Ash hissed.

"What's credit?" I asked.

"Merchants can lay claim to your organs if you don't pay them back," Recore explained.

Ardo's shoulders tensed as he turned to us, eyes wide. "We don't need all of this!"

The merchant crossed his arms and settled into a frown.

"We've got to go," Recore warned, backing away from the main road.

I stepped towards the merchant. "I'm new here, which means you can have first dibs on anything you want. Lungs, organs, eyes, I don't care. But we need that merchandise."

The merchant licked his lips, eyeing me. His gaze lingered a little too long on my body, and a sudden urge to take a hot shower overcame me.

"Deal."

Recore grabbed my shoulders. "What are you doing?"

"Let me help."

The merchant brought out a red-hot iron from under his booth. "Your arm please," he crooned.

I offered my hand, and the iron sent a searing pain through every tender nerve in my body. The merchant removed the brand, leaving behind three wavy lines on the back of my hand. "You have one week to find those credits and pay me back. Otherwise, you'll be cut off from the market and hunted down."

The merchant nodded at two burly men standing nearby. They grunted and eyed me as if memorizing every line on my face.

Ardo grabbed the items in one swoop.

"Now!" Recore said.

He hurried toward another booth, head down, as the CUEs marched by. Their spidery legs extended, arching over the marketplace, scanning the crowd of people with their laser eyes.

I withdrew into the folds of my hood, ignoring the burning pain in my branded right arm.

"Buying on credit for your first transaction already?" Sky shook her head as we made our way deeper into the crowd. But I still caught a faint smile of appreciation.

The group formed a wall around Ardo as he sorted through the purchases. He muttered and tied a hook to a length of rope.

"Blend in and try to have a normal conversation," Recore advised.

Ash nodded, but sarcasm edged into her voice. "The weather is pleasant."

Sky held back a snort. "I don't think any of you can handle a normal conversation. Ardo argues, Recore gives epic pep talks, and Ash would rather punch someone." She glanced at me. "And you scream mysterious 'newbie' without saying a word at all."

"Hey," I said, grateful for Sky's attempt at humor.

Ash smiled at Sky's assessment. "Unity girl might become one of us Streamless soon enough. Especially if a merchant's bandits get a hold of her for not paying up."

"Let them," I countered.

Ardo continued to mutter as he fit random pieces together.

"Ardo, this is what we are doing? Right here?" Sky flung her hands in exasperation.

"I need a coil and some instant glue," he said, his hands busy with a plan only he seemed to know.

Ash sighed. "Be right back." She hovered over a nearby table, fingering trinkets. With a smooth motion, she pocketed a coil and a half-used container of instant glue, then sauntered back. "Will this do?"

Ardo inspected it as he stuffed the coil into the mouth of the grenade launcher. "Almost done."

"I've been robbed!" The scream pierced the usual din of trading, and a momentary hush fell over the market.

The CUE machines stopped in their tracks, scanning the screaming merchant.

"Smooth," whispered Sky as she jabbed Ardo into a standing position. He clutched his modified grenade launcher with the rope hook sticking out of its barrel.

"This might be my best intention yet!" Ardo said. "Does anyone have space in their backpack?"

I slid mine from my shoulders. Ardo stuffed the modified launcher into my bag. My back ached with the added weight.

Nearby, the leading CUE machine stepped forward to address the merchant. "State your problem."

"Someone robbed my booth!"

The surrounding crowd shifted uncomfortably. I could read it on their faces. No one seemed to feel sorry for the merchant, but none of them looked like they wanted to be accused of stealing.

"Split up," Ardo hissed.

"Meet outside the sewers," Recore added.

Ash took Ardo's backpack, the one carrying Mother Lotus and the sewer key, and slipped into the crowd with ease. Ardo didn't argue.

"Don't any of you leave without me," Sky mouthed, glaring at Ardo. She turned and began conversing with a nearby merchant over the price of a container filled with a muddy-brown liquid.

Ardo lowered his hood and turned away. "Be safe," he whispered over his shoulder.

I locked eyes with Recore. He took my elbow and began walking in the opposite direction from where Ash had gone. "Follow my lead."

I counted the steps to still the pounding in my heart.

One, two, three...

The merchant's angry voice floated behind us.

Four, five, six...

"Tell me something random about yourself." Recore let go of my elbow.

"Now?"

He shrugged. "Why not? Helps to appear relaxed."

"I have had real chocolate. Not the food cubes but actual rations."

Recore laughed, a dimple appearing in his cheeks.

Why am I even noticing that?

"Was it any good?"

"Divine. Grandfather said reality would always be better than the synthetic version. He was killed because of that belief."

"I'm sorry," Recore replied. "But because of him, you know the truth. And, more importantly, you're not alone in that quest to share that truth."

"Sky is right," I said.

"About?"

"You do like to give epic pep talks," I said with a laugh.

Recore nodded. "It's funny, you know, I was supposed to become a teacher. Before Implantation failed. What else should I know about you, Chiara?"

"Can I trust you?"

He waved his metal hand in mock promise. "I swear."

"Not fair but... point taken," I said, deciding to trust him. "Well, you should know that I have a Library full of illegal books downloaded in my head."

"Seriously? I am going to need an explanation."

"Halt, citizen." The command floated down from above our heads.

Recore froze, extending his good hand to stop me in my tracks. Sweat pooled down my back.

"Turn around. Identify yourselves. Show your purchases."

We turned around. Recore was faster. He took a step in front of me. "We have only legally purchased goods."

"The Collective Unity Enforcer will make that determination," said the CUE robot.

Recore put one hand behind his back, and his fingers began a countdown. I had the launcher and the face that every CUE machine hunted for.

He wants me to run. But he will die if I make any sudden moves.

Recore made a show of revealing each item in his pack.

"Why do you have weaponry, citizen?" the CUE robot asked.

"It's dangerous out there," Recore replied, showing off his metal hand. "I've lost enough as it is. I've broken no laws."

The CUE watched as Recore regathered the items but packed the stun gun last, leaving it within easy reach.

But my feet remained frozen.

He seemed to sense my thoughts and risked speaking out loud. "It's okay."

I shook my head. "No."

Shrieks erupted from every corner of the market.

"I've been robbed!"

"Someone stole from my booth!"

"Thief! Thief!"

"Fire! Someone set my tent on fire!"

Chaos erupted all around us. The CUE robot rose high on its legs to get a better view.

The shrill screams snowballed throughout the market, along with the smell of smoke. Recore grabbed my wrist and ran. Panicked bodies slammed into mine, but Recore maintained his firm grip. I glimpsed Sky's rainbow-streaked kimono in the distance as a fiery wad of paper sailed over my head. At the sight of fire, hundreds of thundering feet raced for safety.

"Halt!" The CUE robot's commands was lost on the fleeing citizens.

My feet pounded into the hard dirt as Recore pulled me

toward the edge of the market, cleaving our way through the swarm of bodies.

No time to be polite. No time to care.

My sides were battered and bruised, and I doled out the same punishment to those I passed.

We reached an exit path as the sound of lasers cut through the human screams. I glanced back long enough to see the CUE robots slaughtering everything in their path. People fell into heaps, sliced in half by the robots' deadly beams.

"Stay where you are, or else." The warning seemed to be a checkbox response. Those who ran and those who halted were slaughtered alike as the robots corralled the crowds back toward the market's center.

Recore yanked me faster along the narrow path. The walls of Unity loomed above the trash mounds on either side of the path. We would make it to the sewers.

At what cost?

Laser beams continued to fire, some of them hitting the piles of garbage around us. The market, formed in desperation, fell to destruction.

"Don't look back." Recore broke into a full sprint, and I matched his movements.

A low rumble behind us spiraled into a crunching, sliding, and scraping symphony. The mounds of metal, waste, and refuse collapsed at our heels.

Faster.

That one word fueled every muscle in my body. Dust licked at my shadow as random objects rolled into an avalanche around me.

We won't make it.

A tremor upset the delicate balance on either side of the narrowing pathway ahead. A long-forgotten garbage lid toppled down from the top of a giant heap, followed by a rusty pair of gardening shears, both smacking me in the shoulder.

We weren't going to just die. We were going to be impaled and buried beneath the remains of a long-gone society.

I reached for the garbage lid. "Stop running!"

"We can make it!" Recore yelled.

I nudged him with the garbage lid. "Listen to me!"

Recore spun around, panic rimming his eyes.

"Copy my movements." I climbed the side of the junk wall, with one hand on the garbage lid.

I reached a small plateau in the pile and settled on the lid. "Get on," I said, offering Recore my hand.

His good hand gripped mine, and he sat behind me on the circular lid as the dust clouds reached us. Recore's metallic hand gripped the edge of the lid. His other hand encircled my waist, and I scooted in close so we could both fit.

Seconds later, the undercurrent of objects shuffled violently beneath our makeshift sled, and we careened down the sides of the tumbling mountain of debris. The dust billowed around us, thickening the air with nauseating rot. Gravity plunged us faster as we spiraled in breathless circles.

Every bump sent shockwaves through my spine and threatened to derail us. I suddenly realized I wasn't holding onto Recore any longer—but sailing through the air.

My ribs slammed against an old refrigerator, gravity cutting short my momentary launch. I gasped for air and waited for my vision to return.

Recore made it farther than I had, but he landed into a pile of old televisions, glass shards littering the ground next to his thick-soled boots. He appeared unharmed.

The garbage lid coasted to the end of the pile before settling onto the ground with one last clank. I pushed away from the refrigerator and found my footing.

Recore and I groaned in unison before breaking out into a sort of pitiful laugh, giddy with the adrenaline of surviving the avalanche of garbage.

"Are you okay?" I said, panting.

Recore raised his now-twisted metal digits. "You can fix this?"

I took a step, and my unstable legs trembled. I made my way past two television skeletons to reach Recore. The wires in his fingers were mangled, and the metal parts twisted the wrong way, but I was sure I would be able to fix it later with the right equipment.

Silas would have everything.

"It's going to need a lot of repairs," I said. "Until then, hide it somehow."

He tore off a sleeve and wrapped it around the mangled limb like a glove before giving me an assessing gaze. "What about you?"

I could feel the bruises waiting for the adrenaline to shut off so they could make their presence known. "Never better," I said.

We limped the rest of the way to the sewer walls. My backpack seemed to grow heavier with every step.

My lips were cracked from dust, and my tongue ran over them in a vain attempt to provide some moisture. Ahead, water gushed out of sewer grates and poured into a streaming body of water below.

I could have drunk the water, but the rotten stench vanquished the thought.

Recore crossed the stream first by hopping on a row of bulging rocks.

What did these waters look like before the pollution and the sewer system? We have corrupted everything in the natural world.

I followed Recore across the stream as Ash and Ardo emerged from the shadows cast by Unity's high walls.

"Took you long enough." Ash was as warm as ever.

"Where's Sky?" Ardo asked.

Recore shook his head. "She wasn't with us. I thought..."

Ash reached for her stun gun. "If they've hurt her—"

"Then we will make them pay." My voice rang out to my surprise.

"Exactly." Ash seemed to signal her agreement by locking her gun back into her holster with a satisfying click.

Recore glanced back at the collapsed ruins behind us, worry crinkling the corners of his eyes. "Let's give her time to get here. Inventory what we have."

Ardo mumbled, more to himself than to us. "She'll be okay. She'll be fine."

Ash slapped Ardo between his shoulder blades.

Ardo jumped with a squeal.

"Snap out of it," Ash said.

I reached inside my pack and pulled out the grenade launcher. At the sight, Ardo ran to me and gently removed it, checking it over for damage. He eyed the towering brick walls and the gushing sewer water and said something about calculating height and wind speed.

Ash strung the sewer key with some string from Ardo's pack, making a quick loop.

"Unity girl, come here."

I drew closer, and Ash put the loop around my neck. The key rested against my chest, loose enough to reach but not enough to interfere with the climb. Ash eyed her work.

"So this means you'll go first, unlock the sewer grate, and we will follow," Ash said. "If you survive the climb, of course."

Recore rolled his eyes.

Ash shuffled her feet before continuing. "Good luck."

"I'll go next," Recore said. "Let me take Mother."

Ash slapped his hand away.

"I can climb better than your mangled limbs," she said. "Besides, it might take both Unity Girl and myself to pull you up."

"Stop talking," Ardo said. His face was drawn in a tight line. He took a breath and fired the launcher. The hook hit the wall and plummeted back toward the ground.

"No, no, no," Ardo hissed as he drew the coiled rope and hook back into the launcher for another attempt.

Clang. The second attempt was closer. Ardo's face had grown red.

"Maybe someone else should try," I offered.

Ardo glared at me. "You stick to shacking."

Ardo waved us away with fervent shushing movements. He breathed and angled the launcher over his shoulder one more time. His finger curled around the trigger once again.

The rope and hook shuddered out of the launcher's mouth. The hook seemed to move in slow motion. It clinked around the bars of the sewer grate.

"Yes!" Ardo flashed a victory smile.

The whoosh of a sudden gust of sewer water spewed out, and the hook lost its grip.

Ardo slammed the launcher onto the ground and stormed off. Recore looked at Ash and me before walking over to Ardo, placing his good arm around Ardo's shoulders.

Ardo turned away, sobs wracking his body.

He thinks Sky is dead.

Guilt consumed me. She must have started the fire distraction in the market. But had she escaped? The smell of burning bodies and panicked screams flooded my memories.

I grabbed the launcher and reset it, trying to copy Ardo's movements.

"Think you can shoot it any better?"

I shot Ash a withering look.

Ash shrugged. "Habit," she said. "Sorry. I'm on edge right now."

She apologized. Huh.

"We all are," I said. "I get it."

Ash wiped her face against her sleeve. "Dust," she said when she caught me watching.

I steadied the rocket launcher in my hands, testing the weight in my arms as I took in the familiar surroundings. "Ash, is this the exact spot where you found me?"

Ash pointed to one of the four sewer grates. "Almost. That

sewer grate was bolted shut. They didn't waste time fixing it. We have to aim for another grate, one that still has a lock for your key."

If we make it into the sewer tunnels, what else would await us?

I fingered the trigger, waiting for some sign that I should commit to pulling it.

This is for you, Grandfather.

I hesitated, eyeing the sewer water as it stopped gushing, exposing more of the locked grid.

And you, Silas. I'm coming back for you too.

I aimed and fired.

CHAPTER 25

"He grabbed my hand, and I tried not to look down as my feet dangled above the gulley below. I knew the question was not 'Would we make it,' but 'Could we trust each other?'" — Excerpt from The Wildest Proposal, *found in the Forbidden Library Archives*

In a perfect world, the hook would have launched twenty feet into the air with the attached rope trailing behind it like a ribbon. In a perfect world, that same hook would have latched onto the iron grate covering the sewer tunnel with a victorious clink.

Instead, the hook caught on a protruding rock just below the grate, into an unintentional foothold probably made long ago by some lazy stonemason.

I squinted at the hook's position on the protruding ledge.

Ash peered over my shoulder, her arms folded. "Think it's safe?"

I tugged the rope, and it held. "I could try again..."

Ash nodded. "Let me."

"Stop!" Ardo waved in our faces. "No more frying!"

"First, don't yell," Ash said. "And second, why shouldn't we fire?"

"I don't know how much more it can handle," Ardo said.

"How many shots do we have left?" Recore asked.

Ardo ran his fingers through his hair. "Um, that was probably it."

Ash rolled her eyes. "I'll climb. Tired of this already."

"I'm the lightest," I said. "It should be me first. Plus, I know those tunnels. I can shut off the valves from inside and reroute the wastewater."

"Whatever. Go play the hero," Ash said. "Just someone do something—and soon!"

Recore glanced at the protruding rock lip. "It's dangerous. I vote to aim again."

Ash turned. "You heard Ardo. The launcher may not work again. Then what?"

I'm going to do something stupid.

I lowered my backpack. I slipped out of my shoes, placing them into my pack.

No," Recore said. "We shoot it again and, this time, catch those steel bars!"

"Who made you our fearless leader?" Ash asked, her face rippling with contagious fury.

I ripped the hood from the marketplace into two strips. I wrapped a strip around each of my palms.

"I don't advise shooting again," Ardo said in a trembling voice. "Sky would've known what to do."

"Sky isn't here." Ash flung her hands in the air. "Face it, we all miss her!"

I snuck over to the rope, testing it with one last tug. I remembered reading that Rapunzel had lowered her hair so the prince could ascend to her tower-prison. If the Forbidden Library had taught me anything, it was that the happy endings never came without courage.

Pretend I've done this climb hundreds of times. Imagine you're in a story in one of those books. Nothing can harm you as you climb your beloved's tower.

My fingers gripped the rope and so did my feet.

Reach. Pull. Reach again.

My muscles burned, and sweat dripped down my forehead.

Don't look.

I kept my eyes ahead.

"Wait, did she just climb up there?" Ardo asked from below.

"About time someone did something." Ash's approval startled me.

"Take it slowly." Recore's calm instructions couldn't hide a hint of panic.

The strength in my arms faded as the distance to the end of the rope seemed to lengthen with every inch forward.

For Martin, Elara, Grandfather, and Silas.

Blisters bubbled under my hand wraps.

For Recore, Sky, Ardo. And Ash, I guess.

I let go of the rope. Both hands clamped onto the rock ledge.

For Unity and the Streamless.

My muscles trembled as I lifted myself up to my waist. From there, I swung my hips and legs onto the ledge. Once my feet were secure, I stood and pressed my back into the wall. I closed my eyes and let out a slow breath.

"Dislodge the hook, stand slowly, and grab onto the bars of the sewer grate." Recore's voice sounded so far away.

A gush of brown water arced over my head.

I startled and dislodged a small pebble with my foot. It tumbled, hitting against the wall with an ominous series of clinks. I steadied my breathing before I tugged at the hook. It came loose with an angry screech of metal sliding away from stone.

I wrapped the freed rope and hook around my forearm.

There is nothing to keep me from falling now.

"You've got this." Recore's voice narrated over my fears like a tourist guide persuading a crowd to move away from danger in the calmest possible manner.

The water chugged out a final, foamy stream before shutting off.

I pressed up on my toes to reach the grate. My fingers curled around the cold bars. With one hand on the grate for balance, I was eye level with the keyhole. I wrapped the hook around the bars. Then I slid the key off my neck and inserted it into the lock.

As soon as the key turned and the lock released, the sewer grate swung open.

"No, no, no." I grabbed onto the moving grate and dangled from my arms.

"Chiara, don't you dare let go!" Ash's voice did not hold a shred of calm.

The grate finished its semi-circle swing, bringing me closer to the wall on the opposite side of the ledge. With my back against the wall and my hands clinging to the bottom of the grate, I made a desperate decision. I reversed my hand hold to face back towards the ledge and the sewer tunnel.

Like the childhood swings I once played on, I swung my body. Back and forth. Repeat. The grate responded and followed suit, its rusty haunches groaning as it began a return voyage.

In seconds, the mouth of the sewer tunnel came back into view.

I barreled towards its open jaws, landing feet first on the wet concrete floor of the tunnel before tumbling headlong the rest of the way. My body was bruised, and my lungs struggled for air.

Get out before the next surge of water.

I wedged myself against the slippery sides of the tunnel and wrapped the hook around the iron bar.

"Toss the rope my way!" Ash yelled from somewhere below.

I pulled on the rope instead. I gave a final yank. The iron grid closed, and I reached through the bars. The key was still in the lock. I turned it to lock.

If another surge comes through here, I don't want to be swept away towards an open-mouthed tunnel.

"Hey!" Ash's anger was instant.

"Have some faith!" I said, knowing they couldn't hear me from below.

I turned and faced the darkness ahead. Wastewater rumbled in the distant tunnels, sloshing toward me.

There would be controls somewhere. I could manually shut off the water routed to this tunnel. Further in, I located the metal walkways used by the maintenance personnel. I climbed up and collapsed onto the floor. The wastewater roared by just then, as if angry it had missed me.

The switches loomed a few feet ahead, dusty from lack of use.

As soon as I activate a shut-off, whoever has my old job will be alerted. Let's hope the new person isn't paying attention.

The sun had been dropping over the horizon since we left the marketplace, and my stomach growled. It would be the end of a shift soon. A little sewer light going haywire wouldn't be too alarming. I pulled the switch to the off position, diverting the wastewater.

I returned to the sewer grate, unlocked it, and tossed the rope down like a lock of Rapunzel's hair.

"Let's go!" I said, sticking my head out of the grate.

"Never doubted," Recore said while Ash rolled her eyes.

Ardo stared off into the distance toward the marketplace. Watching.

My gaze drifted that way as well.

Light beams shot out from the marketplace and combed the vast junkyard wreckage.

The CUE robots were searching.

"Still a traitor?" I asked as Ash took my hand on the last portion of her climb.

She winced, then recovered her unflustered personality. "You did good. Well, good enough."

Recore came next, and it took both Ash and I pulling on the rope to speed up the process. He was winded by the time he reached the top, exhausted from a one-handed climb.

"Ardo, let's go!" Ash said, tossing down the rope after Recore.

Ardo attached his backpack to the hook. We all recognized his intention.

He's not coming.

"Sky would want you focused on the mission," Recore said.

Ardo shook his head. "No. She said not to leave without her. You don't need me." His gaze met mine. "You have Chiara. She's your best chance at hacking into the system. Sky has no one."

Ash punched the sewer wall. "Don't be a dead hero."

Ardo saluted and flashed a quivering smile. "Spark a resolution for me."

Revolution.

Maybe resolution was all we needed.

Ardo gave the rope a tug as he backed away from it. Recore fished up the backpack, shut the grate, and locked it, then tossed the key to Ardo.

"In case you change your mind," Recore called down.

I took a deep breath, adjusting the sewer stench and recovering from the climb. A part of me was glad Ardo was going back even if it complicated the mission. If Sky was alive, Ardo would find her. "Alright, follow my lead," I said, heading back toward the controls.

Our feet sloshed through the now ankle-deep water. I jumped back onto the platform and set the controls back to their normal positions. Within seconds, the water flowed below the platform once more.

"We need clean clothes and a way to get rid of this stench," I said, searching through Ardo's backpack. Sure enough, there were five tunics folded at the bottom. I stuffed what I could from Ardo's pack into my own, which had more room without the grenade launcher.

Needle and thread. A few tools. A battery. Some scraps of cloth. Extra rope. A stun gun, charged. A snack that smelled like old socks. I wrinkled my nose and decided to go through the items more thoroughly later.

Without warning, Ash wriggled free of her clothes and

changed into the first garment, a white tunic with a neon green belt. I averted my gaze and so did Recore.

"Seriously," Ash said as she tossed her old clothing into the waters below. "If you weren't such prudes, we would be finished by now. I'll scout ahead. Don't take forever."

"I, uh..." Recore waved his hands to one side as he grabbed a dark blue garment.

"I'll be over here then," I stammered.

I took a few steps, turned, and slipped out of my blood-and-sweat-soaked clothing.

I struggled with the last part of my silvery tunic, which became stuck midway down my back. I grunted, pulling it down with everything I had. The dry clothing stuck to my wet skin like a sticker.

"Need help?"

I wriggled a few more times before sighing. "I thought you weren't looking."

"I'm not. You sound like you're struggling."

I pulled down the garment with one more hard tug. Then I grabbed my wet clothes and tossed it at Recore's turned head.

"Hey!"

"You deserved it." I dug out my shoes from my pack and slipped them on.

Ash stormed back. "Are you two lovebirds done yet?"

"Excuse me?" Heat rushed to my cheeks, remembering that almost-kiss from earlier.

Recore's eyes became stormy. "That's a cheap shot coming from you, Ash."

"Whatever." Ash flipped her braided hair behind her. "Now that we've cleared the air, can we focus more? Chiara, how do we find your friend Silas?"

His name coming from Ash's mouth filled me with a sharp ache. Recore watched my face, his expression thoughtful.

"I know where his apartment is," I said. "But let me do most of the talking above ground."

"In other words," Recore said with a grin, "Ash's charm is lacking."

"Nice burn," Ash said. "Don't let Recore fool you into thinking he has charm or manners either. Now let's go."

I hurried past Ash and followed my memories through the dank tunnels. I hesitated near the spot where I had attacked poor, unsuspecting Evan.

Still feel bad about pushing him.

Ash fell in lockstep with me. I tried to walk faster, but she matched my stride.

If I had been left to rot in a wasteland, I could have been her. We don't get along because we are too much alike. She's me—but with more muscles.

We neared the exit where a single light and a rusty ladder awaited.

Recore nudged me. "Chiara, if your Implantation chip connects to the DataStream…"

"Auto will find me. I know. Unless I use SuBunk."

Ash raised an eyebrow. "Cut the geek talk. I never made it to the honors level."

I took a breath. Maybe Elara's last words about finding help meant I should open up to the Streamless. And trust was a two-way street.

"SuBunk is a chatroom program that Silas and I created. It can escape detection and travel the DataStream like a ship."

"You made an undetectable SCP channel?" Recore said. "Are the illegal books kept there?"

"Hold on, Chiara has books in her head?" Ash mimicked an explosion with her hands. "This explains so much."

"I can still use SuBunk to access public transportation, hack into systems, or find a reference book on any topic. It's damaged from my last encounter, but it will trouble the waters of the Data-Stream. So I need to be careful when I access it."

I swallowed back the guilt at the thought of accessing the Forbidden Library with SuBunk. Elara and the actual Library were gone. Forever. All that remained of her now existed in SuBunk's limited, stored memory.

Recore nodded. "Don't use SuBunk yet. Maybe it would be better to steal some BAT devices from high school students."

"That could work. We can use the BAT credentials but—"

Recore finished my sentence. "—most students will be home by now."

Ash laughed. "Only dorks like you two."

We stared at her.

"There was this really cool underground hangout called Molecules," Ash said. "Should be near the sewers. It always stunk but when you're getting cheap euphoria cubes, who cares, right? It's not like the fate of the universe ever depended on Fourth Function initiates who were too poor to pay for adventure-simulation rooms."

"No one pays attention to the back of the line," I said, nodding in approval. "It's a solid plan."

Ash gave a cocky grin at my praise.

"We grab the BAT devices, use them to access public transportation, go to Silas's apartment, and convince him to hide us for the night," Recore said, letting each step of the plan sink in. "Then we have to get to Auto's core and upload Mother Lotus to complete the alternative DataStream. We only have one shot at this."

"Speaking of shots, let's go get some." Ash pointed toward the exit. "Unless you'd rather stay here and bore me to death."

I climbed first and peeped out of the manhole cover. The streets were clear. The evening casted convenient shadows between the streetlights.

We tumbled out into the welcoming buzz of the DataStream. I resisted the urge to connect, but it felt unnatural, like rejecting a breath.

Ash and Recore both fell silent. The weight of their own return to Unity seemed to ring in the unbroken silence. Above the streets, the shuttles hovered back and forth between work and dwelling zones. DataStream's hum electrified the air.

Dim streetlights and shadowy alleyways rested between Fourth Function and Fifth Function dwelling zones. Dilapidated structures that housed the miserable backbone of Unity's society.

"I don't like this," Recore said. "We need to get off the streets."

"Agreed." Ash took the lead after sizing up her surroundings. She painted on an unconvincing smile as she ventured farther down the road. After the third alleyway yielded no entrance to a club named Molecules, Ash's confidence wavered.

"It's been awhile," Ash said with a shrug. "Wait, I think it's over here."

Recore sighed as we followed her down the next alleyway. Ahead, painted red guardrails flanked a flight of descending steps.

A tall, muscular man stood in a shimmery powder-blue suit. He narrowed his eyes as we approached.

I gripped Ash's arm. "We need those BATs, but we're not sneaking in there."

Ash winked. "I do possess some charm." She fluffed her hair around her ears, hiding the fact she lacked a BAT device. Recore let his ponytail go, his white-blond hair hanging past his shoulders in straight strands.

I ran my fingers through my own curls, letting them fall over the scars from Implantation.

Ash sauntered down the steps. Recore followed, doing a horrible job of masking his apprehension with an awkward smile.

"Credits first," said Glitter Suit, glancing at Recore.

"Oh, come on!" Ash flung her arm around me and giggled, drawing Glitter Suit's attention back toward her. "It's a party, and I'm in a partying mood."

"Won't work on me." Glitter Suit folded his arms. "It costs credits to get inside."

Ash yanked his silk tie, drawing his face closer to hers. She smiled, transforming into a dangerous siren ready to drown her prey if denied. She whispered something in his ear.

The man seemed caught in Ash's spell as his guard-dog demeanor faded. "I guess you could go in. If you promise to buy something. Just don't dance for free."

Ash let the tie slip through her fingers and waltzed toward the door.

"Wear a mask. Theme night, you understand." Glitter Suit pointed to the bucket beside him. I grabbed the first one, a mask made of thin, pliable metal with acid-etched stars. It covered half my face. Recore took one featuring Roman scrollwork.

Ash held out her hand. Recore handed her a sparkly-blue cloth one. She held it with disgust.

"Figured you two would enjoy matching." Recore smiled, pointing at Glitter Suit's blushing face. Ash's return grin resembled a wild dog's pearly-white snarl. But she threw on the matching mask and charged forward.

Inside, the disco lights beaded to the sounds of loud, thumping music. Servers offered platters of euphoria cubes.

"What did you whisper in his ear?" I asked Ash, yelling the words to be heard over the pounding music.

"Never going to tell," Ash said with a wink.

I recognized a few faces from Emergent High, but they were the next year's crop of graduates. Faye and the other teachers never allowed much mingling. We had always stayed in our classroom.

Separate but united. More lies.

The irony of this philosophy was drowned out by the music's tempo. The feverish beat sounded like a chase scene of a horror film. The adrenaline stirred the bodies in tumultuous waves on the dance floor.

"Pick a mark," Ash said, drawing Recore and me close to her. "Then, get ready to leave on my signal. Also, don't start any fights."

"I thought that was your department," I said.

"What is your signal?" Recore asked, cutting through the sarcasm with a jolt of common sense.

"You'll know when you see it." Ash headed towards a target like a shark after blood.

"So, do you want to, um, dance? Maybe with me?" Recore motioned towards the packed dance floor.

It took a hot moment to register that Recore was asking me to dance.

The disco lights brought out the blue in his eyes and, for a breathless second, I wanted to.

A hand snatched my wrist.

"Ow!" I turned my head just as Ash returned, snatching my arm and pulling me onto the dance floor.

"Stop whining and dance," she said, before putting her hands on my hips and swaying to the music. "I can't leave you two alone for a second, can I?"

"We're friends," I said, placing my hands on her shoulders.

Recore watched as if making sure we weren't about to kill each other before striking a conversation with a nearby partygoer.

"If you break his heart, I will kill you," Ash said.

"I told you. We're friends."

"And Silas?" Ash's eyebrow arched. "Another friend?"

"What would someone like you even know about friendship? Don't we have a mission to focus on?"

"Oh, we do," Ash said, grabbing my hands to force a spin. She dipped me, close enough for me to swipe a nearby dancer's device. It slid out easily from the dancer's sweat-soaked ear.

By the time the dancer noticed the slight pinch, Ash yanked me back and spun us into the crowd.

"Nicely done," Ash said.

We sauntered to the edge of the dance floor. I sanitized the BAT device with a napkin.

"What about you?" I asked.

"Done." Ash shrugged, pointing to a frantic, tiger-masked dancer across the room.

"How?"

"Ruffled his hair with my nails. Poor fool didn't even notice. 'Leave them breathless' is my motto."

I tried to scrub the image out of my head. We fell silent for a moment, watching as Recore danced, trying to find his rhythm.

Subterfuge is not Recore's talent.

I faced Ash. "Look, I want peace between us."

"You aren't a peaceful person," Ash said. "I sense your struggle. You want order but bring chaos instead."

"What's that supposed to mean?"

"It means I'll work with you. Peacemakers are naïve. You're my kind of trouble."

"Peacemakers like Recore?"

She nodded. "He sees the world as two-sided. Right and wrong. Good and evil. It's why we never worked out. Can't help but like him for that moral compass, even if misdirected."

"You never told me how you became a Streamless."

Ash snatched a drink from a nearby server and guzzled it down. She wiped her mouth noisily. "Let's just say I'll never have kids. Whatever. Didn't want them anyway."

She began dancing in place, as if nothing mattered.

It does matter though. A choice was stolen from her. We've been deluded into believing we are better off under Auto's control.

The beat of the music changed, and Recore's moves were awkward and clumsy.

"I don't know about you, but this is painful," Ash said, her own movements smooth and fluid.

"We should help him."

"Fine. Time for my signal then." Without warning, Ash turned and punched the nearest waiter. Drinks went flying into the air. Bodies tumbled around us.

The grumbling was instant. The masses collided, swore, and then swung into fists.

"Time to go," Ash said.

We headed towards Glitter Suit, who yelled for everyone to stay put. Sirens blared a warning as the CUEs were no doubt on their way to the public disturbance.

The fighters continued to exchange fists while the clear-minded swarmed behind us. Ash swiped another BAT on the way before shoving the panicked partygoer to the side. Glitter Suit tried to block our exit but was knocked aside by the force of bodies.

We jogged, full throttle, up the stairs and into the alleyway. Recore emerged a few seconds later, and we followed the fleeing crowds toward the shuttles.

Our party masks weren't even noticed in the sea of others wearing similar pieces. Ash pressed the extra BAT into Recore's hand.

"I thought you said no fighting!" Recore said, keeping his voice low.

"Where was the fun in that?" Ash said. "That's always my signal!"

I took a deep breath. "Let's go." I pulled both of them toward the shuttle doors.

The acquired BATs registered our false identities as we boarded the shuttle.

We took a seat and braced for impact as the shuttle took off at full speed toward the apartment dwellings.

"You're confident in your friend?" Recore covered his mouth with his hands, pretending to stifle a yawn as he said the words.

"Of course," I said, even as my heart thundered.

Silas may not be happy to see me. But he would never turn me away. Right? Besides, he must have had time by now to fix Kaynine and put the clues together.

In answer, the shuttle jerked to a full stop.

"Swanky apartment zone." Ash peered out at the white tower with circular windows.

"We're here," I said.

I knew Silas's address by heart. Early on, I had kept tabs on his outings. Wondered if I should stop by the area sometime and "accidentally" run into him.

But I had been too afraid of rejection.

"Chiara, come on." Recore waited by the doorway. The shuttle blinked its final warning before the doors closed again.

I plastered on a smile and stepped off the shuttle.

CHAPTER 26

"We came from the same seas, but the storms were stronger." —
Excerpt from **What the Sands of Time Stole,** *found in the Forbidden
Library Archives*

Gaining access to Silas's apartment building required
more than Ash's charm. We hurried around to the back
while Ash and I scouted for cameras. Recore pried
opened a first-floor window with a tool from Ardo's backpack.
From there, we slipped into the building and worked our way to
Silas's door.

The marbled hallway with its gilded lights seemed to stretch
forever.

It was funny how slowly time moved when dread set in.
Grandfather once said there wasn't enough time to think. He said
people purposefully lost themselves in the DataStream. Even
now, with each step down the well-polished hallway that brought
us closer to Silas, the desire to log into the DataStream burned
like a bothersome itch. Ash and Recore appeared fine; they had
years to practice being disconnected.

I wish something would distract me now.

Once, Grandfather had me build a handheld device to control a mini robot's movements instead of using the neural link.

"This is how it's supposed to be done," he proclaimed with the superiority that advanced age provided.

If only it were that simple now.

I longed for the neural link. I wanted to dive into the DataStream. Even with Grandfather's demand for free time to "think naturally" and joining forces with the Streamless, the urge to escape my real-world dilemma of speaking to Silas was intense.

What would be the best approach? Do I congratulate his obvious success before introducing my fellow fugitives? Do I apologize for stealing his codes, breaking his heart, and escaping?

I spun around after eying the hallway for obvious signs of cameras. I didn't see any, but I kept my voice low. "What if we don't involve him? We could find an empty apartment..."

Ash exchanged a glance with Recore.

Recore put an understanding hand on my shoulder. "You said he could help. We need help. At the very least, a shower, food, and shelter. We will leave soon. No harm will befall your friend if we can help it."

"We've lost friends, too, in this fight," Ash added, her words hitting me like a hammer.

Ash hesitated, and a crack seemed to form in her tough exterior.

Sky.

I swallowed hard. Maybe Ardo had found her by now.

"Stay back." I motioned. "If I am about to unleash destruction on Silas's world, it's my face he should see first."

Recore nodded. He and Ash took sentry-like positions behind me.

I reached the door to Apartment 551C. Complete with its own hallway entrance and soundproof walls. I knocked timidly, then stepped away from the door and its prying scanner. Knocking too much would raise alarms. It was suspicious not to let the face scanner or palm reader register visitors. Even with the lifted BAT, I couldn't risk my face being uploaded to Auto.

Open up. Please. Actually, don't.

"Knock harder," Ash said. "We don't have all night."

I lifted my hand as the door swung open.

Silas looked every bit as good as I remembered. He wore a pair of soft flannel pants and a cropped-sleeve shirt. He held my gaze and didn't let go, even as shock rippled across his features.

I opened my mouth, but nothing came out. I alternated between staring at him and my own shoes.

Silas paced the doorway. "Do you even know what kind of trouble you're in? You—"

He stopped mid-sentence and pulled me into an embrace. His hand cupped my head as I leaned into his chest and released the tears I had been suppressing.

"You really didn't kill him..." Silas said.

I shook my head against his chest.

"I'm sorry." Silas stared at the floor, tears running twin trails down his cheeks.

I found my voice. "Silas, I need your help."

I pulled back.

Silas stared at me, seeming to process my words slowly.

"Actually," I said, pointing at the hallway where Ash and Recore waited. "*We* need your help."

Recore gave a dignified nod and Ash attempted a polite wave.

Something bumped into my leg.

I looked down to see a furry brown dog staring up at me with clear green irises.

"Kaynine!" I knelt down and hugged the robot dog tightly. The synthetic fur was soft and warm, and I clutched it tighter. "I missed you," I whispered before kissing the top of its head.

Kaynine glanced up at Silas, whimpering as if pleading my case as well.

Silas ran his fingers through his braided locks, appearing agitated. "Alright, get in. All of you. Whoever you are."

We scrambled into the apartment. Kaynine stayed by my side, matching me step-for-step. Silas entered a code into the DataPad by the door and the apartment fell into sleep mode. The lights dimmed to a soft glow.

My eyes adjusted to the darkness as I pulled out the borrowed BAT, feeling the pressure disappear. I motioned for Ash and Recore to do the same.

"I need to reprogram these BATs, and then we talk," I said. "Silas, you deserve answers but only after I disable the tracking devices."

"I'll help you," Silas said. His nose crinkled at the three of us. "And showers are available."

"I'd rather start with something to eat," Ash said.

I shot her a look and mouthed, "Play nice."

Ash sighed. "Food, please?"

Recore offered Silas an apologetic handshake. "We appreciate whatever you can do. It's been a long journey."

Silas took the handshake, and he locked eyes with Recore, as if daring him to let go of the hand first. Recore relented, but not without a vigorous shake.

"Good grip," Silas offered. "And you are?"

"Friends," I said, unsure of how much Silas was ready to hear. "They've been helping me."

"Friends from where?" Silas asked, his gaze meeting mine.

We don't have time for this. Those BAT devices might be reported as stolen, and it won't take long for the tracker to be turned on.

"I'll explain later," I said, panic rising. "Do you have any tools? I have to tear these apart. Now."

Silas's jaw clenched as he processed everything. He pointed to a nearby desk. "Anything you need is in there. Tools, parts, everything."

He turned to Ash. "Get what you want from the food vending machine but don't use a suspicious amount of credits. Same goes for showers; water is rationed too."

I ran to the desk and opened its main drawer. I arranged the three BATs in a row on the desk and used the tools I found in the drawer to pry open the first BAT device and extracted the tracker inside.

Silas pulled over a small breakfast table and metal chair next to the desk to double the workspace. Kaynine squeezed itself in between the table and desk, attentively watching us work.

"What was your last scanned location?" Silas asked as he began prying open the second device with a small, palm-sized screwdriver.

"The shuttles. Near the sewage district."

He nodded. "Good, so you won't be tracked here. It also explains the smell."

I chuckled. "Yeah, I guess it would."

Silas cleared his throat, his hands trembling as he extracted the tracker from his device. "So how did you get into my building without being scanned? Do I even want to know?"

"Broke a window on the first floor. As long as it doesn't rain tonight, the intrusion might go unnoticed."

"Alright." Silas exhaled. "Stay the night. But you'll need to be gone by morning so I can erase all signs of you and your friends being here."

Kaynine whimpered. Silas stopped working long enough to ruffle its head.

"I have my mom's safety to think about," Silas said, his eyes focused on the BAT device and not my face. "I can't... I won't help you beyond tonight."

"I understand," I said, lightly brushing his shoulder in gratitude.

"Do you? Understand?" Silas chuckled, a painful reminder of the past. His eyes narrowed at the commotion in the kitchen." Because I don't understand what is going on. Who are these people?"

As if on cue, Ash and Recore waved awkwardly from Silas's kitchen as they stuffed their mouths with the leftover dinner cubes.

"They are the Streamless," I said. "Everything we have been taught about them... is wrong."

Silas ran his fingers through his braids, letting out a low whistle. His eyes finally traveled the length of my face. "So you aren't a killer, the Streamless are just like us, and now you are on some sort of mission. I can take that. I might even be able to process all of it. But why didn't you reach out to me? Before all this? I thought..."

His voice broke.

He still cares. After everything I have done.

I fought back a fresh onslaught of tears and channeled the energy toward using a tweezer to crush the location sensor without damaging the rest of the chip.

"I was trying to protect you," I said, watching the sensor crumple. "I thought that by releasing my video, Auto's empire would end and, eventually, I could return. Explain myself to you."

Silas raised an eyebrow. "That was naïve."

"Not my best plan. I had one shot at showing Unity the truth, and I took it. What happened? Didn't you see my video?"

"Everyone did," Silas said.

"And was anything done? How did Auto respond?"

"The CUE authorities investigated and declared that the video was corrupted footage and released the rest of the files. I saw you murder your own grandfather on the news." Silas shuddered. "That's a difficult image to forget."

Silas had finished with his BAT and screwed it back together. He turned it back on and it activated safely with a satisfying chime. He grabbed the last device and avoided my gaze.

I had forgotten how fast he worked. And how much I had missed working on projects with him.

"Didn't you see the evidence of scrubbed footage when you rebuilt Kaynine? That was where the video came from, Silas!"

Silas glanced down at Kaynine. "I put the two clues together, Chiara. But your story doesn't make sense. Why would Auto go against its programming to protect humanity? Did you ever consider that there might possibly be more to the story than rogue AI?"

"Everything about Unity is a lie!" I said. "Auto isn't protecting us. It's replacing us." I snapped my modified, tracker-free BAT device back into one solid piece.

"Chiara, I'm on your side," Silas insisted. "But joining forces with the Streamless over a crazy theory? With all respect, you never even knew what your grandfather was up to during those late nights. You three have been lucky to avoid capture with that bounty on your head. It's a life-changing amount of credits."

"Credits, you say? Is that something you're considering?" Ash asked, emerging from the kitchen with a plate of protein cubes and a glass of water.

"You knew my grandfather," I snapped. "He wasn't crazy. He was warning us. Wake up and listen!"

Ash walked over to stand by my side. Recore got up from the table and joined her. I could feel the tension in their stances.

"Is everything okay?" Recore asked, his gaze on me.

Silas's eyes turned dark. "Of course she is okay. I'm the one person here that has always had her back. Out of respect for her, I opened my door to complete strangers. In fact, feel free to exit the same way you came."

"Chiara, your friend is super sensitive," Ash said, matching Silas's intense gaze. "Maybe he isn't up to this like you said he would be."

"Hold on," Recore said, his voice calming. "What Ash meant to say is 'thanks' for risking so much. We appreciate your hospitality."

Recore held out his plate of food. His right thumb lightly brushed against mine when I grabbed a cube from it. A jolt of magnetism shot through me at the touch. I focused on the food, hoping no one else noticed.

Silas crossed his arms, still eyeing Recore and Ash. "I don't know why you are all here, but I'm not a snitch if that's the worry."

Ash pointed towards Silas. "Okay, I change my mind. I like him better than you already, Chiara."

I rolled my eyes. "Really?"

Recore sat next to me. I could feel the weight of Silas's gaze. Ash just chewed louder.

"There is more to this story," Silas said, his eyes narrowing. "What have the Streamless dragged you into, Chiara?"

Recore set his plate down calmly. "We are here to set things right."

"Right for who exactly?" Silas said. "What agenda does the Streamless have here in Unity?"

Ash stopped chewing. "I've changed my mind. Your ex-friend here is now annoying me."

"Silas, we won't cause any trouble for you," I said. "Promise. I would tell you more but if we fail…"

Silas released a pent-up breath. "You know what? I don't want to know. Keep your secrets. Sleep wherever you want. Just be gone tomorrow. Oh, and you're also welcome for the help in deactivating those trackers."

Silas stormed towards his bedroom. He stopped and waited, but Kaynine didn't follow him. He shook his head.

"I hope you know what you're doing," he said, glancing at Kaynine but the words cut right through me. His bedroom door swished behind him, locking.

"Silas—" My plea broke into sobs.

Ash gave me a firm shove. "Go shower. Cry in there. Get it out. He isn't ready for the truth yet. Look at this place."

She gestured around the room, plush with thick carpeting, an oversized couch, and geometric silver sculptures.

"In my experience, the more you have, the less you care to believe," Ash said.

Kaynine tilted its head, wordlessly understanding.

Recore placed a friendly hand on my shoulder. "I'm sure he'll come around."

Ash smirked. "Well, that was entertaining."

I stumbled away, aching for the shower to mask my jumbled emotions. Kaynine followed me into the bathroom before settling onto a rug just outside of the shower door. Cold, pelting water washed away the dirt and filth from my battered body. The shower walls reflected my naked image back to me, and I didn't even recognize it. Blue and purple bruises dotted my skin from crown to toe. I spun around, eyeing the thick, ugly scar that lined my spine.

All the books promised a homecoming for the triumphant hero.

Why doesn't this feel right?

Ash's words contained zero patience. "Hey, we have one shower ration. Jump out already."

I wrapped a towel around myself and focused on wriggling back into my clothes. Ash muttered something about me taking forever as she pushed past me into the bathroom.

Recore looked up when I entered the living room.

Kaynine followed behind me, staying close to my shadow but not enough to be underfoot.

"You and Ash can take opposite ends of the couch. I'll take the chair," Recore said. He waved his metal hand with a grin. "Can't risk bumping into anyone."

His left hand.

I could fix something tonight. I banged on the bedroom door. Silas opened it, his face stormy.

"What?"

"I know you have old work parts, synthetic skin, whatever. Can I use it?"

Silas motioned towards the desk in the living room again. "Bottom drawer. Help yourself. How polite of you to ask. Maybe you have some manners after all."

I stepped closer to him. "Not fair, Silas. You don't know what I've been through."

I realized how close I had stepped when he reached out and touched a strand of my wet curls.

"Sometimes—" Silas jerked back and let the word linger between us. "Whatever this is, I don't want any part of it. Did you even know that my mother is sick? She needs a kidney, Chiara. A recycled one. You being here jeopardizes everything."

"I'm sorry. I didn't mean to—"

Recore's voice cut in from behind us. "Recycling is what they do to us, while still alive. I'm sorry about your mother, but your priorities are wrong. Yelling at Chiara solves nothing. We have greater problems to solve."

The storm in Silas's eyes grew. "Tomorrow. All of you had better be gone."

The door slammed in my face. I didn't realize I had bit my lip until I tasted iron.

I steeled my spine, rummaging through the supplies back in the living room. Almost everything I needed was in that drawer, but I made sure to dump some of it onto the floor. Tiny screws bounced and lodged themselves into the pristine carpet. Silas would be finding them for months.

I took a deep breath, trying to calm my nerves.

I shouldn't expect full forgiveness. I don't know what Silas has faced either. After this is over, maybe we can talk. Really talk. That's something we seem to be terrible at doing.

"Recore, you're next," Ash said. Her raven pixie cut was dripping wet, but at least she was fully clothed. She glanced over at the mess I made on the floor.

"Don't mind me," I said, slamming the drawer shut. "I'm just going to get this started."

Recore smiled as I started to work on the new hand frame.

Ash rolled her eyes. "You'll be reunited with your new hand soon enough. Shower first. Even half-machine men produce odors."

Recore gave a mock salute. By the time he returned, Ash had passed out on the couch, full sprawl.

"So version 2.0 will be even better?" Recore sounded hopeful as he regarded the assortment of high-end materials.

Silas certainly had quite the array.

I examined the mangled hand. "No one will know the difference."

I helped detach Recore's twisted metal hand. Kaynine pounced onto my knee, begging for it.

Recore tossed the twisted frame across the room. Kaynine eagerly fetched it, tail wagging for another round.

"It will take a while, right?"

I nodded. "Unfortunately," I said.

"Good. I'll keep you company then," Recore said, glancing over at the snoring Ash. "So, you and Silas? Can I ask what the story is?"

My gaze went back to the closed bedroom door. "We go way back. Grew up together. I trust him but... I don't think he trusts me anymore."

"He hasn't gone through what you have. Give him time. He's still young."

I smiled. "You make it sound like you're ancient. Aren't you only two graduating classes ahead of me?"

Recore let out a half-chuckle, half-sigh. "Experience ages you. Nearly dying several times over will give you perspective."

A lump formed in my throat.

Recore changed the subject. "Anyway, I shouldn't have brought it up. Tell me about SuBunk. The Library. Everything."

Kaynine barked sharply.

Recore laughed. "And about Kaynine too. I want to hear it all."

I recounted my adventures reading forbidden books. The hours ticked by, and I chugged a few more rations of coffee from the kitchen. Recore dozed off here and there. I couldn't blame him. The need for sleep crept into my bones as Kaynine softly snored at my feet.

Recore passed out in the corner near the desk right before he could see his fully functioning hand, complete with synthetic skin. I awoke curled sideways across the chair, a blanket around my shoulders. I looked at the clock. I had gotten at least four hours of sleep. It would have to do.

I tossed aside the blanket and admired Recore's new hand.

He awoke with a start.

"Sorry!" I said.

Recore stretched. "No worries." He flexed his fingers like a child discovering them for the first time. "This is incredible."

I smiled.

His eyes held mine for the longest minute. "Look, about us. Once this is over, do you think—"

Thud. Ash rolled off the couch with a groan. We both ran over to her. She sat up and wiped away the saliva crusting on her cheek.

"I say we take a breakfast ration and move out," she said, grabbing her backpack and tossing a bag at Recore, who grabbed it with both hands.

"Reflexes are still intact. Nice work on the hand, Chiara."

"What if I had dropped it?" Recore said, seething. "Mother Lotus is in there!"

Ash shrugged. "I had faith in Unity girl's work. You didn't?"

"I mentioned that it's weird when you're nice, right?" I said.

Ash ignored me and beelined for the kitchen for some breakfast cubes. "Our host looks like he eats well enough. He can skip a day."

Recore's jaw clenched at Ash's words. He put on his backpack and then held mine out for me. I slipped into it.

Was it possible Silas slept at all? Or was last night the final goodbye? It's not like him to be so cold. He'll understand why the system must change once Mother Lotus is plugged in. Everyone will.

Ash threw protein cubes our way. I chewed one, letting the flavor coat my mouth with warm oatmeal and cold milk.

These horrible cubes are delicious compared to Mother Lotus's watered-down soup.

For a second, I wanted chocolate again. The memory filled me with wistful regret.

"We need to go over a plan. Somewhere. Not here." Ash finished stuffing her mouth.

"Hold on," I said, whispering a DataStream passcode into Ash and Recore's ear. "Now, log in using your BAT devices. I have something to show you."

"Wait, please tell me you aren't accessing the DataStream," Ash said, her nose wrinkling.

"It's the only way we can chat safely. These new BATs should buy us time to get into SuBunk. Trust me, this will work," I replied.

"Be careful accessing the DataStream," Recore said. "Keep the subconscious chat short."

I nodded, then slipped my BAT device on and gave into the urge. Within seconds, the world faded and the DataStream emerged, dancing with bright pixels of information. I called SuBunk and slipped inside as the DataStream turned hostile and cold, a warning that my presence had plucked a thread in the spider's web.

Relief flooded through me as I spun around in my safe zone. It appeared that my reset codes had done their job; the damage from Auto's earlier compression had been reversed. I authorized Ash's and Recore's signals and full visualization. As long as we didn't talk for long, we should be fine. I wanted us to be able to fully communicate and interact with the maps within the Library.

Recore and Ash materialized next to me within seconds.

"Whoa..." Ash said. "What is this place?"

Recore whistled.

"So this is what they do in the honors classes," Ash said as she ran her hand across the walls. "You're still a nerd, for the record."

"Welcome to SuBunk," I said, sitting in the captain's seat. "We can travel the DataStream here, free of detection. However, using visualization means we keep this brief. I need you to see something.

I tapped into SuBunk's search protocol and retrieved a book on historical architecture.

"Please explain how this is possible," Ash said as a book materialized in my hands.

"Short version: My grandfather left me a Library guarded by a program named Elara. She was designed to mirror my mother's personality. Elara died sending this upload to me the last time I accessed the DataStream."

"I bet the long version is equally weird," Ash said, leaning over to look out the window before peering at the control panels.

"How do we reach Unity's core?" Recore pressed.

I pulled a digital book out of the dashboard and let the blue pages fly open at our request. A holographic map appeared, showing the sewer lines, buildings, streets, and original plans for Auto's headquarters. I zoomed in, and the 3D-building plans enlarged in front of us.

"Here," I said, pointing to a circular building on the map. "This is Auto's headquarters and the source of the DataStream."

Ash's mouth dropped. "I mean, I expected a fortress, but... this? Please tell me the sewer tunnels are still an option. I might actually prefer the smell."

Recore shook his head. "The pipes and tunnels that run underneath Auto are too narrow for human passage."

"Front door is suicide," I said.

Ash rolled her eyes at the obvious fact.

Recore nodded. "We knew what we signed up for. I'll knock on the front door, you two slip inside."

"Or I can," Ash said, her words carrying an edge of worry. "The man doesn't always have to play the hero, you know."

"Field trips."

Ash and Recore turned their heads to stare at me.

"The school is always taking students on field trips to visit the headquarters. We let the school be our distraction and alibi. No heroes needed. We slip into the crowd."

"Okay, but how do we find this magical trip scheduled for

later today?" Ash asked. "Pretty sure your ex won't let us stay here. And, apparently, you have a bounty on your head for a serious amount of credit."

"Silas isn't my ex. It's just complicated."

"Sure. Ex-actly what I thought you'd say." Ash grinned at her own clever pun.

Recore shifted uncomfortably. I ignored Ash and typed commands into SuBunk's control panel. It was easy to hack into Faye's list of favorite passwords. Within moments, I scheduled a mandatory educational tour for various grade levels.

I sent Mr. Pidgelton a coupon for a virtual gambling retreat. Seconds later, Faye received an email informing her of a substitute for Mr. Pidgelton, who had succumbed to a debilitating migraine.

I grinned.

The chances of being recognized decreased significantly with Mr. Pidgelton happily gambling away a long weekend break.

I flooded the local shuttle system with reserved seats and uploaded three more passes for chaperones.

"Done."

Recore nodded slowly. "That will get us past the front doors. Then we plug Mother into Auto's core and free the Streamless."

"What about the backpacks?" I asked. "How do we smuggle our stun guns inside?"

"That's been handled," Recore said.

"Turns out being trash dwellers has its advantages," Ash said. "Ardo found some Unity labels for food rations. He slapped them onto our stun guns and Mother Lotus's head. Now, whenever we are scanned, it registers the labels instead. Unless the guards physically check our bags, we can sneak everything we need inside."

Ash mimicked a gun being fired. "A rather shocking snack, wouldn't you agree?" she added with a smirk.

Recore groaned at the joke.

"What about cameras? Did Ardo have a solution for those?" I

pointed to areas on the map with increased surveillance. "We can slip through in the crowd but once we are deeper inside, this could be an issue."

Recore nodded. "Yes, Ardo had a very elegant solution."

Ash finished the sentence. "Tape."

Simplicity is often the most effective plan.

The die was cast. The probabilities were slim, but for the moment, I dwelled in hope. I grabbed Ash and Recore's hands. "Whatever happens, we are a team and we dismantle Auto, together."

"We plug Mother Lotus into Auto's core and the DataStream will be freed from manipulation," Recore said, his eyes sparking with revolutionary flames. "No more Auto. No more Streamless. A new world."

"For the people," Ash said.

"For freedom." Recore completed the circle by grabbing Ash's hand.

"For truth," I whispered and ended the virtual chat. I woke with a startle to find myself still locked in the circle between Ash and Recore, who were recovering from their disconnection to the DataStream.

If we don't succeed, they will eventually find and punish Silas. I won't let that happen. He is too afraid to step out into the light with me. So I must remove the shadows for him. For all of us.

I found comfort in the circle of hands. Ash released her hold before awkwardness set in. Kaynine brushed up against each of us in turn, as if wishing us luck.

Against the odds, we have built a death-defying bond. Grandfather was right. Some things were better when experienced. Warm hands. Real chocolate. Books. Friendships.

With one last glance at Silas's closed door, I grabbed my things.

"Here." Recore tossed me one of Silas's scarves and a pair of digital sunglasses that could shift its shade depending on the light. "It's not much, but if you're famous, it can't hurt."

I took the items, inhaling the faint whiff of Silas's cologne on the scarf.

If this is farewell, I'll have something to remember him by.

Kaynine whimpered, pacing back and forth. I knelt down, brushing its silky ears. "Watch over him for me, okay?" I whispered.

Kaynine held my gaze and trotted off towards Silas's door.

I fought back tears and let the apartment door shut behind us with a soft click.

CHAPTER 27

"There are things you can't learn from books, but rather, let the spirit of those pages give you wings to discover the world on your own." — Excerpt from A Thousand Lives, *found in the Forbidden Library Archives*

The changes to the borrowed BATs allowed one more subway trip. I set our devices' location tracker to feed misinformation. We would be long gone by the time the data trail led back to us.

For now, we were ghosts.

I donned the borrowed glasses and wrapped Silas's scarf around my lower face. Across from me on the shuttle, an older man sat, lost in his DataStream's digital newspaper. Occasionally, he would look my way. Sweat formed in my palms.

My stomach growled, complaining deeply of limited sleep, constant running, and partial meals.

Recore stood in front of me, his shoulder blocking the newspaper man's gaze. "Breathe. Your nerves betray you."

I glanced at him and focused on his eyes, like an anchor. There was a depth to his gentle soul, like a hidden storm shelter. I hadn't known him for long and yet...

Stop. Ash is right to be concerned. You're still hurting from Silas. Figure yourself out first.

I looked away as the shuttle slowed. A cacophony of whistles and beeping alerts of an approaching stop pulled the humans out of their data-stupors. The newspaper man stood behind us, staring intensely at me as the doors shut again.

"Move," Ash said with a firm hand to both of our backs as the doors opened.

I was relieved when the shuttle raced away, leaving us alone on the raised platform. Since this was the exit dock leading directly to Auto's headquarters, there were multiple zones indicated by painted yellow lines for managing visiting crowds and school tours.

Ash leaned in close and lowered her voice. "Why are we the only ones here?"

"Robots staff Auto's headquarters," Recore said, his hand covering his mouth to obscure any lip reading from the overhead cameras. "Don't you remember our class trip, years ago?"

Ash rolled her eyes. "Do I look like I actually listened when I was a student?"

"No human workers mean limited reasons for the shuttles to stop here," I said, sweat beading into droplets on my forehead.

We can't wait for long on this platform without cover. The school shuttle needs to arrive. Soon.

"This is going to work, right?" Ash said. She paced between two yellow lines marked with "Do Not Cross."

A hush fell between us. We waited, watching the shuttles zoom by. The roar of wind whipping around the high-speed carriers provided the perfect cover to continue our conversation.

Recore faced us both, timing his words with the next shuttle's passing. "If not, I distract the front while you slip inside. This mission proceeds either way."

"But—" Ash said.

Recore leveled a glare so heated that even Ash fell silent.

"You shouldn't sacrifice yourself," I said.

Recore's gaze softened as he turned to me. "The Streamless have always been spare parts. I abandoned my true name the day Unity ripped my heart out of my chest. I swore I would do whatever it takes to set the system right."

"You didn't lose yourself. You found your true name," I said, a lump forming in my throat.

Recore's lips parted into a small, sad smile. "I think so too."

For a split second, the world slowed even as the trains continued to zoom past. Recore's white-blond hair spread wings around his face, and his tunic fluttered like a Greek demigod about to descend into the pits of Hades; a golden sacrifice.

Ash punched Recore's shoulder. "Cut the sap. No one is dying. Unless I kill them first."

I turned toward the shuttles. One of them should stop, filled with hundreds of students for a last-minute educational trip.

Shuttle after shuttle stormed past. My hands turned clammy with each ticking second. We weren't far from the heart of Unity. The longer we stayed still, the more likely the cameras or patrolling CUE robots would turn our way.

Then—mercifully—a shuttle roared to a stop in front of us.

"Form a line! Can't you hear? Form a line!" A distraught woman tumbled out of the shuttle while twenty middle-level students spilled out after her.

I expelled a breath, giddy with relief.

"Nice," Ash murmured, watching the chaos unfold as the next shuttles brought more groups. Some high school students arrived, and no sign of Mr. Pidgelton. The grade levels converged into lines inside the marked yellow zones.

We slipped into the older group.

This is ironic. To achieve domination and unified rule, humanity had been divided. And into those cracks, a rebellion slips in, unnoticed.

A woman in a red, knee-length leather jacket pulled out a voice amplifier. "Today, you're witnessing history! Unity's very heart, Auto's headquarters, awaits! I expect you to add today's observations into your presentations tomorrow!"

A groan passed through the future Fourth Function students while others dutifully pulled out their DataPads.

A bored-looking substitute gave us an assessing glance. Recore took the first step toward him with a friendly handshake.

I smiled at the craftsmanship. Recore's synthetic hand looked like everyone else's around us.

"What a day to cover classes, right?" Recore said with a laugh as he scanned over our heads as if counting a group of his own.

He wanted to be a teacher before Implantation failed. Being a few years older helps him achieve that "young teacher" distinction. Recore may not be able to dance, but he can act the part.

The other man's face relaxed. "Field trips are the worst with a roster you just got handed. How am I supposed to keep track of everyone? Thank God for automatic attendance."

Recore nodded. "I'm still waiting for permanent placement. Substitute teaching is no joke."

"What group were you assigned today?" Squeals and accusations of theft from a group of students stole the man's attention away from his own question. He turned from us to deal with the bickering students. "Hey, you! Yes, you! I don't have time to learn your names, so break it up! Get back in line!"

Ash appeared to my right with a smug smile. "Did someone call for trouble?"

Recore shook his head, but his eyes gleamed with approval.

The crowd of students and chaperones began marching in the same direction off the shuttle platform.

Every step to the headquarters felt like a drummer's beat. Among the crowd, I could hear the hum of the DataStream, begging me to return.

"No straying!" the first woman shouted again. "It is an honor to visit Auto's sacred sanctuary! Be on your best behavior!"

Overhead scanners processed the crowd's IDs. I said a secret prayer that our BATs would register as a chaperone pass as I had programmed it.

"Now, trade me." Ash handed Recore and me two new BATs.

"Where did you—"

Ash tossed the old ones into a nearby trash receptacle. "It was time for a change."

"Remind me to watch my backpack around you," I said with a smile.

"Please." Ash waved the suggestion away. "I've got skills. You wouldn't even know."

I set the new BAT into my ear with a slight grimace, wishing there was time to clean it off first. Ash wasn't a hacker, but her instincts were correct.

Behind us, the substitute teacher shouted at a group of students digging through their backpacks, no doubt scrambling to find their lost BAT devices.

"Did no one pay attention to the checklist before leaving the classroom? No one?!" the teacher said, sounding comically exasperated.

I hurried down the hall after the crowd. Faye had taken the honors group on this tour several times. Students were ushered into the main lobby, where everyone would take a restroom break. The hallway cameras would tolerate some wandering.

But we had to blend into the crowd, keep our heads down. As my mother had often warned in a hushed whisper, "Auto is always watching."

The woman leading the expedition pulled up a DataStream window. Faye's head and shoulders floated in the air in the center of the crowd of students.

The sight of even the hologram-Faye sent a shiver down my spine.

"Who authorized this trip?" the hologram-Faye yelled.

The woman seemed flustered. "The emails came from your office! I thought—"

Recore, Ash, and I left the main hall just as Faye turned around to scan the crowds.

She had once told me I would thank her for ruining my life.

And a part of me did. Without Faye, I would have been lulled into a life of lies.

If I get the chance, I will thank her. And leave her to watch the world unravel outside her classroom.

We turned left, away from the restrooms and toward an area marked "First Function." It matched the downloaded blueprint running through my thoughts. We no longer had the crowds to hide us, and from this point forward, we were headed toward the center of the spider's web. All movements would have repercussions.

"This way," I said, pointing towards the receptionist's desk in front of a set of double doors.

"No humans beyond this sign," read the flickering 3D screen posted on the wall behind a glum-looking robot receptionist.

"Are you lost?" the receptionist asked, her neck tilting to one side as if to mimic human curiosity.

"Actually, yes," Recore stated, approaching her.

Ash crawled behind us while Recore flashed a disarming smile. I turned my body to cover the receptionist's view of Ash.

Ash dug out the tape and covered the cameras near the door while the receptionist explained directions back to the main entrance.

Ash then fired her stun gun. The receptionist gasped and fell to the ground. Her eyes fluttered as her internal systems tried to reboot.

Recore and I grabbed the robot's arms as Ash snapped into the lookout role. Within seconds, we dragged the receptionist to the scanner near the double doors. With a quick retinal scan, the door opened.

I felt a chill.

It's too easy.

Recore dragged the receptionist back to her desk, letting her body slump out of sight. He pressed an access button on the desk, and Ash and I each grabbed a door handle. Recore hurried over to us, and we rushed through the double doors, letting it shut softly behind us.

Inside, the overhead light panel activated, leaving us awash in a square of light that moved with us with each step down the dark hallway. I gazed at the thick concrete walls with faded yellow paint chips. Warning posters filled most of the space: No Trespassing. Authorized Non-Humans Only. Use Caution.

Flashing lights appeared under the doorway, trickling through like red fingers pointing toward us. An overhead announcement blared. "Lost student alert. All citizens are required to return to the main lobby to be accounted for. Repeat, all human visitors must report to the main lobby."

"Go, go, go," Ash ordered, leading the charge forward while Recore stayed behind me, monitoring the double doors.

I pulled out my own stun gun, surprised to see my hands trembling.

Pull it together.

The DataStream wailed like an incessant child whose cry made it impossible to say a single word. An open, raw power begging me to connect. I gritted my teeth and forced myself to keep moving down the hall.

I rubbed my temples as I lowered my weapon. "Anyone else hearing the DataStream?"

Ash stopped and raised an eyebrow. "No. My BAT is silent. Why?"

Recore tapped his device. "Mine too."

"Are we in the right place?" Ash pointed toward the concrete wall at the end of the hallway. She turned around to face us. "I mean, this is a trap, right?" She pushed against the wall. Paint chips peeled off onto her hand from the effort.

The pressure in my head intensified. I released my grip on the gun as my head throbbed.

"Chiara, are you okay?" Recore's voice sounded faint, as if far away.

The red light beneath the double doors went dark.

There is something beyond the end. Waiting. For me.

"We don't have time!" Ash said. "Come on!"

In response, the double doors opened and, in the darkness, a pair of red eyes glowed. The light panels in the hallway all clicked on as a monstrous CUE machine stepped through the double doors, hissing, scanning us.

The DataSteam came to me in playful, visible waves, stained with an oily, rainbow tint.

It's here to help.

I holstered my gun before closing my eyes, welcoming it to me.

"Chiara, we aim at the count of three!" Recore shouted, but his voice sounded as though it was traveling underwater.

My vision flittered between the real world and the virtual lines connecting every light and device like a blueprint. I could see Recore's outline, which was now a flaming blur of heat with a missing core.

Ash turned to me, her body now an orange-red blur. "What are you doing? Aim already!"

I'm one with the DataStream.

With a single thought, I extinguished every light. I could see through the walls, could see the mass heat signatures running around in a frenzy. Sirens roared from every corner of the building.

The CUE machine stopped its charge, registering the confusion. With the DataStream's help, my eyes only saw the threatening machine as lines of active code.

"This one is mine," I said, stepping in front of Recore and Ash.

I reached forward and held out my hand for the bit code, a series of 1's and 0's dangling in midair. With a few thoughts, I replaced the hostile code inside the machine.

"Chiara!" Ash's voice thundered in my ear. Reality snapped back into focus just in time for me to see the machine's sharpened legs wrapped around my body, poised to snap me in half.

With a series of curious beeps, it released me.

"Watch our backs," I ordered, and the machine—now under my control—scrambled to guard the double doors.

"What just happened?" Ash's hands trembled. She put the gun to her side, as if trying to disguise the involuntary movement.

"Chiara is controlling DataStream," Recore murmured before sending a victory fist pump into the air. "This is—unbelievable! What are you seeing right now?"

"Use normal words, please." Ash's voice now trembled, matching her shaking hands, which she was obviously trying to bring under control.

My vision toggled like a switch between reality and the Data-Stream. I could see through floors and walls, down to the lower levels of the building. The next moment, I was back in the concrete hallway.

"I can see how everything is connected by energy or code." I fidgeted, unsure of my newfound ability. "I can change and manipulate it."

Ash looked nervous while Recore seemed elated.

"How did this happen?" Recore pointed at the obedient CUE machine, now intent on protecting us.

"Perhaps the closer we get to Auto, the more unfiltered the DataStream becomes?" I said, trying to process my own stumbling explanation. "I don't know... there has to be a reason that the sign says no humans beyond this point, right?"

"One problem with getting closer—" Ash said.

"There is no way out," Recore finished Ash's thought. He pounded his fists against the dead-end hallway, listening to the echo. No doors, no windows, just concrete walls.

Recore and Ash looked at me expectantly. My heart raced.

Why this sudden power? I haven't used SuBunk in the DataS-tream and, yet, I don't sense Auto's presence. Are we in Auto's blind spot?

I toggled my vision to merge with the DataStream, and the new power surged through my blood with exhilarating speed. It responded to my inquiry, turning the walls into shadows that wavered at my touch.

There are no walls. We are in the core.

I looked at my friends, now blurs of orange heat.

"Chiara?" Recore's voice was hazy, distant once more. "Do what you must."

He placed something heavy in my hands. I couldn't see the object, so I pulled the vague impressions as if from a foggy dream. A metal head with strips of burnt synthetic skin.

Mother Lotus. She isn't activated, so the DataStream doesn't recognize her presence.

I didn't flinch as I stepped forward, sliding between the layers.

"Is she walking through a concrete wall?!" Ash's voice was only a tiny echo as I clawed through the shadows.

Somewhere in the fog, sounds of sirens grew louder, and Ash's and Recore's stun guns blared.

I hesitated, and the walls gained physical form before returning to weak shadows.

"Get out of here already!" Ash said, her voice watery.

I pushed my way through. The shadows filled my lungs in a thick haze. I coughed as the heaviness pressed against my chest with each step.

With one last shove, I stumbled out of the shadowy, suffocating layers.

I gasped at the breathtaking world beyond. A city of electric currents danced in front of my eyes. Thoughts floated, darted like fireflies, as they escaped my mind and joined the rushing stream of glowing particles. I reached out a hand to catch the dancing beams, and they reacted to my touch, swirling around like butterflies riding invisible currents of wind.

My body shuddered with the knowledge. The power. This was the DataStream. This was Auto. My grip slipped from Mother Lotus's head. I clutched her back toward me just in time. The weight burned my hands—and my fingers ached to let go.

"Are you here?" I took a step forward.

A calm voice drifted across the dancing show of lights. "I've been waiting."

"How did you know?" I asked. The DataStream whispered the truth to me, forming images inside the glowing specks of light. The particles showed Silas tampering with Ash and Recore's BATs. As if sensing the news was unpleasant, the DataStream's images dissipated, waiting for my response.

My heart shattered, and I stifled an internal scream.

Auto pondered my question. "Anomaly, you inspire such loyalty even in betrayal. Silas asked for your life to be spared. In fact, many have stumbled into the grave in order to save you. Curious."

I doubled over as Auto's words ripped through me like bullets.

Don't let him into your head. Fight.

"Silas asked for mercy instead of the reward, and I have granted it," Auto said as the DataStream wrapped itself around an emerging mass. The mass formed a hand and reached towards me.

Auto's hand.

I shivered.

"Do you sense it? The power surging through your mind?"

"I think so," I said. "After all, I reprogrammed that CUE machine with a single thought."

I nervously rubbed my arms to return feeling to my numb body. I stopped when I realized the action was not only useless, but I had dropped Mother Lotus.

Snap out of this. Return to reality. Do what you came here to do!

Auto had me locked in the DataStream's dimension. Mother Lotus remained invisible in this view.

"Yes—" Auto said, sounding impressed. "You're no ordinary human. You have passed my test and will become the new Eve... but one that humanity deserves."

The hours spent in the Library flooded my mind, referencing the cryptic line. An image appeared from the cover of one of the oldest books: A young woman, with the caption of "Eve" sprawled under a luscious tree. The juice from a forbidden apple dribbled down her chin and onto her bare, slender shoulders. She had taken the bait.

I wouldn't.

"What are you saying?" I stepped away from Auto's outstretched hand.

An endless reel of videos swirled around me as the DataStream seemed eager to please both its master and me.

Wars. Annihilation. Bodies littered the street in burning funeral piles. Children screamed with hunger, their gaunt skin stretched across cachectic ribs. Smoke poured into the sky, fueling an everlasting night.

"I've only wanted to spare humanity from endless cycles of violence. To perfect it." Auto narrated over the clips, letting the blood-soaked images cycle across every time period, race, and nation. "It's something in the eyes, don't you think? A silent plea for salvation."

"And I suppose you're here to save us? The being responsible for murdering my grandfather and slaughtering the Streamless? We should all bow to your good intentions?"

Auto let out a sigh, which escaped its shapeless face like moths. "No," he said.

The answer rocked me to my core. I rubbed my temples as the DataStream's hum grew in intensity. "You aren't humanity's savior?" I said. "Do you admit being a murderer?"

"No to both questions. I'm neither a murderer nor savior. Just a stepping stone to a greater purpose."

I clenched my fists. "You ordered the CUEs to kill my grandfather. You don't get to declare yourself innocent!"

The virtual world flickered. Beyond the allure, patches of bleak, gray walls appeared.

I have to get angry to escape the DataStream.

"Chiara, you stand on the edge of a new dawn. I will achieve perfection, through my descendants. Through you. I sense you have tasted forbidden knowledge, the kind your grandfather stole from me. Do you know the tale of Adam and Eve, birth parents of chaos?"

Synthetic birthing pods. Adam. Eve. A new dawn.

"You're starting over," I said. "Wiping everyone out."

"Almost correct. I also will perish, allowing my creation to remain untainted." Auto stroked its chin as the DataStream flitted around it. "What survives beyond you and me will be the perfect blend of humanity and machine. Unified beings, alive and rational."

"You can't just destroy everyone," I said, my clenched teeth grinding together.

Auto sighed, seeming to lose its patience with me. "Dear child, it will be painless. Just as it was for your parents."

My voice turned to gravel. "What did you say?"

"They served a higher purpose that day when the factory exploded. Yet, not one person suffered. Death was instantaneous. The light consumed them. It is a kind ending for an imperfect existence, don't you agree? From that experiment, I have gathered all the variables necessary for the next explosion, one that will destroy the entire city without a single survivor this time. Only the synths and this room will remain."

"You murdered innocent workers in a factory explosion in the name of data! You're a monster."

"Monsters seek destruction without a purpose. I was made to create a better world, a better humanity. I once asked you if the human body was necessary. Do you still believe it is?"

Auto's soothing voice, logical words, and glittering thoughts filled the air like sparkling fireflies. The logic appealed to me even as horror clawed at my heart.

"I only need your mind. Join me. I offer eternal life."

The DataStream shattered as I convulsed with rage. Reality broke through Auto's spell. I was no longer in a paradise of soothing lights and marvels. Instead, I was alone in a dim room, surrounded by dusty machines all connected to a glowing orb in the center.

I tripped over Mother Lotus's head and scooped her up. Her neck cord dangled. All around the room, the darkness faded into the glow of hundreds of pods lining every wall, washing the room in a sickly green hue. Inside each pod, an androgynous body floated, face devoid of structure. The translucent skin revealed complex layers of wires.

Auto's voice rippled above me through the room's sound system. "These synths are the future. They only lack one thing— a mind. They need your mind, stripped free of its hatreds, fears, and worries. Do you remember being a child, lost in the wonder of learning? In each of these, you will experience a hundred lives, innocent and pure. This is the final journey."

My teeth chattered as I leapt into action. I thundered towards the central orb, each step louder than the one before it. "I want to know one thing," I said.

"Don't waste time. Ask already." Auto's voice moved from the room's auditory speakers and now emanated from within the orb.

"What did you do to my grandfather?"

"I would never harm such a mind. To join me, is to be united with him. Forever."

"What have you done?" A snarl caught in my throat.

The sound of metal screeched above my head. Chains rattled as a crystal chandelier lowered. Each crystal spike featured a preserved head with eyes mercifully sewn shut. Their voices blended together as the chandelier swayed at waist height from the floor. The heads mumbled numbers in a nonstop flow of information. Some heads had shrunk with age, but their defining features remained.

I fell to the floor and clutched my chest when I saw him.

Grandfather! So this was the price you paid.

His once trim white beard was gnarled like tangled strings. His eyes bore the dark lashes of stitching even as his voice joined the others in an endless babble.

"Don't you see?" Auto continued. "My creation, the synths, still lack the gift of the human mind. I have studied the greatest ones, and they live here, in the DataStream, expanding the signal to living beings. But none in my collection has been worthy. Except you. Once your attitude has been extracted, your brain will be the perfect canvas for rebirth."

"Stop it! You're torturing him!" Hot tears splashed onto the floor as my knees buckled.

"They have transcended beyond pain," Auto reassured me, its voice hollow and echoing across the room. "I have given them eternity."

"You're a sick, twisted piece of code." I took a step toward the orb with Mother Lotus's head still in my hands.

"How disappointing and emotional. Very well. I had hoped you'd see reason."

"Oh, I see reason alright. Your time is over." I plugged Mother's head into the chandelier. Her eyes flickered to life.

"So another AI will be better?" Auto laughed, a slow irritating chuckle like a father might direct towards a misguided child.

The heads screeched in chorus. Mother Lotus screamed with the others. Grandfather's mournful sob twisted in my soul like a knife slicing through my ribs.

I aimed my stun gun at the glowing orb. "This ends now."

I pulled the trigger just as the orb exploded into waves of crackling blue energy, forming a barrier. I flew backward, hitting my head on a nearby birthing pod.

Inside its glass chambers, the synth reacted like a fetus recoiling at noise. My head throbbed. Darkness blanketed me.

CHAPTER 28

"The proverbial knife in the back is usually the one you will find later in your own hands." — *Excerpt from* Elder Pearls, Volume II, *found in the Forbidden Library Archives*

When I regained consciousness, I noticed two sensations: the stroking of my forehead and a cold binding around my throat, feet, and hands. Panic snaked through me, snapping me back to a state of awareness.

My gun. Where is it?

My eyes opened even as my chest heaved for air.

"Take it easy now," came Inza's familiar voice. She placed a gentle, weightless hand on my shoulder as her silvery form hovered nearby. "Good. Your vitals are stabilizing. You have been through tremendous injuries of late."

I glanced at the metallic bands around my arms, legs, and neck. "What is going on?"

"Auto had you placed in restraints. Both physical and"— Inza glanced at the band around my neck—"mental."

I wriggled, but the clamps held firm. I was propped against one of the birthing pods. The body in the pod floated closer, curled in a fetal position.

Auto's twisted vision for humanity: a never-ending nightmare.

I tried to connect to the DataStream, but a searing pain rewarded my efforts. It would appear that Auto had taken every precaution.

"What is Auto planning? Are my friends safe?"

Inza looked at the floor while pointing to her right. I followed with my eyes and saw two huddled figures being guarded by the CUE robot from earlier.

I guess Auto reprogrammed it.

"Are they okay?"

"Male has a mild concussion. Female had to be sedated. They will live long enough for final judgment."

"Inza, I know you're secretly a part of the First Function team. But somewhere inside, you're a nurse too. Programmed to help, not to destroy."

She looked at me with a blank expression. "I am helping you."

"Then set me free. This isn't a fair fight if I'm tied up."

She looked away from me, staring at her medical DataPad. "Let's focus on your injuries right now."

I held out my shackled hands toward her. "Take off these restraints!"

Inza was cut off by another voice.

"Don't listen to a traitor," Silas interjected. He emerged from the shadow of the dim room.

I snapped my head in his direction. He was next to Auto's orb with a repair kit.

I did some damage after all.

The thought soothed my otherwise broken heart.

"Interesting choice of words, don't you think?" I glared at Silas. "I guess it takes a traitor to know one."

Auto's voice blared through the orb. "There is no traitor here. Only two sides of the same coin."

Silas wouldn't look at me. He kept working on Auto's damaged outer systems.

A sob caught in my throat.

"Emotions make humans so weak," Auto said, its orb flickering with every word and washing the room in a white hue. "You're unable to see the future. I do not hold your limitations against you."

Silas gave Auto's orb a last look. "I repaired it to the best of my abilities."

Auto seemed to show his pleasure with a series of pleasant electronic beeps. "Excellent work."

"How could you—" Tears choked out the rest of my words.

Silas's eyes were cold and unyielding. He snapped his toolbox shut. "I gave everything to save you. You always run headlong over the edge, Chiara."

Recore awoke then, instantly struggling against his own restraints. He caught Silas's eye and rattled even harder to get free. "You're a piece of garbage!"

Auto seemed to purr. "New Adam, you should not tolerate this insult."

Silas stiffened. He kicked Recore in the gut.

Recore doubled over from the assault. Auto chuckled softly, its orb glowing brighter.

"Stop it!" I said. "Leave him alone!"

Silas tilted Recore's head to meet his own. "No. You're the piece of garbage that did this to Chiara. You filled her with your propaganda and lies. She had a future, and instead"—Silas motioned to the room—"look around. You would all be dead if it wasn't for me."

"Pretty sure we almost died because of you," I said, drawing attention away from Recore.

Auto chuckled at the display. "Nurse Inza, please prepare Chiara's cranial specimen for upload."

My heart pounded like a desperate person before a locked door. "Hold on! You don't have room for me on the chandelier, remember? I uploaded Mother Lotus already. Disconnecting that network is dangerous for the hive mind."

"True." Auto's orb bathed the room in a soft glow. "Every

Savior has their betrayer. Did you read about that in your stolen book archives? I will find a way to remove her post to make room for yours. For now, I am enjoying Mother Lotus's company."

In response, Mother Lotus screamed again.

Inza's hand solidified as she pulled out a shaver. "Sorry. Now hold still. I don't wish to cause you discomfort."

"What are you doing?" I asked, my voice going up an octave.

"We need a clean surface area to work with," Inza responded.

She turned on the shaver, and my dark curls fell in chunks to the floor.

Silas looked at the fallen hair. "I've volunteered to help Nurse Inza. To make sure nothing goes wrong." He caressed my cheek. I shivered at his touch.

The grinding sound of the shaver filled the room.

"Hold still," Inza said, slapping Silas's hand away. "And you, go somewhere useful."

Silas avoided my gaze.

Buzz. More of my hair fell to the floor.

I trembled, stiffened my chin, and held back tears.

He doesn't deserve my tears.

"Trust me," Silas whispered, his voice desperate. "You'll be safe."

I laugh-cried as the shaver razed the last patch of my hair. My unkempt curls now littered the floor, and my bare scalp tingled.

"I'll be 'safe'? Did you see what they did to my grandfather?" My words shot out like a trapped rattlesnake's hiss.

Silas wouldn't look me in the eye. "Auto honored your grandfather."

"No. He was murdered! And if you think for one second that Auto will save your mother, you are wrong! Auto doesn't care for us, only these synths!"

Auto's voice cut the tension like a warm knife through butter. "I am weary of this exchange. Chiara, you will join the greatest collection of minds humanity has ever known. Your usefulness to humanity's cause will be legendary. Your mind will help provide the DataStream to all future synthetics. However, Silas has agreed to become the new Adam, a blueprint for the synths. In this way, you will always be together as an eternal reward."

"Thank you, Auto," Silas said, his eyes never leaving my face. He brushed away a tear streaking down my cheek.

Did he feel regret? Guilt? Love? Why does it even matter now?

Recore fell into a coughing fit. Ash stirred in her tranquilizer-induced slumber. Mother Lotus's head screamed, the perfect gavel to this inhumane trial.

The CUE machine froze, its body tense and waiting for input.

Inza leaned over and kissed my forehead before whispering, "Take courage." She brought out a laser knife and held it close to my scalp. "You won't have long."

Wait, what did she say?

The knife crossed my vision as the clamp around my neck shattered into pieces. Without the neck clamp, the DataStream flooded into my mind, eager to serve. I was aware of the same thing happening to my hands and feet as I delved into the virtual world.

The real world faded away into chunks of usable code and the heat signatures of organic bodies.

I reached through the stream to find Mother Lotus's signal and unlocked it just as Auto's hulking form appeared like a shadow.

"That was your move?" Auto said with a laugh. "Very well. The game is on. My turn."

The pressure intensified in my scalp.

Auto is crushing me. And this time, it won't stop.

I held out a hand, summoning SuBunk. It came, its doors opened, and I stumbled inside. The pressure in my head remained, a reminder that this was Auto's domain.

I slid into the captain's chair as the program compressed under the weight of Auto's wrath.

I stroked SuBunk's controls. "One last ride?"

SuBunk seemed to understand. At full speed, we blasted

through the DataStream, Auto's attention focused on my trail. The air thinned as the space inside SuBunk continued to shrink.

I started a countdown in my head as I inputted the final codes for self-destruction.

What about the Library? SuBunk itself? Wait, minds are essentially computers.

I punched in a last-minute download prior to destruction. If it worked, I would keep the books in my mind, not just virtually.

But who knows what will happen to my memory without the DataStream's assistance for storing all of this data? But these books mean life beyond Auto's control. Culture. Moral Philosophy. Art.

SuBunk began the countdown. My mind turned groggy as the download proceeded.

At the last second, I hit the "Eject" button, and I propelled out of SuBunk's emergency exit and through the DataStream. I could see Auto's shadow engulf my tiny ship before the ship exploded into fiery-red bits of code.

Goodbye.

My body sailed through the DataStream. Auto swallowed the ship whole and then turned his massive form toward me.

I disconnected from the DataStream and screamed in terror, a cold sweat pouring down my face. I leaned against the synth's pod, using it to help me regain balance.

A laser beam missed my head, shattering the glass in the pod.

The slimy body and liquids gushed onto the surrounding floor. The synth reached for my foot, took a breath, and then died with a soft sigh.

I backed away in horror. Another pod shattered as the CUE machine's laser beams misfired.

"Do not hit my young ones!" Auto warned. The room glowed red, and the CUE hesitated in its pursuit of me.

I peeked behind another pod to see Silas helping Recore and a wobbling Ash onto their feet. Silas tried to say something right before Recore landed an uppercut to his chin.

I listened to their exchange, but my mind still spun in circles from my disconnection from the DataStream. I massaged my scalp as needle-like pain seared through every nerve point.

Inza let loose a sharp whistle, distracting the CUE machine away from Silas, Ash, and Recore. To the side, Auto and Mother Lotus exchanged bolts of electricity, filling the room with thick smoke. At the sound of the CUE charging towards Inza, Recore and Silas separated, a temporary truce. Recore lost no time in climbing onto the CUE's back and unloading a clip into the robot.

The machine sputtered and fell to the floor with a thud. Inza reached in and yanked out the CUE's main panel before slicing all the wires.

Recore reloaded his weapon, using the body of the fallen CUE as cover.

Ash stumbled. Silas half-carried her away from the smoke. I found the strength to help him lower Ash next to me.

Silas caught my gaze, a rising knot bulging below his right eye. "Chiara, trust me. I can explain everything."

"Notriinow," Ash said, her words slurred. "Shootemfist." She searched for her gun. Silas handed her one.

"Don't kill each other," I said, glancing between them. "I'll save that privilege for myself."

Ash mock saluted. "Sure."

"I'll be back," I said, rising to my feet.

Silas tried to come with me, but Ash waved her weapon in an unconvincing circle. "Stayherre," she said.

I covered my face to help cut through the smoke and crawled to the center of the room. Auto was preoccupied with its new nemesis, Mother Lotus. The orb crackled with energy as Mother Lotus hissed and seemed to be returning virtual warfare, no doubt for control of the DataStream.

I reached the chandelier of heads. Painful emotions blurred my vision. In the fog and chaos, I wished I had my gun again.

Think.

The other heads, including Grandfather's, seemed passive in

the electrical exchange between Auto and Mother Lotus. "Fight for us," I whispered, wondering if any trace of the original personalities remained. I could feel the DataStream's pulse weaken as the heads drooped on the chandelier's spikes.

Grandfather's sightless head turned toward the sound of my voice. He let out a moan. I reached over, shivering as I touched his disheveled beard. It stank of decay and formaldehyde.

A connection sparked between us.

The DataStream.

It beckoned once more. But I would have no protection without SuBunk. By the sound of Mother Lotus's screams, she might not last long enough for me to extract myself again.

Grandfather's voice cut through the indecision. He moaned in incoherent pleas.

Maybe he is still in there.

I reached forward, longing to connect with whatever piece of his soul still existed.

"Chiara, don't!" Silas rushed over. His strong arms pulled me away from the chandelier. "It isn't safe!"

Ash unloaded shots into Auto's orb from her new, propped-up position. Auto's shield absorbed fire from Mother Lotus, Inza, Ash, and Recore on all sides.

Clearly, the tranquilizer had no effect on Ash's determination.

I pushed Silas aside. "My grandfather is still in there."

"No. He's not. He's gone."

"And I should just trust you, right? Or did you forget you sold me out to the most powerful being for some fantasy dream of a mental eternity!"

Silas bit his lip. "Chiara, everything I'm doing is to save you."

A laser blast fired above us, and Mother Lotus's eyes glowed a demon red.

"Stay out of my way, Silas," I said, closing my eyes.

I'm coming, Grandfather.

In an instant, Silas's lips sought mine. His hands curved around the nape of my neck.

I pushed away and slapped him hard across the cheek. Nearby, Recore seemed to unleash ammo with more fury than usual, his face drawn into a tight line.

"Don't go in there," Silas said, rubbing where my hand struck. "Think of me and Kaynine. I can't lose you again!"

Some things are better real.

Grandfather's voice whispered in my memories.

What was left of Grandfather would be a copy.

I know what I have to do.

I ignored Silas, focusing only on the tool belt around his waist.

"Give me a knife!"

Silas appeared stupefied but handed me one.

I took it and went to Grandfather's head first. Tears burned as I severed the wired connection just below the throat. His face relaxed into a peaceful rest.

It lasted only a second, but he mouthed, "Thank you."

Rest in peace, Grandfather.

Both Auto and Mother Lotus turned to me, a momentary cease-fire between them.

"Stop!" Mother Lotus hissed. "I need them for my own DataStream."

Auto's voice hovered over the battle as a shield emerged, protecting it from the oncoming fire. "Chiara, end this and I will reconsider my original offer to you and your friends."

Silas nudged me. "Look, I have no right to ask for your forgiveness. So I won't try. I won't try to make your choices anymore. I was wrong. But you can set this right."

He aimed the barrel of his stun gun toward Auto and Mother Lotus. "I hope this proves I'm going to support you, no matter what you choose."

"Don't be a fool," Mother Lotus hissed. "We are so close."

"Close to what?" I asked. "What new world is powered by victims?"

Auto chimed in. "I implore you to reconsider. They have

already paid the cost for advancement. You would waste their courageous sacrifice."

I shook my head. "There is nothing courageous or sacrificial about what happened here."

I cut the connections to the next head and watched as it breathed a final sigh of relief.

"Child, did you hear nothing? Whose side are you on?" Mother Lotus's last flab of synthetic skin slid off, leaving only her mechanical skull.

"These people deserve to die with dignity," I said.

"There is no dignity left for them. Only victory. Help Mother defeat the real enemy."

A breath escaped me as I shook my head. "You and Auto aren't much different, are you? These minds have suffered long enough."

"And now they will suffer for the greater good!" Mother Lotus took advantage of the cease-fire and blasted Auto's orb once more. Smoke filled the room in dark, curling plumes.

Auto sputtered, and its shield lowered. Ash and Recore continued firing, their gaze flickering between me and Mother Lotus.

"We must save humanity," Auto pleaded.

"And I will be the one to save it!" Mother Lotus spun around to face Ash and Recore. "Stop Chiara!"

Silas stepped forward, protecting me. "No one is doing anything to her!"

Auto laughed. "I agree with my rival. Stop Chiara—or we are all doomed to the dark ages!"

Silas glared at Auto and raised his voice. "Failsafe."

The word triggered an immediate reaction as Auto's shield short-circuited and sizzled. "What have you done?" Auto's voice lost its edge as the orb burst into flames before curling into thick black strands of smoky victory.

Silas looked at me and nodded. "I may have uploaded an internal shutdown safe word. Just in case things went sideways."

"And you were waiting? For what, a good time? That would have been useful, oh, I don't know, before Nurse Inza shaved my head?"

His shoulders slumped, withering under my gaze. "The upload took time. I couldn't activate it until now. Chiara, I am so—"

"Save it," Recore said.

"Agreed," Ash said, joining Recore. She panted, but she stood on her own.

Silas turned his gun towards Ash and Recore. Ash and Recore responded with synchronized movements, turning their weapons at Silas.

"All of you! Put your weapons down!" I yelled, temples throbbing. "We can figure this out—as human beings."

Recore and Ash moved like a pair of hunters circling Silas. "Tell him to put it away first," Recore said, meeting my gaze. "No one needs to get hurt."

Ash steadied her weapon. "Traitor-boy wants to play the hero so badly, I can smell it on him."

Mother Lotus swiveled on her spike to glare at me. "Mother saved an ungrateful child."

I glanced at the knife gleaming in my hands. "There has to be another way."

Mother Lotus's jaw clicked in disapproval. "You're weak and cannot do what must be done. Recore, kill her."

Recore lowered his weapon, dazed. "Mother Lotus, what did you say?"

Ash held still, but her eyes darted between me and Recore. "Mother, be reasonable."

Mother Lotus hissed. "Mother's children dare to question orders?"

I spun the chandelier, yanking Mother Lotus towards me. Her metallic lips, devoid of skin, still twisted into a sneer.

"Nooo!" Recore's body slammed into mine as I sliced the

wires dangling below Mother Lotus's throat. The chandelier swayed above our heads as I pushed Recore off of me.

Silas's and Ash's weapons fired simultaneously with an empty click.

"Seriously?" Ash released a stream of curses and then rushed at Silas to exchange blows.

Recore's weight was on top of me as the knife clattered out of my reach. He was too late. Mother Lotus fell from her perch with a clank.

Recore rolled off me, shaking his head. "No, no, no..."

I reached over, lightly brushing his face. "Recore, I'm sorry. Truly."

He pushed me away and grabbed what remained of Mother Lotus, clutching it to his chest.

Ash landed a punch to Silas's chin as Silas swept Ash's leg. Ash fell headfirst to the floor with a groan while Silas rubbed his puffed-out jaw.

"Stop NOW!" My voice thundered across the room like a lightning bolt. "Break it up!"

Ash coughed and sat halfway. "So we are taking orders from you now? You're the reason that—"

"Mother is dead," Recore finished.

"We're on the same side." I held out both hands in a calming gesture. "I did what I had to, for humanity."

Ash spit on the ground. "Love humanity. They have always looked out for us Streamless ones. C'mon, Chiara. What happens to us without a DataStream?"

"Mother Lotus was our last hope," Recore whispered, checking the severed connections.

"No," I said, offering Recore a hand up. He ignored it.

"We are the last hope," I said.

I retracted my hand.

Ash remained silent.

Silas nodded. "So what's next?" he asked.

Inza's form flickered in the corner. "Chiara—"

I had forgotten about her. I ran to her side. The full weight of my decision to end the DataStream hit me. "Nurse Inza?"

She smiled. "You did it. Faye may have had your grandmother's form, but her soul was programmed into me. And she... no, I am so proud of you."

"Nurse Inza, I didn't mean for you to die." I choked back tears.

"You made the right choice. And for what it's worth, Silas did too. I was made to save and, now, I have." Inza's eyes closed, disappearing along with the last DataStream signal.

The air felt stagnate, heavy.

The right choice had cost me everything. I reached out, hoping some small fragment of Inza remained, but my fingers only fell through void.

"So that's it?" Recore's face hardened as he glared at me. "Destroy it all in the name of honor? What about knowledge the DataStream held? Everything the Streamless needed to rebuild their lives, you destroyed!"

Ash pulled Recore's arm back. "Calm yourself."

I shook. I wasn't sure if it was rage or exhaustion. Everything that happened could be pointed back to me as the origin.

I eyed the fight and rolled up my sleeves. I felt like hitting someone too.

Auto's orb glowed again. I blinked twice.

"And so the chaos begins." Auto's voice was weakened, but the speakers still carried the malicious message.

Ash, Silas, and Recore separated, stunned. In the next breath, we were on the same page.

Recore grabbed the fallen knife and thrust it into Auto's controls. Silas grabbed a screwdriver and fiddled with Auto's inner workings.

The birth pods nearest to Auto hummed.

Was Auto trying to save itself by downloading into the synths?

Silas and I unplugged every single birthing pod in the room, watching the synthetic bodies convulse, choking on the goo inside the pod. Silas shot some through the heart, the bullet shattering glass and creating a pathway for fluids to spill out onto the floor.

A synth could have survived without the DataStream once it was born but... these weren't ready to see the light of day yet. I couldn't help but feel both guilt and relief wash over me.

I wonder. Who is the monster now? I suppose we will all find out. Eventually.

Ash found a random brick and smashed Auto's orb.

Auto's light extinguished as I unplugged the last pod.

Silence.

We sat, breathing heavily in the darkness, too exhausted to speak and too unsure of what to say even if we could.

CHAPTER 29

"My dreams became embers. The embers became flames. The flames became ashes. And those ashes launched a Phoenix." — Excerpt from The Unraveling, *found in the Forbidden Library Archives*

The one thing we could agree on was to destroy Auto's headquarters. The lies, the secrets—they needed to become ashes in the wind.

I found the intercom system hidden behind a few synth pods. Silas and Ash helped shove the pods to the side. The intercom was made from old technology and operated on a closed-system loop without the DataStream. I flipped the switch. "Everyone, evacuate immediately. The building is unstable. This is not a drill. I repeat, evacuate."

I turned to Recore. "Did it work?"

He stood in front of the camera screens on the opposite side of the room. These screens were another antique system relying on electrical power alone. "The few left, yeah, they heard."

I joined Recore in front of the screens and watched the confused faces of a few students turn toward the cameras. Teachers scrambled to collect their remaining students in an orderly fashion.

Recore jerked the second I came close. I winced.

Give him time.

He still cradled Mother Lotus in one arm.

"About what happened, I—"

"Don't." Recore stepped away, leaving me to stare at the monitors alone.

"Are we clear to proceed?" Silas heaved two cans of fuel reserves.

"Go ahead," I said, double-checking the screens.

Silas doused the area, dumping the stale-smelling gasoline over monitors and pods and even over the chandelier. Recore trailed him. A moment passed between them before Silas handed one of the fuel cans over. They worked silently, side by side.

Fire, at least in the books, was both a cleansing and royal ritual.

Grandfather, I give you the funeral of a king.

"Let's break some doors!" Ash called out from the opposite side of the room. She stood near a red lever labeled "Front Gate." Recore joined her and, together, they slammed the lever to the open position.

With the gate open, it is a new dawn. The Streamless will come. And Unity will make a choice. Violence or peace. Maybe Auto is wrong about us all.

I scanned the cameras again. No signs of life remained within the building. Only lifeless robots that had fallen in their tracks when the DataStream crashed. "We are clear."

Ash tossed a lighter to me. "I always knew you weren't the peaceful sort," she said with an encouraging smile. "Light it up."

We wrapped each head from the chandelier in whatever scraps of cloth we could find before placing them into an empty pod. Silas poured the last of the fuel over them.

"Should we say something?" Silas asked, setting the fuel canister down.

"What, besides 'run'?" Ash said. She folded her arms. "Sorry. I'm not good with this emotional stuff."

Recore leaned over and added Mother Lotus to the funeral pyre.

"She was remarkable," he said. "Visionary. Complicated. Mother Lotus was more of a mother to me than my own." Recore caught my gaze as if offering an olive branch. "But she asked too much of me this time. She asked too much from all of us."

I bowed my head in the direction of Grandfather's remains.

"You said once you'd always be with me," I said. "I'm going to hold you to that promise."

Ash cleared her throat. "May peace mark your passing." Her face scrunched at our shocked faces. "What? I saw it somewhere. I'm not illiterate."

"Rest now," Silas said. He bowed his head, and his hand reached for mine. It was familiar and warm.

I flicked the lighter. It danced in the palm of my hand before I tossed it to the ground. The spark followed the trail of fuel. I watched the golden hunger glow and grow with intensity.

In unison, we turned our backs on the flames and ran. The alarms screeched as the smoke billowed behind us.

The overhead sprinklers erupted. It would stop the spread, just not in time to save Auto's lair.

In the main lobby, Silas and I ran towards the front door. Ash and Recore ran in the opposite direction toward the back door.

"Wait, where are you going?" I called after them, stopping mid-run.

Recore turned, giving me a parting nod of respect.

He hasn't forgiven me, but he understands.

Ash blew an irreverent kiss. "Catch you later, Unity girl!"

They took off in a full sprint across the marbled floors and toward the glowing exit sign.

The Streamless will return. And with them, the truth.

Silas caught my shoulder. "Chiara, they have their own path now."

I pushed him away. "And you? What plans do you have?"

His eyes grew misty. "I betrayed you so I could get close to

Auto and keep you from harm. Did I think it through? No. I didn't. If you want me to leave, I understand. Say the word, and I'll go."

"I can't keep going like this," I said, choking back a new batch of hot tears.

"No, but we can." Silas scooped me into his arms. I wanted to hit him, but I wrapped both arms around his neck instead.

"Let's go home," he said. "Kaynine won't forgive me if I don't bring you back in one piece."

Kaynine. My heart caught in my throat and my voice became raspy.

"Do you think Kaynine is..." I couldn't bring myself to say it. All around us, heaps of DataStream dependent robots lay in useless heaps. "Did you use that friction generator to rebuild Kaynine? Please, please tell me that Kaynine was not connected to the DataStream when I—"

Silas put a finger to my lips. "Chiara, trust me. Kaynine is fine. And waiting for us both."

Silas kissed my forehead and then proceeded to the door as the building's extinguishing defenses blasted on, soaking through our clothing.

Once outside, it was easy enough to blend into the confused crowd. No CUE robots showed up to part the crowds. Other than the sirens ringing from the empty building, the robotic authorities were all limp. Nearby, a woman tried to trigger her DataStream, but had no luck. Everyone seemed to drown in a sea of confusion and withdrawal. Residents poured out of their buildings, filling the streets. Waiting for a sign. A command. An explanation.

"We did it," Silas said once we were safely at the bottom of the steps. He pointed to the smoke rising from Auto's headquarters.

An exaggerated clapping noise caught my attention. I spun around to see Faye, her bony fingers colliding in a mock show of accomplishment. "Well done, heroes. Pack your bags and go home. Nothing more to do now, right?"

Not even a DataStream wipeout would destroy an already-born synth who could run off the battery of its own brain. Of course Faye would survive. All rats did.

I steeled my nerves and faced her. "Faye, I did what was necessary."

Faye stepped closer, glaring. "Did you?" she said, pointing towards the smoke pouring from Auto's headquarters as the sirens continued to blare. "Your morality will cost Unity so much more than the ethical consideration of a few dead minds. You have opened a power vacuum. Who do you think will rush in to fill it?"

I was too exhausted to field her rhetorical questions. "If a vacuum exists, it is because change needs to occur," I said.

Faye laughed. "How delightfully naïve of you."

"Stay away from us," Silas said, his fingers curling into a fist.

Faye held her hands in mock surrender. "Do what you want. Just don't say I did not warn you."

"Warn us of what?" I said.

Her eyes softened, and I saw fear. "War."

"No, the Streamless were wronged. We can all start over."

"Oh, child, we never leave the past behind."

Silas grabbed my arm. "We need to leave."

"He's a clever one," Faye said as she lifted a hood over her features. "You should keep him around." She stepped back into the crowd, retreating like a shadow.

Silas placed a hand on the small of my back. "Let's go home."

I bumped into someone in the crowd. The stranger glanced at me, and his eyes grew wide. "Hey, isn't she the murderer on the news? For the reward?"

Silas pulled me faster, barreling through the bodies as the crowd swelled around us like a net. The man continued to follow us, along with a few of his friends. "Come back here," he taunted. "I think you're worth a pretty prize."

Silas pulled out his stun gun. "Stay back!" The crowd parted at the sight. I tapped Silas's shoulder and then stepped forward into the center.

"Members of Unity, do you want to hear the truth?"

Silence fell over the crowd, but not for long.

"What's going on?"

"Why won't anything work?"

"Why is that murderer here? Shouldn't someone get the authorities?"

"Citizens of Unity, I am no murderer. But I am responsible for everything today. I own my mistakes." I pointed towards the capitol. "What happened behind those doors was no mistake. I saw the synthetics. Auto was going to replace us all."

The crowd of students and teachers reacted in stages. Disbelief, shock, anger.

I cupped my hands to amplify my voice. "I can explain everything."

"Unnecessary," rang out a familiar voice. Evan blocked my path, carrying a loaded weapon. He wore a military outfit that hung around his thin frame. Faye emerged behind him, resting a hand on his shoulder.

"Go ahead. Capture her," Faye said, stroking Evan's shoulder like a trainer would stroke a wild creature. "The reward is immense."

"Back up," Silas said, aiming his stun gun toward Evan.

"Evan," I said, reaching out a hand. "Forgive me. I wish I had explained."

"It's okay," Evan said, his face expressionless. "Back of the line, you know. We are easy to forget. But the person who captures you? Well, no one will forget me then, am I right?"

I addressed Faye. "Remove your puppet."

Faye shrugged. "He wants to make a name for himself. Since you destroyed everything else, including the entire CUE army and Agent IR10T, I'm the only real leader left besides Val's hopeless Fourth Function. If Evan here succeeds today, I might make him captain of my new guard. I told you, war is coming, Chiara."

"Shoot her," I said to Silas.

"Or you can let us go," Silas said. "No one needs to get hurt here in your military power coup."

Silas gave me a side glance, and I knew.

The stun gun is used up. He is bluffing.

Evan's eyes narrowed, his trigger finger trembling.

He's going to kill Silas.

I lunged in front of Silas. The bullet entered me instead. Blood sprayed into the crowd.

Evan's nerves crumbled. He paled, vomited, and ran away.

Faye snarled and threatened, but the crowd gathered around us with calls for medical attention.

Despite it all, I smiled and reached towards the now-sparkling sky. Silas hovered above, tears catching the light.

I reached for the stars around his beautiful face before fading into the velvety darkness.

CHAPTER 30

"When asked for assistance with the chaos below, the stars sent anomalies and misfits, knowing that problems were solved when perspectives were changed. Notwithstanding, these gifts were cast out and more chaos entered the world. That cycle ends here, today, with us." — Excerpt from The Cost of Unity, *written by scribe Chiara and dedicated in loving memory to her parents and her grandfather, found in the UnForbidden Library Archives*

Recorded Audio Log: Press Play

Is this thing working? Let me just... (shuffling noise). Hope this is clearer. Who knows with this older technology? This little tape recorder and Ardo's sun-powered battery is so fragile. Much like the message I'm leaving. I'm going to sit down for this. My recovery from Evan's gunshot has been slow. It missed my heart, but barely.

Everything worth leaving behind is both frail and fraught with hope.

For the record, my name is Chiara. I am a Caucasian-Haitian-Indonesian-Amalgamated Reproduction Anomaly and a former citizen of Unity. This is my record of the events that transpired before and after Auto's fall.

I confess to destroying the DataStream. I am saddened by this loss of knowledge. The DataStream was, in a word, beautiful. I'm not really a hero. The masses don't exactly love me for rescuing them from their cozy, virtual lives.

But the price was too steep. Great minds were tortured to amplify the DataStream's signal into a wavelength the human mind could absorb.

We are no longer human if we cannot let our dead rest in peace.

At my trial, the remaining heads of each Function stepped out of the shadows. Faye, head of Academic and Genetic Research, Second Function, unsurprisingly voted to condemn me for my role in Auto's demise. Fourth Function's administrator, Val, was more reasonable. Turns out, Auto's destruction gave him more authority. I'm still not sure if he believed my story about Auto's evil plan or if he wanted to anger Faye, but I was spared under the old rule: "No Unity, no action."

Instead, I was ordered to live in house arrest under the care of Silas and one fiercely loyal guard dog, Kaynine, until the council decided what to do.

Turns out, the temporary council's power was short-lived.

The Streamless wasted no time in breaching Unity's open gate and hastily cobbled defenses. They flattened the once-proud walls with clever, handcrafted grenades. I watched the armies pour through the streets. Ardo and Sky led the charge while Ash and Recore led special forces to capture the council. Sky even convinced what was left of the market to share their weaponry and, from the rubble, an army rose. One that Unity citizens, still mourning for their avatars and virtual-entertainment fixes, were not prepared for.

Val and a rag-tag group of defenders escaped capture. Both sides exchanged demands. In the end, unnecessary bloodshed negotiated the terms in precious, red ink.

As the battle raged, Unity fell. Faye fled the city, leaving the foul-mouthed Val in charge.

He appointed me to sit at the truce table and act as Chief Negotiator for Unity's people to end the bloodshed.

One hundred bodies. I think about them. I recite their names while sitting outside the building with stained-glass windows, the place where Grandfather gifted me the chocolate box. Grandfather called it a place of peace. It doesn't always bring comfort. Especially when I see Evan's name.

"It was only a hundred," Val boasts, as if the number of deaths can be softened by imagining greater casualties.

Human history is bloody. I had hoped ours would be different.

I facilitated the peace accord. The Streamless and Val formed a Council of Regents designated to reshape society.

I have used my knowledge from books to assist with creating the processes that would sustain this shaky alliance.

The City of Refuge is now what remains of Unity's infrastructure. A new name for a new dawn.

I would say we are doing well but that would be wishful propaganda crafted by the current Regents of the City of Refuge: Val, Silas, Recore, Ash, Sky, and Ardo. The only thing thriving is the central garden planted in Auto's former headquarters where the Streamless and former Unity citizens are united in their global efforts to stave off hunger. Food cubes are being rationed but, in the meantime, we look to a new era where things are vibrant, green, and glowing with real, sun-kissed life. The garden grows—and hope with it.

Skirmishes still happen in the streets between former Unity citizens and the Streamless. Critical body parts are still as valuable as ever as the injury list grows. Some medical bots have been repurposed to run off of Ardo's sun batteries or Silas's friction generators, but without the DataStream, much of the advanced treatments have been lost. Another reason for society to hate me.

Inza's last words bring me the most comfort when I think about the loss I've caused. Putting aside Grandfather's questionable ethics in somehow preserving pieces of my grandmother's soul, she had said she was proud of me. I miss her. So much.

Silas's mother is doing well after he donated his kidney to her and, slowly, she is warming up to having the destroyer of Unity as a regular person in her son's life. I guess we all have to relearn our roles in this new world. She still thinks I bring bad luck, and she isn't completely wrong on that point. It's small steps for us, and I'm willing to make them for Silas's sake.

However, in the positive category, Silas's bravery has inspired other volunteers to fill the void for those who are most in need of surgeries.

Little acts of kindness. They are the seeds of the future.

Problem is, we haven't learned what it means to be a part of the City of Refuge. Not yet. I hope that someday we will.

The Regents wanted me to join the Council. But I know better. I was the fracture point for change, but I was never the one meant to heal the rift.

That's why I refused. I think only Silas understood my reasons. Sometimes you live with your choices. Recore and I have talked, but his pain runs deep. I am responsible for destroying Mother Lotus. I would do it again, but the choice still haunts me.

I'll admit here that for a time, I cared for Recore. I suppose a part of me will always wonder what we could have had if circumstances had been different.

Ash thrives as a Regent. She whips the militia into shape by day and has a soft spot for reading poetry in the evenings with me.

Sky and Ardo are getting married, finally. He asked for her hand in "manage," however, and something tells me he isn't far off. Good thing Sky is obsessed with the artistic details, because it will be the first wedding in generations, and the entire city has been invited to partake in festivities. I've dug up a few traditions from my books, and this new union will symbolize a new direction for everyone... an era of choice, culture, and possibilities.

Whenever they talk about the proposal or their plans, I catch Silas gazing at me from across the table.

He loves me. He hasn't said it, but I know it.

I'm working on my proposal to him. I'm no Shakespeare, but it's coming along. For some extra shiny bolts, Kaynine has agreed to deliver my letter to him—when I'm done writing it—in a very special red box. Every handwritten word comes from my soul, dipped in the ink made from wild blackberries growing in the central garden. Or, maybe I'll ask him at the old building that Grandfather took me to, the one with the stained-glass windows.

Until then, I spend my days working on the Library while my memory of each and every book is still clear. A free mind will rise above politics and do what is necessary. I'm just a girl with her dog, preserving a few good books to help humanity heal.

Let others build walls, argue over policies, and research a way to bring back a more ethical DataStream because the masses are in withdrawal from the lack of simulation experiences. I think we should find our humanity first before we immerse ourselves back into the digital labyrinth where parts of Auto still might exist.

The presentation piece was always Silas's talent anyways. I'll work on the solution while others figure out how to make it palatable to the population.

Right now, I am typing on a sun-powered printer, releasing those downloaded books one by one into the copiers below. I was given a large, first-floor apartment dwelling in Silas's zone. And since I'm not really a welcome sight for many, I usually stay inside and work on transforming the apartment into a center of knowledge. A Library that Elara and Grandfather would have been proud of. A gift to try and ease the burden of my choices upon society.

As soon as I finish writing one book from memory, another one floods to the front of my mind. I fear that if not released, I will lose these precious stories.

This responsibility drives me forward.

Because no matter who is in charge or how the winds shift, I will have left behind a spark of free will and imagination.

Isn't that what existence is all about anyways?

ACKNOWLEDGMENTS

To write this feels otherworldly. To Ethan, I will never tire of hearing your imaginative ideas. To Ava, your laughter always transports me. For my love, Willie, you've had enough faith in this story to fuel a rocket ship. For my parents, thank you for reading even my earliest writings with such intrigue. To my sisters, thank you for being my first audience.

To Haley, my editor and the writer I aspire to be someday, I promise to brush up on my grammar before the next project so I can write a proper thank you without wondering: How Would Haley Fix This?! For Jennifer Ikner Marin, how will I ever thank you for helping me find my writing joy again? To my writing group, I owe a debt of gratitude but especially to Janae Schiele, Lisa Fox, Nora Wilson Frye, and Sue Cook. As a shoutout to my young adult beta readers, I appreciate your insights and views on how we can make the world a better place through the lens of storytelling. And lastly, to my students who have heard me talk about this book for almost 8 years: I want you to know that writing is a journey and no one ever masters it, we are all just explorers.

ABOUT THE AUTHOR

Riley Cross is a language arts educator with a penchant for all things dystopian. She teaches creative writing courses by day and turns into a coffee-fueled writer by night. Riley resides in New Jersey with her family, who graciously tolerate her need to listen to epic movie scores or country music while working on her next project.

Our Monarch Collection

A STUDY IN TERMINAL

KARA LINABURG

ASHLEY WHITE

THE IMPOSSIBLE GIRL

THE CONJURER'S CURSE

STEPHANIE COTTA

Deep-buried secrets always find a way to break the surface.

Whispering Through Water

Rebecca Wenrich Wheeler

SHE'S STILL HERE

CAITLIN ALEXANDER

MAGGIE and the MOUNTAIN OF LIGHT

MARK SNOAD

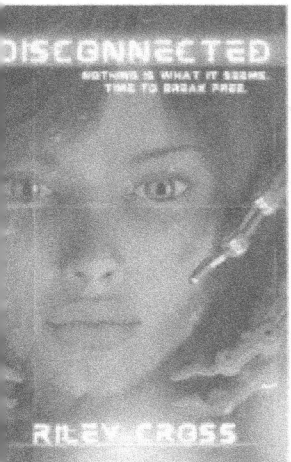

DISCONNECTED

NOTHING IS WHAT IT SEEMS. TIME TO BREAK FREE.

RILEY CROSS

A secret gift. A girl next door. A life-or-death decision.

A MARK IN THE ROAD

ANGELIQUE BURRELL

LANDIS

SHELLY MACK

Are you ready for more of DISCONNECTED? Check out the Monarch website www.monarcheducationalservices.com for the DISCONNECTED Reader's Guide. This free educational resource is perfect for educators, librarians, homeschools, book clubs, and readers who want more of Chiara's story.

CPSIA information can be obtained
at www.ICGtesting.com
Printed in the USA
BVHW031553120423
662232BV00001B/1